RECKLESS HOMICIDE

RECKLESS
HOMICIDE

Ira Genberg

st. martin's press
new york

Design by Maureen Troy

Library of Congress Cataloging-in-Publication Data

Genberg, Ira.
     Reckless homicide   /   Ira Genberg. — 1st ed.
         p.   cm.
    ISBN 0-312-17974-X
    I. Title.
    PS3557.E4246R4   1998
    813'.54—dc21   97-37110
                                                  CIP

First Edition: January 1998

10 9 8 7 6 5 4 3 2 1

FOR ROSEMARY, JACK, AND ANNE

RECKLESS HOMICIDE

CHARLIE WASN'T SUPPOSED TO have left Carolyn alone with Ronnie, who smoked, drank, and wore his slick, greasy hair in a ponytail. He wasn't supposed to have been taking his shirts to the cleaners. But how could Charlie have known his daughter would leave an open bottle of perfume on her dresser inches from Ronnie's burning cigarette? How could he have known the perfume's vapors would ignite?

One in ten million, testified engineers for the perfume company when I asked them the odds, but secret internal studies showed that company executives, alerted to far riskier odds, had refused to change the formula, figuring it was cheaper to settle case by case with the victims' families. Eighty percent alcohol, I argued to the jurors, that's what made the vapors ignite. And what about those three other girls whose bodies burned when their perfume bottles, exposed to heat, had exploded? Not one warning on the label, not one bit of conscience in that foul-smelling company. Reckless homicide is what I called it.

"Carolyn was the kind of girl you'd want as your daughter," I told the jurors. "A dedicated student, star soccer player, editor of her school paper. More than all that, she had a kind and generous soul. She respected everyone, and everyone respected her.

"You heard the undisputed testimony of her friend Ronnie, who was lying on the bed with Carolyn, both of them fully dressed, when they heard a soft crackling and smelled the smoke billowing upward and saw it blacken all it touched. You heard Ronnie say the fire moved in awkward surges toward the neighbor's Persian cats crouched in the room's far corner. When Carolyn broke from Ronnie's grasp, she headed toward the cats she'd promised to watch.

"The fire wouldn't wait. It rolled onto the fallen drapes, then swelled into a brilliant orange-yellow tidal wave that engulfed the stunned animals. We're told their cries turned to humanlike howls while their kicking legs disappeared in the

haze. Carolyn, surrounded now by thickening smoke, tried frantically to maneuver her way out of the room. The carpet under her feet burst into snapping flames. It burned off Carolyn's toes, then whipped upward."

I felt my legs wobble. My voice, while laced with outrage, grew weak. I peered with blurry vision into a sea of faces. "For thirty seconds of unimaginable horror, Carolyn writhed, shrieked, lurched. We know from Ronnie that her eyes reeled, her mouth stretched open, and her ears melted. Her long, curly blond hair became a coil of burnt wire. The searing fire penetrated her skin, and drove relentlessly inward. Carolyn collapsed to the floor, the fire cooking her insides."

I caught my breath, and fell silent. I, too, was consumed by the fire. This was no ordinary trial for me. Carolyn, sweet, beautiful Carolyn, was my only brother's only child.

THE GYM IS DEVOID OF ALL BUT the scorching heat, which falls from the roof, shoots up from the floor, drips off the metal rims. As aspiring composers are uplifted by Mozart, Charlie and I are inspired by the sounds of leather bouncing against wood, touching glass and swishing through nets of rope. We play for hours with pain in our joints, saliva on our lips, a lightness in our heads; we push and claw with the ferocity of warriors defending their village. Charlie is still as quick as a diamond's light. His forty-two-year-old face is aglow, his breathing hard, his eyes emanating a savage, natural gleam as free and un-corrupted as a baby's smile. I smell my brother's breath, his face inches away, his chest bumping against mine. Charlie straightens himself as if to shoot, then bursts past me in a blur along the baseline, twists in the air, and spins in a reverse layup. "Game," he calls out. "Another one?"

"It's been three hours," I protest.

"We used to play ten hours."

"When we were eighteen," I note.

"Don't you miss the crowds, Michael?" Charlie shouts back. "God, all that noise turned me on. Added a foot to my vertical leap."

"I thought it was the cheerleaders who made you jump."

Charlie laughs. It's good to see him laugh again. He has this rich, deep laugh that hints at the wildness in his soul. Unlit dynamite in dry, hot grass, someone once said after Charlie tackled a trash-talking opponent. The name stuck. Twenty years later, he's still called "Unlit" by those who knew him at Boston College.

"Let's go shower, okay?" I ask, but it's more of an order, politely put.

"Where are they now? Don't you ever wonder?"

"Who, the cheerleaders?"

"Yeah." Charlie smiles, but it is the faint, tired smile of an old man recalling a lost love. Charlie's cheeks turn a sickly ashen gray. He sinks gently to the hardwood floor. I know what's happened. The vision of young girls has reminded him of Carolyn. It's been a year of hell for Charlie since Carolyn's fiery death—screaming nightmares and Seconal pills, followed these last two weeks by his humiliating discharge from the airline. For days after Carolyn burned, Charlie would sit in Carolyn's fire-ravaged room merely to breathe in a lingering odor of hers, touch something she had touched, soak up the air that once surrounded her.

He's not alone. I, too, inhale the stink of burnt ashes; but no fire is anywhere to be found. Orange-yellow flames are always on the outer periphery of my consciousness—chasing, circling, consuming me amidst the sweet, sickening smell of Carolyn's perfume. "You didn't make the perfume flammable, Charlie. You didn't put the cigarette next to it. You weren't the one who put no warning label on the bottle," I rush to say, but Charlie can't hear. He's slumped forward as if shot in the back of his head. He's fallen into one of his trances, his eyes riveted to a spot on the floor. I gently nudge my brother's pale, rawboned body, its flesh having been stripped so rapidly that friends who haven't seen Charlie in recent weeks are astonished once they recognize this easily startled soul with the rumbling stomach and loose pants, hunched shoulders and tangled, unwashed hair, as the former war hero and local basketball king Charlie Ashmore.

I drop to my knees and rub Charlie's shoulders. "You okay?" I ask over and over again. In time Charlie raises his head. "I need my job back," he whispers, his smoky blue eyes, deep as tunnels, penetrating my soul with a familiar thrust. "You're the only one I trust to talk to them."

"I represent the airline," I groan with a dismissive wave of my hand. "How many times have we been through this? I'm their outside counsel. Hell, Charlie, I even sit on their board. That's why you want me to talk to them, and that's why I can't."

"Yeah, I know," grumbles Charlie. "The shit about the bar's ethical rules."

"It's called a conflict of interest."

"Don't be anyone's lawyer, not mine, not the airline's. Just talk to them, one human to another. You can be human, can't you? Those lawyer rules you keep talking about, they don't make null and void you being human?"

"Those rules are there for a reason. To protect people from people like me."

Charlie's eyes close for an instant. "Been flying since Nam," he says flatly, as if a dull pain is robbing him of his energy. "Flying is all I know. All I'm good at."

The slight trembling in Charlie's voice annoys me. That trembling is there for a reason. He's a master at manipulating me, and he's doing it now. We both know that, try as I might, I cannot avert my eyes from a grieving mortal even when wisdom requires it; the helpless are a necessary challenge to me. The relief of innocent suffering is inextricably bound—foolish as this might be—with my pure, untrammeled vision of heroic conquest, which looms above me like a soft, hazy light guiding me down the path to everlasting life. "Maybe it's best you're not flying anymore," I fight back.

Charlie shakes his head. "You know how a holy man gets one with God in his best moments? That's how it's with me and my jets. In Nam, those babies saved and killed and got rid of evil. Like God does."

"There were a lot of gods there. Most of them false," I say curtly.

"It felt good the way people were always hanging around me there, trying to get close to me. As if some of what I had might actually rub off on them."

"You're trying to suck me in, Charlie. It's no good. Only be cruel to give you some reason to hope."

"More cruel not to have hope." Charlie shrugs. "How else can you stay sane?"

"Victims create themselves. We saw that with Daddy, right? Create in your mind a world where you're not a victim, and you won't be one."

"You've never felt utterly worthless," Charlie sighs. "It's like having a parasite cruise through your bloodstream, sucking up a little bit more of you hour after hour. Remember what Daddy said? The purpose of suffering was to purify one's self on earth. So innocent death must be the ultimate fulfillment of God's will."

"You sound like a deranged preacher."

"Come on, what death is more innocent, more pure, than suicide? A leap of faith, an act of rebellion, all in the same moment."

"It's a pitiful surrender, if you ask me. What Daddy did was a pitiful surrender."

"I think about what Daddy did a lot since Carolyn died."

"It won't work," I say gruffly. "All this talk about suicide. I can't help you with the airline. I spoke with Ted Nash, the guy in personnel who signed your termination letter—"

"A two-sentence letter," Charlie snaps. "You'd think after eighteen years the bastards would've given me more than two sentences. Eighteen—"

"He told me, off the record, the airline suspects you were using drugs."

"Bullshit!"

"What do you call Seconal?"

"A doctor's prescription. And no one at the airline even knew I was taking it."

"Get another lawyer, Charlie. There are plenty that know the employment laws. That's not even my area of expertise—"

"I don't have to take the Seconal. Helps with my blood pressure. Also helps me sleep. Mainly for the sleep I take it. Ever since Carolyn died."

"That's a year, Charlie."

"I have to sleep, don't I? If Carolyn were still alive, I wouldn't know what the hell Seconal was. She was only sixteen years old, for Christ sake."

"How often do you take the Seconal?"

"You've never lost a daughter, Michael. You don't know—"

"How often, Charlie?"

"Don't start playing lawyer with me. I don't like it. Even your voice changes."

He's right. Many of my habits as a lawyer—cynical glances, false outrage, impatience with irrelevant or inconsistent remarks—have, despite my best efforts, bled into my other life. No conversation, however casual, is immune. But I persist: "C'mon, Charlie. How often?"

"Never took it within twenty-four hours of a flight. Only at night and only if I wasn't flying the next day."

"How much?"

"Twenty-five milligrams. Sometimes fifty. Fifty is what the doctor prescribes."

"That's fifty too much. For a pilot, I mean. I can understand—"

"Nobody else, Michael. You go over Nash's head. Straight to Philip Brandon."

I arch my back. I need that steaming hot, shooting water pounding my hair and face, rolling down and soothing my weary flesh.

"I'll go with you to see Philip if that would make it easier," Charlie offers, refusing to yield. Like a drowning man, he respects none of the rights or sensibilities of those able to rescue him.

"Charlie, I don't need you to go with me. I don't need to go." I climb to my feet.

"That stuff about drugs is all bullshit. I've never failed a company drug test. Never failed an FAA test either. It was the plane, not me. They tested me the day after the flight to Minneapolis. I passed."

"That's a day late. And what Minneapolis flight?"

"I got fired a week after that. We went into a high-speed free-fall. Got caught in some heavy winds. Everything was shaking. Floor, controls, the yolk. Passengers got thrown into the aisles. Lights went crazy. I heard screaming and instruments whirring and glass breaking."

"Jesus, you've never told me this before," I scold him gently.

"We hit a freezing rain. The elevators stuck. Couldn't straighten the plane out. Thank God the stabilizers kicked in."

"Didn't you tell anyone the plane was screwed up?"

"I wrote it in the logbook. I talked about it with the crew and the lead mechanic on the ground. I did everything I was supposed to do."

I drop back to the floor, cup my hands around his head. My eyes are a bit moist. I believe him.

DIANA WELLS IS blessed or cursed with a delicate chin, dimply cheekbones, cornflower-blue eyes, and a little girl's full lips, all of which accentuate a look of fragility some mistakenly associate with weakness. Though without an ounce of fat, her body lacks the hard, muscular tone other women of comparable beauty often develop through training, thereby reinforcing Diana's image of lightness. Silky black curls slide across her soft shoulders and wave gently against the smooth, olive-tinged skin of her upper forehead whenever she turns her head.

She turns to me now. It's five in the morning, and we're fully dressed, unable to keep our eyes closed. Her darkish skin often reminds me of a tranquil, sun-drenched day at the beach; but the restless, impatient air about her at this moment swiftly removes any such illusion, suggesting instead the falling of night over a jungle nervously awaiting the next strike of a big cat. Dozens of men have made brave promises to this woman they could not have possibly kept, many set forth in love notes now stored in cardboard boxes crammed into a dust-filled, forsaken attic closet.

"I can't let you do it," I hear her warn me. "You'd be putting yourself at grave risk." There's no compromise in her voice.

"The only one at risk for the grave is Charlie," I reply, pleased with my clever twist of words. Words are my life.

"You can't prevail on Philip Brandon to do what's not in his interest to do," she insists. "You could be sanctioned by the bar. You could, on top of that, piss off Philip enough to lose him. Brandon Air Lines keeps half the firm's lawyers busy."

Of course, I know that. I also know I wouldn't have Brandon Air Lines as a client if Charlie hadn't fixed me up with Philip ten years ago. Charlie knows that too. If he and Philip hadn't played ball together at Boston College, I wouldn't be making seven hundred thousand dollars a year, and I wouldn't be sitting in this two-million-dollar mansion. Charlie knows that too.

She leans forward. I smell her lightly scented perfume rising. "You've got a reputation, Michael, that few other lawyers have."

Diana's artful in her flattery, her voice and demeanor betraying no hint of fraud or shame. Ordinarily I'm easy prey to those who claim to be in awe of me, a character trait I can't seem to abandon, but at this early hour, a bit dazed yet wired, I test her and myself: "I know you don't like Charlie," I say, knocking her backward.

She flushes with the indignation of a priest wrongly accused of selling his office. "I'm looking after you," she rages.

I nod gratefully, but there's a ring of skepticism in my voice when I say: "I understand, I do." It's awkward talking ethics with Diana. She's working for me and sleeping in my bed, a circumstance we've steadfastly denied to all curious partners and associates; and all are curious. Sure we can justify it, and to ourselves we do. We're both single. We're genuinely in love. Yet—and here's that phrase again—I've got a conflict of interest sleeping with her, as every associate wanting to make partner in our firm will unhesitatingly point out. If we are candid and straightforward about our love for each other, all hell will break loose. The associates will scream that Diana—the most talented trial lawyer of the group, a fact they blithely ignore—will make partner instead of them because she's sleeping with the firm's most powerful partner. They'll accuse Diana of sleeping with me merely to get ahead and claim that I, wanting only to satisfy some perverse lust, am being taken for a ride, however pleasant for the moment. Even my partners will fear Diana's passing them in time. They make it impossible for us to tell them the truth.

So there it is. While claiming to protect me from a conflict of interest, she overlooks an equally obvious conflict when she's involved. To make matters a bit more touchy, she's eligible for partner in six months despite having been in the firm only a year. I'd persuaded my partners long ago to count all her nine years at the U.S. Attorney's office in New York as time toward partnership here, contending she had more actual trial experience than any lawyer in our firm except me. I wasn't sleeping with her then, but how would that decision look to those associates who have routinely worked twelve-hour days for nine years, given up prepaid vacations time and again, suffered through insomnia, high blood pressure, divorces, and child-sharing arrangements, labored beyond midnight while stricken with nasty viruses, all to be among those select few rewarded with admission to the inner sanctum of partnership that confers upon its members the things they all want more than love or inner peace: money, recognition, prestige. Sure they despise the way they're worked to death, but they pray, with God's help, that someday they'll be able to do to others what's been done to them. Funny how every night after seven they go into each other's offices. To reassure themselves of their sanity, I suspect. The trick is, they must learn to love their masters without hating themselves for loving them.

It was Diana's idea that we sleep together, though I hardly objected. She had a compelling rationale: All the partners and associates, having incorrectly concluded we were sleeping together, were in their subtle little ways punishing us for it, so why not at least get some good from it? Contagious germs of information speculating on our whereabouts, our intentions, our sexual practices, were disseminated to all who'd listen, and all did. No one believed our denials; the more vigorously we claimed innocence, the more defensive we appeared. "So let's do it," Diana decided, those four words rolling off her tongue with the easy self-confidence of a mother telling her son to stop mowing the grass and come in for some ice cream. No objections expected or considered. The rumors had given her an exciting courage, she explained a moment later. Maybe the rumormongers understood better than we did; she'd smiled, but not a casual smile—a broad, happy, all-teeth-showing smile that gave me courage too.

I've come to despise many of the associates I once liked. They've torn out pages from Diana's case files. They've hidden books she's needed. They've refused to help her with research, or cover for her when she had two depositions in different places on the same day. They are united in their belief that if she makes partner, one of them won't. I know who the ringleaders are. They won't make it here. I'll give them a long list of reasons—none linked to Diana—for their coming demise.

I'm annoyed Diana can't grasp my loyalty to Charlie when she finds so charming my loyalty to her. "I owe Charlie," I say a bit roughly. "More than you know."

"You just gave him six months of your life, didn't you?"

The perfume case. Four months preparation, two months trial. I won six million for Charlie, but collected not a cent. The company declared bankruptcy. One more bullet to Charlie's bullet-torn body. To her I say: "That was a tough six months for him too."

Her eyes flash with the fiercely metallic glow of a tigress protecting her young. "Don't let him screw up your life, Michael."

"I'm not letting him do anything," I reply testily. "I'm trying to balance all the considerations, that's all. I want to do the right thing, not just what's best for me." I peer directly into her face. Her eyes have lost none of their luminance; they seem only to be protruding a bit more. She doesn't want Charlie here. He's more than merely in her way. He's a scowling face, a constant reminder that we are breaking every ethical rule while falling back on ethical rules to refuse him. Then I think: If Charlie got his job back, wouldn't he more likely leave? I look at Diana curiously. Maybe she is protecting me, maybe her motives are entirely pure.

"The right thing to do," she says with a measured caution, "is what you've always done. Stay on the straight and narrow path."

Ethics again. I don't inflate my hours as others do, don't coax clients into filing weak lawsuits, don't represent anyone if I have a conflict of interest. I turned down Texaco and a million-dollar fee because I represented a mom-and-pop shop that *might* have had a claim against Texaco, and quit an even bigger case when the client asked me to destroy documents. Neither of these deeds endeared me to my money-driven partners, which reassured me of their rightness.

"I'm not going to decide anything today," I tell her. "I'm going to sleep on it another night or two."

She smiles wanly with a narrow, admonishing stare; then to be certain I get the meaning of her look, she glances at her watch. I smile too. Sleep on it? Sleep I can't have until I decide what to do about Charlie.

We are bunched together in one small nook of my two-thousand-square-foot living room, which I had built despite my architect's objection that it overwhelmed the house's other rooms. But doesn't every grand house need one massive room people will remember years after having seen it? I've always been drawn to the beauty of this room. Four satin wing chairs in the room's center look upon four large walk-in bookcases sporting hundreds of books. Six fourteen-foot arched windows allow light to flood the room, bounce off the crystal cubes of the Waterford chandeliers, and rest upon the two-foot-thick gilded crown molding. On white-hot afternoons, the light drifts across the overmantle of Greek design and flirts with the elaborately carved mahogany cabinets on either side of the twelve-foot grandfather clock. Statues of young boys and swans flank a Steinway piano. Mahogany-paneled doors lead to the room's three exits. It is, in short, a room that strikes some as a wing of a museum. Where are the little ropes marking off the room? some like to joke. They know the black marble fireplace has never been lit, the Persian rug seldom touched. They don't know I often move the furniture to one corner now, roll up the rug, and dance with Diana to Sinatra albums. She's given the room a jolt of energy.

Diana leaves her chair, sits on my lap, and hugs me, all, it seems, in one swift, graceful motion. She rubs her cheeks against mine as if readying herself to take me. Talk is done for the morning.

I BUILT THIS house without the usual horrors—the contractor stealing money, going broke, or disregarding the drawings. It wasn't luck. I built this house the way I try lawsuits: with attention to detail, then more attention. I diligently interviewed several contractors and architects before making my selections; worked closely with the architect before the plans and specifications were completed; drafted a comprehensive contract for the contractor to sign; made certain the contractor paid his subcontractors by issuing joint checks where appropriate; paid the contractor not one penny more than he'd earned; and reviewed the work's progress every day with the contract in hand. I was friendly to the workers, believing my humanity would not only make them work harder, it would absolve me from the guilt caused by their low wages. If workers were still there in the evening, I'd drive to the nearest McDonald's and bring them back hamburgers and Cokes. After a while they began to request french fries, then some sort of dessert, and occasionally extra napkins, which to my unending dismay they invariably left scattered on the property; but all that was long ago.

After Paula died, I kept the house despite the strange looks from friends who concluded I was either distraught with grief (and couldn't part with the last possession of consequence Paula and I had shared) or viewed this house as a tangible, everlasting monument to my success; neither possibility raised their opinion of me. I have this way—some kindly call it determination—of doing what I want to do despite others' opinions, believing (often unwisely) I possess some rare insight into the way thousands of tiny considerations come together to make a decision wise or unwise. Now I'm glad I still have this house. Diana is here, and life is good again.

The truth is, Grace keeps me in this house. She's had enough trauma these past few years, so we're not moving. She's ten years old, plays Beethoven and Bach with a power and sensitivity that nearly move me to weep, and has the generosity of spirit to shoot hoops with me in the backyard when she'd rather be gossiping with her girlfriends about who liked which boy and whether he deserved their attention.

I remember when Grace was the size of a pebble in Paula's body. I remember paralyzing waves of nausea, breakfasts of warm toast and bubbly Cokes, sleep broken by long, rambling conversations into early mornings, white-coated men wheeling Paula into the delivery room, followed by wild, bestial roars and gasping, sucking breaths.

In the early years of our marriage, Paula and I held on to each other in public, helped each other with the routine drudgeries of life. Our telephone rang constantly. We were invited to parties of every kind, asked to organize dozens of fund-raising campaigns for charities. The intensity suited us; bursting with possibilities, we fully expected our love to overcome any unforeseen obstacles. This was the great irony of our decline. There were no obstacles; nothing ever blocked our path. As the years passed, we found ourselves nightly exchanging reports on bills, telephone calls, people seen, people avoided, the maid's petulant remarks. We grew weary of the minutiae. Our lips barely touched when we kissed, our eyes focused elsewhere. Acts of generosity—an unexpected back rub, a special meal, a surprise vacation—became rare, and we brooded with the silent rage of those who received their promised checks a week late.

Paula was tired that last year, each day more grueling for her than the last. The doctors found the cancer a week after Grace's most extravagant birthday bash, a nonstop four-hour free-for-all at a wild water amusement park with twenty running and jumping five-year-olds, all having the stamina to drive to their knees the most dedicated group of cross-country runners. The cancer brought us back together. The intensity of our love shot back into our blood.

Paula died for months. Stretched out on her narrow hospital bed like an ungainly corpse, she underwent an hour-to-hour series of tortures not unlike those of victims burned, stabbed, and clubbed by their demonic captors.

Her tubelike arms shook; her forehead glowed from delirium-inducing fevers; her lungs grew weak from the raspy screams that shot past her dry, blistered lips. *Make me die, Michael, make me die,* she would whisper with the foul-smelling breath of decay. I hung on to her arms and legs when the unforgiving pain sliced through her bony ribs and bolted her body upward. I wouldn't let her die. I carried away her excretions, wiped her forehead, listened to her senseless mumblings, and watched her shiver as if death were gripping her whole. *How much longer, Michael? How much?* I wouldn't let either of us surrender to the pain-free existence we craved. I persuaded myself she would live, and never faltered in that belief, no matter the evidence to the contrary. I let nature take its savage, uncompromising course. Her screams grew more animal-like as her body shrank. Her hair fell out, her eyes emptied of all spark. She left this world a shriveled, nearly bald slab of flesh with the twitching limbs and wailing cry of a newborn.

Jeanne, our twenty-two-year-old baby-sitter, takes Grace to school, picks her up, watches over her until I get home. She makes sure Grace is fed and kept out of harm's way. Even the kindest of baby-sitters are tantamount to guards who oversee prisoners in holding cells, making sure nobody gets in, nobody gets out. Whenever I miss dinner, Grace complains the food was burnt, chewy, or dry. "I'm the only kid I know who wants Pepto-Bismol for dessert," she likes to say with a chuckle. She, like me, knows that humor can be effective. Last week she swore Jeanne's batch of abandoned doughnuts killed a stray cat found on its side by our garbage can, the cat's eyes wide-open from shock.

While Grace needs me, I need Grace way more. She's the one rock I cling to when being pulled from the shore. She stabilizes me, keeps me on firm ground. Not something that can be said about many her age, but Grace has a sense of purpose and priorities. But for the Grace of God, I have often mused these past two years.

Grace has no idea I see her this way. It would surely spook her. She likes to run free, and be reassured every night that all is under control. I read to her thirty minutes every night. Not twenty-nine, no, Grace won't put up with that. We've agreed to thirty minutes, and rules are rules. Thirty-one minutes doesn't offend her, though. Rules can be bent a little, and she knows how to bend them. She holds on to my watch, and as thirty minutes nears, she won't look at it, often sliding it under her blanket until I demand to see it. By then, an hour or more has usually passed.

She's happy that Diana's here: none of the jealousy I expected from one so tender and vulnerable. They talk about boys too, and apparently Diana has tips valuable enough for Grace to impart to her buddies. This allows Grace to be a leader, a position naturally suited for her anyway. She's popular with the boys, her buddies tell me while giggling a bit, and no wonder. She did inherit from her mother the fine features and thick blond hair one unconsciously associates with women in the movies.

Uncle Charlie's her "special friend." He cooks her grilled cheese sandwiches and tells her ghost stories in the dark. They play the crazy word games Charlie used to play with Carolyn, and have a pact of some sort to keep some of the stranger words a secret. It's their way of bonding, I figure, so let them have their fun. They have their own words for everything. A plane is a "flying shark," a watch a "personal clock."

Grace has made these last few weeks bearable for Charlie. Charlie doesn't like living in my guest room, eating my food, imposing on my routine; but he has nowhere else to go. No job, no money, no wife who'll have him. Ruth threw him out, claiming he wouldn't talk to her; Charlie complained that talk led to tears, and tears to shame.

I watch Charlie with Grace, and I remember that Charlie raised me. Only two years older than I, he was more of a parent to me than my parents, who never got the hang of giving. Charlie gave what my parents couldn't: warmth, direction, genuine affection. Money, too. He paid back my college loans while I studied law. What favor have I ever asked of Charlie he didn't oblige? I can't think of one, not one.

AT BRANDON AIR Lines, Philip Brandon sets the rules and proclaims the limits of good and evil. He is above morality, above truth, his every whim to be followed without debate.

Philip's rise to absolute power is, as companies go, a relatively recent event. Until his retirement two years ago, his father—"King William" to the staff—decided all company policy, leaving Philip to oversee the operating details. William remains the airline's largest single shareholder, but is now content to watch from the sidelines as Philip calls the plays.

Philip is working day and night to be worthy of his new exalted status and, some say, to outdo his father. Through a lightning-strike series of acquisitions, he has transformed the company from one primarily having routes along the East Coast to the nation's third largest airline with routes to every major city in the world. It hasn't come easily, though. Philip has had to borrow heavily from banks and investment houses; fire scores of experienced managers from the acquired airlines; contend with rising salaries and fuel costs; and pay massive legal fees not only to fend off a rash of hostile takeover attempts but to persuade the FAA and the SEC that his buying spree violated no laws.

Philip is waiting for me. I enter the airline's chief conference room, expecting to see only Philip, but sitting beside him is Roy Brooks, the airline's Executive Vice President, a fancy title for a man who merely does Philip's bidding, and does it with a vengeance. I regard Roy's presence as a barrier deliberately erected to prevent me from persuading Philip to do whatever it is I want. All Philip knows is I'm concerned about freezing elevators on the Jarrad 99s.

The mahogany table, topped by a thick slab of Venatino marble, comfortably seats forty-two. As is his habit, Philip sits not at the table's head but with an air of modesty takes his place toward its middle like royalty preparing to mingle with commoners. Roy sits with the stiffness of an officer in the presence of his commander. The two men have little in common. With his gaunt cheeks, tender chin, and midnight-blue eyes, Philip carries the patrician look of his father and grandfather, whose millions have launched him to the peak of the airline industry. Roy Brooks, who comes from rougher stock—Baltimore ironworkers and hotel housekeepers—worked his way through college and across the company's shifting terrain inch by inch over thirty years of twelve-hour days. Despite a thick, flaccid waist, Roy has the powerful build of a former linebacker who no longer exercises regularly. His round, full face is made rounder yet by his nearly bald skull. A driven man, Roy drinks coffee by the hour, smokes a pack a day, and limits his vacations to every few years, fearful, I suspect, that subordinates will undercut him in his absence. On his third wife, his second heart surgeon, and his first job, Roy firmly believes—as expressed to me after a few bourbons—that Philip Brandon is more important to him "than wife, surgeon, or God."

Philip rises slowly when I enter the room. He doesn't immediately offer his hand to me; when he does, he conveys his unhappiness by his weak grip and averted eyes. He turns to Roy.

"Have you looked into Michael's complaint about the elevators?" asks Philip in the hoarse whisper of a man fearful he'll learn about that which he has no desire to know; yet I suspect Philip's fearful whisper is part of a scheme to convince me he's without knowledge of any problems and is interested only in finding the truth. That's not how Philip functions. He already knows the answer to his question or he wouldn't have asked it in my presence. Does Philip actually expect me to believe he and Roy haven't discussed this matter, haven't rehearsed their presentation to me?

"Jarrad says there's nothing wrong with the elevators on the Ninety-nine," Roy predictably reports. "They've run every test they know of, and the elevators don't stick. Even at thirty below zero."

"I would have expected Jarrad to say that," I comment. "If they admitted the elevators were defective in any way, they would be stuck with them."

Philip allows a small smile. He enjoys word play like "stuck with them" when the complaint is sticking elevators. His smile lasts only an instant. If the elevators do stick, and Jarrad won't take the J99s back, what is he to do? He's bought hundreds of J99s to service the airline's primary eastern routes. If he shuts down the J99s, he'll lose a billion dollars in three months. The airline's credibility will take a long, twisting dive. Loans will go unpaid. The airline's stock price will plummet. Everything the Brandon family owns—the airline, real estate, food chains—will be at grave risk. The airline, at the heart of the family empire, is collateral for all else.

A billion dollars in three months. Let's say we sue Jarrad for its refusal to take back the planes. Litigation of this size and scope will take, at a rock-bottom minimum, two years; by that time, the airline's a truncated shadow of its former self. Let's say Jarrad voluntarily takes back the planes. The airline still loses its billion dollars; it'll take at least three months to find, lease, and service that many replacement planes. Either way the airline takes a knife to its neck. That's why Roy's stiff and Philip's cold. That's why I'm sure they've rehearsed their presentation. They forgot about me, though. They forgot I might prepare too.

"I've had all the logbooks sent to me by the Records Department," I begin. "I've found twelve complaints so far of elevators sticking. And there are logbooks still on planes I haven't seen yet."

"How did you get those . . ." Roy sputters with such venom he can't finish his sentence.

"I called the Records Department. It wasn't hard. I get documents sent to me from those people all the time, Roy. Is something wrong?" I ask innocently.

"That's twelve too many," Philip concedes generously. He's going to work with me to a point. He doesn't want me storming out of the room. I know too much already. Aware of my passion for the truth, he must not let me leave believing the public's safety has been compromised.

"It is twelve too many," I concur. "Particularly when you consider the Jarrad Ninety-nine has been operational only four months."

Philip's chest tightens. "They service most of our eastern routes." He knows I know that. Maybe he has no facts with which to persuade me. Maybe he's appealing to my loyalty.

"Jarrad won't take them back," Roy chimes in. "They went ballistic when I even mentioned the possibility. They said they'd see us in court first. After we'd spent four million in legal fees."

I'm about to say, *So you asked Jarrad to take them back, Roy? There's no problem, but you asked them?* but I'll save the cross-examinations for later. I'll stick to facts now. "One of those twelve complaints came from Charlie Ashmore. He reported elevators sticking on his flight to Minneapolis. The ground crew looked at it and confirmed the sticking."

Philip gazes upward as if seeking divine guidance. "What is it you want, Michael?"

"Charlie was fired because of that flight. But it was the plane, not him."

"We're not rehiring anybody," Roy squawks. "We made a decision based on the evidence—"

I wave my hand at him. "I'm not asking you to rehire Charlie on the spot. I'm here to say we need to report this defect to the FAA."

Philip jerks backward, as if retreating from a bloody corpse. His body shakes, then stiffens as if to protect itself from a blow yet to come. The FAA, if told of the twelve incidents of sticking, might halt the flying of the J99s until all can be thoroughly inspected under its supervision. "We'll handle this internally," Philip manages to say. "If the problem is as bad as you suggest, then we'll go to the FAA."

Roy grins with a shake of his head, his slightly crooked, tobacco-stained teeth in full view. "This is old-fashioned blackmail, ain't it? Either we rehire your brother, or you'll go to the FAA." Roy's eyes, soft at first, light up, their dark blue turning to the shimmering blue of a burning match. His voice turns cold and powerful, vibrating like a mighty instrument at full throttle. "Your brother's a drunk or a druggie. He's got no business flying. If you're worried about safety, then get the fuck out of here and go play your lawyer games with somebody who's stupid enough to play with you!"

"Who are you representing here?" Philip asks in a low growl. "Charlie or the airline? Do I need to bring in my own counsel to—"

"No, of course not." I'm being double-teamed here. Roy wants to know if I'm a whistle-blower, and Philip wants to know if blood is thicker than cash. The airline, all here know, has made me and my partners rich beyond our wildest dreams. "I'm not representing anyone," I explain. "Not the airline, not Charlie. As a board member, I'm here to get to the truth," I say evenly but with sufficient force that Philip sags slightly.

"Very noble," remarks Philip in his most cutting voice. "And who appointed you our truth-seeker?" I feel the heavy weight of Philip's eyes measuring me. "You're our lawyer, and you owe us your complete loyalty. That's what all your lawyer rules say, right?"

"I am giving you my complete loyalty. If the Ninety-nine has a design defect, it needs to be corrected. The public's safety demands it."

"Let me get right to it, okay?" Philip asks, but it's not intended as a question. Philip doesn't ask; he answers, he takes, he does. "I spoke at length today with Ted Nash, and based upon the evidence available to him, he had no choice but to terminate Charlie. Ted wasn't aware Charlie and I knew each other, so he saw no reason to contact me about it."

"What specific evidence does Nash have?" I inquire.

Philip folds his hands, rests them upon the familiar marble-topped table. "On that near-disastrous flight to Minneapolis—you know which one I mean, don't you?" Philip's voice carries no hint of derision, but the words themselves have a taunting quality.

"You mean the flight where the elevators stuck?" I shoot back. "The one I just told you about?"

"I mean where the jet dived three thousand feet, for whatever reason," Philip says quietly. "The copilot said Charlie was drowsy, tuned out, had slow reflexes. Slurred his words. Drugs or alcohol is what the copilot figured."

"Did he blame Charlie for the dive?" I probe.

"Not directly, no."

"Was he asked how Charlie, if he was drowsy and tuned out, managed to recover the plane from that dive?"

"Don't know," concedes Philip.

"You will admit, won't you, that recovering a plane from a speeding free-fall takes enormous skill and enormous powers of concentration?"

"I don't have to admit anything," Philip snaps. "I'm just telling you what evidence Nash had."

"And I'm just trying to determine how solid that evidence is."

"I don't like where this is going," Philip grumbles. "You're the airline's lawyer, Michael. I pay you to—"

"You're not paying me for this meeting."

Philip turns his chin upward as if this conversation oozes a distinct smell he wishes not to breathe. "The copilot wasn't alone. A flight attendant on that same flight said Charlie's face was flushed, and she confirmed the copilot's impression that Charlie's speech was slurred. Said Charlie was tripping over his words."

"Did either of them see Charlie use drugs or alcohol?"

"Not that I know of."

"And neither will deny the free-fall happened right after heavy winds kicked up, will they?"

"Nobody's saying there wasn't turbulence, or that Charlie didn't do a helluva job in getting the plane back on course. But we do know that two crew members thought Charlie was on something and the plane took a dive. Another thing, Michael. I don't want people thinking the airline can't make a decision. Or else everyone who gets fired is going to want an investigation or a rehearing."

"What's more important," I object, "procedure or substance?"

"Let's get off the lawyer bullshit," Philip snaps. "Maybe you're in the dark, Michael, but I know firsthand how barbiturates fuck you up. My wife's on them for insomnia. Makes her dazed and sleepy as shit. She slurs her words too. No reflexes, no coordination. See my point?"

"Emma," I say, referring to his wife by name—basic courtesy demands that one of us personalize her—"is not Charlie. I'm sorry for—"

"My point is, comfort separates you from reality. If you have indoor heat, you don't appreciate how cold it is outside. Barbiturates strip away the reality of things."

I don't ask why Emma's taking barbiturates; it will likely drive Philip to elaborate further on the evils of barbiturates, which will in turn strengthen his resolve to keep Charlie from the cockpit. The more time a man is allowed to defend his position, the less likely he'll be to yield it.

I know his problems with Emma go well beyond slurred words and poor reflexes. He knows I know. He's asked me to recommend divorce lawyers, and he's said more than once he'd leave Emma if he didn't think she'd get custody of his daughters, one of whom drinks a quart of wine a day and is failing tenth grade while the other, a former cheerleader who smokes dope for breakfast, has twice had pregnancies aborted after short-lived romances with running backs. I wonder if Philip's children have learned from Emma, or if Emma, exhausted by her children, has surrendered to them.

I shake my head at Philip to convey my disappointment. "This is Charlie we're talking about, your friend for over twenty years, the Charlie you've always had faith in. What's happening with Emma is, of course, going to affect how you see things, but you've got to recognize that, put it aside for the moment, and deal with the issue at hand on its own merits. Don't punish Charlie for what's hurting Emma."

Philip shifts uneasily in his chair. He's been in awe of Charlie since their college years when Charlie led the conference in scoring. Charlie was everybody's hero then, Philip Brandon another face in the crowd. "Nash said—"

"That's in the past," I cut him off. "It's time now to conduct a thorough, no-holds-barred investigation. Let's see if other pilots had similar problems. Let me chat with the copilot and attendant who—"

"Chat? You mean cross-examine, don't you?" Roy bellows. "You mean an all-out, kick-their-butt cross-examination that'll make them wish they'd never opened their mouths. By the end of this so-called chat, you'll have them telling us they caused the turbulence, not God."

"Don't either of you want to know if something's seriously wrong with the plane?" I press them.

Philip wears the implacable expression of one considering the consequences of a controversy not of his making. "Every pilot who has a lapse blames the plane. You know that, Michael."

"Charlie's had a perfect record for eighteen years. He's got the FAA's highest rating. Doesn't that all count for something?"

"Of course it does. But when public safety is involved, the airline must error on the side of caution," Philip maintains.

" 'Error' is the right word," I brood.

"Nash had—"

"Forget Nash. It's with you now. The point is, Charlie's as good as any pilot you have. I could bring in here a hundred pilots to say they've never flown with anyone more skilled or more responsible than Charlie. But the airline, we couldn't get anyone but that one copilot or one attendant to say they've seen Charlie drowsy or slurring his words."

"I still don't know which side you're on," Philip sulks. "You've got all those 'I's' and 'we's' in there."

"If you'd look at this objectively, you'd realize I'm protecting the airline.

It's unfortunate but not surprising that Charlie intends to sue the airline for breach of contract, for defamation, and for whatever else his lawyer can come up with. But if the airline investigates and finds Charlie's right, he can be reinstated, and there's no lawsuit. If the airline finds otherwise, it adds to its evidence and strengthens its argument of due diligence. Probably knocks out any punitive damage possibilities. The airline has nothing to lose and much to gain."

"Are you threatening me?" Philip's voice rises with every word.

"I'm advising you," I say firmly.

"A lawsuit means publicity. Publicity like this about the J Ninety-nine will kill us," Philip groans with the eerie voice of one about to look death in the face. He breathes deeply, exhales slowly. "Charlie's always been a little wild. Unlit Charlie, we used to call him."

"You're sounding more than a little desperate," I mock him.

"Don't push too hard, Michael. Remember who pays you."

"I've tried nineteen cases for the airline, Philip. I haven't lost one. That's also worth remembering."

"I expected a better attitude from you."

"Same here."

"Maybe money's not as important to you—"

"I'll keep my investigation short and focused, Philip. I'll keep you advised at every step."

"Have you gotten a drug test for Charlie?" Philip asks abruptly.

"Do you want me to?" I sense a crucial change in direction. My bones tingle with the excitement only victory can bring.

"Get me a negative drug test today, and we'll bring him back," Philip pronounces. "But no second chances. Understood?"

I lean across the table and seize Philip's hand. "I won't forget this."

"Yeah, yeah. Well, the evidence is kind of flimsy, and Charlie's had a perfect record, so what the hell? I can be as reasonable as the next guy, right?" Philip mutters aloud, his hand still locked in my hard grip.

SHARP PAINS STAB AND TWIST MY insides as I step into Dan Palmer's small waiting room. Charlie rises stiffly from a soft leather chair, his body absorbing the pain on my face.

"The test came back positive, Charlie. One half a milligram of Seconal per liter of blood. The lab checked both blood and urine. Palmer says it's a real low level, but positive nonetheless."

"I needed more notice." Charlie trembles. "I take the Seconal at night. How many times have I told you that?" He's accusing me of something, though I'm not sure he knows precisely what it is.

Our voices are as low as whispers. "Philip wanted you tested today. I wasn't in a position to argue—"

"I'll take it again, Michael. Let me—"

"According to Palmer, if you took the Seconal last night, then you took between fifty and a hundred milligrams. You told me you took between twenty-five and fifty, and the doctor's prescription limited you to fifty."

"I tried to sleep without it. Gave up around four o'clock. Took my fifty, slept until nine. So what's your definition of night? For me it was late at night. For someone else it was early morning."

"None of this will matter anyway. The airline won't look kindly upon any test showing even the slightest trace of a drug. In fact, Nash will jump on this as proof he was right to fire you."

"Give me twenty-four hours, Michael, that's all I ask. I'll pass the next—"

"Won't do any good. All the airline needs to see is any test you failed."

"Then don't show it to them, Michael. I had no notice!" he races on. "I'll never fail another drug test. Promise you. Never!"

I hesitate a moment. "Quit completely?"

"Yes, yes, completely," Charlie swears. He's drawing ever closer. His hands grip my shoulders.

"How do I know you can?"

"My promises are always good. You know that. Like money in the bank."

"There's been a lot of bank failures lately."

Charlie lets loose a guarded smile. "I'll dump all that shit in the garbage. Tonight."

"Tonight?"

"Tonight, Michael. I swear it on Daddy's grave."

An icy chill runs down my back. I'm being sucked into a vortex of deceit foreign to me. I cast my eyes downward, unable to look directly at Charlie. "I'm splitting in half," I mumble loud enough for Charlie to hear. I ache to help my brother, I ache to keep myself whole. I have this unequivocal duty to advocate zealously on the airline's behalf that compels me to disclose the failed test. Although I've never questioned this duty, I ask now: Is it a mere technicality, or a moral imperative born of honesty and fair play? Does it permit exceptions when fair play would be achieved if this duty were disregarded?

"It's not your job to decide who's guilty or innocent, is it?" Charlie pushes me. "Lawyers aren't judges or juries. They're supposed to figure out how to win, right?"

"There's more to being a lawyer than winning or losing."

"But that's all I ever hear lawyers talk about," Charlie retorts. "Besides the money they make."

"I've never deliberately misled a client, Charlie. I'm not sure I ever could."

"If Philip wants more tests, he can make me take them. He's the ultimate judge here, not you. All you can do is recommend."

"And conceal highly relevant evidence, right?"

"Don't get so worked up—"

"I'm accountable, Charlie, whether it's my ultimate decision or not."

Charlie looks into my face, but he's looking way past things of the flesh. "Do you believe in me, Michael? Believe I will quit?"

"I do," I answer truthfully.

"So justice wouldn't happen if you told them about this test, would it? I'd be out a job, and the airline out a good pilot."

I'm at war with myself. I can't win. "Take another test tomorrow," I relent. "Let's see what happens. If it's positive, it's over. I give up on your being rehired. If it's negative, we figure out what to do next. Something that makes sense for everyone."

RUTH ASHMORE IS drawn to her style of suffering; it permits her a martyr's pride and stands between her and real pain, the kind that paralyzes thought and action. She is reminded by even the most oblique connections to Carolyn—a song on the radio Carolyn once hummed, an old acquaintance waving hello—to take a few long swallows of Wild Turkey to ward off the paralysis and light her cheeks with that soft, pinkish glow. From Carolyn's death there has taken root in Ruth's soul an amorphous yet unyielding bitterness that emanates outward and hangs perpetually about her like a silky, impenetrable web.

She's wearing the long, flowing auburn dress that matches up with her thick, shoulder-length auburn hair. She knows I'm drawn to sensuous elegance. She knows most everything about me, having spent a year committing to memory my every habit, every desire, every minute physical feature, all to master my heart and mind one day in the manner God occupies the souls of His most devoted servants.

She almost made it. Twenty years ago we would nightly press our naked flesh together with unabandoned adoration. We'd sleep curled around each other, wishing to be cut off from the outside world as are hunters in wild, uncharted lands. Harvard was our love nest—I a first-year law student, she a sophomore literature whiz. Every instant apart during that glorious year seemed wasted time. Leaving Ruth was sufferable only when she begged me to stay. Love, we knew, had its own incomprehensible laws, to be disobeyed at one's peril.

Now we kiss each other lightly on the cheek when we see each other, as dutiful in-laws do. Today her kiss is a bit longer and harder and closer to my lips. Her hands caress, not merely touch my shoulders. After we sit, she inches toward me on the plaid sofa I gave her and Charlie on their tenth wedding anniversary. She has that Wild Turkey glow. Her knee is touching mine. This is deliberate, I think. Nothing Ruth does is without purpose.

We used to play this game, "the most and the least." She would ask:
What do you like about me the most?
You know me so well, I'd always answer.
And the least?
You know me so well.

She starts the game we haven't played since that year at Harvard when I say: "Charlie needs you. He won't come right out and say it, but . . ."

Her lips tighten. I watch the joy fall from her body. "He won't come out and say anything," she grumbles. "That's the problem. All we have are forced, choppy conversations. Like strangers huddled together in a train station."

"He's talking plenty now."

"To you, maybe. He always liked you the best," she adds with a bitter laugh. "I always liked you best too."

"You belong with Charlie," I admonish her.

"I was with you first," she points out with a mischievous chuckle. "The way I remember it, you didn't want to keep dating because you needed to study more. But you're out of law school now. And you're single again."

"I still have a brother," I observe acidly.

"He'll be divorced soon. So will I."

Not on my account, I scream inside my head. "It'll kill him, Ruth. I mean, literally."

"Life isn't easy for anybody, is it? I teach kids who are rich, smart, and don't give a shit about literature."

"You're angry with Charlie—"

"Do you blame me?" she cries. "He swore up and down he wouldn't leave Carolyn alone with that boy. Swore to me! The one time I asked him to stay home with her . . . the one time . . ." Her voice trails off. "Anyway, I don't miss Charlie. I don't sleep on his side of the bed, don't read over his cards, don't eat any of the things we'd eat together. I used to think divorce was a sordid arrangement only for those irresponsible, irritating types who had no breeding. Now I know divorce is a good thing if you need it. I'll take no alimony from Charlie, and give him half of everything we've got. No fuss, no muss, no big lawyer fees." Her hand touches my knee in the way friends pat one another, but the intensity of her gaze dispels the notion she is merely seeking a listener.

"He's talking about suicide again."

Ruth shrugs. "So what, Michael? You'll save him, won't you? You save everybody. Except me, that is." She forces a brief, stiff smile that conveys her disappointment in me. "Anyway, just because your dad killed himself doesn't mean Charlie will. It's not the kind of thing that's in the genes."

"Funny, though, how Charlie picked up all of Dad's habits—the way

Dad would put his hand to his cheek, how he'd wink at you when he was telling you a confidence, the way he'd shake his finger when he caught you stretching the truth."

"Your dad was the one stretching the truth, God rest his soul. Hiding it, actually. If anything's in your family's genes, it's hiding the truth. So far you've overcome that."

"Charlie took a drug test this morning. He passed."

"He failed yesterday," Ruth replies with a cutting smile. "He told me last night. Bitched about not being warned. I hope you got him another doctor."

My eyes blur in confusion. "He went to his own doctor. He wanted to . . ."

"Of course he did. That way the airline can't trace the first test."

My eyes widen slowly. She's right. Charlie's a few steps ahead of me.

"Charlie's not a saint, you know. He probably does more of that Seconal shit than he tells you. Exactly how much, I don't know. He's like one of those drunks who hides his liquor."

"Is he doing more than fifty a night?"

"He's living with you, not me. I should be asking you. But if I were a betting girl, I'd bet he's at a hundred a night, and will keep doing a hundred if he gets his job back or not. He's hooked on that shit. He can't sleep without it."

"I don't believe that."

"You always see the best in people," she sighs as a parent does when scolding and praising in the same instant. "Nice but dangerous. Here, very dangerous. You shouldn't help Charlie this time. He's not fit to fly." She looks at me as if a great fog were descending between us. "He's not the same man he was before Carolyn died. I don't care how many tests he passes."

"He's not the same man since losing his job either."

"He doesn't have to be a pilot. It wasn't one of God's Ten Commandments, was it?"

She pushes herself off the sofa and leaves the room. No warning, no excuse me, a push and she's gone. Moments later she returns wearing a full-length white robe barely thick enough to conceal her flesh, moist from what I take to be a nervous sexual tension. I notice her body tremble slightly as she sits beside me. No pretense any longer. Her knee is solidly lined up with mine. "I'm not wearing anything under this robe."

I'm silent, impassive. I know of no words that will spare her total humiliation. She can interpret my silence in a light most favorable to her self-esteem (I was frightened or undecided or loyal to Charlie), and continue about her already depressing life.

"Aren't you going to say something?" she asks softly. "Like, you shouldn't have told me that, or hey, take it off, honey. Don't be like Charlie, okay? Talk to me." Her face is darkening along with her mood. The Wild Turkey is turning on her. She's growing tired and sullen.

I almost speak, almost cry out. For an instant I do want to strip her of that robe. I do want her flailing about beneath me. Isn't she splitting from Charlie now, physically and spiritually? Isn't she alone, wounded, crying out for me? I look at her, look hard. She still has that sleek, athletic body of twenty years ago.

"Just go," she says finally, her voice shaky.

"I came to talk about Charlie," I mumble, returning to my senses.

"Sometimes I think I married Charlie to get back at you."

"Don't rewrite history, Ruth. You loved Charlie—"

"Charlie cut my heart out. Don't let him cut out yours." She breathes in deeply, her eyes cast downward. "Don't let him talk you into hiding that first test. It'll corrupt you."

"What makes you think I'll hide—"

"Charlie needs you to, that's all. What Charlie needs from you, he gets."

"I never said I'd hide—"

"Go, Michael. It's time for you to go. I can't look at you anymore."

SENSUOUSLY CURVED BRANCHES drooping from wide-trunked, hunchbacked live oaks come together to form a series of arches decorated by patches of ghostly gray Spanish moss. My Jaguar kicks up dirt and dust as it rocks under the arches and past the rain-blackened cabins and ramshackle trailer homes concentrated along these bumpy, winding roads. The farther from home I drive, the more arid the land becomes. Gone are the spiderwebs glistening with dew. Birds resting on endless wires of telephone poles overlook blighted trees and brown grass, the unforgiving monotony occasionally interrupted by a tiny church or flea market. Sawed-lumber signs nailed to trees warn passersby to *Get Right With God.* Sweating women with rolled-up pants halt as the Jaguar rolls past them.

I smell wild crab blossoms, see cotton drying on platforms of inch boards. I'm reminded of college summers when Charlie and I would sweat half-naked beside each other in the blistering heat, our smell mixing with the mules' steamy, ammoniacal odor as the humming plow cut into the sandy soil. There's long been a physical closeness between Charlie and me that few men have shared and which cannot be underestimated in figuring our emotional bond. In the late afternoons when the cotton was dry and the long-snouted gray weevils were thirsty, we'd mop the cotton with poison. I remember the look and smell of the poison, I remember the weevils struggling to breathe. Visions of death flood my brain: a chicken's head is snapped off, its body dashing madly in the dry grass; a brownish-green bullfrog emerges from the shadows of a decaying log, its tongue flickering; hogs are stabbed through the heart, their blood squirting out to the rhythm of hideous cries, their flesh plunged into boiling water.

Nothing new. I'm seized by these visions of death every year I come to this cemetery: when I'm sitting in the dirt, or standing in silence, or leaving flowers by Daddy's unmarked grave.

"Did you get rid of the Seconal?" I ask Charlie. Seconal reminds me of death too. All powerful drugs do.

"All of it," Charlie answers firmly and without equivocation. I know he's not lying.

"It's over then, completely over?"

"I'll never use Seconal again. Clear enough?"

"And no other drug, right?" I'm covering all the bases, as I've been trained to do.

"No drugs, period. All I want from this life is to fly," Charlie pleads with that wounded look that invariably squeezes some artery leading to my brain. "I'm not like you. I've got limits."

"What do you want, Charlie? My sympathy or my contempt?"

"Your forgiveness."

I park the car, and we walk the last hundred yards over rocks, between trees, on uneven, muddy earth. As required by his will, Ben Ashmore is buried on the edge of this abandoned meadow among snakes and mice in the crawling, thick underbrush that almost chokes the rotting cedar boards identifying the dozens of black corpses. Forever isolated in alien territory, far away from all he knew. This was the pain and relief Daddy desired; this was where his rapid flight to insanity ended. In his last year most had shied away from him, unwilling to be drawn into that narrowing circle of acquaintances who might later be held responsible for his condition. The ordinary defenses to the aging process—intellectual curiosity, artistic integrity, an enduring love—somehow eluded Daddy's grasp.

We sit with arms folded around our knees. "Daddy killed himself because he hid the truth about who he was," I say. "Lies killed him." I say this for my benefit as well as Charlie's. I repeat it to myself: *Lies killed him.*

"Maybe Daddy liked being who he pretended to be." Charlie drops his arms, stretches his legs. "What would any of us be without our lies? Could we stand the pain of living?"

I won't let him glorify mendacity. I must press his face against the glass, and make him look inside. "You never could stand Daddy being unhappy, could you? Even now you can't. You'd always persuade yourself that Daddy should be happy, must be happy, so he was happy. That's how you learned all the subtle ways of concealing the truth from yourself. Truth was your enemy." I stare hard at Charlie. He must not be allowed to fool himself. "Truth was, Daddy ran away from himself. It would've been easier for him if he'd died in one of those Warsaw sewers."

"The evil was so incomprehensible it paralyzed him." Charlie pardons Daddy as he often pardons himself. "If God was a Nazi soldier, what was he supposed to do? Maybe by denying he was a Jew, maybe by deliberately committing a sin, he was looking for God. Only the true sinner knows God."

"I'm not surprised Mama died a month later. She never understood how she'd tortured Daddy until he killed himself. He didn't want to be Ashmore. He was Aschenmaker. He was a Jew."

"He didn't have to give up his name. He could've said no to Mama. Like I said, maybe he liked not having to be a Jew. Mama made believe she was a Jew to marry him, and almost died for it. The Nazis hated her for touching Jewish flesh, and the Jews hated her for converting back. She was in sort of a twilight zone."

"She put us in a twilight zone, too. We've always been Jews among Christians, and Christians among Jews. We've never quite fit in anywhere."

"She saved his life, Michael. So what if he had to change his name? She got him out of Germany."

"He had to leave his mother and brother behind. He never knew how they died. You can't help but imagine the worst."

"No truth is an absolute, is it? The years pass. The light pales."

"Daddy went crazy. That's an absolute. All the illusions that make life tolerable, he just let them go. He got too close to the raw truth, too vulnerable to death. Truth is a powerful and dangerous thing."

"I remember that time Mama brought us to church. The minister asked all Christians to rise, and Daddy stayed in his seat. The minister spotted Daddy, and called him to the altar. While Daddy was sort of shuffling up there, the minister yelled out for everybody to pray for Daddy's soul and sing for him. Remember that?"

We look at each other and chuckle. It had been a funny, if not pitiful, sight. Charlie climbs to his feet. "Just like this," he says, imitating the minister's exaggerated gestures and sly grin. "There was all this moaning they called singing, and Daddy's knees buckled," Charlie goes on. "The preacher kept waving Daddy to walk faster. When Daddy finally got up there, the preacher grabbed Daddy's hands, and held them up. That's all that bunch needed. Everybody started shouting and clapping, and Daddy's face got all screwed up, and he just bolted like a horse at the gate. Just goddamn bolted!" Charlie laughs loudly amidst the vast silence enveloping the meadow. He runs a few steps to and fro, as if he's Daddy sprinting from the church. "He was in hell right there! He was looking into the face of depravity and redemption and he wanted no part of it! Never forget that, the way he pushed the minister away and streaked out of there like a goddamn racehorse!"

The vision of our father dashing wildly out of the church makes us laugh as we often had as children while sitting at the dinner table, our faces turning red, our chests bouncing, much to the displeasure of Ben and Sara Ashmore, who would watch with hard stares and shaking heads. The momentum of our laughter, as it had years ago, feeds on itself. It echoes in the distance, grows noisier, makes our sides rumble. I clench my hands, stiffen my face, and struggle to breathe naturally. I'm among the dead, yards from Daddy's grave! I must control myself. What if someone hears us, what if the dead can hear?

Upon spotting my predicament, Charlie is seized by a vicious spasm of laughter. I feel the ground vibrating, see Charlie's contorted face. The more I clench and stiffen, the higher climbs the pitch of my laughter; my lips widen, my body shakes, and my head bobs. I can't overcome this nameless, horrifying sensation causing my body to shake uncontrollably.

Charlie's laughter turns to howls of inhuman pain. He falls to the earth and sobs with the same passion he'd laughed, his belly still shaking and twisting. Water streams from Charlie's red, swollen eyes.

. . .

I DO MORE than Philip requires. I arrange for the entire crew of the Minneapolis flight to be flown to my office, and in one day I interview all of them. I ask straightforward questions and get direct answers. Patti types my notes, which I present to each of the witnesses in the form of affidavits. I tell them to change any statements they find inaccurate or in any way inconsistent with what they've told me. Every crew member signs his or her affidavit without making a single change.

All of them praise Charlie's recovery of the plane, and all, except Sexton and Dilman, claim Charlie was at all times alert, focused, and in complete command. Sexton himself, while saying precisely what I'd been told he'd say, wavers when asked if the elevators might have caused the plane to dive. "Anything's possible," he finally concludes with the lack of conviction that seems to pervade all his remarks. Dilman, though more certain of herself, observed Charlie for no more than thirty to forty seconds, and readily admits she's "no medical expert" and "could have been wrong" about Charlie's condition.

I write a report to Philip attaching all these affidavits and Charlie's second drug test. I am confident, I say, that Charlie should be reinstated immediately.

I SLEEP IN a twilight state, half-awake, too weary to move, the sort of vague uneasiness one feels after taking a pain-killing drug. My dry mouth tastes like rubber.

"You can't sleep?" I hear Diana whisper.

"I've had better nights. You?"

"You keep moving. It's hard to sleep."

I turn on the lamp and sit up against the brass headboard. "I saw Philip Brandon today. Charlie got his job back."

Her chin inches upward, her eyes full of wonder. "I didn't think Brandon would do it. I figured one strike, you're out."

"There were no strikes," I say slowly. "I only gave him the test Charlie passed."

"Michael, no," she exclaims softly. She pushes away the sheets and sits beside me. "This isn't smart, and it isn't safe."

"He's done with drugs, Diana. I know Charlie better than anyone. He keeps his promises," I say without looking at her.

"You still owe the airline complete disclosure. This isn't like you."

I shrug as if sufficiently wise to know which rules can be ignored. "I changed my mind at the cemetery," I explain, my vision a bit blurry at this early hour. "I wanted to forgive Charlie, and this was my way of doing it. No one ever forgave Dad, not even Dad."

"If you're so sure of Charlie, why can't you sleep?"

"I'm worried about me." I chuckle lightly. "I don't want to corrupt myself. Something Ruth said." I turn toward her, my eyes starting to clear. She's worried, I can see that. Lines cross her forehead, swirl below her eyes. "Charlie will be okay. I don't know if he was on Seconal when that plane dived, but if he was, he still recovered it, didn't he? Even when Charlie drank, he could go out and score twenty points. Charlie can do miraculous things drunk, sober, or on Seconal."

"You're a fool, but a good fool." She leans toward me, pulls on my shoulders until I'm flat on my back. Our lips touch lightly at first, as if exploring virgin territory, then her tongue glides deeper. I'm ready, she's got me ready, but she stops and takes a moment to examine me as she would a fine work of art—with a look of earnest pleasure and noble satisfaction. I close my eyes, absorbed by her breath, the light scratching of her teeth.

She has me in her mouth. I'll be lost soon. She'll make me come with the usual piercing howls, and an hour later she'll have me enter her. This is how she likes it. I last longer.

I try to push her away, but Diana refuses to budge. She has a supreme energy about her in lovemaking, akin to a great athlete at the peak of her powers, and can be extraordinarily kind and extraordinarily ruthless in the same motion. A powerful tremor shoots up my back, dividing me in two. Slowly I realize the bed is squeaking as if tortured and I'm thrashing about like a hooked fish. I cannot fight any longer. I erupt, my strength spilling out, to be resurrected at Diana's pleasure.

She lies on top of my shivering body. She's remarkably fresh and sweet, her flawless, velvety-smooth skin a seductive yet daunting sight. Her soft hair tickles my face as she twists back and forth, her firm breasts swelling and rubbing against my chest. "Are you ready, Michael?" I feel the hardness of her nipples and the smoothness of her thighs, and behold a radiant joy in her eyes. We're swaying side to side in a slow, bumping dance. "I'm ready, Michael, I'm ready." I push her away, then force her under me.

We rise and fall in unison. I reach for her two rear mounds of flesh, dig my toes into the mattress: my turn to be as cruel and kind as Diana. I thrust myself deeper, harder, faster. I seem to be descending at unimaginable speeds. She lets out a sweet, urgent gasp that inspires me to an even greater frenzy. I ride her as if she were a magnificent, savage animal in full gallop. I need to exhaust and conquer her, toss her off the mountain, and watch her float helplessly into my arms.

Her gasps turn to short, high-pitched screams. Now she thrashes and heaves. Water rises in her eyes. I imagine water inside her too, turbulent water, the breaking of sharp ocean waves. Her fingers are driving into my back, her motion and smell overwhelming me. If only I could lock in this moment as a camera freezes its subject, keeping it pure and everlasting— but my legs are weakening and my face is puckering up in rapture and agony.

Long after our convulsions end, and our lust is momentarily extinguished, our hips rock gently back and forth as if keeping in rhythm with the beat of some distant drum pounding slowly inside our heads. "You won't ever run out on me, will you?" I ask with a small chuckle; but I mean her to take this question seriously.

"I already know you work sixty hours a week."

"Paula would've left if she hadn't gotten sick. Maybe she was smart enough not to accept it."

"I'll gladly wallow in my stupidity," she laughs quietly while burying her head in my chest.

"You've left every other man in your life."

"None of them were you. They all whined about how much I worked. All needing to be pampered. Wore me out. I look back at them now, and see they were nothing but distractions."

"You're not one for small talk, are you?"

"Neither are you."

I stroke her thick hair, twirling the silky strands in my fingers. "Have you ever used a man for nothing but sex?"

She looks up at me, and smiles. "Distractions aren't all bad."

"So the answer is yes?"

"I've had my one-hour bimbos. No name, no telephone number. No promises. Probably not half as many as you."

"I hope not," I laugh, but I'm not amused.

"You've had me checked for AIDS and everything else. Anything else I can do for you?"

I let go of her hair, and look away. "Whenever I took Paula somewhere,

I'd make her pay for it. I'd work longer hours that weekend or that night while she slept alone. I didn't mean to punish her. I—"

"Did she actually expect to walk away without a scratch?"

"Don't make fun," I say softly. "I've never blamed her for wanting to leave me. A sort of joyless chasm got between us and kept widening. I don't want to screw up with you, too, Diana. How do you get over an addiction?"

"THERE'S GOING TO be hearings, Michael. About the J Ninety-nine."

I turn in the darkness and glance at the red numbers on my alarm clock. I struggle to focus. "Hearings?" I say. "When—"

"Father had dinner tonight with friends on the Hill. The Transportation Subcommittee on Aviation wants to look into the goddamn elevators. Some sonofabitch has been complaining to them," Philip growls.

"Who?"

"That's what I called to ask you."

"How would I know?" I reply testily. "I don't have any friends on the Hill."

"They're going to start with the FAA people. I think we'll be okay with them. They don't know any elevators have stuck, and besides, they'll be busy defending their decision to approve the plane."

"That they don't know might lead to bigger problems," I advise Philip, whose apparent disdain for the truth—except when it can be shaped to suit his interests—offends me, particularly when that disdain is paraded naked in front of me, implicitly suggesting I share his contemptible view of reality. "If the Subcommittee concludes there is a serious problem, and the airline has hid it from the FAA, there could be claims of criminal fraud."

"We can't let that happen," he says with a shaky voice.

"What exactly does the Subcommittee already know?" I ask him.

"Somebody's complained, that's all, and they feel it's their duty to follow up. I wasn't so goddamn worried about it until you came up with this criminal fraud angle."

He sounds angry for my having given him proper advice, but I suspect it's fear, not anger, that's chilling his soul. "We need to prepare ourselves for all possibilities," I say. "And if you weren't worried, why are you calling me at two A.M.?"

"Most of the airlines contract out their maintenance work," he broods. "We don't. We do it all with our own people. We're committed to safety, and pay the extra monies to insure it."

"I'll mention that to the judge before he decides on the sentence."

"What are you saying, Michael? That spending the extra money to do our own maintenance work means nothing?"

"If the Subcommittee thinks the airline has deliberately concealed a defect, then yes, it means nothing. If it goes beyond the Subcommittee and into the courts, same answer."

"How do we get these hearings stopped?" Panic is creeping into his voice.

"There's nothing a lawyer can do," I rush in happily, content to keep my distance from any improper schemes. "It's all political." Philip knows, better than I, all the nefarious ways of undermining a Subcommittee's work: discredit accusers, blackmail key Subcommittee members, call in favors to party leaders.

"Once the news breaks, we'll get some lousy publicity no matter what happens. It'll probably hit the papers by tomorrow afternoon. That's the real reason I called you. To help me figure out how to keep our stock price where it is. Any big drop will get the sharks swimming. National's been eyeing us for months now."

"I'll clear my schedule," I assure him. National Air Lines, a smaller but cash-rich airline, competes head to head with Brandon on key cross-country routes. Swallowing up Brandon Air Lines would make National the country's largest airline.

"Do that, Michael." He falls into a momentary silence before whispering with the dazed heaviness of one awakened from a deep sleep: "I'd rather be shot in the head than lose this airline."

"I believe you," I reply, as does a friend to a mourner upon first hearing of the mourner's loss. Shame, I know, can drive a man to do things he would otherwise consider beyond the pale.

PHILIP BRANDON IS, to himself, an economic unit whose primary task in life is to remain a productive asset. His eyes are unblinkingly fixed on the company's bottom line, which for him soars far above the flesh and blood of those who contribute to it.

I suspect money matters to Philip not for what it can buy—that's the least of it—and not merely as confirmation of his worth; rather, it denies the animal in him, counters decay, and proves his entitlement to everlasting life. Unlike character, money can be measured with precision. It creates a distance between men; it frees those who have it of obligations lesser men cannot avoid. Money endures. Money binds the past to the future. Money links the generations.

In my years with Philip, I've noticed that in his peculiar way he strives not only for money but with equal fervor for a moral purity that will protect him from a potentially crippling guilt inspired by his business-driven need to destroy his competitors and keep down his workers' wages. Constant movement is the magic, cold efficiency the music. He's on a treadmill of sorts: The more he strives, the less he enjoys; the less he enjoys, the more he strives. He tells me he thinks incessantly of work—in the shower, at parties, during golf. Every meeting, whatever its purpose, is a business opportunity. The more money he makes, the more he's worshipped. Money and religion merge.

The great irony, as I see it, is that this superhuman leader of men is at heart a child with no tolerance for uncertainty. Uncertainty leads to helplessness, which in turn leads to death. The greater Philip's uncertainty, the more he's driven to the security of order. I suspect he wants what every child wants: to bond with an omnipotent guide that will eliminate his terror of helplessness and bring him inner harmony.

I've seen Philip with his father countless times, and from the sum of those experiences I've come to understand that Philip is a captive of his father, the all-knowing ruler who praises his son generously not to build his son's belief in himself but to bind his son to that praise with suffocating tightness—if that hasn't been the intent of King William's words, it has surely been their effect. I believe Philip would unhesitatingly sacrifice all his wealth neither for the airline nor his soul but for a few drops of praise from King William, as would a parched desert traveler surrender all his possessions for a long drink of cool, clean water.

Philip travels alone. He's drawn to no political party, no church, no grand idea. No one has his complete trust; no faith is he driven to defend. All he has is the sacred duty to keep the family business in the family, to keep the name of William Brandon alive.

King William is not here today in the flesh; but everywhere his presence can be felt. Life-sized oil paintings of William framed by magnificent swirling golden leaves hang in the lobby and in every conference room.

Despite all of William's influence, neither he nor his son can slow the ominous momentum of the Subcommittee, whose members—without having yet heard sworn testimony from any witness—have supposedly let it be known, off the record, they have "hard evidence of a serious defect" that might require "a major fix" to be done "under the FAA's supervision." Brandon Air Lines stands to lose more than any other airline if the J99s are grounded. No other airline has nearly as many J99s, which accounts for the heart-stopping drop in Brandon's stock price from sixty-one dollars to forty dollars per share. All Philip has done to expand the airline—which made the purchase of the J99s necessary—may now come tumbling down upon him with the force of heavy boulders rushing down a steep mountain.

The free-fall plunge in Brandon's stock price has inspired National Air Lines to buy huge chunks of Brandon's stock. National, it seems, has been working feverishly but quietly (if National's intentions become known, Brandon's stock price will zoom up, making it more expensive for National to keep buying stock) with bankers and brokers, several of whom have leaked the news to Philip, whose gratitude (and business) they will want if the takeover fails.

According to Philip's sources, National is pledging its entire airline as collateral in return for billions of dollars in loans with which they will buy control of Brandon Air Lines, then make a tender offer to buy the remaining shares at a premium. National, it seems, is sensing a kill. Its officers are personally buying Brandon's stock—a sure sign of confidence—which they will likely sell back to their employer when it makes its premium-price tender offer.

Upon gaining control, National won't likely talk about profits, political influence, or monopoly power; the acquirers generally emphasize "synergy," "asset deployment," and "growth." National will immediately repay many of their loans by selling off a necessary share of Brandon's assets: This is standard procedure in the merciless world of takeovers. What allows this entire plan to work is one core reality: Brandon's stock price has fallen below the market value of its assets.

Philip looks like hell, but that's no surprise; he's been headed that way since I've known him. In the last ten years Philip has aged twenty. His once sparkling white teeth are a pale yellow, his wavy almond-brown hair of years earlier a thin, dreary brownish-gray. Blackish-blue wormlike moles with spiderlike hairs creep along the back of his neck. No longer does he have a swift gait, and hands still capable of a powerful grip shake at odd times. His six-foot-two-inch frame is perpetually slumped forward, his once massive chest losing its muscle.

"I haven't slept in two nights," he confides in me. "I've considered every possible way of getting our stock price up, but nothing works because there's no time. There's no time to downsize the airline, no time to put together a cost-cutting package investors would like, and no time to put out a plan for higher future earnings."

Philip's weak voice and dull eyes signal that kind of all-pervasive exhaustion that acts to confuse a man and make him highly suggestible to reckless impulses. I suspect he'd be breathing a bit easier if King William were dead. Failure wouldn't be so life-threatening.

"I've called friends at other airlines, at our main suppliers, at investment houses. I've been in touch with pension fund managers and bank presidents. I can't find any white knight to come in and buy our stock. I've begged, Michael, and I hate to beg. I've told them I'd buy it all back in two years at a guaranteed profit, and put all of it in writing. Everybody's afraid of what might happen at these hearings. Everybody but National. They're gutty bastards," he says with grudging admiration.

"They may be gutty, but what company is spotless?" I ask, but it's more a call to action.

"I've had people crawling all over National's annual reports, tax returns, SEC statements," he lectures me as a teacher would a student. "So far nobody's come up with anything to discredit National as a manager. If we could just find something juicy, I'd send a letter to our stockholders warning them not to sell."

"They're going to take the highest price they can get," I say bluntly. "Once National makes a tender offer, it's done."

A pale, brittle look sweeps over him, wrinkling, then with the passing seconds, disfiguring, his face. He'd been aware for days of the airline's predicament, but not until this moment did the momentous consequences of any decision made today seem to sink fully into his consciousness. "If I wasn't so deep in debt, I'd borrow every dime I could, and buy back all the stock I could. But nobody will lend me anything. I'm at my limit," he groans. "I don't know what else to do. I've had friends trying to stir up dissension at National over their buying up of our stock. So far, it's not working. But I'll keep them at it until the last bullet is fired."

We sit underneath the three towering chandeliers of the chief conference room, light spilling off their oval crystal tubes onto the marble-topped mahogany table. I imagine the average observer would find ludicrous (or appallingly wasteful) the sight of our sitting alone beside forty empty chairs.

"You never know what might happen," I observe, but with little enthusiasm. Corporate intrigue grates on my sense of fair play.

He leans forward and speaks to me as one utters a prayer. "I've even considered getting some of our people on the boards of big charities. To blunt the bad publicity. Or maybe start a minority hiring program, and make a big thing of it. But that'll only help us long term, if there is a long term."

He's out of ideas, I think. It's time to unveil my grand plan, lead him from this emotional terror. I suspect he'll be grateful for my idea, and despise me for having conceived it.

"National is breaking the law," I tell him with genuine conviction. "Takeovers are not generally illegal, but when they take place within the same industry, they run the risk of hurting consumers. Especially here, where you have two big players combining. Competition is reduced. Prices naturally rise. This is exactly the kind of behavior the antitrust laws will not tolerate."

"Antitrust laws?" he muses. "That gives us treble damages, doesn't it? We could win billions." His face, aglow for a moment, sinks back into a familiar gloom. "That'll take years to get heard, won't it? Won't we have to go through all the pretrial bullshit first?"

"We get the Justice Department to intervene," I say with the excitement of a child about to complete a most difficult puzzle. "Justice can stop National here and now."

"No," he says adamantly. "I don't want Justice snooping around. Before you know it, they'll be investigating us too. Once you get them in, you can't get them out."

I slump back in my chair. Seeking to extinguish the blaze coming toward us, I overlooked the potential fire to my rear: Wouldn't Justice, which is more thorough in its work than the ordinary Subcommittee and less subject to political influence, likely find in the course of its investigation that the airline has deliberately concealed evidence of sticking elevators from the FAA? How the webs we weave come back to trap us.

"Let me run this by you," says Philip in a way that puts me on guard. "We can release some info on earnings tomorrow that'll show big growth. Make the stock jump, at least in the short term. But maybe that's all we'll need to get past this."

"You mean, lie about earnings? That will get you in prison, Philip." He has, at last, confronted head-on his years-long pretense of moral purity, which, having come squarely into conflict with his need for security, he has now abandoned completely.

"I can worry about prison later. In the meanwhile, I'll have the airline."

"I won't be part of that, Philip."

"You and Father," he groans with a roll of his eyes. "You both expect me to play by all the rules. And expect me always to come out with all my body parts."

Having anticipated an objection along these lines, I'm mildly pleased to be lumped with King William, which not only softens the blow but lends credibility to my position. "How is your father taking all this?" I seize the opportunity to ask.

"Very worried. I hate to see him this way."

"Do you want to hook your father in by phone, get his input?" I inquire not so innocently.

His eyelids droop, partially covering the two black dots, the size of pinpoints, that appear to have been pricked into his globe-shaped eyes by some tiny weapon. His mouth, locked in a bitter grimace, is the first to be altered, forcing his lips slightly upward into the faint smile of a soldier struggling to rally the troops while a fresh wound gushes blood. His sunken cheeks depress inward, betraying an utter agony. He has that sense of vulnerability about him that comes with having a father one perceives as invulnerable.

"You haven't told him everything?" I probe with a knowing look.

"He knows all about National and, of course, about the hearings."

"Does he know the elevators do have a sticking problem?"

"No," says Philip sharply. "And I don't want you misinforming him or anybody else about that. There isn't a problem. If there was, I would've told the FAA about it."

"Save that speech for the FAA," I say more harshly than I intend. "It doesn't work with me."

He loosens his blue silk tie, then snuggles back into the chair's cushion as I imagine one does before revealing all to his therapist. "I was given one mission in life: Make this airline grow. By the time I was ten, I was learning about stock options, employee health plans, fuel costs. None of those supposedly free, untroubled childhood moments, nothing to draw on when I got stressed out." He takes a breath, straightens his back. "Michael, we need to get these hearings stopped before they ever start. We need to find out who their Deep Throat is, and rip his heart out."

"You mean kill him?" I ask in awe.

Philip's eyes flash as if sunlight, having penetrated the ceiling, is bouncing off his jet-black pupils. He peers at me with a wicked power that only those who are prepared to sacrifice their souls possess. "Figuratively, not literally." He lets loose a small smile. "Once we know who he is, we can discredit him. If nothing's wrong with him, we'll make something up, then make it happen."

"Plant evidence?"

"Who are you, Snow White?" he chuckles. "You need to join the nineties, Michael. I would've expected a big-time lawyer like you to be a bit more worldly."

"Is 'worldly' your word for criminal?"

"Help me find their Deep Throat," he barks, but I detect a soft, pleading undertone. "Use every contact you've got."

"I'm your lawyer, Philip. Not a hit man."

His eyes, I notice, are moist. His chin has dropped a few inches, and his breathing is strained. "My father dedicated his whole life to building this airline. He expects me to build it further, or at least keep it where it is. Losing it altogether is unthinkable. God, if National gets us, the Brandon name will be gone. It's one thing simply to die, Michael, but worse yet to have your name erased. What greater death is there?"

I leave my chair, walk around the table. At this moment we're not adversaries; we're two friends seeking to improve our lives. I touch Philip's shoulder. "The crazy thing is, the hearings which got National buying our stock are probably the one thing stopping them from announcing a tender offer. If the hearings get started, and the Subcommittee tells us to ground the J99s until the defect's fixed, our price will drop further, and make the takeover that much easier. So National is bound to wait, and this gives us time." Time for what, I'm not sure.

Philip's eyes have that soft glow of gratitude. He grabs my hand and squeezes. "It gives us time," he echoes faintly. "Maybe enough time to get your partner Randy involved. He'll have a clearer vision than you, Michael, of what has to be done here. He'll be open to more options."

So much for friendship. Philip's dumping me for Randy, who he correctly sees to be a lawyer with a "clearer vision" of all that can be done without regard to those pesky little rules that are designed to limit one's "options" in the marketplace and in life.

"MISTER ASHMORE, I'M SORRY TO interrupt you—"

"I'm in conference, Michelle," I tell the receptionist gently. "Hold all my calls."

"I know I'm supposed to hold them," she replies with a frustration of her own. "But this woman sounds positively frantic. She says she's your sister-in-law."

"I'll take it in my office." I put down the phone, then turn to my audience of clients and associates. "I'll be back in a moment," I excuse myself. I try not to be sheepish, wishing to convey, without having to tell an outright lie, that this is not merely a personal call but one of great urgency involving a matter apparently bigger than the one we're discussing. No matter how many cases I've won, I still play games when necessary or useful.

I stride down the hall, unhappy I've been pulled from my meeting. This better be important—but maybe it is. I walk faster. Ruth has never called me at work.

I reach for the ringing phone. "Ruth, what's the matter?"

"Have you talked to Charlie today?"

Her voice betrays a hint of panic. Michelle was right to interrupt me. "No. Why?"

"The divorce order was signed this morning. His lawyer called him, and he called me. He was screaming at me. I couldn't calm him down. He said he wished he were dead. I could almost feel his chest shaking."

"Where is he?"

"He was just leaving when he called me. Off to New York. I begged him not to go, Michael. He was in no shape to fly. But he went anyway."

"I'll talk to him when he gets back."

"Do that, Michael."

"He'll be moving out next week. To an apartment by the airport," I mention. "Signed a short-term lease. He was getting better, Ruth, but still had hopes you'd change your mind."

"Don't let him fly for a few days. I'm worried to death about him."

"I told you this would happen."

"It's my fault?" she asks bitterly. "You're the one who got him back in the air," she huffs.

"Okay, so there's enough blame to go around," I retreat.

"Let's not forget Charlie. Give him most of it."

"I'll talk to Charlie tonight. I'll see what I can do."

"Don't let him fly for a while, okay, Michael? Make him stay put."

AT 10:27 P.M. the oldies station is playing Dylan's "Like a Rolling Stone," which it interrupts in midsentence to broadcast the emerging details of a crash: *Brandon Air Lines. All passengers and crew feared dead. From La Guardia Airport. Six miles north of Washington National. Spectacular ball of flames.* My car skids, swirls, and slams to a halt. Cars behind me honk as they dart past me. The light changes once, twice, many times. More honking, more cars whizzing around me. I grip the wheel. Slowly I move my foot from the brake to the accelerator.

I don't know where to go, what to do. I scream out, and scream again— not words but unintelligible, animal-like howls of fear and grief. It is as if the car is driving itself toward the crash site.

I park a mile from the crash site and stagger from my car. All my limbs are trembling, making it impossible to walk at a normal pace. In time I come upon a portrait of organized chaos: ambulances, fire trucks, and police cars rush in all directions; trained dogs sniff piles of debris for explosives; mobile cranes hoist out chunks of the aircraft from a crater; Red Cross workers hurry food from industrial catering trucks to the investigators; nurses comfort the bereaved; cameramen photograph battered pieces of metal brought to a central clearing; and policemen order crowds gawking at dismembered corpses to stay behind roped-off areas. Ghoulish scavengers are known to have chopped off the fingers of corpses to steal tightly fitting rings.

I'm the airline's counsel, I tell them. They call for confirmation, then let me past the ropes. From a police car phone, I call home. Maybe Charlie decided not to fly, maybe he flew some other flight. Charlie can't be dead; he has too much spirit about him. The baby-sitter says Grace is asleep; Charlie isn't there.

I walk with police officers around the crash site. Covered trucks unload body bags in front of a giant canvas tent filled with decaying flesh. Investigators with test tubes collect blood while state troopers and policemen carry corpses on stretchers. Pathologists, stenographers, and morgue attendants process the dead. The victims' personal possessions are tagged and placed in plastic bags. Priests administer last rites.

The ninety-ton aircraft has been stripped: Its engines, wings, nose, and tail lie in heaps of debris strewn over fifty square yards. The forward section of the fuselage is dug into a ten-foot-deep, gravelike crater sixty feet long, circled by mounds of soft earth. Bits of outer wings, shattered flaps, and sheared-off ailerons decorate the crater's outer edges. Mutilated corpses are scattered throughout the nearby frozen thicket, some body parts hidden by layers of stuffing that have burst through torn seats.

Teams of accident investigators from the National Transportation Safety Board's Office of Aviation trudge through the thicket like soldiers on a forced march. Sharp-edged fragments, broken fuel lines, twisted hunks of aluminum and steel, tangled control cables, sliced suitcases, smashed hydraulic pipes, and spaghetti-shaped electrical wires conspire to block paths in every direction. The cold air—twenty-eight degrees and dropping—is made colder still by gusty winds. Yet they endure.

I've tried enough crash cases to know what they'll do. They'll examine every tear and break in the aircraft's structure, inspect all electrically powered units, and record the positions of the landing gear, flaps, and trim tabs. All of them pilots or former pilots, they are adept at separating in-flight structural damage from ground-impact damage. With magnifying glasses they'll study surface areas for paint or oil smears, or nearly invisible scratches, any of which might have resulted from one part of the aircraft lightly sliding over another, a sign of midair breakup caused by depressurization. Next they'll compare the corpses' ground positions to the airline's seating plan for clues as to the cause or sequence of the aircraft's breakup. The early word is that nothing has been found. A similar analysis of the aircraft's scattered parts reinforces the notion that the aircraft did not disintegrate in flight.

I need to go into the tent, see if Charlie's there. It's not a move I make easily. I've been here three hours before I tell the police officers escorting me around the site that I might have a relative among the dead. They look at me curiously but with a sense of compassion missing until now. I'm no longer a pain-in-the-ass lawyer they've got to watch; I'm now a victim too. I'm a person.

They surround me as I enter the tent, smell the burnt, rotting flesh and witness the severed heads and limbs. A bitter fluid rushes upward to my throat. Sharp pains cut through my chest. I fight to stifle the vomit and to remain upright. I look closely at the mangled flesh. Faces grotesquely disfigured, bodies ripped into pieces of shapeless flesh, crushed heads mingled with internal organs. Some are burned beyond recognition, probably identifiable only by dental records. Not one is graceful in death.

So many bodies of black men, black women. They come rolling in, one after the other, in all shades of black, in all ages and sizes. I hear Charlie at the black cemetery, hear him pleading and promising. I recall every word, every wounded look. My eyes roll backward, my eyelids half close. My legs are limp. I'm not grateful to be alive. I feel no sense of good fortune or invulnerability, merely a weakening of that inside me I can't name or touch.

No Charlie, no Charlie, I mumble as I circle the tent. A sense of relief settles inside me, but only for a moment. Pilot hasn't been found yet, an investigator says.

A burnt coil of blond hair comes into my view, and all memories of Carolyn are upon me. With near-perfect clarity I numbly watch the fire envelop and consume that dear, helpless girl. How many times have I seen and heard her die screaming? How many times have I listened to or read Ronnie's eyewitness account? Or the fire investigator's postdeath analysis? With each reading, my imagination has grown more vivid; new details are supplied, new perspectives developed that cut closer to the bone. "Her eyes just sort of bulged up and out like she'd gotten stabbed in the neck," I remember Ronnie telling the jury. "God Almighty, I swear that fire just ate her up." I shudder ever so slightly as these words bounce off my brain.

Did the fire eat up Charlie? Painstakingly I construct a vision of Charlie unharmed. Charlie's in front of me, a basketball in his hand, that familiar gleam in his eyes. Charlie's alive. To the Charlie I will to life, I speak with such emotion I grow hoarse.

As I leave the tent, reporters dash toward me. I look downward, increase the pace of my walk. "Look up, sir!" someone shouts, and by habit I raise my head. A camera light flashes. "What's your name? Who are you looking for?" a reporter demands, his tone suggesting—and meant to suggest—he has an unqualified right to know.

"Fuck you," I mutter, slicing through their human wall.

More telephone calls from the squad car. Executives at the airline confirm that Charlie piloted the downed jet, but I resist their condolences, clinging to what I perceive to be a rock-solid probability that Charlie, having taken Ruth's advice, backed out at the last moment. As the hours pass, I become convinced that Charlie is still in New York. The divorce order saved his life.

Night turns to morning, morning to a drizzly afternoon. The nurses feed me, the investigators occasionally check with me. They know who I am; they've seen me at my best. A wet, icy chill captures me when my eyes seize upon the darkened face of one of my police escorts. I should go with him, he says. I nod and follow.

We enter the tent. Charlie's body is mostly intact. A leg's missing, an ear is cut off. Someone's talking to me. Found hanging from a tree. Neck and arms got caught in long, twisting branches.

I can't keep looking. I don't mean I won't; I can't. My mind is swirling as if on a flying roller coaster in hundred-and-twenty-degree heat. Blackness is in my eyes. I try to push it away with my hands, find a ray of light. I'm falling. Not even Daddy's suicide has prepared me for this moment. My shoulder hits the ground. Dirt pops up into my face. I'm down, but I have the sensation that I'm still falling. I am, I'm still falling.

I'M PILOTING A small plane flying low to the ground. The plane is shooting a thick and noxious pesticide that kills all insects below—insects resting on plants, crawling on the ground, flying among the trees. Winds blow the pesticide miles off course, destroying insects by the tens of thousands.

I find no joy in this mass slaughtering of the insects. I'm paid to do a job, and being a diligent, hardworking soul, I do it thoroughly. I kill every insect I can, even those that aren't near the plants I'm sworn to protect. I kill them all because I can't distinguish the good from the bad, and after all, they are only insects. While the plane rests on the ground, insects creep along its body and wings. Those that make their way inside eat into the electrical wires until they nearly disconnect. The next time the plane takes off, it rises only thirty feet before dropping to the ground.

Bruised and bleeding, I try to force open the door, but it's rammed shut.

To my horror there comes into the cockpit thousands of insects from a multitude of species. They sting and bite me in every part of my swelling body. I'm screaming, writhing, flailing my arms. Jointed legs, pairs of wings, antennas, compound eyes—this is all I see. Hornets fly into my face, scorpions crawl down my legs. The unrelenting assault is merciless. Every square inch of me is covered with insects back and front. Soon I can no longer scream, as they're down my throat, filling my lungs. They suck out my blood, eat the flesh off my bones. Their revenge is complete.

"IN A WAY it's a very positive dream," Diana says. "The bugs caused the plane to fail. That's what you think happened, isn't it? The plane had bugs in it. Charlie was only doing his job."

"No, it's a dream about me. I killed all those living things that could've been saved. I had no spirituality, so the bugs ate my flesh."

"What a gruesome way to look at it."

I'm on my feet, pacing up and down the living room floor. "Can you confess away your sins if you've got the heart of a sinner?" I ask with a slight shiver. "Isn't the sin always with you then?"

Diana shakes her head slowly, her eyes closing a bit. "It tears me up to see you doubting yourself like this."

"Should I tell someone what I've done?"

"You didn't commit any crime, Michael. You believed in your brother, and helped him get his job back."

"They'd all be alive if I'd listened to you."

"You made an error in judgment, okay? One mistake doesn't make you evil."

"It makes me guilty."

"It makes you human." She rises from her chair, and rubs her cheek against mine. Diana is for me a natural cleansing force, a brisk salty-ocean breeze against my face. "You're allowed to be human," she says softly.

NOTHING IN FOCUS: The wide-board oak floor shakes as if rocked by a moving earth, the overhead light that's burned brightly all night flickers and dims, and the double-thick Sheetrock walls gyrate in a deadly dance. I push myself off the bed with the heavy stiffness of a body caked with rust. My fingers, as rigid as sticks of wood, clumsily pry open my eyes as I stagger forward, then fall to the floor with a hard thump. Escape from this swirling, sweaty, all-consuming, sucking black hole that blurs the line of reality and illusion is still possible: One dive into a speeding car, and I'm free.

Maybe I should draw Charlie until the sun rises—Charlie swimming with a fury against the ocean's tide, Charlie playing Mozart at the piano, Charlie screaming from the fire's cruel heat. Draw, draw, draw until Charlie's out of my system!

For hours I sit naked without pen or paper, staring aimlessly at the ceiling. No energy to look for paper. Any obstacle, no matter how small, bogs me down like a boat caught in a great mass of seaweed. The color's left my cheeks, and past my shriveled, paper-dry lips comes a foul breath. I don't want to eat. It's a battle merely to chew food. Sometimes I let the food stay in my mouth until my lips reach a tilted glass of bourbon, an act I achieve with a dogged determination reserved for few other activities. No food, I think, no friends either. Either they urge me to "get out," which I find demeaning, or they coddle me, claiming my immobility is understandable, thereby encouraging my descent into unworthiness; yet I can't remain alone for long periods of time, so hell, I let them come. I receive as guests the very people who deepen my despair. Nothing seems permanent, good, and unalterable; no one can relieve me from the crushing responsibility of choice and the ever-present temptation to blame myself.

THE FUNERAL HOME is littered with flower bouquets and hordes of acquaintances who come to pay their respects or, more likely, to be part of the spectacle. Anchors and crews from local TV stations ring the outside of the building. On my request, Charlie's casket remains closed.

I want to be alone, but can't refuse those who feel the need to console me. Having already wounded beyond repair more lives than any decent God would have allowed, I wish to hurt no one else. My body—seized by a dull, paralyzing despair—slumps at the shoulders and bends forward in the way of a man forty years my senior; my vision, narrowed by an empty, cold stare, is colored by a newly acquired cynicism. I listen (as one does to garbled background noise) to the mutterings of well-meaning, hovering souls whose rapidly aging bodies will soon be hurling them toward funerals of their own; and I respond merely with slow nods as if these motions are accomplished at great sacrifice. Looking upward, I inhale the hot, suffocating mist of a spicy perfume steaming off the neck of eighty-year-old Aunt Joan, whose cracked lips squeeze a lit cigarette. Her hair, dyed a reddish-brown hue reminiscent of a wasp I swatted last week, drops in ringlets around her neck. "Sorry for your loss," she repeats several times before being mercifully led away by her son, who dutifully echoes her remarks while puffing on his own lung-poisoning stick of tobacco.

My firm's lawyers, at the funeral en masse, offer condolences with feigned sadness, many of them already counting the dollars that will come to them shortly after the inevitable avalanche of lawsuits descends upon the airline. I dread these coming lawsuits—Charlie's performance and my own maneuverings will be subject to the most savage assaults.

"What do you want me to say?" I hear a man break through. "There's not much time left."

I turn to face the rabbi. How do you pay tribute to a man who killed all his crew and passengers? The rabbi is looking for help, for an angle. He needs to put the right slant on this horrifying disaster. "Talk about God and forgiveness. Talk about how Charlie loved his family. He was a war hero, you know. Flew extra missions in Nam so others wouldn't have to risk their lives."

"That's good, that's good." The rabbi wears heavy-rimmed glasses which brush up against his bushy eyebrows and touch his thick, graying beard. He's bald on top, a few thatches of hair by his neck all that remains. "Was he a practicing Jew?" he asks earnestly.

"He didn't go to school on the holidays. That's about it."

"What about since then?" the rabbi questions with a disapproving tone.

My voice turns cold. "Since then? He figured, since then, he wasn't more closely connected to Jews than to other men, and he wouldn't listen to rabbis who said God had chosen the Jews not by merit, but simply for service, because however modest that claim, it was still demeaning to those not of the faith, wasn't it? To those not burdened by demanding spiritual obligations? Charlie wouldn't be a man apart. It was the only way he could look God in the face."

"You sound so angry," the rabbi mumbles, his eyes cast downward. "This is a difficult time—"

"Charlie never liked the synagogue," I say abruptly. I didn't either. The air was stale, the words made no sense, and Mother kept wanting us to believe in Jesus because she didn't feel safe believing alone. But drinking the blood and eating the flesh of Christ, even in a purely symbolic way, sickened both of us. Christian statues and relics were graven images, so what choice did we have?

"If I didn't know you were a Jew, I'd have thought you hated . . ." The rabbi's voice trails off into a dark silence.

I glare down at the man whose head barely reaches to my shoulders. "I don't hate anyone. When God tells me the Jews have a monopoly on the truth, I'll believe it then." I walk past the rabbi, who's muttering he'll do the best he can. He'll do the best he can for God, I think, not for Charlie. Who is Charlie to him?

I drop into a deeply cushioned chair within earshot of the funeral director. The funeral director—with the soft, somber voice typical of his trade—speaks quietly with mourners who might someday be a source of business while keeping a respectful distance from the home's most expensive casket, a finely grained, solid mahogany box he sold to me without having to shame me into it. Carolyn's here, too, I think. She was brought to this same funeral home fourteen months ago—same mahogany casket, same rabbi, same mourners. Maybe she's with Charlie in that casket. Maybe that's why I won't let anyone open it.

I climb out of my chair and labor toward Ruth, whose eyes are fixed on the casket. I touch her shoulder, ready to forgive her for the pain she inflicted on Charlie in his final hours. After all, Ruth is suffering too. I keep my hand on her, believing we are experiencing a rare private moment that can be had only by those who have shared a great victory or a devastating loss, when, without turning her head, Ruth says: "I blame the crash on you. Charlie was too doped up, too proud to know better. You betrayed him."

My hand drops, my body shrinks backward. This morning's bold, splashy headlines leap back into my consciousness: PILOT TOOK LETHAL DRUG DOSE. Autopsy tests reveal that Charlie took a life-threatening dose of phenobarbital, a white crystalline barbiturate used as a sedative and a hypnotic. Sabotage, explains the *Post*, has been ruled out as a cause, no evidence having been found that any bomb or incendiary device was discharged, or that any passenger was intent on murder or suicide.

"The harder you tried to rescue Charlie, the harder it was for him to rescue himself," I hear Ruth say. "I know, Michael, because before the Seconal, there was bourbon. I'd sneak into his closet and empty out the bottles. He'd buy more. I'd empty them too, and he'd buy still more. He wore me down. But I think he respected me for what I tried to do.

"You did for Charlie what he did for your father. He sympathized, he forgave, he pampered. He convinced himself—no, he lied to himself—that everything was okay. Lying helped Charlie, not your father. For a while lying kept your great family secret a secret—that nobody could save your father. And now we know that nobody could save Charlie either."

"It wasn't lying. It was hope."

"He used you, Michael. You were a fly in the spider's web. He ate a little part of you whenever he was hungry. He'd act desperate, and you'd buzz right in."

"That's a strange way to look at it."

"Aren't you angry with Charlie, even a little? He promised us, didn't he?"

"Hasn't he been punished enough?" I scold her.

"I'd rather we be angry with Charlie than ourselves. Guilt can eat you alive."

I bend forward, my voice down to a whisper: "I do wonder, Ruth. Charlie was a creature of habit. If he'd wanted to calm down, why didn't he take Seconal? That's what he was used to, that's what always worked for him."

She reflects a moment. "Maybe he couldn't get the Seconal quick enough. Or maybe he didn't plan to take anything, but somebody offered the phenobarbital to him."

"He could've gotten the Seconal anytime he wanted through his doctor," I point out. "And Charlie would know exactly how much to take."

"And if he was suicidal, it was my fault?" Her voice, tinged with a mocking cynicism, contrasts with the weariness of her expression. Her thin neck is bent backward. Red veins crisscross the whites of her eyes. Bits of sleep cling to her eyelashes.

"I didn't say that." The mourners are gathering for their journey to the grave site. I take her hand, and labor toward the door. "I don't know what happened," I confess.

A raw, drizzling cold at the grave site, much the same weather as the moment of the crash. I hold Grace tightly, my arm extended around her back, my hand clutching her far shoulder. She mustn't be allowed to fly from me as Charlie did. The rabbi stands by Charlie's grave and talks about God's mercy, mentioning Charlie by name only once.

I tremble slightly as I carry Charlie's casket with five others to a naked spot of dirt yards from Carolyn's grave, wondering all the while if Charlie knows where he is. I'm the last to let go of the casket. A moment later the casket thuds against the carved-out earth and the rabbi cries out that in a world without evil, a man could never truly aspire to be righteous.

Long after the ceremony ends, I remain there with Grace, inches from the six-foot hole that is now Charlie's home. Grace's limbs are stiff, her feet dug deep into the wet dirt. She stares numbly at the casket.

Dıed on impact: words re-
peated countless times to assure me that Charlie's death was instant and
painless. *On impact*, I whisper to myself every so often. Friends counsel me
to avoid media reports of the crash, but I can't stop myself from absorbing
and memorizing every detail, however trivial.

Mass murder—inadvertent certainly, but the corpses were visible, and
each time I absorb the full force of my complicity with Charlie, I'm seized
not only with contempt and loathing for myself but with an everlasting and
limitless terror that I'll be crushed bit by bit and delivered to some blacker-
than-black hellish cavern. No light slices through these impenetrable layers
of gloom. Charlie led me to evil and I followed. To rise to innocence,
mustn't I accept and declare my guilt?

This wasn't a mere error as Diana would have me believe. An error is
adding up numbers incorrectly or dropping a fly ball. This was a moral
failure, a breakdown of character carrying with it a sense of annihilation
more terrifying than death. Try as I might, I can no longer recall the precise
instant I decided Charlie must be given another chance. Maybe I don't want
to know. Maybe that's why this and other mysteries are now shrouded
behind layers of shifting denials and baffling distortions.

In a windowless room overflowing with paper and airline parts, I listen
to every word spoken by Charlie in the last hour of his life. The cockpit
voice recorder, commonly called the black box, is at first a jumble of voices
and static. For two hours I concentrate on sorting out voices, absorbing
basic information. After that, I'm free to imagine the terror Charlie felt as
the angle of the dive sharpened and the altimeter's white figures whirled
down the scale amidst blinking lights and howling horns. I'm in the cockpit

as cold, swirling winds rock the plane. Down it goes at frightening speed. Shrieking passengers are hurled headlong to the front of the cabin, their broken bodies piled in a heap, while I'm helplessly pinned against the windshield by massive invisible forces. I see the plane explode on impact, hear the deafening collision of steel and earth, feel the sizzling heat, smell the burning flesh. Blood encircles, then engulfs me.

One remark of Charlie's unnerves me. Moments before the crash, he says to his copilot: "The up and down is stewed." What is Charlie trying to convey? Charlie's voice is relatively even—no panic, no shouting. "The up and down is stewed." I know the word "stewed" often means "drunk," and barbiturates make one act and feel drunk. But who's drunk? Apparently the "up and down" is. Who or what goes up and down? The plane. The pilot. Only one interpretation seems reasonable: The pilot is drunk. Seconds later Charlie mutters those same words in response to the copilot's question: "Are you okay?" Does the copilot mean Charlie's looking and talking as if ill, distracted, or under the influence of drugs? Or is the copilot, with the storm winds increasing in strength, seeking reassurance from Charlie they're not in danger, the phrase "Are you okay?" meaning "Are we okay?"

I take home a copy of the tape's transcript, read it over and over until my mind grows blurry: my way of holding on to Charlie a while longer, not unlike a child who, on his first day of school, won't let go of his mother. I not only know from memory every word spoken by Charlie on that last flight, I can't get the words or the fire or the blood out of my mind. For hours I lie in bed, unable to move or sleep. This defeat isn't dry, flat land but an ocean having many levels. Suffering has no limits.

At morning's light I wrap a square white woolen tallith around my shoulders, put tefillin on my left forearm and above my eyes. Wearing a plain black yarmulke, I bob my head in prayer as Daddy did the night before he killed himself. For a moment my entire body quivers as if in a dance with God. I'm alone, in hiding. Like God, I think.

"IT'S FOR YOU. " Diana hands me the kitchen phone. "Randy Chapman. He says it's urgent."

I take the phone reluctantly. Diana forces a smile.

"I just got off the horn with Philip Brandon," reports Randy. "He got tired of waiting for you to return his calls."

"I *am* in mourning."

"So is he. He thinks you may have killed his company. He gave me a blow-by-blow account of how you talked him into rehiring Charlie. He ain't a happy camper, Michael."

"He made the final decision."

"Oh, great, let's just tell him that. I'm sure he'll be persuaded."

"Any suggestions?"

"Pray he doesn't fire us. We won't have much of a firm left if he does."

"Who else knows about this?"

"Everybody. Philip called Clay Webb on some tax matter, then cried on his shoulder too. Cried and yelled, to be accurate. Philip's out of control."

"Is there panic in the firm?"

"Big time. Everybody's talking about who'll get the axe if the airline goes elsewhere."

"Are they upset with me?" I ask cautiously, as if once let go, these words cannot be retrieved.

"Again, big time. They are pissed off—"

"Who's they?" I interrupt.

"They is every partner and every associate. Throw in a few paralegals too. They seem to believe you weren't thinking of them when you risked the firm's relationship with its biggest client to help out your brother. A decision that momentous should have been discussed by the partnership first."

"I didn't think I needed partnership approval to talk to my own client. I never did before, did I?"

"You never did anything like this before. You had to know if things went badly, you were putting the whole firm at risk. These people got families. They need their jobs."

"If it weren't for me, they wouldn't have jobs here in the first place. Brandon Air Lines is here because of me."

"They don't think that way, Michael. All they see is Brandon leaving because of you."

My hands clench, my eyes burn. I slam down the phone. Violence has seeped into my blood. I tremble to think my values can vanish with such ease at the touch of adversity.

Water fills my eyes. I hear loud, sobbing gasps coming from my throat. My body shakes as if possessed by demons, my face turns the blue of a baby in need of oxygen. Not even Diana's embrace can stop these convulsionlike spasms. I weep for what I did, I weep for what I fear I've become. Mercifully, my body defends itself by shutting down after an hour. I fall into an uneasy sleep, fully dressed on the kitchen floor.

FOUR IN THE morning. I keep my eyes open, the images of death easier to control while awake. The phone is disconnected, the radio thumps a soft rock. Every tune I hear this hellish week will be forever associated with terror and grief.

I must go back to work. Hot showers, movies, sympathetic friends: All have failed to relax me. Every day by noon I've been bone-tired.

I pull up to my building around seven, then mindlessly circle the streets for an hour, torn between a desire for solitude and a need to declare my grief. I leave my car in the midst of a thunderstorm that floods sewers, drives water down streets at high speeds, and soaks my clothes to my underwear before I, deep in engaging meditation, head for cover.

I enter my office dripping wet. I'd gladly surrender my life for Charlie's, I tell my secretary Patti upon seeing her, to which she mutters a few words about how she loved her sister and could understand—but I'm gone before she finishes her reply. It's not until I flick on my light that I realize I've left her in midsentence.

I sit at my desk staring at words I don't fully comprehend, almost as if my native language has become foreign to me; yet I can do nothing but remain here, a smothering heaviness having infiltrated and captured my body. I can't recall names of people I've known for years; I forget phone numbers I dial regularly. Concentration on even the smallest tasks is blocked by an overwhelming disbelief. I'm a car without a driver plunging down a slope.

On my desk I put an eight-by-ten photo of Charlie holding a basketball, his free hand pointing a thumb upward. Even I recognize my memories of Charlie contain shades of denial—Charlie makes every shot, honors every promise—I cannot completely overcome. Denial, I muse, is at times necessary. I need to deny wholeheartedly the possibility that Charlie, wanting to die, chose at a critical split second not to expend every effort to recover the plane.

I have all the victims' files in front of me. Of the 120 killed, 96 were black, a statistic that adds yet another dimension to my misery. Blacks from all parts of the country were flying into the District for this year's National Baptist Convention. Black church and community leaders, swift to act, have called upon the FAA to sanction the airline. Had the passengers not been predominantly working-class blacks, they charge, the pilot's condition would have been more carefully examined; and the FAA would have brought sanctions without having to be asked. The FAA has thus far refused to sanction Brandon Air Lines, claiming the cause of the crash has not been finally determined.

A short knock at the door, and Randy's inside my office before I can reply. "Glad you're back," Randy says. "We need to figure out what to do."

"They're still pissed off?"

"It's gone way beyond that. They want assurances they won't be fired. And they want to renegotiate the points."

I deliberately raise my eyebrows, wrinkle my forehead. "Renegotiate?"

Randy, sitting opposite me, stretches out his legs. "That's what I said. No way. We just finished that in December. Once a year, I told them. But they said things have changed, and anyway, we're both paid too much."

"It'll set a bad precedent."

"Horrible. Anyway, we're not overpaid. You and I started this firm with nothing, right? For two years we barely fed ourselves, and for two years after that, we were near bottom. They all came on board after the engine was built and the ship sailing."

I nod. Randy and I met fourteen years ago working Saturdays pro bono for the homeless, the abused, and the elderly. We formed the kinship of those who do battle for all things just and good. One sunny afternoon we impulsively decided to leave our suffocating, come-to-our-church, do-as-we-do, wildly rich blue-blood firms to begin a practice with a few small clients and a bunch of high-interest loans. For years we did everything together: drove to work, ate lunch, brainstormed, plotted, watched each other's trials. We feel no urge to apologize to our partners for our incomes, no matter how high they may go.

"They've gotten together and elected Clay Webb as their rep to talk to us."

I slump back in my chair. This is beginning to sound like a full-blown rebellion. That crash, I'm slowly understanding, was a blast of fire to the partnership's collective skin. Yet Clay is a reasonable soul. Lacking a litigator's killer instinct, Clay is content to draft agreements, form corporations, negotiate loans, and attend board meetings. I imagine that shuffling papers is all the law means to Clay and his three daughters in college, who deride his relatively unglamorous work and slavish devotion to the few clients he's managed to acquire, though they accept without hesitation all benefits that flow from the money he earns.

"We need to give Clay something, or at least pretend to," Randy advises. "Give him some stature so they don't elect somebody else who might breathe a little fire."

Exactly what I'm thinking, though I'm glad Randy articulates it first. This sort of scheming is beneath me.

"You okay?" Randy asks. "You look like shit."

"I'm okay," I say dully.

"You should see a shrink. Get one of those antidepressant drugs."

"I'm okay."

"Stop kidding yourself, Michael. Get well, and do it quick. I need you now."

RANDY'S OFFICE IS immaculate, his papers arranged in orderly stacks, his initials engraved in gold on his paperweight. His clothes are custom-made, his briefcase of the finest leather. On the edge of his black leather chair he sits with arms resting on a gold-trimmed mahogany desk. His hair, still full and dark with a few sprinkles of gray, is neatly combed. His large, catlike eyes rest full on Clay Webb's face. Two oil paintings of sailboats hang above the six-chair conference table near his office's rear door.

"No one's perfect, and no one rules perfectly. We're all sinners, all holy men," he tells Clay with the sardonic smile of an experienced street hustler.

Clay Webb waits on a cushioned chair across from me, and smiles nervously. Since he stopped smoking, Clay has noticeably gained weight. His stomach bulges slightly; his hips are wider and more fleshy; and his pectorals sag like a woman's. His body's only stiffness forms across his lips, which hardly move even when he speaks with emotion. Pockmarks scar his face (an unwelcome remnant of childhood acne), and his few remaining hairs, clumped in tiny bushes around his ears, are covered in the main by the temples of his silver-rimmed glasses.

"There's been a lot of frustration around here building up for a long time," Clay says after an uneasy silence. "You guys alone decide how the points are divided up, and you guys make most of the money. Nobody but you two thinks the system works. The rest of us want an elected committee to decide the points."

"This isn't a democracy, Clay. It's a business," declares Randy.

Clay shifts his body back and forth, trying to get comfortable. "Why can't it be both?" he whines.

Randy's face darkens. He edges forward. "This isn't about democracy anyway. It's about money," Randy sputters, a vein near his temple pulsing madly. "They think we're greedy, but they're the greedy ones! Their lack of gratitude, it's astonishing. We're being devoured by the wolves we've fed!"

"They have no complaints about how much they make, but how much compared to you two guys," Clay fights back.

"I think they make too much compared to us!" Randy shouts at him. "Nobody works harder than Michael or me. Nobody has been here longer. Nobody has more talent. And nobody but Michael brings in much business. And I manage this place. Make all the hard decisions. In the last year alone, I got us the lowest rental rate in town, got five top lawyers to come here with their clients, and bought us the best computer system for twenty percent less."

"All they want is a fresh look at the system," Clay observes quietly. "Let somebody else decide the points. If you're right, you've got nothing to worry about." I believe Clay has no desire to blame, punish, or wound; he wants merely to forget whatever wrongs have been committed and start again in a new direction.

"If it's more money they want, let them go out on their own like we did, and see how well they do."

"They will, Randy, and your threats will only scare them away faster. Loyalty's a dead concept in the business world."

"Not in my world, it's not," Randy states with conviction.

"Michael wasn't loyal to them," Clay mumbles, his tone reflecting his ambivalence.

I remain silent, my appetite to do battle having been weakened by Charlie's death, the same circumstance that has likely emboldened my partners to seek concessions from me. They smell my weakness, yet they will go only so far. Money, the guiding force behind their talk of injustice, chills their commitment to all-out war.

"There's another thing," Clay mentions uneasily. He turns to me. "You're not going to like this."

"Spit it out," commands Randy.

Clay looks back at Randy. "One of the associates asked Diana when she first knew Michael was talking to the airline about his brother. She said she always knew, then apparently launched into a heated defense of Michael. The long and short of it is, the associates and many of the partners want her gone. She kept vital information from the partners. Her loyalty is to Michael, not the firm. She's a disaster for morale, and that's the last thing we need now."

I break my silence. "She's staying," I bristle. "End of discussion."

"It'll weaken you if she stays," says Clay. "It'll prove to them you put your own needs above the firm."

"Why don't they fire me if they're so upset?"

"If they fire Michael," intervenes Randy, "they might as well fire me too. There won't be a firm left anyway."

Clay raises his arms as if to signal a halt. "C'mon now, nobody's thinking about firing Michael. He founded this firm, for God's sake. I'm just saying, as a PR matter, it would be smart for Michael to let Diana go."

"Jealousy," I muse aloud. "Every partner wants her body. Every associate wants her talent."

"Every associate is afraid she'll make partner instead of them because you're sleeping with her."

"Like I said, Clay, end of discussion. What's next on your agenda?"

Clay sighs with a shake of his head. "The partners think you owe them, Michael. They're afraid they'll all be sued if the airline has to pay out millions of dollars to the victims' estates. Brandon might just be mad enough to sue you for getting him to rehire Charlie. If you're liable for malpractice, then we're liable too."

"Brandon's not going to sue us," Randy asserts bravely.

"We'll need to contact our insurance carrier," advises Clay glumly.

"What for?" Randy snaps. "Michael didn't commit malpractice. He made a recommendation that could have been accepted or rejected. In hindsight, it would've been better rejected, but that's hindsight. Like I said, none of us is perfect."

Clay, not easily moved to anger, removes his glasses and looks squarely at Randy. "Neither of you can reform, that's what the problem is. Every time you've been challenged, you've not only knocked us down, you've arrogated even more power to yourselves to guard against the next challenge. We must have limits, don't you think? You stay in power because we let you. Because we've all been afraid. We're as guilty as you are."

Randy's face flushes with a most intense shade of redness, revealing that inner turbulence of indignation he invariably feels whenever lectured or challenged by an inferior. "We built this firm," he cries out. "Long before you came here, we—"

"It's not in your interest to be reformed," Clay says, the tightness in his voice reflected on his deeply wrinkled forehead. "You love this unmitigated power to be arbitrary, don't you? To rule the lives of all fifty-five lawyers here? It makes your lives vital. Without it, you'd be bodies without faces."

Fury has its hold on Randy: It's in the hot glow of his eyes, the sweat on his neck. "You want to take over our firm, don't you?" Randy growls.

"It's not your firm. It belongs to all the partners. That's the point neither of you can get into your head."

Randy shoots in Clay's direction that deathlike stare that frequently incites fear among the weaker-hearted, but Clay is growing stronger. With the moral assurance of a God-fearing priest, Clay pronounces: "A man who sins while trying to be holy has still sinned, right?"

"Pack up your goddamn things and get the hell out of here!" explodes Randy.

"I'm fired? I'm—"

"Fired!" yells Randy, this time a note of glee creeping into his voice.

Clay falls backward ever so slightly, as if withdrawing from a bloodied dog found in the street, its head crooked from the impact of a speeding car. He peers directly into my face, looking for a reassuring nod, a warm smile, even as small a gesture as eye contact.

I don't turn away. "We're all a little bit on edge, Clay. I don't think Randy meant what he just said." Firing Clay would either incite a greater rebellion or cause a swarm of others to resign in fear. We need Clay, and Clay needs us. Where will he ever find a job that pays him two hundred thousand a year when he brings in a hundred thousand in business? We fire him, we fire his family too.

"I meant it," Randy chuckles. "But I guess I don't mean it anymore."

Clay Webb stands up, then leaves the room. Not a word, not even a nod. He's gone before we have time to reconsider.

WHENEVER RANDY CHAPMAN marches briskly across the oak floors that separate the lawyers' offices from the secretarial bays, the lawyers in his sight strain to appear busy, and their secretaries, absorbing their tension, type faster, answer their phones on the first ring. Randy Chapman isn't a man to be made unhappy.

Unlike most men, Randy is not only comfortable with the burdens of power, he believes he has the right and duty to rule. Limousines, four-star hotels, a corner office with floor-to-ceiling windows: These luxuries, having been showered upon him with uncommon regularity, are now viewed by him as God-given privileges. His wife and children have come to believe that money enters the family checking account automatically, as if by divine decree.

In the past week of swirling accusations and closed-door conferences, Randy has come to see each partner either as friend or traitor, depending upon his willingness to succumb to Randy's view of the firm's best interests. Those who don't swiftly acknowledge his value or who foolishly repeat statements he's made to them in confidence are banished from his kingdom of grace—at which time he becomes preoccupied with his newest enemy's supposed plot against him. He reads evil intentions into these partners' most harmless statements, interprets their every facial expression in the most unfavorable light.

In moments of joy, Randy has a child's unbounded enthusiasm. He flatters, grins, touches with genuine affection; people gravitate to him, albeit cautiously. Today he's a stiff body with the burning eyes of a man betrayed by his wife. He enters my office without knocking, a subtle sign of my diminishing status. "We need to inspire fear in them," Randy says coldly. "If they sense weakness, they'll go for our throats. Maybe get some rumors started that we'll fire anybody who presses us too hard."

"I'd rather inspire trust."

"Don't you want some revenge, Michael? For them trying to make us feel guilty?"

"They don't fear us anymore, not as much as they fear a lawsuit. If we try to intimidate them, we'll incite a bigger rebellion."

"Don't wimp out on me, Michael."

"Maybe we have paid ourselves too much. Maybe that's why we got this rebellion."

Randy remains on his feet. He points a shaking finger at me. "We got it because of the crash. The crash gave them the excuse to come at us."

"We are where we are," I say flatly.

"If fear won't work, then we've got to give them something. I'm not willing to take a pay cut, and neither should you."

"If you're referring to Diana, no."

"You got us into this, Michael. Do something to get us out."

"I'm willing to give up points. It doesn't mean you have to."

"Yes, it does," Randy groans. "How can I justify making more than you? Look, I need that money. I've got five kids, all of them in private schools, and Kay is adding two wings to our house, which still won't be half as big as yours."

"No."

"I don't give a damn if you're screwing her, Michael. Maybe they do, but I don't. I just want a deal."

"I need her here. She's the best lawyer we've got."

"Won't she still sleep with you if you fire her?" Randy snorts. "Blame it on me. Say I made you do it."

"She's not an idiot. Sometimes you—"

"Okay, okay," Randy concedes. "But who says she's not using you to make partner here? Everybody else seems to think that. Prove them wrong. Fire her, and keep screwing her."

"She provokes you, doesn't she? Because she won't bow down, won't kiss your behind?"

"She doesn't need to. She's got yours to kiss, right?"

ALL THE SIGNS were there: rage, guilt, a need to free herself. I missed them, though. I spent all day with Ruth at the funeral, and said not one word to her about the media—how it cons, distorts, exploits. I didn't warn her; she didn't warn me. I stare again at the *Post*'s front page: EX-WIFE CLAIMS PILOT, FIRED FOR DRUG USE, SHOULD NOT HAVE BEEN ALLOWED TO FLY.

The article runs down two long columns and continues on page two. Quotes from Ruth are everywhere. She blames the airline for "criminal negligence" and "gross stupidity." They "knew Charlie was hooked," but "Charlie was pals with the right people." An obvious reference to Philip Brandon, though it might be construed to apply to me as well. Ruth mentions no names specifically but leaves a trail of bodies to account for their actions. I drop the *Post* on the floor. I will eventually be engulfed in this tidal wave. I shudder. It's coming, I know in my quivering gut it's coming.

I summon Ruth to my office in the voice of a drill sergeant, then hang up before her reply. No one's ever betrayed me this way. The signs were there, but why blame myself? Why always blame myself? Ruth arrives within the hour, and is hurried into my office. I remain in my chair. "Sit," I order brusquely.

"Is this going to be a lecture?"

"Call it what you want, but you've guaranteed yourself top billing in every lawsuit filed against the airline," I reprimand her. "You'll be hounded by lawyers and the media for as long as these cases last."

"I just told the truth," she replies without a trace of remorse. "That's more than I bet you'll do."

"What you told was your version of the truth in the light most damning to Charlie, to the airline, and to me. You got us all, didn't you?"

"I'm not the one who—"

"What goes around comes around, Ruth. Sooner or later they'll come up with the divorce order and argue suicide. You won't be looking like a hero then."

"What should I do?" she asks after an awkward silence.

"Don't say another word to anyone about Charlie or the airline or what you think went wrong. Before you're called to testify, you see me. We'll go over everything. Every question and every answer. Understood?"

"I won't lie, Michael."

"I won't ask you to. Just behave yourself in the meantime."

"This thing about the divorce order," she remarks cautiously. "It makes it more likely it was pilot error, doesn't it?"

"Don't mention it to anyone, especially not the media," I advise sternly. "Not unless you're asked directly about it. I don't want you to lie."

"Sure you do. You just can't say it." She breathes deeply, and looks away. "Charlie knew how I felt about you. He was in pain. It took root in his gut and festered like a bleeding sore."

"This isn't the time or place," I say sharply.

"He wasn't angry with you, just me. He was a good man," she adds, as if a tribute is necessary. Maybe one from her is.

"That's not the way the media sees it."

She shrugs, then continues as if compelled by some inner force. "In the beginning Charlie did so much for me. He'd draw my bath, cook dinner, take me to the symphony. Funny how his kindness repelled me. I should've been grateful, of course, but the more he played the angel, the more I felt like Satan. He followed me, watched me, sat too close. Like a child clinging to his mother's knees while she's stirring a boiling pot. He was underfoot. Suffocated me with kindness. I didn't deserve all his attention, you know. It got so bad that sometimes I'd actually grip my hands around my neck when we were making love, so hard I thought I'd choke. I had to believe I was a victim. Being made to suffer despite my innocence. I had to believe that, or the guilt would've crushed any little pleasure I could get from him. Charlie made it so unbearable for me, I had to tell him."

"About what?"

"About how I loved you, not him. He cried a little, then apologized for crying and went to sleep. No nasty words, no yelling, no chance for a fight. The next morning he asked me what he could do to make me love him. Tell him, and he'd do it. What do you do with a man like that? You want to beat some sense into him."

"Or get to your knees and thank God."

"You were never afraid to leave or stay or take. You'd weigh the risks and benefits. Like a lawyer, I guess. Always the lawyer. I need that, someone not to worship me. Not to expect much from me."

"The way I remember it, you asked Charlie to marry you."

"I never should've. A little girl's decision, that's all it was. Hate ruined our marriage, Michael. I hated you, I hated myself. After a while, Charlie knew he could do nothing to change that. I'd mope around, I'd sulk. I was a horror to live with. I had to divorce him."

"He never said a word to me about any of this," I whisper in mild disbelief.

"Of course not. Male ego." She rises, walks toward me. "Do you ever imagine when you're driving home that I'll be there at your front door, just waiting?"

"Sit down, Ruth." I glance at my watch. Maybe I should've had this conversation by phone.

"Why do you always make me feel like I'm renting your time?" She pouts. "It's a lease vaguely worded and impossible to enforce, you know. Pretty soon you'll be sending me memos. No return calls, not even one-word answers, just short memos unsigned."

"I'm not the one, Ruth. Now, please sit down."

"I think of you by my door, Michael. You've got candy or flowers, and you're begging my forgiveness. As it should be." She allows herself a small smile.

"I'm not the one—"

"To bring me back? From my own little hell? I'm not asking for all that, Michael. Just a touch of kindness. Is that too much to ask?"

"I didn't know I was so cold," I reply with a heavy sarcasm.

"That's why I'm telling you. So you'll know to return my calls, maybe even call me once in a while. So you'll know not to challenge my every statement like I'm a witness against you. I'm not against you," she protests. "You don't know how fragile I am."

"I don't challenge statements to be cruel. Just to get at the truth," I say in true lawyerly fashion.

She is right above me now. "You know how a victim needs to talk about a crime she's endured? I—"

"What crime have you endured?" I inquire harshly.

"Not being paid attention to by the one I love. The worst crime," she mumbles.

I'M INVITED TO participate in a CNN panel discussion on airline safety. I tell the show's producer I can't comment on Flight 555's crash or any positions the airline might take concerning it. "That's okay," he assures me. "We won't ask about the airline's legal stuff. It's more about the whole industry, what can be done, what can't be."

"I'm not a pilot or an engineer. You might want someone with a more technical background."

"We've already got technical people. We're looking for a broader spectrum."

I call Philip. He thinks I should participate. "I'd rather have somebody there from our team than nobody at all. And who, better than you, would know the right things to say to keep us out of trouble?"

I go to a local CNN conference center, and am hooked up by satellite with four other centers, all of us able to see the others on video screens, the moderator directing us from Atlanta. We spend five minutes debating mildly the FAA's record on safety when the moderator abruptly asks me: "Since the pilot on Flight five five five was your brother, do you know what he meant when he said 'the up and down is stewed'?"

"I was told I wouldn't be asked about Flight five—"

"You were told we wouldn't ask about the airline's legal positions. I was right there when our producer told you that, and we'll certainly honor that. But we're not talking about legal positions now. We're—"

I've been ambushed. I fly into a rage: "Honor the spirit of your agreement, sir. No questions about this recent tragedy." I won't speculate on national television about what Charlie meant. A month or a year or five years from now, I might need to argue an interpretation different from whatever I spill out at this instant.

"I didn't mean to upset you," says the moderator, a gray-haired gentleman in his fifties who looks the part of a conservative, well-bred family man. "It seemed only natural to ask. There are those who believe Charles Ashmore took those massive quantities of phenobarbital because he intended to die, then take his plane down with him."

I'm astonished by the accusation. I'm about to call it ludicrous when a female panelist from New York, earlier introduced as a clinical psychiatrist (that should have alerted me, but I was expecting her to comment on passengers' fears of flying), inquires: "Wasn't your brother experiencing a high degree of instability? I understand he had a daughter die right in his own home a year ago, and on the very day of the crash he found out his wife's divorce petition had been granted."

"He was not unstable," I argue strenuously, but state no facts in support of my position. I don't want someday to find my remarks twisted and used in some lawyer's brief to the court.

"But are those observations correct?" the moderator weighs in. "About the divorce papers and his daughter?"

"And there was his father's suicide as well," the psychiatrist marches on. "Wasn't he found hanging from a living room chandelier?"

These people have not a scintilla of mercy. *That was my daddy too, you bastard, that was my own daddy hanging from the chandelier.* How do they manage to chat so casually about matters so painful to a human in their presence? Charlie found Daddy first. He untied the knot, and carried Daddy back to his bed. It wasn't until Daddy was under the blankets that Charlie let out a hideous shriek.

I must answer. I can't let Charlie take this relentless assault any longer. "My brother Charlie held planes sacred the way some people hold their families sacred. He'd never let a plane go down on purpose, not in a trillion years. If he'd wanted to commit suicide—which, I assure you, he did not—he would've done it in private, alone, without endangering anyone else. Charlie was a war hero, you know, not only because he flew better than anyone, but because he flew in the place of others so they wouldn't be at risk."

"He seems," the psychiatrist pontificates, "to be a man understandably full of rage. As you say, he had to risk his life for others, and got nothing in return. He lost his daughter, then his wife. He had a suicidal father and a mother—correct me if I'm wrong—who once worked for the Nazis and didn't want him to be raised as a Jew. This has all the trademarks of a man headed for the cliff."

"You have all the trademarks of a scandal-sheet reporter," I answer fiercely. "My mother never worked for the Nazis, and never objected to Charlie being raised the way he was. Your whole analysis—"

"Was it suicide or an accidental OD?" the moderator jumps in.

"Suicide, never. No suicide note, was there? Charlie would have left a note. We were very close. Did everything together. I would've known . . ." I'm babbling now. I must control myself. I glance at my watch. This is torture.

"So you think it was an accidental OD?"

"Charlie died from impact," I declare, "not drugs."

"But when you put it all together, plus the gibberish he was talking right before the crash, you can't so easily dismiss the possibility of a suicide in one of two ways," persists the psychiatrist. "Either he took that huge amount of phenobarbital to kill himself alone, or he took it just before boarding the plane knowing he couldn't properly operate the plane in his condition."

Sitting beside the psychiatrist in New York is a former federal prosecutor who veers off in another direction, as if the time has come to discuss more practical issues: "If the pilot did intend to take his own life—and I respectfully emphasize the word 'if'—do you believe the airline is morally or legally responsible?"

This isn't a panel discussion; it's an inquisition. "There was no attempt at suicide here," I repeat with complete conviction. "But if it's a purely hypothetical question, I'd say no company can be held responsible for a criminal act of one of its employees. That's black-letter law."

We run out of airtime. I don't thank the moderator or say good-bye to the panelists. I switch off my mike, walk away. I'm coming to believe Diana was right on the money to call me a good fool; unfortunately, I seem to be perfecting the art of it.

BOUND AND GAGGED in a makeshift tent. My accusers, wearing judges' robes and executioners' masks, refuse to tell me the nature of my crime. I'm found guilty. Gradually the tent turns to icy, surging waist-high water driving me down a dark slope. Human blood and excrement splash into my mouth. A narrow patch of light. I grab on to a rough metal prong workmen use to return from the sewer to ground level.

I fall. This is real. I'm on the bedroom floor, dazed and weak. I hear Diana scream, and sometime later—how long, I don't know—men in white clothes breathe air into my lungs, then rush me to a hospital.

Four doctors examine me. No bumps, bruises, or diagnosable illnesses, they conclude. Yet I writhe with pain, I sweat, I speak as if my mouth is stuffed with cotton. They shoot me with painkillers. Diana combs my wet hair. I inhale deeply and shiver.

They admit me for the night. This illness, having come on with such swiftness, mystifies the doctors, who won't admit to their confusion. My pain is real, the symptoms visible, but the force behind it invisible to all their high-tech machines.

"Should we get a specialist?" Diana asks, her voice holding steady from what I suspect is a concentrated effort.

"We don't even know what specialty. Everything hurts," I groan. These shooting pains have about them the supernatural quality of a divine mistake, an evil spell meant for someone else.

They stick needles in my arms, run test after test, and order me to move my feet. Like a crippled man in a walker, I stumble down the hospital's corridors holding on to Diana's arm, my head slumped forward. Somewhere in my body there must lay the earlier cells of the earlier me, a person in whom I once had great faith but at the moment can't reconstruct.

Diana helps me back into a bed whose raised iron arms make it seem more like a baby's crib. I look up at her. "Am I going insane?"

"You're ill, that's all. You'll be better soon."

"Am I going insane? Like my father?"

"You've been through so much . . ."

"They'll find out soon. Maybe I should tell them."

"You have nothing to tell. The guilt is all in your head."

"Daddy . . ." Grace is by the door. She edges inside. "Daddy, can I see you?"

"Sure, honey," I manage to say. "Come in."

"You two be alone for a while," Diana excuses herself.

Grace climbs over the iron and sits on the bed beside me. I lean toward Grace. I cup her cheeks, the shape of balloons her first three years of life, then stroke her curly hair. I can't measure my feelings for Grace as I measure so much of what I do.

"I don't want you to ever work again," Grace says. "Can't we just be poor, Dad? Is that okay?"

I smile a moment, but my lips freeze when I notice her soft, finely featured face contort, her slender lips jut forward with a slight tremble. My entire body absorbs her every sorrow-beaten ache, every wrenching stab. My chest muscles constrict so tightly I fear I'll stop breathing.

Grace stares at me for a long while. "What's wrong with you, Daddy?" Her cheeks have turned a sickly pale. I'm no longer her once powerful father.

"Nothing, honey. It's—"

"You're scaring me, Daddy!"

"I'll be okay, honey. I'm just a little tired."

"You never looked like this, never."

"I'll be—"

"You got to get better. You can't die!"

I shake—maybe it's Grace's fear, maybe my own, but I shake hard enough for Grace to shriek and the nurse to dash into the room with a needle that penetrates my shoulder and stays there long enough for me to close my eyes and sleep.

HOURS LATER I awake, thinking of Grace. She's all the family I have left. I'm angry at myself for having frightened her so, and this anger gives me a renewed jolt of energy. I sit up in bed, and remember how I fed Grace those first few years and drove her to all those Disney movies. I've always been her primary parent. I taught her to play soccer and piano, went to all her games and recitals, helped her every night with her homework. Grace and I have always been a team.

By midafternoon my head is erect, my back straight. The doctors gather to examine me. Clear eyes, normal appetite, swift walk. The doctors are delighted with themselves. Something they did must have worked. Go, they say, go home.

I've returned from the grave.

Two kinds of clients: those who go to rich lawyers, figuring they must be good; and those who seek out their poorer cousins, figuring their fees must be reasonable. The large conference room at Ashmore & Chapman is intended to attract the free spenders. Designed by Randy, it's fit for royalty. Brass chandeliers, carved antique tables, silk wall coverings, and a gleaming black and gold marble floor covered in its center by a ninety-year-old Persian rug emphatically convey the intended impression.

Twenty leather chairs line the center table. I sit at its head, nearly blocked from view by ever-higher stacks of logbooks, maintenance records, equipment drawings, and correspondence. Roy Brooks and Jim McKinney sit with hands folded like schoolboys.

"Give me your assessment, Jim," I order quietly.

McKinney nods and straightens his back. As Chief Pilot, he's one step below Roy Brooks and in charge of pilot training. On my instructions, McKinney has reconstructed Charlie's flight path in painstaking detail from data collected by the black box and the flight data recorder. A tape deck, the FDR records with accuracy to one tenth of a second a plane's airspeed, altitude, direction, pitch, and G load as well as the performance of its engines, flaps, rudders, and control yokes. Embedded in shock-proof insulation within a fireproof, waterproof, crash-proof steel sphere the size of a beach ball, the FDR was found, undamaged, in thick brush by a plumber's wife after the airline offered ten thousand dollars for its recovery.

"Charlie's right on course the whole way," McKinney begins, his hand gesturing with each sentence. "At a hundred miles out, he's at twenty-five thousand feet going four hundred forty knots. At thirty-five miles, he's at ten thousand feet, same speed, and perfectly intercepts the localizer. At six miles, when the trouble starts, he's at one hundred fifty knots and three thousand feet, right where he should be. He's right in line with the localizers, the outer marker, and the glide scope. Up till this point, he's done everything right, complied with every detail in the operations manual. If he had drugs in him, it wasn't affecting his flying."

Roy shakes his head with a joyless, cynical laugh. "You guys got your heads in the clouds. He crashed, nose-down, at three hundred knots. And nobody's found a thing wrong with the plane."

"Up till the point of the dive, nobody's found a thing wrong with how he was flying either," McKinney maintains.

"Take a closer look at the Safety Board's report," counsels Roy. "They said pilot error. A 'shocking amount of phenobarbital in the pilot's blood' was their exact words, right? And then there's the position of the stabilizers. They were in the full nose-down position. No sane pilot puts the stabilizers to four point four degrees, especially not in turbulence. And the pilot of a J Ninety-nine can tell the stabilizer's true position at all times even if the electrical system malfunctions."

I can't object. The pointer is actuated by the movement of two drums and a cable running the length of the plane. The cable and drums work independently of the electrical system. Charlie had to know.

According to the Safety Board's report, Charlie went through a sharp upward movement upon encountering turbulence, leveled out, then dived at supersonic speed. The plane had its nose up at 45 degrees when the stabilizers were moved electrically from their normal setting of 2.5 degrees to 4.4 degrees.

I have no answer for Roy. I can only say: "The Safety Board's report is not admissible in a court of law."

"I don't care about *legal* technicalities," Roy grumbles. "Those guys are experts."

I glare at Roy, offended by his tone. "If you read the whole report, it specifically says the winds were high and tricky, and the controllers sent the plane right into the worst of it."

"They also said our pilot should've adapted to the winds, like everybody else did."

"Winds come and go in seconds," McKinney points out. "Every pilot has to deal with his own set of speeds and angles." McKinney leans forward, ready for the next exchange. He's an accomplished pilot whose skills, though revered at the airline, haven't enlarged his sense of self. He is an unpretentious fellow with soft, appealing features: fair, unwrinkled skin, reddish-brown hair, hazel eyes, arched nose. *If Jim says it's so, it's so*, goes a familiar saying among Brandon's pilots.

"Okay, let's go through it," Roy suggests with a familiar edge to his voice. "An explosion? No sounds of one on the black box and no chemical residues of explosives. Birds? No microscopic traces of blood. The rudders? Right at center where they should be. The spoilers? In the retracted position, normal for an initial landing approach. Loss of fuel? No, because the angle of descent would've been about normal with only minor damage. Engine fire? Charlie would've had time to report that, and anyway, no lightning was seen by anybody."

"You haven't mentioned ice on the wings," I say acidly. "You haven't mentioned sticking elevators."

"Freezing rain is perfect weather for freezing and sticking," McKinney adds.

"This wouldn't be the first plane to go down because of ice on the wings," I point out. "Remember that US Air flight that crashed coming out of La Guardia? Ice on the wings. It got deiced at the gate but waited too long in line for takeoff. It iced up again."

"That flight crashed on takeoff, Michael. This one didn't. And the de-icing fluids we got now work a lot better than they did ten years ago."

"Ice can build up during the flight too," McKinney contends. "Icy wings have no lift."

"Hey, I'm not for losing the case," Roy protests. "All I'm saying is, let's get up a winning argument supported by the evidence. If we say it's the plane, we'll get our brains beat out. If we say it's ice on the wings, they'll say the plane would have come down at a somewhat normal angle, not this sharp dive. So I'm telling you, forget the plane. Blame it on the weather or the controllers."

"You mean forget Jarrad."

"Exactly, Michael. Think wind shear. Like you said, there were high, tricky winds. Charlie would've likely encountered a strong headwind that speeded up air flow over the wings and lifted the plane. Then at the center of the microburst, he'd have gotten that downward rush. He'd have lost speed and altitude, right? What's wrong with that argument?"

"They'll say Charlie should've increased power and climbed. He was high up enough to get it turned around."

"The plane could've stalled, Jim. That's what wind shear does."

"Another thing, Roy," I interject. "The airline is paying for psychiatrists and ministers to counsel the victims' families. I'm told the airline is finding out some intimate stuff and using it to fend off lawsuits. Put a stop to that today."

"Who's doing that?" asks Roy indignantly.

"Higher-ups at the airline."

"That can't be—"

"Today, Roy. End it today. Or we'll be getting punitive damage suits and the worst publicity imaginable."

Roy's cheeks redden. "You shouldn't be the angry one," he fires back. "You and your partners are going to get rich from this tragedy while the airline is going to be emptying its pockets."

"I lost a brother," I growl. "No amount of money—"

"I'm not saying you're happy," Roy quickly retreats. "All of us profit from others' tragedies, that's all I meant. Doctors need people to get sick. Lawyers need lawsuits."

"Is Perez waiting outside?" McKinney interrupts upon observing the look on my face. I'm sure it's savage.

I unclench my fists and nod. "All right, let's get Perez in here. Let's see what he'll tell us."

EDDIE PEREZ IS neither white nor black, his skin a copper tan with tiny patches of blue-black along his neck. In his shirt pocket are cigarettes for which he occasionally reaches, but, out of courtesy to us, withdraws before touching the pack. His forearms—made unusually thick, he tells us, by swinging a baseball bat endlessly as a boy in Cuba—rest unnaturally on his lap as he explains: "We sprayed a lot of planes that night with deicer fluid. We had the best stuff on the market."

"All the planes needed deicing, didn't they?" I press him. Perez seems rigid in body and spirit as if fighting to control that which would otherwise rise naturally to the surface.

"Yes, sir. Cold and rainy." Perez speaks English well, a trace of an accent not detectable until now. I'm told he's consumed every grain of information about this country's history and culture his mind can absorb. Despite his knowledge of all things American, I suspect he carries in his soul the dark fear of every immigrant: to be denied the full acceptance accorded to a natural-born citizen, and having abandoned his native land, to be lost as a drifting seafarer in a vast, unforgiving ocean. I suspect every lawyer makes his blood freeze.

"And winds gusting up to fifteen miles per hour?" I won't stop. I won't even let him catch his breath. I have no desire to hurt him, but if it serves my purposes, I will.

"Yes, sir," he answers dutifully.

"Did you actually see this plane deiced?"

"Yes, sir. Did it myself."

"So I need not talk to the crew?"

An almost imperceptible pallor squeezes across Perez's face. He tightens his grip on the chair, and speaks in halting breaths. "No, sir. Like I said, I did it myself. And I wrote it in the book." His accent is growing thicker. I'm hitting a nerve.

"Did you make the logbook entries before or after the flight took off?"

"Before, always before. I give it to the pilot when I'm done."

"What's your point?" Roy intercedes.

"I have a question, not a point." I keep my focus on Perez. "Then you must have deiced the plane before it got to the runway."

"Yes, sir," he replies with a slight stammer.

"How long before the plane got to the runway did you make your entries in the logbook?"

"Ten minutes, maybe fifteen."

"And how long before that did you deice the plane?"

"Maybe another fifteen minutes."

"So the deicing took place about thirty minutes before the plane left for the runway?"

Perez nods.

"And maybe longer?" I push him.

"Maybe."

"Now, Roy, I have a point," I say, looking squarely at Brooks. "Based on the airline's records, the plane sat about thirty minutes on the runway. Maybe the plane iced up again during those sixty or so minutes between deicing and takeoff."

"Whose side are you on, Michael?"

"I represent the airline, Roy."

"It sounds like you're trying to show we screwed up deicing the plane. That won't help us, will it? It would only get the pilot off the hook."

"The pilot's dead, Roy. He's not on any hook."

"You know what I mean," Roy sputters. "I don't want you saving your brother's reputation at the airline's expense."

My body stiffens. My eyes narrow. "It's painfully obvious, Roy, you don't know what the law is, so let me walk you through it. Point one: If Charlie caused the crash, the airline has no defense. It is liable and must pay the victims' estates. Point two: If the equipment failed, then Jarrad, the manufacturer, may be liable. Point three: If the deicing didn't work, maybe it's because there was a design defect or a construction defect—in which case Jarrad pays the victims and pays us for the plane."

"You don't want to get into that," Roy argues. "Once we say Jarrad was at fault, we're dead in the water if we're wrong. We can't very well argue it was the weather or the controllers if we claim a defect in the plane. And Jarrad, they'll claim we screwed up in our maintenance program or some such nonsense, and we'll be scrambling to keep afloat. Can you imagine how bad the damage to our reputation will be if Jarrad gets ahold of all our documents and shows we ain't been maintaining our planes right? You know they'll hire a dozen experts and have two dozen more in-house all swearing we didn't do this or that right. I mean, just look at you with the deicing. You make it look like we didn't do so good when we had a full crew crawling all over our planes for as long as time allowed."

"Whose side are you on, Roy? The airline's or Jarrad's?"

"Fuck you, Michael."

I point at Roy the way an experienced prosecutor points at an accused criminal: straight, firm, and right between his eyes. "If the problem is with the plane, that means Brandon is completely vindicated. And Jarrad's the one who should be shaking."

"You mean Charlie is completely vindicated, don't you?"

"I said Brandon. I mean Brandon."

"The Jarrad Ninety-nine has been operational less than a year," McKinney pitches in. "The newer the plane, the more bugs it usually has."

As a policeman signals a line of cars to halt, Perez raises his hands rough from work and age, his gnarled fingers smelling from tobacco and cashews. "I didn't deice none of the planes while they was on the runway," Perez says. "That's true, but all the others made it. Even another Jarrad Ninety-nine that left about five minutes later and went into Dulles, just a few miles away."

. . .

"I DIDN'T DO nothing wrong," Rod Hansen wails as if cornered by a wild dog. "How come you got me here?"

"I'm taking statements from everyone. No exceptions."

"Do I need a lawyer?" asks Hansen warily. He brushes back his grayish-brown hair, longer and wilder than that of most men his age.

"Did you follow all the standard procedures?" I interrogate.

"Yes."

"Then no, you don't need a lawyer. I'm not here to trap you or trick you, Rod. There will be plenty of other lawyers who will try to do that. I'm here to get the facts, then help you shape your testimony to benefit you and the airline to the greatest possible extent within the bounds of the truth."

"I'm more used to physical combat than this kind," Hansen remarks with a wry smile. He was an all-city tackle in high school, and apparently likes to work into conversations with strangers the highlights of his football career and the knee injury that allegedly prevented him from becoming a college all-American. In the next ten minutes he tells it all to me down to the dates of his surgery. I let him go on. Maybe if I let him confide in me about this, he'll confide in me about other things too.

When he nods a bit sheepishly, signaling an end to his football tales, I ask: "Did you brief the pilot and copilot on all anticipated weather conditions?"

"Sure. About an hour or so before the flight. I went over the maps and charts with them."

"What did they show?"

"Thirty percent chance of a thunderstorm coming into D.C. around midnight," answers Hansen with the rough-hewn style that has served him well as the airline's chief dispatcher at La Guardia.

"The storm turned out to be worse than you thought," I jab him.

"Worse than anyone thought. And it wasn't supposed to hit for an hour after Flight five five five landed." His words carry the kind of tension that ordinarily precedes an exchange of punches.

"Did you recommend to Captain Ashmore that he fly as scheduled?"

"I did. And so did our meteorologist."

"When you met with Captain Ashmore before his flight took off from La Guardia, did you notice any symptoms of drug use?"

"Hell no. I wouldn't of let him fly if I did."

"Any unusual or suspicious behavior?"

"None."

"That's good," I assure him. "So you have no doubt this plane was properly dispatched?"

"No doubt."

I nod gently to reinforce the notion we're on the same team. "You spoke with the pilot three times during the flight. The last time was fifteen minutes before the crash. You warned him of thunderstorms and low visibility. And each time the pilot responded coherently, correct? Because if he didn't, you would have reported it right then and there, correct again?"

"Correct on all counts," confirms Hansen, who's coming to realize my goal is to protect him. Hansen's voice perks up, his speech quickens. "I reviewed everything. All weather reports from the various stations throughout the airline's system. The airline's meteorologist's forecast. Everything from the Weather Bureau. Did I tell you I'm trained in meteorology? I know what turbulent weather is like."

"Good."

"I have no doubt the aircraft was properly dispatched," Hansen booms out, now aware these are the magic words. "The pilot had no doubt neither. He knew everything I knew. You know, it's the pilot's call, it always is. He wasn't worried. Even yawned a few times."

Yawned? My blood stops. My eyes widen. I say sharply: "He seemed alert and ready to fly, though, didn't he? You wouldn't have let him fly otherwise."

"Yeah, he was okay. Yawning a few times ain't no big deal. He was okay. I mean, I ain't even positive he yawned. Maybe he didn't."

THE MUCH-DREADED civil lawsuit is filed this morning in the United States District Court in Washington. The news cannot be worse. Brandon Air Lines is the sole defendant; nowhere is Jarrad or the government mentioned. Further, the plaintiffs not only charge Brandon with ordinary negligence, but in additional counts seek hundreds of millions of dollars in punitive damages. The airline, says the suit, was guilty of "willful misconduct" for allowing Charles Ashmore to be rehired and for allowing him to fly while saturated with barbiturates.

The suit is brought as a class action on behalf of the five-person Lee family, all of whom perished in the crash. The death of an entire family is a peculiarly chilling circumstance, one that—to be pragmatic about it—makes the Lee estate an excellent choice as the representative plaintiff. If the court certifies this case as a class action (which it surely and swiftly will since the same facts and same laws apply equally to all class members), then the trial conducted by the Lee estate will determine the fates of all the crash victims. If the Lee estate wins, all the victims win; each victim's estate will later have a separate trial only as to the amount of damages it will recover.

I'll conduct the airline's defense as a general does a war. I've already chosen a team of the firm's best associates and paralegals, headed by Diana, to draft interrogatories, prepare motions, and review the documents supplied by the plaintiffs, Jarrad, and the government. I've commandeered a conference room, stripped it of its furniture, and converted it to a "War Room" for the hundreds of thousands of documents expected to be received. I've hired a litigation-support service to feed these documents into a computer, allowing for instant retrieval of any piece of paper. Most important, I've listed every key witness, each of whom I'm determined to depose at length. These depositions will prepare me for cross-examination at trial and allow me to impeach any trial witness whose testimony is at odds with his deposition testimony. All this will be costly; the hours and fees will pile up with extraordinary speed. I'll try to reduce fees where I can, but I won't compromise my preparation even if I have to work for nothing.

I make my way through the noon traffic out to Great Falls, where Philip Brandon lives. Sick today, Philip has summoned me to his mansion. Maybe Philip's home to avoid the reporters who have camped out across from the airline's headquarters, or maybe Philip wants me to walk one last time in the home he might soon lose to foreclosure. Whatever Philip's reason for not going to work bodes ill for me. My sweat has hardened into a sticky coat.

I have one defense to these utterly depressing events: a complete vision of victory and vindication given life by scores of details—court rulings, witnesses' voices, evidentiary battles, jurors' faces. These and countless other details sustain me from the early mornings to darkness.

I turn my car in to the long driveway. I park by the cobblestone circular path a few yards from the massive stone and brick house that the tour buses invariably stop to see. An elderly, well-dressed black woman ushers me through the white marble entrance hall where bronze statues of ballerinas rest upon a gilded fireplace mantel, antique brass chandeliers hang from a thirty-foot ceiling, and egg-and-dart plaster crown molding stretches around the oval-shaped room. This ancient mansion seems not as grand as it once did, its haunting high ceilings and cold giant rooms having acquired a hint of violence about them. Stone, plaster, bronze, brass—all dead matter—dominate this museumlike morgue.

I'm led to the library, a two-story room with its own staircase to a wrought-iron balcony surrounded by business books. Two purple silk wing chairs (that call to mind the presence of royalty) face a desk where Philip Brandon sits glumly. The drapes on the double-arched windows behind Philip are pulled apart, allowing a broad view of the backyard's rolling grassy acres, which on this day seem diminished by the infinite blackish-gray sky.

"You look horrible," Philip notes.

I drop into the closer wing chair. Philip's rage to the contrary, the crash has, in a strange jerk of fate, saved Philip's airline, at least for the moment. The Subcommittee, believing it would be prudent to wait "until all court proceedings are concluded," has postponed hearings on the J99 "indefinitely." Witnesses, the Subcommittee's Chairman opines, will be "less than candid" while lawsuits are pending. The effect of the Subcommittee's call for inaction has been to kick back up the price of Brandon's stock to fifty-six dollars a share, the folks on Wall Street apparently believing that no Subcommittee, once it loses its zeal to investigate a matter, ever regains it.

Adversity makes for opportunity. The rise in Brandon's fortunes has discouraged National from continuing its buying spree; rather, National has reversed its field, sold en masse its Brandon stock, and reaped huge profits, which it will no doubt store in reserve, to be drawn upon if Brandon's stock price again begins to die. The vultures aren't entirely gone; they're merely out of sight.

None of this, though, makes my news easier to say. "The insurance company's bailing out," I say after a moment's silence. "They say the policy's not in force if the pilot was under the influence of drugs or alcohol."

Philip's voice sinks to a harsh whisper: "So they won't pay up if we lose?"

"It's a little trickier than that. The jury's not going to decide if the pilot was or wasn't under the influence. Just whether the pilot was at fault or not. If we lose, Walker Insurance will refuse to pay, and we'll have to bring suit to enforce the policy, which leads to another tricky question. Does Walker merely have to prove the pilot was under the influence, or that his being under the influence caused the crash? No court in the District has decided this issue."

"Don't let them screw us," Philip rants. Then, in the next moment, he asks: "Can we settle this thing?"

"It depends on how much we're willing to pay," I counsel him. "If we lose at trial, we'll have to pay for each victim's lost future earnings, loss of enjoyment of life's activities, funeral expenses, and the horror suffered by virtue of the death itself."

Philip flinches. "How much are they going to want?" he asks in the sort of hushed voice commonly heard at a wake.

"I spoke with plaintiffs' lead counsel this morning. He said they'd consider something in the range of four million a person."

For a moment Philip doesn't breathe, his cheeks turning a shade paler. "Four hundred eighty million? That's blackmail!"

"We don't have to settle it."

"We can lose, can't we?" inquires Philip, returning quickly to the practical businessman he is.

"Sure we can lose."

Philip shakes his head in disgust. "We should've tried harder to settle this thing before they got lawyers. Lawyers with contingent fees and bullshit about how much money their clients would have made the rest of their lives. Every goddamn corpse would have been a CEO in five years, that's about what we'll hear. We'll get consortium claims too. The deprived spouse, no more hugging and kissing. Yes, we'll hear every sob story known or unknown. You mark my words. We'll hear it all. As soon as we mention money, we'll hear it all."

"They didn't ask for a jury. We should," I say abruptly. Most jurors lack the technical expertise necessary to comprehend the intricacies of aviation technology, and trials of complex aviation cases before juries—with their many evidentiary disputes, shorter hours, and longer closing arguments—are, to the consternation of plaintiffs' counsel, likely to finish weeks later than similar trials before judges.

"A jury will be horrified by even the hint of a drug user flying a commercial jet," Philip warns.

"*If* they believe that's what caused the crash. Remember, juries are sometimes funny about airline accidents. No matter what the judge instructs them, many believe air travel is inherently dangerous and passengers assume the risk of such travel. Anyway, I do my best work in front of juries."

"Juries bring back higher awards, don't they?"

"I'm your lawyer, Philip. Let me decide the litigation strategy."

"I let you decide the strategy last time, and look what's happened. No jury, Michael. That's final."

I can do nothing but absorb the blow, and move on. "We could bring Jarrad into the settlement talks," I suggest. "They have tons of money. And if the plane went down because of a mechanical defect, Jarrad's liable for all of it anyway."

"Jarrad won't pay a dime. They haven't lost a crash case yet, and that's going to give them all the nerve they need to play hardball. And hell, they haven't even been sued, so why would they—"

"They haven't been sued by the plaintiffs. We could sue them, saying the plane was defective."

Philip's eyes lock into mine with an intensity that suggests a powerful inner rage. "We've been through all this," he growls. "No means no. Anyway, if there was a defect, we still lose if we should have discovered it, right?" Philip straightens his back. "Why not sue the government? The controllers told us to land and gave us lousy weather information to boot. Not only that, the controllers were licensed by the FAA, and were using electronic equipment designed to FAA specifications. The plane itself was designed and constructed according to FAA specifications, given a Certificate of Airworthiness by the FAA, flown along air routes designed by the FAA, and flown by a pilot examined and licensed by the FAA. And the beauty of showing it was the government's fault is that it's a complete defense for us. Once we sue Jarrad, we've muddied the waters. We have no clear focus. We'd be telling the jury it was a mechanical failure and it was the controller's poor instructions. They'd be wondering the whole time— well, which is it? We'd look like we didn't know either, or that we were desperate enough to try anything. We'd look like—"

"Alternate theories are commonly pled in litigation," I interrupt. "Anyway, it's very possible the two theories wouldn't be inconsistent. The controller was negligent in directing the pilot into turbulence, and Jarrad was negligent in designing or constructing a plane that failed to respond to turbulence."

"I'm not convinced," Philip says flatly.

My voice turns blade-sharp. "When this and every other airline was sued by the Justice Department two years ago for price fixing, you told me to settle. Go as high as twenty million. I told you to try the case. We won, and paid nothing."

"That time you were right. This time you've got other things to consider."

"What does that mean?"

"Your brother. You're more interested in him than the airline."

"Then get another lawyer." I jump to my feet. I start to walk away, already sorry I've acted so boldly. I need to be in control of this case.

"Sit down, Michael. Don't be so goddamn sensitive."

"You're accusing me of unethical conduct. I won't—"

"Let's look at it coldly, that's all I ask."

I sit down, my eyes fixed on the center of Philip's face. "Here's a cold look. If we don't bring Jarrad in, a jury will have to find the government liable. That won't happen. We're all taxpayers."

Philip looks downward. I watch and hear Philip breathe heavily, anger fueling him as a hard push on the accelerator pumps a car. I know my resistance grates on him. He wants me to be afraid, to ache, to know he has the power to end my life of riches.

I'm tempted to stop arguing, to surrender without further delay. I have to remind myself of my personal worth to keep from bargaining away my professional virtue, driven as I am by that which is more powerful than morality or ethics: raw, unnerving pain.

"If we allege a mechanical failure caused by a design defect, can we still have our pilots flying J Ninety-nines? No, of course not," Philip observes. "The union would be down our throat. What would we do with all our J Ninety-nines?"

"If there's a design problem with the J Ninety-nines, you shouldn't let one leave the ground."

He lets loose an irritated smile. "No company is perfect, Michael. A good lawyer can fish around, allege safety violations we don't know about or that don't truly exist. He can review FAA reports we submit and argue they're misleading. A good lawyer can put into question any company's practices."

"None of that is admissible," I assure him, "unless they can specifically link a safety violation or FAA report to the crash itself."

"Relevant or not, they might be picked up by the press."

"They'll get no documents from me unless they directly relate to the crash. I'll fight every motion for excessive discovery to the death."

"Michael, I suspect many things go on in this company that I don't know about," Philip remarks testily. "I've heard from time to time that other airlines take FAA people on cruises, give them unsecured loans, set them up with girlfriends or prostitutes, or promise them jobs when they leave the government. Maybe we've done that too. Not to my knowledge, we haven't, but I can't pretend to know everything every one of my twenty thousand employees does."

He can pretend. He's pretending now. "If the airline should lose this case," I charge, "better that it be because one employee, acting contrary to company rules, lost control of his plane than the company as a whole lacked a commitment to safety."

"You're misinterpreting—"

"Better that certain facts don't see the light of day."

Philip is tiring. His eyes wander. In time they fix upon me. "I know where you are, Michael. You're over the shock of Charlie's death. The numbness is gone. Now you want him redeemed. A jury can do that for you. A jury can make his death honorable. A jury can raise Charlie's reputation to some heavenly, pristine state. That, for you, would be winning, whatever the verdict."

"If you believed that, Philip, you wouldn't be talking to me now."

"I don't know what I believe," he confesses.

"Let's get our eyes back on the ball, okay? How much will you settle for?" While Philip detests paying huge sums of money to strangers, he has to consider the overall consequences of refusing to pay.

"Losing will damage our reputation far more than a settlement, won't it? Especially if that drug charge gets a lot of play. In a settlement we can paint ourselves as humanitarians."

"We may be able to strike a deal with the insurance company at this stage," I note. "I expect Walker will pay a reasonable settlement, and be happy to be done with it."

"Sixty million. That's my limit," he announces with an air of defiance.

"They won't take that. They won't even respond."

"Get it done, Michael."

"It won't happen. Even if their lawyer folds, settlement is always more complicated with a class. The court has to approve it."

"Let's take them one by one," Philip suggests. "Divide and conquer."

"We're not allowed to talk to the individual class members," I advise him.

"Why not?" he raves. "Why the hell not?"

"Court rules."

"They want to fuck us good, don't they?"

"It's nothing personal. Those rules have been around since class actions were invented."

"I still say they want to fuck us."

"We're alive, Philip. The people suing us aren't. The jury won't be worrying about us getting fucked."

"They never do, do they?" he sneers. "And what about your brother's estate? Settle that one too. For zero."

"I'm the executor."

"Another conflict of interest, right, Michael?"

"I've got two years to sue. I'm going to wait and see what happens. I'm opting out of the class."

"I repeat. Another conflict of interest."

"I'll set up a meeting with plaintiffs' counsel, and let you know what happens." I rise, shake Philip's hand, and leave. Through one room, then another. Into the white marble hall. I can't recall later how I left the mansion. On my way back to the office I pull my car over to the side of the road until my head clears.

THIRTY MINUTES PASS before Sam Lockwood's secretary makes her way to the reception area. She acknowledges me with a gloomy nod; with a flick of her wrist, she motions me to follow her. Tall and stiff, she walks and bends like a wounded dinosaur. She offers no coffee or soft drink, as secretaries in my firm are trained to do with visitors. In her mid-fifties with uncombed gray hair, a bulging abdomen, and thick-rimmed glasses hanging on a string around her neck, she looks as if she's on her way to a barbecue, her pants baggy and worn, her blouse slightly discolored at the collar. I'm grateful she doesn't speak on our short walk to Lockwood's office.

"Mr. Ashmore," she announces with the enthusiasm of a doctor forced to tell a patient's family that all hope is lost.

Sam Lockwood flashes a boyish smile. He is short, muscular, with a thick neck and a bulldog face. His breath reeks of tobacco, and his sandy mustache, a hint of gray streaking along its bottom, partially covers his upper lip. "It's a true pleasure," he gushes, extending his hand. Looking back at his secretary, he orders coffee and Cokes to be brought in immediately.

"She's getting a little long in the tooth," he tells me when we're alone. "I've had her for fifteen years. How do you fire someone you've had that long?"

I shrug. I can't fire anyone either.

The secretary returns with a tray of the requested refreshments, including cream and sugar. We thank her. She nods with a joyless smile and disappears.

Lockwood's in high spirits. The court granted his motion today, certifying the case as a class action. He's already counting his money, I bet. I sip coffee as Lockwood cheerfully discusses his son's baseball team and his daughter's school play. Lockwood is trying to build a rapport between us; he's a genial fellow, but I have orders to follow.

"I've spoken with Philip Brandon. He'll never go anywhere near your number, Sam. Maybe I can get him as high as forty million, but I can't promise that unless I have a commitment from you that forty million will do it."

"Forty million?" Lockwood gasps. "That's four hundred forty million off my number."

"Your number's not in the ballpark."

"It's a fair number," insists Lockwood. "We'll get more than that if we win. We might get punitives too. Who knows how big that number will be? We'll be asking for another four hundred million."

I push forward. "This case won't get tried for three years, if that. None of these families want to wait that long to get their money. Judging by their personal circumstances, I'd say they need the money now, today. Most have lost a wage earner, in many cases the principal wage earner."

"It's not only money they've lost," barks Lockwood, whose charming enthusiasm of moments ago has vanished.

"All the more reason to get things done quickly. A long, drawn-out lawsuit will only extend and intensify their suffering."

"Your concern is very touching."

"I lost a family member too. I speak from the heart—"

"You speak from the airline's heart. And that's apparently as hard as stone. Forty million, that's an insult."

I study the lines on Lockwood's forehead, the tightness of his lips. Is he truly offended or merely negotiating, having deliberately started far higher than his real number to give himself room to maneuver? From conversations with lawyers who have done battle with Lockwood, I know Lockwood rarely tries cases. I suspect Lockwood, like so many, has a fear, though well hidden, of the courtroom—losing diminishes him, tears at his insides. He's part of that new breed of litigators proficient with paper, skilled in negotiations, absorbed in pretrial discovery. They don't try cases, they manage them. Ninety-five percent of civil cases settle, making inevitable the emergence of these "settlement lawyers," who seek always to wear down their opponents so that settlement will become attractive on their terms. Three quarters of a million Americans are lawyers, thirty thousand new ones graduating each year. A lawyer rarely litigates against the same lawyer twice. The need to be cordial and in good faith has vanished.

"I don't mean to insult you, Sam. But you need to hear where the airline is, and where they'll go."

"You haven't said where they'll go."

"They won't go anywhere until you move, and move big."

"I might go to four hundred even," Lockwood hedges.

Lockwood can be pushed. He's represented crash victims in the past, but in the main has sued doctors for malpractice. Rumor has it that Lockwood, while capable of insightful observations and pointed questions, lacks the energy to sustain such thinking over the marathon course of a giant case wherein grueling, acrimonious depositions grind on fifty hours a week.

"Four hundred won't do it," I say.

"Maybe three hundred sixty, but that's about it," Lockwood groans. "To get less than that, you'll have to try the case."

"Don't kid yourself, Sam. The airline won't hesitate to try it. There were storms, you know. If the jury finds no negligence, your people get zero."

"I might go a little lower, but not much. Three hundred twenty, maybe. But after that, you'll hit a rock wall."

I stand up. "We can't get anywhere with those numbers."

"Aren't you going to counter? You came here at forty, and you're still at forty. I've come down one hundred sixty million. I've taken huge steps."

"You'll need to get under a hundred million before a counter makes sense from the airline's perspective."

"Then the airline's got a lousy perspective. Their ass is hanging out there wide open, and they don't have the good sense to throw a blanket over it."

"Do you really believe a judge or jury will find the airline negligent when the plane went down in the midst of a storm? You need to think about that, Sam. We're going to throw every resource we've got into this case."

"We won't be intimidated," declares Lockwood, but his voice lacks conviction.

"All I ask is you use your common sense. Call me when you're ready to talk further."

"There won't be any further talk until you talk first," yells Lockwood as I depart. I find my own way out.

ANOTHER DUBIOUS FIRST FOR
me. Isabel Castino, the United States Attorney for the District of Columbia,
has called to invite me to her office for a "short chat."

A prosecutor all her working life, Isabel has been recently elevated to
the District's top federal post by Clinton, who, like so many others, has
become enamored with her boundless loathing for evil and her ruthless
determination to eradicate it. Legend has it that she was forced to watch
Castro's butchers break her father's ribs with baseball bats, burn the skin
off his back, then shoot him through the head at close range. Hours later
the six-year-old Isabel was smuggled onto an overcrowded, rickety boat that
tossed and bounced for days before reaching Miami. Her mother and sister,
who made it onto the next boat, drowned two miles from shore.

Until her federal appointment, Isabel was for twelve years a rarity in the
seamy, combative, low-paying world of assistant DAs. An articulate, impec-
cably mannered Ivy League law school graduate, she could have joined any
firm in the District. Not one would have refused an impressive, light-
skinned Hispanic lawyer they could have paraded in front of select clients
and judges; all would have in particular embraced Isabel, whose sharp wit
and pleasant look enhanced her "marketability." Yet, turning from money
and prestige, Isabel dived into the grimy, in-the-trenches work of protecting
the District's decent, hardworking folks day after day, week after week, from
murderers and cocaine traffickers, gunrunners and AIDS junkies. She got
conviction after conviction, unconcerned, she once told me, with "the ni-
ceties of the bar's ethical bullshit." She would, she said, keep her "priorities
straight," which meant putting in prison, by any means possible, all those
who "screwed with" the law. Whenever more radical Hispanics accused her
of collaborating with the police—agents of the white power structure to

some, an occupying force to others—she would take great pains to praise publicly the "men and women who risked their lives for little pay," flatly declaring that no prosecutor could do his or her job without them.

Isabel and I aren't friends. I publicly exposed her darker side at the trial of a Korean boy charged with raping his date. The boy spoke little English. At the police station Isabel informed the boy of his Miranda rights, then had him thrown into a cell with a burly prisoner accused of mutilating young boys. Within an hour the Korean boy confessed to his crime and was rewarded with a cleaner cell and a smaller cellmate. At trial I, working pro bono, had the boy's confession excluded from evidence; the Miranda warnings given by Isabel were not translated. "This boy hardly understood English," I told the court. "Ms. Castino had to know that because she was in the same room with the boy's interpreter. This was a deliberate effort to evade the law." Isabel was left with one witness: a sixteen-year-old Korean girl with a history of prostitution and drugs. The boy was acquitted.

Isabel sits not at her oval desk but in one of two soft leather chairs she's moved closer together. Her way of showing she's forgiven me, I think, though I don't need to be forgiven. She played dirty with that Korean boy, and paid for it.

To the side of her desk sits her scarred, oversized brown vinyl briefcase, a familiar sight in the halls of our local courthouses. I sense she takes an instant dislike to those lawyers who, unlike me, march around those same halls with alligator-skin attachés or gold-trimmed Bally leather cases, the cost of one exceeding six weeks of Isabel's pay.

"I read about you some months ago," she begins. "Your reckless homicide case. Quite a victory. I meant to call you, but something was always getting in the way," she claims in the rapid, excited speech of one late for an appointment; but Isabel, I know, is habitually in a rush. "I was intrigued," she adds graciously. "It's a wonderful way of getting at murderers without specific proof they ordered or committed the murders. The perfume company didn't want a death to take place, but you got the court to rule it didn't matter as long as the death resulted from grossly unacceptable conduct done in plain disregard of the harm caused. It was brilliant," she exults.

My back is straight, my eyes alert, my manner businesslike. "There was case law already out there that, when pieced together, arguably supported the same result," I say with appropriate modesty.

"But you had to recognize that, then figure out how to piece the right language of those cases together," she says. "Not an easy thing to do when not one statute mentioned reckless homicide as a criminal or civil wrong. You made new law, and you did it by using nothing but your own genius."

All this praise is making me wary. Isabel isn't known for her generosity toward members of the defense bar.

Isabel leans toward me. Her wheat-colored hair, pulled back, is tied in a ponytail. Her skirt, dark and thick, is edging up her thigh. "Don't you see how it works for us against the drug kingpins? Those bastards create an atmosphere where murder is not only condoned, it's encouraged. Murder is necessary and honorable, it's how their minions advance their careers. Now we don't need to tie the kingpins directly to these murders. All we need show is the kingpin created an atmosphere that told these murderers it was okay to kill under certain circumstances. The same would be true, of course, for corporate executives who sent out signals that it was okay to ignore the public safety."

Funny how things you do get twisted around by others in ways you could never imagine. Reckless homicide was a theory I used in a civil case to get a verdict against a company that knew its perfume would explode whenever brought close to a flame. Isabel wants to borrow my theory to convict drug dealers and business leaders for murders they didn't know were about to be committed.

I'm growing restless. I'd come here nurturing the distant hope that Isabel had secret information about the crash and, wishing to make amends or merely help a colleague in grief, would pass all of it along to me with the usual warnings of "confidentiality" and "appropriate use." After all, the feds are heavily involved. Not only do they have a compelling interest in the safety of air travel in general, they have spent weeks specifically investigating this crash. They undoubtedly know things I don't.

I decide to push the door open. "You mentioned the perfume case. The victim there was my brother's only child."

She nods. "And it was your brother Charlie who died in that crash."

I take another step. "The autopsy said Charlie was loaded up on phenobarbital, but he'd never taken phenobarbital before. I thought maybe someone wanted the plane to crash, and that's why you called me."

She rises from her chair, her ponytail swishing from side to side. She has a marathon runner's slender frame and deep brown eyes that invite confessions from friends and foes alike. "I'm suspicious by nature, you know, like any decent prosecutor." She flashes a smile. "Every time a plane crashes, especially these days, I take a look at all the possibilities." She begins to walk to and fro, picking up speed with each change of direction. "But no, it wasn't anything deliberate. Just to be absolutely sure, I had the FBI thoroughly check the backgrounds of everyone on that plane, and nothing showed up. I had FBI and CIA people combing the site as well. They were wearing NTSB jackets so nobody would ask why they were there. Believe me, if there'd been a hint of sabotage, I'd have gotten hundreds of agents involved." She stops, glances at me, then resumes her march. "I've got to proceed based on the evidence before me, not on some wild theory. We've got a pilot here, already fired once for drug use, who crashes his plane after stuffing himself with barbiturates right before takeoff. Not a pretty picture."

I stay still, stay calm, but I'm searching for air to breathe. When she spoke about having to "proceed based on the evidence," she meant evidence of *criminal* conduct by the airline.

"No other explanation flies," she says, her play on words deliberate. "The Safety Board's report is thorough, unequivocal, and consistent with the evidence. The airline should never have let a known drug user get on that jet with a ton of drugs cruising through his veins." She pauses a moment, and says, with a modicum of sincerity: "I'm sorry for your loss. I really am."

"Thanks." Isabel, I fear, has the ability to argue anything with passionate conviction even when she knows she's wrong—the hallmark of a mature lawyer, a good liar, or both.

"That's why I called you. To tell you in person rather than have you just get them in the mail."

"Get what in the mail?" I ask, but I think I know.

"I've given a lot of thought to this. Convening a grand jury, I mean, down at the Superior Court. I've got responsibility for any crimes committed in the District, federal or not, and that's where the plane crashed. I'll be sending out subpoenas by week's end."

"There was no crime committed by the airline." I raise my voice. "Not here, not anywhere."

"Not the usual kind, no. But we have over a hundred deaths. I considered criminal negligence, I considered involuntary manslaughter, but they just wouldn't do. There was something missing. I thought murder, why wasn't this murder?"

She looks at me for a sign. I tighten my jaw. I glare. I fear she wants revenge of some sort.

She looks away, then continues her discourse on the law according to Isabel Castino, the District's chief law enforcer. "Not first-degree murder," she concedes. "That requires proof of deliberate and premeditated malice. We don't have that here. Nothing in cold blood."

I shake my head in a way that signals my disappointment in her. "You don't have second-degree murder either," I say sharply. "That's a killing in the sudden heat of passion."

"I'll tell you what I do have, though. Reckless homicide. A theory of law given to me by none other than the airline's attorney himself. That's a little eerie, isn't it?"

This is more than I can stand. Not only will my client be indicted, it will be indicted on a unique theory I developed to help Charlie. Helping Charlie has of late become a drive down the proverbial road to hell. I, too, rise from my chair. "Overzealousness, the most dangerous quality there is, especially in a prosecutor," I preach loudly. "Anyone whose life ambition is to be a prosecutor ought to be refused the job on that ground alone. Anyone who prosecutes out of anger or revenge should be locked up until too old to prosecute."

"Is that what you think?" She is astonished I have the audacity to accuse her. She's apparently angry at the airline for having killed so many innocents, and she's undoubtedly still angry at me for having humiliated her in court. She's not astonished at all, I realize.

"It's exactly what I think," I tell her forcefully. "A murder case? That's insane. The pilot hit bad weather. Your controllers told him to move to the east, and that's where he encountered wind shear."

"The view here is, if he hadn't been drugged up like he was, he could've handled it. Others got through the same storm okay."

"Do you know the first thing about Charles Ashmore?" I'm shouting now. She needs to hear me shout. She needs to know she can't cast aside all that's fair and honorable merely to seek headlines, and go untouched. "Charles Ashmore flew over three hundred combat missions in Nam, then flew two dozen more to spare others from having to. Does that sound to you like a selfish, irresponsible guy who'd risk the lives of his passengers and crew? For God's sake, until the night he died, Charlie hated to be even a minute late at the gate."

"People change," she says with a nonchalance that strikes me as truly reckless. "Things happen to them."

"There's no malice here," I rant. "No intent to harm. No—"

"If the conduct is reckless enough, malice can be implied." She's not ready to yield.

Neither am I. "The perfume case was a civil matter tried under the civil laws. There's nothing in the criminal code about reckless homicide. Not one statute even mentions it."

"The airline was reckless as hell," she persists. "Grossly deviated from all acceptable standards, don't you think? That's just the kind of depravity and wanton disregard for human life that needs to be punished with the same vigor as deliberate murder."

I stiffen. Maybe she'll get away with it. She has the right facts to make new law, and she has the resources of the world's most powerful government. If the whole truth be known, the civil courts in the District have recently held that a reckless disregard for human life is the equivalent of a specific intent to kill. It seems a small step from these rulings to a criminal verdict based on the same principles.

"What exactly are you looking for?" I demand to know.

The glee in her voice alarms me. "I want the folks ruling the skies to know they've got a public trust. I want deterrence, that's what it comes down to. Fines won't make them blink an eye. Prison terms will. Second-degree murder gets you life. The same principles underlying certain second-degree murder convictions are present here. Complete disregard for human life."

"You're crazy," I mutter aloud. "Who do you want to put away for life?"

She moves in short little jump-steps. "The higher up, the better."

"This is bad faith, this is abusive litigation!" I shout as if trying to stop a car wreck. I slam my fist against her desk. "You go forward with this, and we'll go after you personally," I swear. "We'll seek every sanction the law allows, and then some."

Her body trembles, only slightly, but enough to tell me I've made an impression. Maybe it's fear, maybe anger. "Don't you ever threaten me." She recovers quickly.

I stare at her with the sort of awe with which one beholds a raging fire. "The jury will see you for what you are, a petty bureaucrat trying to make a name for herself, trying to capitalize on a horrible tragedy. It's absolutely disgraceful!"

"Get out!" shouts Isabel at the top of her lungs, her forehead as scarlet as her cheeks. "Get out!"

I shake my head at her as I would at any lunatic, then leave silently. My

insides tremble as I walk down the narrow corridors, Isabel's words still
ringing in my ears.

"DOES THE U.S. Attorney think we intentionally crashed the plane?"
Philip asks incredulously. He drums his fingers against his custom-made
desk, none of his wealth and power able to console him now.

"I only know she's subpoenaed nearly a million pages of our records," I
tell him.

Philip breathes tight little breaths. "If this airline is indicted, it'll scare
away customers by the millions. Our stock price will get beat to shit. Our
key people will be out looking for greener pastures. Reporters will be con-
tacting us on the hour for statements. Our reputation will be in the toilet."

"This is a proud and public-spirited airline," I support him. "We can't
let some wild-eyed government lawyer bring it down. I say we devote whatever resources necessary to fight this."

"This is a nightmare," Philip groans. He reaches across his desk and
inhales a bag of potato chips while I cast my eyes downward as one does
when wishing to avoid witnessing a painful collision. Philip has been consuming food and drink in extraordinary proportions since learning a grand
jury would be convened to investigate the crash. "How could anyone bring
criminal charges against an entire airline because one pilot crashed one
plane, and in lousy weather too?" inquires Philip in the same bitter, dis-
believing voice. I'm sure he thinks real crimes are committed only by psy-
chopaths, dishonest brokers, and violent gangs, categories in which Brandon
Air Lines cannot be made to fit.

Philip flips the empty bag into a circular container, its rim painted a
bright orange. He looks back at me, his gaze a bit more focused. "I don't
want them finding anything in those records about the elevators sticking,"
he decrees.

I lower my eyes, fold my hands. I won't do it. I can only sink so low and
no further. I won't violate all I am, and I won't break a slew of laws designed
to protect the public safety. No CEO of a major airline should condone
such conduct, much less suggest it. If I had the courage to do it, I'd report
him to the FAA, and be done with the airline.

He sees my resistance. His tone becomes conciliatory. "Technically, destroying records would be wrong, but the reality is, the elevators had nothing to do with this crash. You know that."

"No, Philip, I—"

"You don't need to say anything. Do it, that's all. We both know every piece of paper we've got will be minutely scrutinized. Somebody is bound to say we had a known defect that we didn't fix and didn't report. I don't want some goddamn government lawyer claiming criminal negligence for something that had nothing to do with this crash. And if Jarrad winds up in all this, I don't want them saying our maintenance program was worse than shit."

I shake my head slowly as if resisting a powerful invisible force, an internal tornadolike wind of sorts. I know my firm will soon be blown apart. I am, like Philip, fearful the end is near. But, unlike Philip, I won't give up who I am to keep what I have.

WE'RE IN MY bed, a familiar place made less familiar these last few weeks by a physical parting: I sleep at the edge, rarely turning to face Diana. Not that I have the slightest anger toward her—it simply is too much effort by day's end to look into her face and respond to the nuances of her expression.

Tonight Diana has curled her body around me, a signal she wants not only to be in physical contact but to talk as well. Communication for Diana—sexual, verbal, emotional—is all part of an interactive package. She leans her chin lightly against the back of my neck and says in nearly a whisper: "Ruth needs to talk to you. She can't go before the grand jury unprepared."

"She says she is prepared. She'll tell the truth, and that's it."

"Let me go see her," Diana urges. "Maybe she'll listen to—"

"You're dreaming," I say, slowly breaking away. "You're the last person she'd listen to. Guilt by association." I kick away the sheets and stand, a small grunt revealing the pain of movement.

"I'm going to see her," Diana declares roughly.

"To do what, Diana? Make her say something to the grand jury she doesn't want to say? What if she tells the grand jury you tried to get her to lie? No way, Diana. It's too damn dangerous. Ruth is getting stranger every day."

Diana slides to the edge of the mattress, lets her legs hang over the side, then angles herself to face me directly. "Do you want to save yourself, Michael?"

"Am I worth saving?"

She nods with a wince as I throw back my arms. I know what she sees: exposed ribs, shrinking chest. I'm dropping pounds again. Too many too quickly, flesh escaping from my limbs as if I were on a crash diet. My eyes seem larger (but more hollow) when viewed against my thinning cheeks and sharpening nose. Even my voice has thinned, as if emptied into a funnel, the heaviness filtered out. "You can't be helped if you're not receptive to help," she pleads.

"Are you a lawyer or a shrink?"

"I'm family, whether you realize it or not."

A bitter weariness has captured me. "What do you want me to do?"

"I told you. Go see Ruth, or let me go. Beg her if you have to."

"Ruth won't respond to anything but a declaration of love."

"You never used to give up so easily." She frowns.

"I used to think I was worth fighting for."

She hops off the bed, her survival instincts fully aroused. "Michael, let's put all that aside for a minute, okay? We can get to your soul later. Let's save your career first. Let's focus on that."

I stand with the stillness of a marble statue. "She won't help us, Diana. And the more we push her, the harder she'll push back."

Tᴀᴇ ɢʀᴀɴᴅ ᴊᴜʀʏ ʀᴏᴏᴍ ɪꜱ ꜱᴜꜰꜰɪ-
ciently long and wide to accommodate tables and chairs for each of the
twenty-three grand jurors chosen to decide if probable cause exists to
believe a crime has been committed. Their forty-six eyes are upon Ruth,
who shifts her weight back and forth in the witness chair, her loose-fitting
ankle-length black dress (suitable for a grieving widow) easily shifting with
her.

The door is not closed all the way—presumably not slammed shut by
the last grand juror to enter—and keeps opening bit by bit; air from the
vents and the door's own creakiness combine to create the door's slow
motion backward, ever widening my field of vision. I stand there, an innocent bystander, and listen and watch. It would not have been proper for
me to open the door, of course, but I haven't opened it. Nor will I shut it.
I have no obligation to shut it. Anyway, I'm more overcome by a need to
hear and see Ruth than by any inclination to comply with the very strictest
interpretations of the rules regarding the secrecy of grand jury proceedings.

Ten feet from Ruth stands Isabel Castino, the grand jurors' desks assem-
bled behind her in a theaterlike semicircle. I've told Ruth she can't be
"compelled to testify about communications with Charlie" (unless they took
place in the presence of others), but I fear she wants someone to pay for
Charlie's death, even if it's Charlie. Ruth looks a bit pale, a bit tight, as
Isabel moves closer. Ruth knows the odds are stacked against her. She
knows she can't have a lawyer present or learn the testimony of other witnesses. The grand jury is "the prosecutor's sword," I've warned her. It cuts
in total secrecy, it cuts bloody.

I hear Isabel speak as if declaring an undeniable fact, but the words are in the form of a question: "You were aware that your husband, Charles Ashmore, had a drug dependency, weren't you?"

"I tried to get him to stop," Ruth confesses the way a saint admits to a failure to convert the heathen.

"To be specific, he was dependent on barbiturates, wasn't he?"

"Yes. Seconal, to be exact. He took fifty to a hundred milligrams a night—if he wasn't flying the next day." At least she adds that. Maybe she's decided to be fair to Charlie, though she sure isn't indulging him. Too late for that, anyway. Charlie has killed people.

"How did he obtain this Seconal?"

"A doctor's prescription. It was all legal."

"Did he ever advise the airline he was taking a prescription-strength barbiturate?"

"Not that I know of."

"Kind of reckless, wouldn't you say?"

"Not a policy I'd recommend." She stops herself. Even to Ruth that must have sounded too flip, a bit cruel.

"For how long prior to his death was your husband hooked on these barbiturates?"

"I never used the word 'hooked.' "

"He took them every night he could, didn't he?"

"Yes."

"So he was hooked. For how long was he hooked?"

Ruth shrugs as if to signal her surrender to this greater, more knowledgeable force. "About a year or so. Ever since our daughter's death. Carolyn died in a fire."

"Oh, yes. Started by perfume vapors mixing with a lit cigarette. The reckless homicide case." Isabel seems pleased to have the grand jurors hear the words "reckless homicide" in connection with another case; it gives the prosecution's theory a certain legitimacy, an established feel. She doesn't mention the perfume case was a civil matter. "After your daughter died, your husband was visibly unstable, wasn't he?"

"Mostly sad. He loved Carolyn very much."

This isn't what Isabel wants to hear. She wants the good stuff—breakdowns, fights, wife abuse, hallucinations. Charlie was dangerous, on the edge, near collapse. The more visibly unstable Charlie was, the more irresponsible was the airline for rehiring him.

"He needed drugs, didn't he?" Isabel presses her. "I'd say that alone made him a bit unstable, wouldn't you?"

Ruth inhales a series of short, rapid breaths, then lets them go. Will she fight or yield? I pray she doesn't entirely abandon the role of the grieving widow—for her sake as well as Charlie's. "Charlie was a good father and a good man. He was very giving," she says with a slight shiver. I like that shiver, whether it's real or not. She wants a little pity, I figure. That's why the shiver. Now I pray that shiver brings tears to the eyes of the most hardened souls here.

Isabel's arms are tucked tightly by her sides, her right hand holding on to a pad with scribbled notes. "Your husband was let go by the airline just a few months before the crash, wasn't he?"

"Yes."

"Because the airline suspected him of drug use?"

"Yes."

"Even though your husband never told the airline he was hooked on barbiturates?"

"He never told them, no."

"At some point, then, the airline could tell your husband was on drugs even without him admitting to it?"

Ruth nods. "When Charlie's plane took a dive on a flight to Minneapolis, his copilot and a flight attendant reported him for drug use."

I grow queasy. My breath turns short and hot. Ruth is giving in too easily. *Fight*, I want to scream out. *Fight!*

"So the airline not only knew he was on drugs—"

"Suspected, not knew. But, of course, they were right."

Isabel gathers herself. "Okay, so the airline correctly suspected that your husband was not only on drugs generally, but had actually been on drugs while flying one of their planes, which he nearly crashed into the earth, is that all correct?"

Ruth grows still. The shiver is long gone. "That's why I was glad they fired Charlie. And why I was so mad when they rehired him. You can't take a hundred milligrams of Seconal night after night and be a pilot."

"Did you inform anyone at the airline of your husband's drug habit?"

This is it, I think. Here we go. These are rough, tricky waters. I'm back to prayer. Please, Ruth, your Fifth Amendment rights. Like I told you. I start saying the words. *I refuse to answer on the grounds . . .*

What kind of reaction will Ruth get if she takes the Fifth? Isabel will surely be contemptuous, the grand jurors suspicious. No one in this room will view her the same way again. Taking the Fifth is no admission of criminal guilt, but some or all of the grand jurors will inevitably see it that way. Why should she expose herself to such humiliation and contempt and danger when she's done nothing wrong? I want her to ask for a halt to the proceedings, walk across the room, open the creaky door yet further, and consult in the hallway with me; but that, too, would inspire contempt among her audience. She remains in her chair, she's about to speak. She can't summon up the courage to resist.

"No," she answers hesitantly, then slowly adds two crucial words she knows won't go unchallenged: "Not technically."

Isabel leans in with a wrinkled brow: "What does that mean?"

"Not technically, because he's not directly employed by the airline."

"What's his connection, then, to—"

"He's the lawyer for Brandon Air Lines."

"Michael Ashmore? You told Michael Ashmore of your husband's drug dependency?"

"Michael was Charlie's brother."

"What exactly did you tell Michael Ashmore?" Isabel's tone now has an urgent edge to it.

"That Charlie was addicted to Seconal. That he couldn't sleep without it. That he couldn't cure himself. That he shouldn't be allowed to fly until he was cured."

My forehead burns with the scorching blood-heat of a rising, infectious fever. My eyes blaze, my cheeks flush. It's deliberate. She's not giving in; she's selling me out. It's goddamn deliberate.

"What was Michael Ashmore's response to all that?" Isabel presses forward.

I'm ready to pace these halls like fathers years ago paced the hospital halls while their wives gave birth. Either that or simply run to the exits, and keep running. Maybe that's what Ruth wants. Maybe she wants me scared and helpless while she takes control of our fates, a reversal of our usual roles. "He already knew Charlie was addicted," she explains. "Charlie, you see, was living with Michael after he got fired. Michael was right there with him night after night."

"So Michael Ashmore knew firsthand—"

"To be fair to Michael, he truly believed Charlie would kick the habit. Charlie swore to Michael he would." My fists clench. If she wanted to be fair to me, she would never have mentioned my name at all.

"He simply took his brother's word for it despite all the evidence to the contrary?" Isabel sums up.

"Michael did have Charlie take a drug test," she volunteers. "Charlie passed."

Isabel has probably seen a copy of the test in the airline's records. Probably meant very little to her. Charlie could have been drugged out an hour after the test. "But you still wanted your husband not to fly?" she asks, knowing the answer.

A sickly pallor creeps across Ruth's face. Unwittingly—or perhaps deliberately on some unconscious level—she has opened the door to a potentially devastating series of inquiries: Did Charlie take any other drug tests? Did he fail any? Were those failed tests reported to the airline? She knows Charlie tested positive for barbiturates, but doesn't know if that test was given to the airline. Thank God I never told her what I did. Of course, she herself never reported the failed test to the airline. She's probably worried to death she, too, has committed a crime of some sort. "That's right," she answers after a long, torturous pause, then zips open her pocketbook and takes out the two letters requested by the prosecution's subpoena *duces tecum*. I've told Ruth these letters, written to her by Charlie a week before the crash, are privileged and the prosecution has no right to them. Yet they say nothing of importance. She told me she'd bring them, and decide what to do when she got there. "I brought the stuff you wanted," she sweetly offers. She's trying to distract Isabel.

It works. Isabel briefly reviews the letters and, finding nothing of use, carries them back to counsel's table. Turning to face Ruth, she veers off to another subject. "Let me get the timing of this straight. At the moment you told Michael Ashmore of your husband's drug dependency, Charlie had already been fired by the airline, and was seeking to be rehired?"

"Yes. I was telling Michael not to help Charlie get rehired. Michael had a lot of influence with Philip Brandon, the head of the airline."

Pain has left my limp body, replaced by a weak-kneed numbness that only the truly vanquished know. I'm a witness to my own coming demise.

"Let me get something else clear in my mind. Your husband was living with Michael Ashmore at the time this whole effort to get your husband rehired was taking place?"

"Yes."

Isabel's voice hardens. "Then Michael Ashmore must have observed on his own your husband's drugged-out condition at the very time he—"

"I don't know what Michael observed. I wasn't there."

"When your husband was living with you, you observed what was happening to him, didn't you?"

She nods. "When you're on Seconal, it's like being drunk. You're lightheaded, drowsy, slur your words. You get a little off balance." She's talking way too much, ignoring everything I've told her: *Answer only what you're asked. Don't volunteer information. Don't speculate. Don't give opinions. Be concise.*

"And, I take it, that was how your husband reacted to Seconal?"

"Yes."

"Pretty easy to observe, wasn't it?"

"Pretty easy, yes."

"Michael Ashmore's no fool, is he? He could observe those symptoms just like you could?"

"He couldn't have missed them if Charlie was still taking a hundred milligrams a night."

"He couldn't have missed them," repeats Isabel in a raised voice.

"*If* Charlie was still taking—"

"And you say Michael Ashmore had influence with Philip Brandon?" Isabel interrupts her.

Ruth catches her breath, and says as a policeman reports a traffic accident: "He's Brandon's golden boy."

"And it was Philip Brandon himself who dealt with Michael Ashmore about this matter?"

"As far as I know, Brandon made the actual decision to rehire Charlie."

Isabel smiles broadly. She has enough now to bring Philip to this room. All the lawyers on this planet couldn't persuade the lowliest judge that Philip Brandon is being called merely for harassment purposes. It isn't often the CEO of a Fortune 200 company can be made to testify in a grand jury proceeding; but this will be one of those rare times, and Isabel, I'm sure, will make the most of it.

RANDY IS WITH me today. The door to the grand jury proceedings is again ajar—though today it is not by happenstance. I told Randy how the door had come to be open while Ruth was testifying, and he quietly opened the door himself, turned to me with a wry smile, and said: "Looks like that same grand juror forgot to close it all the way." I let Randy have his way. He's in charge now. He has more energy, more fight in him.

Randy's here because Philip wants him here. Philip is deliberately avoiding me, and each time we talk by telephone he seems more annoyed, closer to an outburst. Randy's his hero now.

Last month Philip, with borrowed funds, purchased millions of shares in a Chicago-based airline while letting it be known through planted leaks he was seeking a controlling interest; this revelation, as expected, caused his rival's stock price to rise, which in turn drove others to compete for the endangered company, pushing the stock price further upward. Pursuant to Randy's master plan (which, unashamedly, took a red-lettered page from National's playbook), Philip suddenly reversed his field and became the principal seller. Brandon Air Lines netted a cold twenty million dollars. I sense the obvious: Philip likes Randy's straight-to-the-throat style, his willingness to blur the shifting lines of moral correctness.

No Randy Chapmans on this grand jury, though. These grand jurors—largely blue-collar workers and homemakers—won't identify with Philip Brandon. Philip is too rich and powerful to exist for them as flesh and blood. From a prosecutor's perspective, Philip is an easy mark, a human sacrifice to the centuries-old rage of the have-nots.

Unlike any of these grand jurors, Philip can afford to talk to as many lawyers about as many subjects for however long he desires, a circumstance well known to Isabel. "Before coming here today, you had an attorney prepare you, didn't you?"

"I spoke with Randy Chapman."

"Not Michael Ashmore?" inquires Isabel with a bit of surprise. She wants the grand jurors to sense a split among the airline's elite.

"I've known Randy as long as I've known Michael," says Philip in the most casual voice he can muster.

"But Michael Ashmore has long been the airline's chief attorney, hasn't he?"

"He has." Philip shrugs. "He still is."

Isabel crosses her arms, cocks her head. "Exactly how many hours did you spend with Randy Chapman preparing for the testimony you're giving today?" Nothing wrong with a witness meeting with his lawyer, Isabel knows; in fact, *not* to meet reveals a failure to appreciate the gravity of the circumstances. Yet prosecutors often highlight such meetings to the grand jurors, who often view these developments as evidence of a guilty conscience, or worse, of a wrongful deed.

"Eight, ten hours, somewhere in there."

"You must have covered a lot of ground," remarks Isabel. "Did you review all the records surrounding Charles Ashmore's firing and rehiring?"

"I don't know about all of them. But some of them, sure."

Isabel leans forward, lets her voice rise up. "Actually, you were already familiar with them, right?"

"Somewhat."

"Because you were the one who made the decision to rehire Charles Ashmore, weren't you?"

"On the advice of counsel, I did."

"And that counsel was Michael Ashmore?"

"Yes."

Isabel glances down at her notes. Philip is not another Ruth Ashmore: He's sticking to narrow, concise answers. He isn't volunteering information, giving opinions, or indulging in speculation. Randy has prepared him well. I imagine Randy and Philip locked in some secret little room frantically considering all possible questions, then agreeing upon the answers most favorable to the airline.

"What precisely did Michael Ashmore advise you?"

"That we rehire Charles Ashmore."

"Did you know at that time the airline had just a few weeks earlier fired Charles Ashmore for suspected drug use?"

"Yes."

"And that two airline employees had come forward to say that Charles Ashmore had conducted himself, while on a flight to Minneapolis, as if he were drunk or on drugs?"

"Yes, but Michael had looked into all that, and assured me the overwhelming evidence was to the contrary."

"Really? Even though Charles Ashmore had almost dived his plane into the earth on that very flight?"

"There are lots of reasons why a plane might dive."

"Pilot error being one of them?"

"One of them," Philip grudgingly admits.

"And you knew, of course, that the person making the recommendation to rehire Charles Ashmore was his brother, didn't you?"

"Yes."

"Didn't that cause you any concern?"

"I've always known Michael Ashmore to be of the very highest moral character."

"Moral character or not, didn't you consider the very real possibility of bias? They were brothers."

"On twenty-twenty hindsight, I guess I should have. But no, not at the time." Philip's shoulders slump a bit. He draws his fingers into a ball, then lets them loose.

I'm sure this is precisely how Isabel envisioned this encounter: a corporate titan clenching and unclenching his fists while being forced to admit his involvement in a deadly crash. "It wouldn't take twenty-twenty vision," Isabel mocks him. "You could be almost blind and see that now, and almost blind and see that then."

"Is there a question?" Philip huffs.

"There is, sir. Did you ever have anyone review the investigation made by Michael Ashmore?"

"I had Roy Brooks look at Michael's report."

"No, sir, I mean more than that. I mean, did anyone ever talk to witnesses Ashmore talked to, or talk to those he didn't talk to?"

"I don't believe so."

"Did anyone confront Charles Ashmore himself and find out what he had to say about his plane's dive, about his drug problem?"

"We left all that to Michael. He was our attorney."

Isabel raises her hands as if to call for a halt. "Okay, so everything was left to the pilot's brother. Except the final decision. That was your call."

"My call," Philip agrees. "Same facts, same pilot, same advice, and I'd make the same decision tomorrow. It wasn't a crazy decision, you know. Planes do crash, as scary as that is."

Isabel turns toward the grand jurors. Her eyes seem to have grown larger. It's a risky, theatrical move, but she pulls it off. "What's scary, sir, is your attitude," she admonishes in a loud, angry voice. "Full of unrepentance and blindness."

"I'm deeply sorry for what happened," explains Philip in a voice that strikes me as a bit cold. "I'm just not willing to blame the airline for reckless conduct like you want me to."

"So you'd make the same decision again? You don't see the recklessness in *that?*"

"No, I don't," Philip maintains. He can't back off now.

"Then God help us all!" booms out Isabel, as if declaring victory. She turns again to face the grand jurors, whose troubled expressions reflect the fear she has instilled in them.

THE CIVIL CASE won't settle anytime soon unless the airline raises its offer, I tell Philip. Lockwood will likely drop to what the airline considers reasonable numbers in the months before trial, I'm about to add, when Philip says: "I'm going to have someone else handle Lockwood."

A short silence, then I ask hesitantly: "What do you mean someone else?"

"Just that. You're no longer our counsel. You got us into this awful mess, and I'm not about to let you make it worse. I told you from the very beginning you couldn't be the attorney for both the airline and your brother. That's still true."

"I'm the best lawyer to handle this case," I plead. "Nobody knows the facts like I do, and nobody has handled as many crash cases."

"You're out of this case. That's done. Even if you'd settled it, you'd no longer be representing us."

"I don't understand," is all I can think to say, but I understand perfectly. My faint voice acknowledges that.

"Effective today, your firm no longer represents us. Not in any capacity—litigation, tax, labor, acquisitions, nothing. All your files should be transferred to the firm of Grant and Bird."

"Please don't punish the whole firm because you're mad—"

"I wish you and Randy the best of luck. You've been good to us for many years, and I'm grateful for that. But in the end, I must do what I think is in the airline's best interests. I'm sure you'd do the same if you were me."

RANDY HAS THAT intense blood-look about his face. He closes his door, then walks behind his desk. I straighten my back, cross my arms. I brace myself.

"We need to fire twenty lawyers," Randy says as if repeating a decision already made. "Ten now, ten in a month." Randy rattles off ten names. All these lawyers work hard, have talent, and have families to support. "I'll tell them myself," he declares. "One by one. It won't be a day at the beach."

"We don't have to fire them," I answer gamely.

He allows himself a brief, cynical laugh. "No matter what you do for them now, Michael, they won't ever be grateful. And with Brandon Air Lines gone, there'll be lawyers here with absolutely nothing to do."

"We'll find other clients," I insist, but my voice has the hollow echo of a whisper into a microphone. A month ago I would have jumped to my feet, flailed my arms, pounded Randy's desk; now I remain still. I need Randy. He's one of the few friends I have left.

"We need to fire people right now, Michael. Don't you see what's going on? Lawyers here aren't talking about anything but lawsuits and hiding assets. Everybody's guarding their clients like a tornado is coming their way."

I slump back in my chair. "Every one of those people you fire is going to hate me, not you." Without it having to be said, we both understand that a month ago Randy would not have dared dictate to me.

"I picked these ten carefully. For your info, not one likes or respects you anyway. Their collective opinion of you has dropped with the speed of a shooting comet," Randy adds, another ball of fire thrown to scorch my already burnt body.

I wipe my forehead, lower my eyes. Ninety-four degrees on this July afternoon. The air-conditioning system, which has worked well for a decade, broke down hours ago. I long for this enervating heat to evaporate like steam from boiling water, to be replaced by winter's chill. Outside Randy's floor-to-ceiling windows, cars overheat, dogs sleep, steam rises from the street. Nerves everywhere are on edge.

"Next year we'll be looking at higher rent, higher associate salaries, and no Brandon Air Lines. Nobody criticizes Ford for laying off workers when sales drop," Randy reasons.

"Ford has shareholders to report to, we don't. We're the owners. We can do the right thing, even if it costs us a few dollars."

"I'm telling them tomorrow. Partners will each get three months severance, associates one month. I think that's generous."

"I think it stinks."

"No Brandon Air Lines, that stinks too."

Randy's treating me exactly how he'll treat those lawyers he'll fire: with an uncompromising, businesslike spirit. I remain slumped in Randy's leather chair, arms still folded, wishing I were in my office where all the power symbols are mine. "Forget morality, okay? Cold dollars say, if you start firing lawyers to make a little more money for ourselves this year and next year, you kill our future. Why would any good young lawyer risk coming here? How will we keep up high standards of quality? Keep clients?" My questions shoot forth like bullets from a machine gun. I'm in command for the moment. "And I don't care what other partners say now, they'll be edgy about this place too. They might be next. Believe me, we'll have trouble keeping our partners too."

"You're in no position to make threats."

"Power comes and goes, Randy. It's a very fragile and elusive commodity. You can't have it unless others are willing to let you have it."

"Maybe I'm not explaining this right," Randy offers. "No money's leaving. Nobody being fired has any clients worth a damn. Besides, what loyalty do we owe these people? There isn't anybody here who wouldn't leave if a better deal came along elsewhere," he says as nonchalantly as one mentions the time of day. He stops to inhale, then with measured caution, he pronounces: "Diana's in the next group of ten to go. It was a long time coming. I'm not sorry."

"I'm not surprised."

"That she has to go?"

"That you're not sorry."

"Do you know how much time and money she's cost us?" Randy frowns. "Besides you, she's all people talk about. She's killing us."

"Blame the victim for the rape."

"You've been selfish, Michael. You've heard all the rumors, and you continue to do whatever you're doing—"

"I'm not doing anything."

"Oh, come on," Randy laughs with a roll of his eyes. "I can hardly blame you for what's happened. She's come on to you, I can see that. That's what I've told everyone. Hey, if she were on her back for me, her legs spread, that pretty little ass of hers moving around, I don't know if—"

"You'd better stop," I cut in. Here I draw the line.

Randy chuckles and grimaces in one motion, the way one does upon opening an occupied bathroom stall. "I'm only saying she's come on to you. I've seen the way she looks at you with that dreamy expression in her eyes. Don't you think people notice you go to lunch with her almost every day? Best restaurants in town. Who are you kidding?" Randy's voice, betrayed a moment ago by a nervous edge, grows stronger. "You don't know how bad it is. People here want to know precisely what you and her are doing, how often, and why you haven't stopped. They talk about you two with the kind of emotion you'd expect at weddings or funerals. Maybe you don't see it, but I'm protecting you."

"I won't stand for this!" I yell with the pain one feels the instant a bone breaks.

"What choice do you have?"

"You'll break up the firm, Randy."

"The firm's going to break up in some way, big or small, whatever we do. I'm trying to keep it small. Funny how breaking up a firm is like a divorce, isn't it? You think it can't happen, then it must happen, and when it does happen, you're left wondering what you could've done to stop it."

"You don't care what happens as long as your income doesn't drop." Randy, I think, is akin to those men in power who invent theories (and sometimes facts) to support their right to rule, and at the moment they tie the rope around their victim's neck, seek to glorify the holiness of their act, trading their executioners' tools for judges' robes.

"I'm not expressing myself very well, am I?" Randy shakes his head. "I want the best for you, Michael, and for the firm too. I don't mean to be attacking you. If that's what it's been sounding like, I'm sorry. I'm a little upset, that's all. We both are. Take everything said here with a grain of salt."

Randy's confession of sorts reassures me. Maybe I've judged him too harshly. I, too, need to confess, and Randy's remorse frees me to confide in him. Anyway, don't I owe Randy a full explanation, or as we lawyers say, full disclosure? He's been my partner virtually all my working life. We can talk to each other in ways few men can. We understand the law and lawyers, know when to fight, when to retreat. We appreciate each other's talents, know each other's limits. If I can't tell Randy, whom can I tell?

"I made a mistake, Randy. I did something I shouldn't have done."

"Go on," Randy urges softly. He has a look of concern that I know is real.

"I didn't give the airline everything. I investigated Charlie's fitness to fly with an open mind, interviewed everyone with any connection to the Minneapolis flight, and never tried to put words in their mouths. It was all straight up, except for that one thing."

"What didn't you give them?"

"I gave them statements from all the witnesses, gave them all of Charlie's records, gave them the drug test Charlie passed. I did a thorough job,

Randy. In mind and heart I believed recommending Charlie's rehiring was best not only for Charlie, but for the airline too." I'm rolling now. I want Randy to know I've done good, that I *am* good. My need to be understood has washed away any intermittent fears of treachery. "I admit, though, I pushed this rehiring on Philip. He didn't want to do it." I'm not perfect, I've made mistakes, but that's something Randy can understand and forgive. I'm showing remorse. What fair listener won't see my predicament?

"What did you withhold?" Randy presses me. Like all trial lawyers, he wants to get right to the core of it.

"A drug test Charlie failed."

Randy's eyes widen. "You knew he'd failed—"

"In all fairness to Charlie, I'd rushed him. He had no notice."

"He wasn't supposed to have notice!" Randy shouts. "That's the whole point of drug testing!" His cheeks are turning crimson, his eyes burning.

I'm being lectured on ethics by a man who embezzled a client's monies and who, after nearly being caught, still had to be persuaded to return the monies. I think the seriousness of his crime (or the potential criminal consequences of it) has finally sunk into Randy's consciousness; the mere mention of the words "Hudson Escrow Fund" causes his body to sag noticeably. Having promised never to raise the episode again, I restrain myself from launching a counterassault, though not without difficulty.

I suppose I expected Randy's support, no matter what the circumstances. I expected friendship to triumph over money, loyalty over facts. Maybe I am guilty. Maybe I did kill all those people. Maybe now I've killed this law firm. Is there no end to my destructive power?

"You stupid son of a bitch," Randy says in awe.

My body sinks like a ball of lead. Who are my friends? I wonder. Who? After forty years I still have to ask.

"LIKE FINDING OUT your buddies were taken from their beds at sunrise and shot by a firing squad," is the way one partner sums it up. The description sticks. "Shooting at Sunrise" is the commonly accepted way of referring to the ten firings. Randy, the partners agree, had to do what he did. I'm the villain. I must be punished.

Every decision I've made in the last decade is analyzed and magnified, then used as further evidence of my selfishness or lack of judgment. Whatever I currently support, the partners reject. Even my generosity is assailed, as many partners now consider my pro bono activities an annoying distraction, proclaiming proudly, like terrorists taking credit for a bomb blast, that their goal is to make money, not give it away.

Randy hires a marketing director, a slim, articulate, blond-haired woman in her early thirties who performs those functions virtually all the partners would have once found to violate the bar's Canons of Ethics, but now accept by pointing out that all forms of marketing have become widespread and therefore necessary to compete effectively for business. The director has over the years developed a network of media contacts upon whom she calls whenever her employer conducts a seminar, wins a lawsuit, or adds a partner. She speaks of broadening the firm's client base, drafting a firm brochure, defining business objectives, and cross-selling services to existing clients.

It's "no longer enough to do good work and join the right clubs," she says in her only reference to the quality of our work, which I mention to her is supposedly the basis of our existence. Those firms who don't market their services "will go the way of the dinosaur," she reminds me softly as she scoots away, not in the habit of chatting pleasantly with the unconverted. At our weekly firm meeting she suggests that every lawyer devise individual marketing plans and submit them to her for her review and comment. That evening she is busy compiling extensive databases that track our clients' business and personal preferences. With the passion and attention to detail of a football coach diagraming his team's plays, she orchestrates which lawyers will speak to which clients about which subjects at an early evening cocktail party having the correct blend of food and liquor. She attends no meetings, closings, negotiations, trials, depositions, or other activities involving legal work. "I report directly to Randy," she mumbles when I suggest she witness firsthand the product she is selling.

Despite all her frantic efforts, our marketing director cannot stop the bar's official gossip column from reporting that A&C is in a downward spiral, having recently lost several partners to other firms. The firm's prestige, as well as its pocketbook, is taking a beating. Is there any doubt I must be punished?

For years I've remained distant from all but a select few of my partners in the manner of an army officer preparing to assign men to a suicide mission—not because I care nothing for them or believe myself above them, but because I have little time or reason for chitchat. I know now I must talk to them, humanize myself as if they were jurors I must persuade. Despite all my work, all my fatigue, I allow nothing to interfere with my efforts to forge instantaneous intimacies; I inquire in detail about my partners' families and tell years-old war stories, all of which is painfully transparent and embarrassingly awkward to those forced to listen. To my surprise, I'm drawn to those most contemptuous of me, to those whose cold pity is reinforced by an unswerving opinion that I am continuing to act selfishly by failing to confess wrongdoing and accept punishment of some sort, preferably a major cut in income. Fear has robbed these lawyers of every ounce of affection and gratitude.

I'm utterly alone. In the days following the firings, I go to fast-food restaurants miles away, bearable only because no one knows me but unbearable for the same reason. Rebelling against all the advice I've ever given clients, I defend myself to friends and partners in humorless, self-pitying terms, arguing my merits as a person and bewailing my cruel fate. At times I speak with raw panic, with numb hands and buckling legs. My efforts to prove my innocence fail miserably. I'm forced into solitude at the very time I need a human touch. Even to be seen with me is dangerous, as it raises suspicions of collaboration. Kindness is taken for weakness.

I am a bundle of contradictions: While vehemently denying any wrongdoing, I seek mercy for any wrongdoing, however minor, I might have committed. My weakness exhilarates those who no longer fear me and are happy to remind me—all for the firm's greater good—of my despicable deeds, which grow more despicable as the days pass.

I watch from a distance as they dismember me with such remarkable cruelty I feel disconnected, as if watching myself watching them. Duty, honor, decency: These are the new code words for murder.

LIKE WATER FROM a broken toilet, the partners' fear and anger stream beyond established boundaries, betraying their stench to all discerning guests of Ashmore & Chapman's extravagantly arranged recruiting party, an annual ritual performed every summer at great expense for the sole purpose of enticing our brightest law clerks to accept offers of permanent employment. Clerks are praised, particularly in front of their spouses, and the firm's high standing in the legal community is modestly pointed out with feigned reluctance. The false gaiety of years past, as awkward as that was, is more comfortable than this atmosphere of feverish whisperings and bitter gazes. My home—where the party is held each year—once a source of pride among the partners, now fuels an ever-rising resentment of my riches.

I retreat to a quiet corner of my living room with orange juice in hand, politely fending off the silly smiles of clerks who lack the necessary poise to create the impression they desire. This party—designed to reveal to prospective associates the firm's gentle, human side—has the unmistakable gravity of a three-ring circus moments after the star trapeze artist has fallen to his death.

I'm no longer immortal, no longer immune from a fall from grace. Inspired to demonstrate a new egalitarian attitude, I do suddenly what I've never before done: I gravitate toward young associates and paralegals and speak cheerfully of the firm's bright future, further alarming those who know only desperate circumstances would cause a senior partner to find it necessary to persuade such lowly employees of the firm's potential.

"Is the firm in a lot of trouble?" asks one wine-drinking paralegal. "There's been rumors a lot more people will be fired. Are things really that bad?"

My brain empties of spontaneous thought like a Danforth Quayle on national television unable to say what he'd do if the President could not continue his duties. I look back at the mildly intoxicated woman who, apparently emboldened by the alcohol, flashes a knowing smile.

I turn away with wonder: Do we all have a touch of the murderer in our souls?

Mʏ ғɪʀsᴛ ᴛɪᴍᴇ ɪɴ ᴛʜᴇ ᴡɪᴛɴᴇss chair. I'm looking upward at Isabel Castino, who has that glow about her all confident interrogators enjoy. I strain to recall what I tell my clients before they testify. *Find a comfortable position and stay with it. Don't squirm. Don't mumble. Don't look away. Make friends with the jurors by looking directly at them.* Twenty-three hard faces are examining me, waiting to see if I'll crack. I squirm, and look away. I mumble something about the Fifth Amendment, and refuse to answer her question. I forget the exact phrases I'm supposed to say, but the point is plain to all here. I'm a lawyer relying on lawyerly tricks to evade telling the truth.

I don't feel safe. I know Randy's been called to testify and Philip's been made to appear a second time; but I don't know what they were asked or what they said. All this secrecy is maddening.

Isabel wants to do to me what I do to others sitting in these hard wooden chairs: expose the witness's cruelty and arrogance, then dehumanize him as a warrior dehumanizes his victim before dealing the death blow. Fear hastens fatigue, and fatigue works against the witness, draining his spirit to resist. Knowing all this doesn't seem to help. I'm as tired and frightened as any ordinary witness. Like many of them, I crave mercy and forgiveness, deadly desires for those who sit in these hard chairs. How terrifying to discover I can be taken apart, opened up and exposed to her probing touch and cold glare. I cling desperately to the Fifth Amendment, my only shield against this onslaught.

When I'm where Isabel is, I, too, am a relentless seeker of those specific facts necessary to shape a truth most compatible with my theory of the case. Jurors watch, judges take notes, court reporters transcribe. When the witness is contradicting himself, or conceding the guts of my opponent's case—

when he's melting before me like the Wicked Witch in Oz—all my feelings of inferiority are swept away, all my creative impulses spring to their peak. At these moments I reach a level of fulfillment unknown in my other life, inspiring a profound inner peace.

Isabel is my other self torturing me. In this sacred chamber Isabel can inflict suffering without guilt or shame not merely because it's her right and duty but, I suspect, as a result of her innate talent to convince herself of the absolute moral rightness of her cause, whatever may appear to be the facts or current state of the law. Facts and law don't seem to get in her way. All good advocates understand that facts are dependent upon fading memories and subject to varying, conflicting interpretations, while laws, necessarily inflexible, cannot always take into account the specific nuances of a particular situation; even an unobjectionable law, applied to a certain set of facts, might lead to an unjust result. The more self-righteous among us (Isabel qualifies) believe that no person of conscience can obey all laws in all instances; if every law is to be regarded as sacred, nothing will be forbidden.

She's picking up steam. The questions are coming faster, her voice rising, her body bouncing to and fro. She knows too much. She knows precisely why Charlie was fired, precisely what Sexton and Dilman told me, precisely what I argued to Philip to get Charlie rehired. She's coming dangerously close. She asks about Charlie's Seconal habit. She asks about Charlie's doctor. Then, in a moment of pure exhilaration, she asks who Dan Palmer is.

"I refuse to answer," I say, now getting the hang of it after two hours of repetition, "on the ground that my answer may tend to incriminate me."

"Did Dan Palmer, at your direction, administer a drug test to your brother, Charles Ashmore, which turned out to be positive for Seconal?"

"I refuse to—"

"In the course of your investigation on behalf of the airline into the fitness of Charles Ashmore to fly, did Dan Palmer, your own personal physician, give you written results of a drug test Charles Ashmore failed, and did you deliberately withhold this test from the airline when you recommended that Charles Ashmore be rehired by the airline?"

I squeeze the chair's wooden arms, then hold on as if the chair is about to take flight. I know now with hideous intimacy the hot fear and icy chills of the witnesses I interrogate. I'm on the other side, unable to get back. The earth is splitting.

· · ·

DIANA WANTS ME to persuade Palmer to lie. It's too late for Palmer to say there was no test; Isabel knows about the test, though she doesn't actually have the test itself. If she had it, she would've shoved it in my face and let the grand jurors gaze upon it.

What are the possibilities? Palmer could say he no longer has the test results, but discarding such records would be contrary to good medical practice and to Palmer's own policy to keep such records for as long as his patient lives. That's where Diana sees an opening: Charlie wasn't his patient, and Charlie's dead, either circumstance a basis for Palmer's letting the records go. If no written proof of the test exists, Palmer can claim memory loss as to the test's results. After all, his office has probably run a thousand or more tests in the three months since one of his nurses stuck a needle in Charlie's arm. Or Palmer can go a step further: He can recall that Charlie passed the test.

Another scenario: Palmer gave the test to Charlie, and Charlie, not I, withheld the test from the airline. Palmer didn't even tell me the test results, as his duty was to inform Charlie, not me, regardless of who made the appointment. Any other course of action would have breached the doctor-patient relationship. Charlie, for his part, kept me in the dark; or to juice it up a little, Diana suggests I say that Charlie told me he passed the test.

Diana's fairy tale has its problems: I have to commit the crime of suborning perjury, and Palmer has to risk his entire career by committing perjury. I have also to explain why Charlie, if he passed Palmer's test, took a second test, and why I submitted only the second test to the airline rather than both tests. To all this Diana says: The prosecution has no hard evidence of any wrongdoing by me.

The only people alive besides Palmer, Diana, and me who know about the failed test are Ruth and Randy. While Ruth knows for certain only that Charlie failed the test, and Randy knows more (that I withheld it from the airline), we nonetheless conclude that Ruth betrayed me. She has a motive, however twisted. Randy has no incentive to harm me. Not only are we still friends, he jeopardizes the entire law firm when he puts me at the center of the action. That, Randy won't do. It's good to know our friendship rests on a foundation of solid self-interest.

The inevitable call comes. The moment I hear Palmer's voice, I know some unhappy news is about to be delivered. This is the telephone call I've always dreaded, the one whose silent ring has awakened me from many fitful sleeps. Twice I have Palmer read word for word the subpoena commanding that he testify and produce records of all tests "administered by him" to Charles Ashmore. By the call's end, I am virtually breathless. Never have I destroyed—or asked anyone to destroy—evidence in connection with a lawsuit. Those lawyers in the blistering heat of combat seduced by their all-consuming need to triumph, and caught in their act of misplaced passion, have suffered disbarment, fines, even imprisonment. I advise Palmer to do nothing until I determine the best way to proceed.

The subpoena has been drafted poorly. The term "administered" is left undefined; ordinarily a lawyer would request tests administered by the doctor or anyone under his employ and/or control. Since a nurse from Palmer's office drew Charlie's blood and collected his urine, a plausible argument could be made that Palmer supervised but did not administer the test. Palmer told his nurse what to do, when to do it, and how quickly to have it done; he also chose the laboratory, called for the results, and notified me moments later. What precisely does "administered" mean in this context?

"Do you still have the records of Charlie's test?" I question Palmer hours after our initial call.

"I don't know. I'll have to look." He's allowing himself some room, I think, until he adds: "They should be around here somewhere."

"You told me your secretary was giving you problems."

"She couldn't file worth a damn. Nothing was ever where it was supposed to be. Fired her a few weeks ago." The room comes back into view. "I had samples sent to the lab of Charlie's blood and urine. Probably got copies of the lab reports." I take "probably" to mean he would conveniently misplace those copies if directed to do so, but in an uneasy voice Palmer adds: "I imagine the lab does too."

"Is it possible the lab never sent you copies of the results, but merely gave them to you by phone?"

"I did call them. But they always send written copies later."

"We were in a hurry, if you recall. You had the lab send copies of the test directly to me. Maybe they got confused about—"

"I guess it's possible they didn't follow through."

"Would the lab send you copies of the test results tomorrow if you requested it?"

"Sure."

"Do you know anyone at the lab on a personal basis?"

"My girlfriend's sister works there."

"Could she send you copies?"

"I don't see why not."

I cannot find it in me to take that final step—would she send you the lab's *only* copies?

"Do you want me to get copies from the lab?" Palmer asks. His voice is subdued, tinged with a quiet nervousness that persuades me the doctor does understand; yet neither of us is prepared to reveal to the other his readiness to break the law.

"Not yet, no, not yet," I reply after an uncomfortably long silence.

Palmer is one of those old-fashioned souls who believes in returning favors. Two years ago his wife sued for divorce, claiming "irreconcilable differences." Married to Palmer sixteen months, she wanted the house overlooking the Potomac, the silver Mercedes, his certificates of deposit, most of his stocks and bonds, half of his IRA, and generous alimony payments for the remainder of her years. At her deposition, I asked if she had committed adultery during the sixteen months of their marriage. On her attorney's advice, she refused to answer, relying upon a Maryland statute considered the civil equivalent of the Fifth Amendment. Having invoked the statute, she could not stray from it without losing its protection. If she were to deny committing adultery with any particular man or with more than one man, she would be required to answer my initial question. I inquired if she had committed adultery with two men, then repeated the question eighteen more times, adding one man with each new question. On her attorney's advice, she invoked the statute's protection with each answer. As I rose to cross-examine her at trial, I waited until the courtroom was silent, on edge, then boomed out in an indignant voice: "Mrs. Palmer, isn't it true that during your sixteen-month marriage to Dr. Palmer, you committed adultery with twenty different men?" Had she said no, I would have been entitled to read her deposition testimony to the jury; but, as in her deposition, she refused to answer, and the stunned jury (one woman juror let out a low gasp) awarded her no alimony and a minute portion of the couple's assets. For this result Palmer has been everlastingly grateful, and upon his own solemn, misguided vow, would do "anything" for me "at any time."

"Can they force me to give them confidential medical records?" Palmer inquires.

"The District has no doctor-patient privilege. Even if it did, the privilege dies when the patient dies."

"I'll look around," he says. "Maybe they're not here."

I walk to Diana's office. I slump into her chair. "I think Palmer will do it if I beg him," I say. "But if things go south, Palmer will be the first to see the inside of a prison. If Isabel's out for blood, she'll give Palmer immunity and come after me."

"Palmer's loyal to you, isn't he?"

"Loyalty fades in the heat," I reply. "Anyway, Palmer could fold on me, loyal or not. He'll be asked a hundred questions about what lab he sent the samples to, what they did, how long it took, who he talked to. How many witnesses have we seen screw up even when they're telling the absolute truth? They get nervous, they forget, just plain screw up," I whisper, my body growing stiff as if readying itself for a casket. "They'll subpoena the lab next. What if Palmer's contact over there doesn't honor his request, or just can't get it done?"

"Did Palmer send you a bill?" Diana ponders, not wanting us to miss anything.

"No bill, no invoice. He did this as a favor."

"I wish my doctor was that nice."

"Save him a million dollars, and maybe he will be."

She juts out her chin like a boxer issuing a challenge. "Maybe it's time for him to save you."

Palmer calls. He's found the test. He claims to be sorry.

"No, that's okay," I reply gamely.

"I could lose it again. It's pretty messy around here."

I withheld that test from the airline out of love—the kind of pure, everlasting, unconditional love that must always take precedence over obligation, legal or otherwise. I trusted Charlie the way I loved him. It went beyond anything he ever did or said, went deeper than any gut instinct or well-considered judgment. It was blinding faith, the kind that makes men believe in a divine presence.

I won't condemn Charlie. Some connections can't be broken; they persevere beyond time and space and rotted flesh. Charlie's dead, not gone.

Palmer's waiting. I'm stalling. I'm not any ordinary lawyer, I tell myself. I've worked for homeless refugees, for kids on the street without fathers, for battered wives. I've donated my time, paid their legal expenses, sacrificed my sleep and good health. All my life I've been committed to the poor and the weak and the innocent; all my life I've set the highest standards for myself. To instruct Palmer to destroy the failed test would poison my soul, ruin my power to pretend I am who I aspire to be. If I can't pretend, all hope is lost.

"Dan," I say as if announcing my own death, "tell the truth. That's all. Give them the records. Let's be able to keep our heads high."

"Sure," he says. I discern a note of relief in his voice. Maybe even a tinge of respect.

I hang up the phone. I won't live an ordinary life again, I think. No nights without the sweats, no meals without a slight gagging sensation.

I WATCH THEM search my house. FBI agents in blue sanitary slippers and yellow rubber gloves rummage through bedroom drawers, explore closet shelves, inspect cabinets. They're looking for phenobarbital and fingerprints and writings showing that I knew: about Charlie's depression, about his drug habits, about his coming divorce, about anything. They play videotapes, examine photos, shake out clothes.

I'm ill—not figuratively, but in a real physical way. They're touching intimate things, violating sacred rituals, intruding on personal space. Will they find anything to hurt Charlie or me? I stand for two hours like a coach watching his team run its final play in a one-point game. My body's a taut string, my breath short.

I've seen this sort of thing happen. Many of my pro bono clients have lost everything because a car swerved into them or a bottle exploded in their faces: unintended, helpless victims forever trying to untangle their lives and, on some unconscious level, blaming themselves for being in the wrong place at the wrong time. Now I'm one of them. Maybe I'll need a lawyer too, some powerful figure who will fight my battle and reassure me I've been wronged.

I go to my office to search my files before they do. I have a few hours head start, and I plunge right in the way I dive into the waves before fully absorbing the ocean's temperature. I have Patti bring in all files from the War Room and from her secretarial bay. Diana's with me. We divide up my office, then attack the stacks of paper.

Something's wrong. An hour passes before I realize it. I ask Diana: "Have you seen the logbooks? They're not with the stuff from the War Room."

"No." Her eyes narrow. She's worried. "Have you gone through all—"

"I've gone through everything from the War Room." I'm in a hurry now. I can't wait for sentences to be completed.

We look through everything from everywhere in a fury. It's like one of those cartoons in which papers are flying in every direction at super speed. But we see no humor in it. The logbooks are gone. Not just any logbooks— the logbooks that prove the J99 has serious sticking problems with the elevators. *Gone* is a general, inclusive term for what has happened; *stolen* is the better, more precise description. *I'm being set up.* I look at Diana. Her face is as white as I've ever seen it. We've reached the same terrifying conclusion: I'm on my way down.

I imagine Ruth alone with her Wild Turkey. She's laughing, yet her eyes gleam with a demonic hatred. If she can't have me, she'll kill me, right? I underestimated her dedication to my demise.

The investigators are here. They search with a cold-bloodedness that reminds me of the bureaucrats who built the Nazi machine. They aren't as thorough as they were at the house; I guess even zealots get tired. They're done in fifty-two minutes. They pick out a few papers, which I have copied for myself before they leave.

I close my door and telephone Ruth. This must stop, I think. This insane vendetta of hers must be held up to the light, examined, discussed, and brought to a civilized end.

She's surprised to hear from me. Her voice rises with curious delight.

I remain somber. I tell her about my ordeal before the grand jury, the missing logbooks, the coming testimony of Dan Palmer. She denies having any contact with the prosecution since her appearance before the grand jury. As to the missing logbooks, did I think she'd broken into my office? She laughs at what she calls my "paranoia." It's a bitter, noisy laugh that rings in my head long after we say good-bye.

"So tell me about you and Diana. Tell me." Her voice has retained the bitterness of her laughter; but it has a grinding hardness to it that suggests pleasure in the shadow of cruelty.

"Diana's with me four, five nights a week." She, of course, was told that long ago by Charlie. This is what lawyers do: They state the obvious but make it appear as if concessions are being made.

"Give me some details, Michael. Does she like it on top, or is she a missionary girl? How long does it usually last? Does she make a lot of noise? More of a screamer than a moaner, or just one of those well-behaved Episcopalian girls who keep their lips tightly locked and just sort of burst quietly inside?"

"Give it up, Ruth."

"I recall—correct me if I'm wrong—that you used to like some oral action. Both ways, right? Does she oblige you in that regard?" asks Ruth with a contemptuous snort.

"You need professional help."

"Just tell me how often you two do it. You're so busy, she's so busy, and there's Grace to reckon with. Where do you two find the time? Grace is up early, and you must both be awful tired late at night."

"Does it annoy you that I'm not entirely miserable?"

"No, I can live with that. I can even live with your faking happiness. All of us have to do that sometimes. But actually being happy, that's not what I have in mind for you."

"You didn't have that in mind for Charlie either."

She ignores my sudden assault. Nothing will throw her off her demented course. "Do you know what bothers me most? No matter how big a jerk you are, I'll still forgive you. Stupid, isn't it? My biggest fear is you'll die before I do."

"That's my biggest fear too."

She doesn't laugh. "I think you're hurting inside, but won't let me see it."

She resents my spirit now, the very quality that once drew her to me. "You need to get over your anger," I counsel her. "Move on."

"The greater the pain, the easier the anger," she says. "Anger is therapeutic. It's necessary."

"Anger begets anger," I say ominously. I want her to feel some danger too.

I report the conversation to Diana, who listens attentively and nods without expression, sufficiently wise to avoid making her pleasure known. "I don't hate her," Diana notes a moment later.

"No, but you wouldn't be grief-stricken if she were found somewhere without a pulse, would you? Nothing painful, something that got her in her sleep. Didn't even wake her."

"Oh, stop it," she chuckles. "You make me sound awful."

"You're not awful."

"Thank you. Not exactly a rave endorsement, but I'll take it." She nudges my ribs. "Hey, you, let's go home, okay?"

We haven't made love but once since the crash. Pain and painkillers have robbed me of energy and desire. We get home early, we listen to Sinatra, then I take my Demerol. She does everything: dinner, dishes, laundry. She makes sure Grace does her homework and brushes her teeth.

I sleep. That's why I take the Demerol: Nothing else will knock me out. Diana worries I'll get like Charlie. Demerol, Seconal, what's the difference? she broods whenever the opportunity arises.

I feel skin rubbing against me. Diana is near. I can smell her fragrance, feel her knees on either side of my waist. Her hands rub my chest. I open my eyes. She smiles and whispers: "Any way you want me. Anything you want me to do." She stretches out on top of me, her whole body massaging my whole body.

I'm coming alive. The Demerol is fading. Diana sits up, places me inside her. She sinks toward me, arches her body, and rhythmically flows back and forth. In the beginning I'm merely content to hang on, but now I'm ready to recapture my old self. With a burst of strength I shove Diana off me, and we reverse positions. This is my night, I think. Anything I want, any way I want it. I grip her shoulders, dig my feet into the mattress.

I enter her with familiar ease. I start slowly, but soon I'm flinging myself to and fro with what seems to be a jolting power. Maybe the Demerol's still working, maybe it's fooling me or I'm fooling myself, but I seem to be overwhelming her. Her breasts are rising and sweating, her eyes spinning beneath dampening hair.

She's pushing against my chest, but I won't be knocked off balance. My hands stick to her shoulders. I hear her furious intakes of breath, I feel our chests thumping against each other. I'm in a rocking, blissful, crazy free-fall, but crazy is making me sane. I gaze upon Diana's contorted, puckered-up face, and I see love there. Lust, pain, excitement too, but love outshines all else. Diana turns her body sharply once, twice, again. She knows exactly what to do to make me lose all control. I surrender. I'm crazy but not invincible. I come with a throaty roar.

I return to my senses after my fluid has been drained from me. "I hope Grace didn't hear me."

"It's two in the morning. Nothing's going to wake her. Remember how she slept when that heat detector accidentally went off? We had two fire trucks outside, sirens blasting away. She didn't move a muscle."

"I wish I could sleep like that." I can joke about anything now, even my insomnia.

"You'll sleep tonight," she chuckles.

"Grace didn't hear," I assure myself.

Diana turns toward me. "Grace asked me today if I'm going to be her mother."

"What did you tell her?"

"I told her the truth. I don't know."

"What do you want the truth to be?"

"You know." She breaks into a smile. "You just like to hear me say it."

I do.

"What do you want, Michael?"

Rising up, I kiss her full on the lips. My arms lock around her waist. I pull her toward me. We roll across the bed. We kiss again. The truth is, I don't know what I want.

A WIDE-SHOULDERED, thick-chested sheriff comes to my office wearing the solemn expression of a pallbearer. He hands me a large brown envelope. "I was told not to arrest anybody," the sheriff says in a squeaky voice as high-pitched as that of a fourteen-year-old boy. I take the envelope back to my office, shutting my door before carefully unsealing it. I expect the papers inside to be another group of subpoenas directed to airline employees. The sheriff's comment concerning his instructions "not to arrest anybody" merely reflected his confused state of mind.

My heart sinks as if injected with lead. The sheriff correctly understood the papers he was delivering. I'm dizzy, in disbelief, the way I imagine a soldier feels when a bullet knocks the air from his body and his blood streams toward the dirt. Vomit shoots upward and accumulates at the base of my throat in globs so thick it causes me to gag as if I were choking. This is what it feels like to die, no, this is worse. Death doesn't make you burn with humiliation, doesn't make you wish you'd never spent a day on this planet.

I've been indicted—not the airline, not Philip, but me and me alone. I read with a quivering stomach. The indictment charges me with the murder of one hundred twenty people. I took "affirmative steps to have Charles Ashmore reinstated as a pilot," says the indictment, "at all times knowing full well that Charles Ashmore was a heavy barbiturate user, was terminated by the airline for that very reason, and would be unfit to pilot a commercial jet." The indictment declares further that I accomplished this deed by using unfairly my "influential positions as the airline's general counsel and a member of its board of directors" and by "engaging in a deliberate and calculated campaign of deceit and fraud, which included, but was not limited to, the concealment of critical evidence." Proclaims the indictment: "The pilot's predictable and continuing use of barbiturates was the foreseeable and proximate cause of the deaths of all one hundred twenty victims." The indictment alleges not only "reckless conduct creating a substantial and unjustifiable risk of death" but "a depraved indifference to human life," and seeks as punishment for such transgressions "life imprisonment, without parole."

For nearly an hour I remain rolled up on my sofa. Having long believed this world would never scar me, I am without the necessary reserves to respond. I gather myself, straighten my back, stand. Soaked with sweat, I shake my body as does a cat who's been doused with water.

However difficult, I must appear outraged and confident. I wander aimlessly into the halls seeking shelter, but within seconds return to my office, shut the door. I don't yet have the strength to pretend. Another hour passes before I sneak into Diana's office.

Diana's body stiffens. Her face turns a hellish white, as if I were covered with blood. "What is it?" she falters. "Tell me." I hand her the indictment. She drops into her chair, studies the thick document slowly. Every so often she mutters, "I can't believe it," the way one does upon learning of a family member's sudden death.

By the time she's finished, her eyes are wet. She looks at me in agonizing silence, then gives me back the indictment as if holding it too long might make her an accomplice.

"Castino's the criminal here, not you. She's twisting everything."

I nod. I have to believe she's right. She is, isn't she? This isn't how the reckless homicide theory was supposed to be used. How strange and dangerous the law can be. Reflecting the images of its makers, the law is like a sheet of glass: transparent, hard to repair, easily broken. Its edges are sharp.

I need to see Grace, need her touch. No one else can give me the same sense of permanence. Grace has always been quick to forgive, slow to judge.

That's how she is tonight. She listens with an intense gaze as I tell her I "might" be in a trial, "might" have to defend myself, "might" be away for a while.

"You won't go away," she pipes up. Her face is the bright cherry-red of a child who's been holding her breath. "The bastards!"

"Grace," I caution her, but her defiance energizes me. It's love, isn't it? Her love lifts me straight up. I want her love to cover me, purify me.

"Bastards!" she cries sharply.

"Yeah, they are, aren't they?" I force a smile, hoping to break the tension. I need to protect her as well as inform her.

"You're not going away," she declares. "Not for one day!"

I stretch out my arms and embrace her. "I'll fight, Grace, don't you worry about that. This whole thing is wrong." I have to fight. Not just for myself but for Charlie too. We're in this together, Charlie and me.

"Don't worry, honey," I say again. What will happen to Grace if I lose? A dark chill slithers down my spine. I can't bear to consider the possibilities. There's Diana too. How long would she wait for me? How long would I want her to wait? They're not indicting me alone, I begin to realize. They're condemning everyone I hold dear.

I will fight. No deals, I swear to myself. I look into Grace's eyes and nod the way I do when something good is about to happen. She squeezes my shoulder. For an instant we are the same age.

ISABEL WON'T AGREE to bail. No bail in murder cases, she says, especially where the indictment alleges multiple murders. Diana argues I'm no threat to flee or commit a crime, so why not let me stay at home during the trial? I've got roots in the community; I'm not going anywhere.

They negotiate back and forth about the day, the hour, the minute I'll be taken into custody. I watch, I listen, I keep quiet. Diana knows what to say, how to say it. Isabel isn't generous. She'll give me a week at home, then have me escorted to the arraignment hearing. If I don't get bail, I'll be taken to Lorton Penitentiary and kept there until the trial ends; the jail adjacent to the courthouse is overcrowded. If I'm convicted, I'll remain at Lorton. I'll be used to it by then, Isabel jokes. Nobody laughs. It could be worse. Isabel could have me arrested this instant, allowing me no time to get my affairs in order.

My indictment makes last night's eleven-o'clock news and this morning's *Today* show. On our way back to the office, we pick up a *Washington Post*, hoping my troubles are buried in the back pages. PROMINENT ATTORNEY CHARGED WITH MASS MURDER IN AIRLINE CRASH, the *Post* proclaims on page one. Thank God there are no photos of me. Thank God I refused all interviews.

I've told Jeanne to keep Grace away from all radios and televisions, but I know Grace will soon learn how despised her daddy is. Children have a way of learning such things even when they don't want to know.

I get strange looks from the receptionist and the secretaries as I make my way to my office. I imagine I inspire that certain awe in them that all pure evil evokes. *Didn't kill anyone on purpose*, I want to scream out, but screaming will only heighten their fear of me. My partners, made of sterner stuff, have long taken the view that one's character, like one's religion, is not to be considered in the conduct of commercial pursuits. For once I'm pleased they are mercenaries disguised as officers of the court.

Randy's already in my office. He's sitting on my sofa, pen in hand, legal pad on knee. Notes are scribbled wildly up and down the top page. I sit at my desk. "Any thoughts?" I ask casually. I want him to think I'm composed, still capable of leading this firm.

"It's done," he replies. No smile, no embrace, nothing from Randy but strained stiffness, averted eyes, distant tone, all exuding anger. "The partners want you to take a permanent leave of absence. At least until the trial is over," Randy clarifies.

"I won't take any leave of absence," I snap. "It'll send the wrong signal. You're compromising my defense, Randy. Playing with my life."

His face softens a bit. "It's not me, Michael. I voted against all of it."

"A vote? When I wasn't there?"

"They didn't think it was appropriate for you to be there."

I feel my face twist, seized by a violent spasm. "I'm a partner, aren't I? Don't I have a vote?"

"That's what I said. You had a vote and a right to be present at every vote. But the truth is, the vote wasn't close. Your vote wouldn't have mattered. Anyway, you weren't here this morning, and your secretary didn't know how to reach you."

"They can't do that!" I rant, rising from my chair.

"They did it," replies Randy with a decisive finality. "And they did it lawfully, did it according to the partnership agreement. Look, I don't think what they did was right, but all this publicity is killing us. Mass murder, for Christ sake. A silk-stocking firm like this one doesn't want the smell of—"

"You son of a bitch," I growl.

"I voted against it!" Randy swears.

"But you didn't fight for me, did you? You didn't fight." I glare at Randy but say nothing more, apprehending with painful clarity that Randy's influence, at its peak only months ago, has virtually disappeared.

"You need to get your head straight."

"My head is straight."

"Until your case is over, your head won't be straight. If you don't see that, you're in worse shape than I thought."

"Exactly when was it decided there'd be a vote?"

"Last night. When the news broke out. About the hidden test and the indictment. Of course, I already knew about the test, but it's national news now. I said we should wait until you got to the office, but a lot of eyes were rolling. They all know you'll be gone for a while, no matter how it comes out. So what are we really talking about here? Pride, maybe?"

"I don't want the jury thinking my partners agree with the prosecution."

"Nobody here wants to be associated with your trial, Michael. Too seamy for them. And they don't want to pay you when you're gone. That's no surprise, is it? Charity from these greedy clowns? Did you expect—"

"Not charity, but a little compassion. If not compassion, some minimal degree of loyalty. They've all lived quite well off the millions of dollars I've brought into this firm year after year."

"They have. But every year's a new year. Next year you won't have the airline, and probably never will again."

I shake my head with a deliberate slowness while my breathing, though I try to control it, is picking up speed. "I know why Philip was pissed off at me. But why fire you too?" I ask, fishing for anything I can hook. "You got those hearings put off, didn't you? He owes you."

"The crash put those hearings off, not me."

"C'mon, Randy. You didn't argue the plane was okay, and the cause of the crash confirmed that?"

"I'd like to take credit, but no, I didn't talk to a single Congressman."

"I don't want a leave of absence," I groan after an uncomfortably long pause. "It sounds like I'm being forced out."

"Michael," he sighs, as if speaking to a stubborn child, "they don't want you here. It's not only the airline. No client is comfortable with you. They're all calling here, asking for other partners to do their work. Diana must go too," he adds for good measure. "She and nine others. Not just her."

"Not just her," I note acidly. "Is that supposed to make me feel better?"

"It's not my job to make you feel better. The partners believe this is the best course for you and for us," declares Randy, back to that distant voice, the words "you" and "us" sticking to my brain. "Truth is, the leave of absence was a compromise. It was that or have you flat-out fired. There'd be no firm left if I refused to do either." His voice trembles slightly. He's becoming human again, I think. He finds it difficult to tell me how low I've dropped, but my insistence on staying has forced him to say what he otherwise would have kept secret.

This is my firm, but I no longer belong here. It's humiliating to stay, humiliating to leave. "I'm going to take more than a leave of absence," I announce gamely. "I'll make it a clean break. That's what everyone wants, isn't it?"

"A leave of absence will be enough," Randy observes halfheartedly.

"Just give me back my capital account," I say. "I don't want charity."

"There's no need—"

"This must be played to the media as solely my decision," I announce firmly. "To devote full time to my defense. Absolutely nothing about this vote, absolutely nothing!"

"Of course, but—"

"No buts!"

"You deserve more than just your capital account, that's all I meant to say. Take what's yours, Michael. Take your percentage of the accounts receivable. I'm certain the partners would throw in another hundred thousand lump-sum payment on top of that. Take it, okay? You'll need the money."

My eyes widen. I *am* being fired. Randy wouldn't have mentioned a lump-sum payment unless the partners had already authorized it. Nobody gets a lump-sum buyout in return for a leave of absence.

He looks down, scribbles a few notes. He knows he's given himself away.

"I'll take the money," I say with a sharp edge. "I'll take two hundred thousand, plus my accounts receivables, plus my capital account." Randy's right. I will need money.

"One hundred thousand," Randy insists. "That's as high as the partners will ever let me go. Take it now before they change their mind."

I waver a moment. The trial alone will probably last six to eight weeks, and cost a half million in fees alone. Beyond that, I'll need an exact model

of the J99 constructed to scale; photographs of the cockpit's interior enlarged to ten feet tall; the flight recorder readout reproduced in various
colors; and a computer-animated movie made of the flight's final four
minutes. Add another three hundred thousand to the bottom line.

As costly as all this will be, it might only be the beginning. The civil suit
against the airline will likely be amended to include me as a party. The cost
of defending against that suit would push me to the edge of bankruptcy; a
verdict against me would surely render me insolvent.

"Take it, Michael. I don't know how long I can keep it on the table."

"Okay." I nod, then dismiss him with a wave of my hand. He leaves.
We don't shake hands, don't even look at each other. We are embarrassed
we've gone down so meekly, though I'm not surprised. Small defeats have
become a way of life.

The next day I get my hundred thousand, plus another hundred thousand
for my share of the receivables and the capital. Both checks come in a plain
white envelope. No card, no note, nothing but cold cash. That's all I ever
was to them, I think. They'd leave me for dead if it meant another nickel
in their pockets.

I can't stay here another day. My loathing for my partners has grown
steadily since the crash, leaving no room for the smallest kindnesses. Their
grating voices and inane smirks heighten my daily tension. I'm of the same
blood with men everywhere who wish for the day their oppressors will hang
from burning trees, their necks stretched, their skins on fire. At times I can
actually *see* the flames engulfing them; I can *hear* their screams. During
these breathtaking reveries, a crisp biting rawness (like a frosty wind whip-
ping across a sweating neck) seizes my entire being, plunging me into a
peculiar blend of joy and despair.

Within hours I have hand-delivered to each partner a brief letter thanking him for his "unqualified support during this most difficult time. Re-
grettably, though, I must now turn my full attention" to my defense. No
one replies to my letter. I'm ignored. No luncheons, no sorrowful good-
byes, no exchanges of phone numbers. I gather my books and files, stuff
them in suitcases, and go; but not fast enough. The brass plates on the door
have already been changed. Chapman, Knowles, Ross, Marnon, Lehrich &
Webb are the new stars here—the sheer number of names a sure sign the
firm's power base is dangerously fragmented. I'm livid they lack the common decency to allow me a dignified exit. Soon my name will be removed

from firm stationery, firm books, firm pension plans: I'm a ghost who won't return.

I don't know where I'll go if I'm found innocent. What firm will have me no matter the verdict? Not long ago I could have joined any law firm in the country and been given a hero's welcome. I've waited too long, believing I'd never have to go.

THE WOUNDS KEEP WIDENING. Brandon Air Lines rehires my old firm two days after I leave. The nine lawyers to be fired with Diana stay with the firm; indeed, none are ever told they made the dreaded list. Diana alone is let go.

I find in every open garbage can, every crawling roach, every report of rape or robbery, a confirmation that the world is disintegrating around me and I, empty and helpless, am a disemboweled shell. Hot and cold flushes cruise through my veins. I brood, I mumble, I stare aimlessly. I'm responsible—not legally, but in some more profound way that connects all souls. I regularly skip breakfast and lunch; fasting, a form of penance, brings on the hunger pains that, strangely enough, calm my soul.

Diana and I set up shop in my living room. We bring in the desk and conference table from my old office, and clear out all the room's unnecessary furniture. We put metal file cabinets in the corners to hold copies of documents we've taken from the War Room. Patti, my old secretary, will be here tomorrow. She's a casualty of the war against all that which reminds my former firm of my odious presence.

Diana and I are working from darkness to darkness. We've put together a comprehensive request for documents from Jarrad; composed a witness list; and considered all potential trial strategies. Diana urges me to concede Charlie's recklessness but contend it didn't cause the crash; blame the elevators and the weather. I can't concede that, I tell her. I can't give Charlie up. No matter the evidence, I cling to the belief that Charlie took no barbiturates knowingly. Something happened, I say.

"You make that argument, Michael, and you'll be laughed out of the courtroom and into prison." I can't tell if she's irate or panic-stricken. Her jaw is jutting forward, her eyes aglow. She's looking at a madman. "You've got not a shred of evidence that Charlie was drugged. If we even hint at that, the jury will think we're as desperate as hell. They won't take us seriously on the issues that matter."

Who is "we" and "us"? I've already contacted three of the District's most highly regarded defense lawyers. All are interested: I'm a high-profile client in a high-profile case who can pay. Before deciding, I want to hear from each of them their most relevant experience and their intended way of attacking the prosecution's case. It's in part a chance to get some good advice free. "You're not thinking of being my lawyer, are you?" I ask directly.

"Nobody knows the facts better than I do. Nobody will work harder."

"Nobody would be under more pressure. I can't let you—"

"And here's the best part: I'm free. You won't have to sell the house."

"If you're free, how do you eat?"

"I'll give up my apartment and live here. Grace will need somebody if you don't get bail."

I want her to move here. Yet I say: "You can't live here. Too many reporters."

"Fuck them," she says with a smile, but there's a fury not far behind it. She's used to doing as she pleases.

"Anyway, it's never wise to get involved with a man being prosecuted for murder."

"Too late for that, isn't it? Now, here's some advice for you: Never face a murder prosecution alone. It gets lonely quick."

We are good for each other. We lift each other's spirits, give ourselves a powerful source of energy. If I drink every last drop of her, maybe I'll be whole again. Still, I worry: "No, Diana. Help me from the sidelines."

"I won't let you talk me out of this," she says fiercely. "I can win."

My head jerks upward. "If you're so insistent," I reply after a moment's contemplation, "then maybe I need to get some specifics. All those years you were a prosecutor, how many cases did you try, how many did you win?" I'm not completely serious, but she can't be either, despite her intensity. What would she do to herself if she lost?

"I didn't keep track, Michael. They weren't basketball games."

"I guess nobody keeps track. Unless they've won more than they've lost."

"If you must know, I did win more, a lot more."

I wave my hand dismissively. "It doesn't matter, Diana. They're not basketball games."

Her eyes light up. She, like me, can't resist a challenge. "I tried one hundred and nine cases, lost only three. Nineteen were murder cases. I won them all. Is that specific enough?"

I nod. "Especially since you didn't keep track," I add with a chuckle, but I'm satisfied. Those are Hall of Fame numbers.

Diana rises from her chair, walks for a moment in a small circle, then comes to me. She sits on my lap facing me, our chests touching as she leans forward. "Michael," she whispers in a hesitant voice sufficiently somber to frighten me, "do you believe we must now tell each other everything? If I'm going to be your counsel, no secrets, right?"

"No secrets," I agree. "What do you want to know?"

"Everything. And I want you to know everything." She inhales deeply, lets it out slowly, as if preparing herself to make an Olympic-sized leap. "Is there anything I could say to you that would make you hate me? You forgave Charlie, so I hope you'll forgive me too."

"Tell me," I order with a sense of urgency.

I hear her heart hammering against her chest. "I started the rumors about us as lovers. Not directly, but with little hints, like wearing the same clothes two days in a row after leaving the office late with you, or by deliberately looking at you in a certain way that others would notice." Her breathing stops, then rushes ahead. She is truly afraid, I think. She must love me in a way and with an intensity I need. "Everything was going so badly for me," she defends herself in a halting voice. "Everybody, except you, seemed to relish the idea of watching me tremble in fear. You were the head of the firm. Your wife had died. And I knew you wanted me. Ever since our ride on the train."

I remember the train. Rush hour, no seats available, Diana and I holding on to the same padded pole. Her body was directly in front of mine, forcing me to stretch awkwardly across her shoulder. Bodies were crushing against us from all sides as the train shook and rumbled. I momentarily lost my grasp, pressing and bumping against Diana as the train jerked, stopped, then roared underground into the empty blackness, cutting through the earth with a frenzied speed. My breathing became labored and heavy, as if our naked bodies, entwined, were working toward climax. Near the ride's end, seats became available. Sitting across from her, I looked too long at her bare, deftly crossed legs, hoping they would separate even for an instant. When I glanced upward, I spotted Diana staring back at me, her lips parted in a devilish smile. She not only knew, she wanted me to know she knew.

I looked away with a sweaty forehead and a tumbling heart; after that, I was hers for the asking.

I bring her closer to me and squeeze. "It's okay, Diana. I don't hate you. You didn't have to tell me anything. I trust you more now than I did before."

"That's why I left New York," she mutters. "The lawyers there were always coming on to me. A joke, huh? They were the very people enforcing the laws against sexual harassment. That's how the idea about rumors came to me. One of the lawyers there said we might as well do it since the rumors said we were. That's when I left."

"But you knew I wouldn't leave you?"

"I'm a trial lawyer, Michael. I'm supposed to know how people will react to my questions."

"You mean commands, don't you? So let's do it, that's what you said. That's a command, not a question." I smile.

She returns my smile. She knows she's gotten what she wants: to defend, in the harsh glare of the national media, a man who recklessly interceded in an internal company matter and imposed his will to achieve a purely personal goal despite knowing—I had to know—he was putting in jeopardy the lives of innocent, unknowing passengers. Now she, too, is at risk. Maybe she'll perform badly, or merely fail to satisfy the dozens of lawyers-turned-commentators who will analyze her every move and remark on it. Maybe she herself will be accused of being a silent participant in the nefarious scheme. And maybe, if all else fails, the media will discover something about her past even I don't know—ten years ago she cheated on her taxes, she sexually harassed a male secretary, she invested in a company that illegally employed child labor. Yet her smile broadens. She touches my face. She has what she wants. Lucky girl.

I WON'T BE a whore. I say no to book publishers and movie producers interested in capitalizing on my misfortune. The money, though big, keeps getting bigger; but I refuse again and again. Juries don't like whores, and neither do I.

The hordes of reporters who call themselves "legitimate" proudly offer no money, secure in their belief that it's their God-given right and duty to interview me. Don't I want the public to hear my side of the story? I refuse their benevolence; they profess to be confused by my stupidity. My phone rings day and night. After a while I learn not to answer it.

We go to round two. They come right to my house and ring the door-bell. They have microphones, camera crews, and tape recorders with them. I close the drapes and hide. I won't let them inside. I won't let them discover Diana or Grace.

Some are more persistent than others. They ring the bell every few minutes for hours. They pound on the door, they yell out my name. They challenge me to show my face. I don't respond with angry words or tearful pleas or obscene gestures. I simply don't respond: a hunted animal clinging to shelter from life-sucking predators.

Isabel has a message hand-delivered to my home, and slipped under the door. She wants to meet before tomorrow's arraignment hearing. I take this as a positive sign. She's worried. She's come to realize this case might turn on her, swallow up what's left of her political career.

My joy disappears with Isabel's first words. She's sitting behind her desk, her back tilted forward, her stare intense. "You should know we have from Dan Palmer the test your brother failed, and we have from Philip Brandon and Randy Chapman all the testimony we'll ever need. We have you cold, Michael."

Randy? I shudder. That makes no sense. She's lying. Not Randy. "I don't believe you," I say coolly. I lean back against my chair, my arms hanging by my sides. I want her to think I'm loose, ready to do battle.

"Believe me," she replies without a trace of emotion. "In return for that priceless commodity called immunity, Brandon told the grand jurors you never gave him the test your brother failed, only the one he passed. Chapman took it another step. He testified you confessed to him you not only hid the test, you knew perfectly well you had to hide it, or your brother wouldn't have been rehired. In fact, it was Chapman who gave me Palmer's name. I wouldn't have found Palmer otherwise because you were clever enough to use a different doctor for the second test."

No clever words come to mind. I'm too wounded, too stunned by Randy's betrayal. I can't make sense of it. Randy has immunity? Why hadn't she offered immunity to me to get Philip? Her letting the airline's CEO and Chairman of the Board completely off the hook is a bright signal she's willing to make extraordinary concessions to put me in prison.

"I wouldn't believe a word those two men said," Diana weighs in. "You may not know this, Isabel, but two days after Michael left his firm, a deal was struck between Randy Chapman and Philip Brandon. The airline, having fired the firm, came back to it. I think it's obvious what happened."

"It's not obvious to me," Isabel answers. "Clue me in, if you can."

"They agreed to go after Michael to get the airline off the hook. Randy saves Philip by lying about what Michael said. In return, Philip saves Randy by rehiring his firm. And you save them both by giving them immunity."

"I see," says Isabel with a contemplative look, but her voice reveals her disdain. "So you want me to give Michael immunity so he can testify against the airline? What the hell, why not give everybody immunity and let them all go free?"

"Why not just let the innocent go free?" Diana retorts. "I'd settle for that."

"That's what I've done. Brandon was deliberately misled, and Chapman and his people knew nothing about all this until long after the deal was done." She turns and looks at me. "You were the worst of them. You engineered it all, and in the most devious way. It makes me absolutely livid that you're one of us, a member of our bar, an officer of our courts." She shakes her head with tightened lips. "I suggest you two stop deluding your-selves and get down to business. Let's see if we can resolve this thing before we put the gloves on."

"No prison time," Diana rushes to say.

"One hundred and twenty people are dead. It's my job to speak for them," Isabel says forcefully. "If I try this case on their behalf, I'm confident the jury will come back with the maximum penalty we're seeking. That's life without parole," she explains as if we don't know. "I'm willing to make you a onetime offer I urge you to accept. Twenty years, fifteen to be served."

"No prison time," Diana repeats.

I join in Diana's objection. "I've got a ten-year-old daughter. Her mother died two years ago. I'm all she has."

"They'll run me out of town if I agree to anything less than fifteen years," Isabel says without remorse.

"You haven't been reading the newspapers, have you?" Diana asks. She's referring to the *Post*'s gracious references to me as a "nationally respected trial lawyer," "community leader," "soldier for the poor." The *Post* has questioned the wisdom of the indictment and the need to seek life impris-onment.

"If you want your body to rot at Lorton for all your living years, be my guest."

"Let's keep this professional, shall we?" Diana intervenes.

My body rotting in some grisly state prison is not only terrifying, it's real. I've heard about the bloody stabbings, the daily rapes, the jittery, brutal guards, the shit on the floor and the swarms of insects it attracts. Show them you're afraid and they'll leave you for dead. It's real, and could happen tomorrow.

Maybe I've misjudged Isabel's thinking. All those dead bodies, all those horrifying newspaper photos, all those enraging television pictures. Maybe she figures she'll have popular support for any efforts to convict anyone who may have contributed to the crash. She needs popular support now. Nothing else will make her removal from office politically unwise.

Isabel's face softens a bit. "You don't think I agonized over this? You don't think I discussed every conceivable aspect of your case with half a dozen lawyers here before making you a target? The facts are plain, undisputed. I've looked at everything. All the civil pleadings, all the thousands of documents. I put a week of solid time into this before deciding to seek an indictment against you."

Diana and I are silent, but our sullen faces reflect our refusal to empathize with Isabel's plight. I find it astonishing she'd expect the slightest gratitude from us.

"If you want a trial, you'll get a trial. But I'm going for it all," Isabel pronounces. "All" means life without parole. "All" sweeps across her desk like wind smelling of sewage. "All" silences the room.

"We believe your indictment is improper on its face," Diana asserts as we're rising to leave. "We'll move to dismiss it first chance we get."

She's talking about the absence of any criminal statute declaring reckless homicide to be a crime. Isn't life a wicked circle? The birth cry mimics the death rattle, the bloody frightened newborn is the shaking tortured man about to pass from this world. Reckless homicide has completed its circle, with me trapped inside.

"See you at the hearing," says Isabel grimly. No good-bye, no think-about-it, no the-offer's-open-till-tomorrow. "You won't get bail," are her parting words. I remember how she had that Korean boy locked in a cell with a child-killer. What will she do to me? I look at her, and wonder if she's thinking about the Korean boy too.

I SAY GOOD-BYE to Grace. We hug, we kiss, but I keep my composure, fearing if I collapse, she will too. I might not be coming home tonight, I explain to her. I might have to stay in a building in Virginia until my trial is over. She seems to understand. She keeps her composure too, though at times her lower lip quivers. Maybe she's afraid if she collapses, I will too.

I hope her mother hasn't ruined her. Paula wouldn't let Grace suffer even when suffering would have strengthened her. If Grace refused to go to bed at her regular time, Paula would allow her to watch television for another hour; if Grace cried because Paula denied her a particular toy that afternoon, Paula would drive to the store that evening and buy it—anything to relieve Grace's misery and hers. For every toy Paula purchased, for every hour she allowed Grace to remain awake beyond her normal bedtime, for every occasion she was about to strike Grace but restrained herself, she made certain Grace knew she was in debt to her, a debt that seemed to accumulate more rapidly than the federal deficit and, no matter what payments were made, could not ever be completely extinguished.

Nothing's changed since Paula died; I, too, yield to Grace's every whim. Yet everything's changed for Grace. She's fragile, I tell myself. She's watched her mother die, she's lost her cousin to fire, and she's heard about her uncle's demise too many times, all circumstances Paula never had to confront. I want to give Grace some sweet memories of childhood, something to shelter her in later years when shelter is necessary.

Two police cars follow us to the courthouse. I'm too jittery to drive. I leave that to Diana, who seems a bit nervous herself. She speeds up, slows down, turns more sharply than necessary. We are already at odds over strategy. She's filed a motion to dismiss despite my reservations, and wants to argue it today; we have nothing to lose and everything to gain, she contends.

I'm worried we'll not only lose the motion, we'll lose some credibility with Judge Henry Meredith as well. Meredith is one of those old-fashioned, be-straight-with-me-or-else judges who enjoys embarrassing a lawyer before all the world if he thinks that lawyer is trying to pull a fast one. He runs his courtroom like a POW camp: He tells you what to do, and you do it; and you'd better hear him the first time. I suspect he holds all unofficial records for finding lawyers in contempt and having unruly defendants gagged.

Diana's motion to dismiss the reckless homicide indictment might anger Meredith—I *invented* the theory, didn't I?—who tends to keep grudges for as long as the offending party is in his courtroom. Meredith will decide the admissibility of all evidence and instruct the jurors as to his view of the law. The jurors, of course, will do more than merely follow Meredith's legal instructions; they'll watch Meredith for clues as to his view of the facts as well. Judges wear official black robes, are learned and supposedly neutral. All they do and say carries great weight with jurors starved for insight.

The Superior Court for the District, while housed in a massive concrete building surrounded by elegant brick pavement, has scattered on its lower floors a series of dark, tiny courtrooms that have the unmistakable air of medieval dungeons with cheap red carpet, four dozen small vinyl chairs, and patches of a thin, grainy wood along its walls. The ceilings, low enough to touch with a short jump, make you keep your head down and voice low, as one does in an obscure cave; and the elevator doors, which remain open far longer than in other buildings, close with a deliberateness suggesting they won't reopen, reminiscent of a casket shut for the last time.

Everybody is tightly bunched together, as in the subway at rush hour. Funny, I didn't fully appreciate the dark smallness of these courtrooms when I tried cases here. I enjoyed the intimacy then, so close to the jurors I could hear them breathing, smell what they'd had for lunch. The judge's bench is within two arms' lengths of the witness chair, which in turn is nearly close enough to the oval-shaped jury box for witnesses to whisper in the jurors' ears.

I'm grateful I'm not in handcuffs, as are most defendants at their arraignment hearings. I look straight ahead as I plod down the crowded center aisle. I'm already weary as I sit at counsel's table eight feet from Judge Meredith. I'm locked in a giant closet filled with strangers who can do me great harm.

By contrast, the federal courtrooms across the square are spacious. Seven chairs (rather than two) surround each counsel's table, which sprawls out below eighteen-foot tile ceilings and across from paneled walls of the finest oak. The halls are appointed with granite floors, marble walls, and comfortable benches. You feel a bit more important there, whatever your role in the process. In the Superior Court, a defendant feels the way he's supposed to feel: like scum to be eradicated.

Isabel sits alone at her counsel's table, though I'm sure she has platoons of lawyers back at her offices ready to do any research or find any files at a moment's notice. She sits alone to convey the impression she's a solitary soldier with limited resources, an underdog for whom sympathy and support are in order.

The bailiff enters the courtroom, firmly proclaiming this court to be in session. Judge Meredith steps through a door behind the bench, nods solemnly, and motions all to be seated. "The formal reading of the indictment," he orders.

"We waive the formal reading, Your Honor," says Diana, rising to her feet. "Mr. Ashmore pleads not guilty to all charges."

"Is there an application for bail?"

Isabel stands. "We oppose any bail, Your Honor. This is a murder case where—"

"I know what kind of case this is," Meredith gruffly cuts her off. "I read the newspapers, Madam Prosecutor. I watch the news. I live right here in the District, not off the coast of Tahiti," he announces loudly, causing a contagious ripple of laughter to wave from the back center of the courtroom to the sides, then up to the first row. "I know you think the defendant here is a murderer, but surely you don't think he's a genuine threat to society. This isn't the usual murder case, now is it? It's more what I'd call a lawyer's murder case. You got a theory of law to get Mr. Ashmore there convicted, but you don't have a gun or an axe or any desire on his part to see people killed, do you?"

"We don't need that under reckless homicide," Isabel protests. "All we need—"

"We're talking about bail here, not whether you got cause to bring the case," Meredith scolds her. "It's two different matters, Madam Prosecutor, and you know it. When I'm thinking about bail, I'm thinking two things. First off, is the defendant going to run away? If we think he is, we lock him up or make the payment so high we know he won't. Second, is he going to commit this same crime again while we're waiting for his trial to start? Well, hell, I know Michael Ashmore myself. I know he's not going anywhere. All he wants is to clear his name. Right, sir?"

Meredith is looking straight at me. He's smiling like a kind uncle who's about to deliver a gift you don't expect. His gray hair, cut short in military fashion, has a few loose strands that hang over his ears, softening further his rounded face.

"I have every intention of being here every day of my trial, Your Honor. Every intention."

Meredith whips his head toward Isabel. "You see, Madam Prosecutor, what did I tell you?" asks Meredith mischievously. "As for committing this same crime again, the odds of that would be in numbers too high for me to count. He doesn't even represent an airline anymore according to what

I hear." Meredith's voice abruptly turns rock-hard. "So forget about the no-bail routine, and give me a number."

"I'll need a moment to consider that, Your Honor," says Isabel respectfully.

"Need a moment? You were so sure you'd prevail you haven't even considered the possibility you'd lose?" inquires Meredith ominously. "You thought I'd just roll over and buy that no-bail, this-is-a-murder-case stuff? You don't give the court much credit for independent thinking, do you?"

"I meant no disrespect—"

"I don't care much what you meant, Madam Prosecutor. The point is, you give me a number, and you give it to me the second this sentence ends."

"Two million dollars," Isabel blurts out.

Meredith glares at her. I don't know why he's going after Isabel the way he is, but I'm enjoying the show. Maybe something Isabel said or did in another case before him, or maybe he simply believes her position to be unreasonable. "Two million, that's all? Why not ten million or a hundred million?"

"This defendant is a wealthy man," Isabel defends herself. "Bail is supposed to be tied to the defendant's wealth."

"I set bail at two hundred thousand dollars," Meredith rules. Then he eyes me: "I have your word, don't I, sir?"

"You have my word."

Isabel rolls her eyes and sits down. I can hear her body hit the chair, an angry collision.

I won't have to go to prison, not yet anyway. For an instant I wish Grace were here to celebrate with me; no, I think again, I won't ever permit her inside this courtroom. I can't stop her from imagining my humiliation, but I can prevent her from witnessing it.

"Your Honor," says Diana confidently, "we would like to be heard on our motion to dismiss the indictment."

Meredith nods. "Make it short, to the point," he instructs.

Diana arranges her notes, then strides to the lectern. "I'll get right to it," she promises. "This indictment must fail as a matter of law. No act may properly be regarded as criminal unless the legislature has seen fit to expressly and specifically define and designate such act as criminal. There's not one statute defining reckless homicide or making any such conduct a crime."

Meredith waves his hand as if brushing off a pesky fly. "We have more than a hundred deaths here, Ms. Wells. The Book of Leviticus commands us not to stand idly by the blood of our neighbors."

"In all due respect, Your Honor, the Bible doesn't address this issue directly, nor does it have any place here if it did." Easy, Diana, easy. Her indignation (part real, part feigned, I suspect) won't convert Meredith. Rumor has it that Meredith is one of those Sunday Holy Rollers who keeps God out of his courtroom because the Constitution strictly requires it; otherwise, we lawyers would need to be quoting Jesus as higher authority.

"There is powerful wisdom in the Bible, young lady. That's all I meant by it. I wasn't citing it as precedent."

Meredith has retreated. It's foolish for a judge to be mixing God and crime in a public courtroom; any such remarks could find their way onto the Sunday morning news shows. Still, I'm uncomfortable. Meredith, while backing off now, might rip our hearts out later.

"I've always believed there is something sacred about the law," Diana continues. "While I don't doubt there are those who want blood and expect the prosecution to get it for them, the prosecution has still got to rise above this sort of misdirected anger, be bigger than those they represent. For all the public's complaining, they hope the government will lead, not follow. They hope the government will go after the real wrongdoers, not the ones most popular to prosecute."

Isabel jumps to her feet. "She seems to be hinting—without a shred of evidence to back her up—that we're prosecuting this defendant for some reason other than the administration of justice, and that's just flat-out untrue. We believe a verdict here of guilty will give meaning to these senseless deaths by sending a message that will be heard in all the law offices and corporate boardrooms of this country. That there is such a thing as accountability. Even for high-and-mighty lawyers."

Meredith allows himself a narrow smile. Everyone derives pleasure from watching a lawyer hang by his own belt. "In this case, we have some advantages we don't usually have, and maybe that's behind all of Ms. Wells's pouting, but that's what's also made me more certain about the indictment's correctness."

She's talking about the civil suit. Usually criminal cases precede their civil counterparts, and the prosecution doesn't have before it the mountains of evidence Isabel has at her disposal. Meredith shifts his weight in his chair.

He stares at Diana. "Are you saying this prosecutor is using her office to achieve some personal goal?"

"I'm saying the prosecution has no legal basis here, which by itself makes this indictment suspect, and beyond that, it's well known that Ms. Castino not long ago took quite a public beating from Michael Ashmore. If Ms. Castino truly wants justice, she'd go after the airline, not the airline's lawyer."

"That was our original intention," Isabel calmly replies. "The airline, not the defendant, was originally the target of the grand jury's investigation. But we went where the evidence led us, and it led us right to the defendant's door. Not only that, but at the same time we were gathering evidence, we were advised by one of this country's foremost legal experts in aviation law that an indictment against the airline would fail on constitutional grounds." Isabel glances down at her notes, a sure sign she's not altogether comfortable with the argument she's about to make. "Because airlines are heavily regulated by a federal statutory scheme, any state laws would likely be preempted under the Supremacy Clause of the United States Constitution. As it was explained to me, an airline couldn't be expected to design and build and fly a plane according to fifty-one sets of standards, one set by the FAA and the other fifty potentially set by juries in each of the states. What would happen, for example, if one state jury found an airline's design criminally negligent and another state found it perfectly acceptable? And because airlines are constantly engaged in interstate commerce, individual states cannot impose varying standards on the airline industry without violating the Commerce Clause. I mention this only to assure this Court the prosecution had no dark scheme of revenge."

"Who was this foremost legal expert?" Diana demands to know.

"You know him well. He used to be your boss," Isabel snickers, then looks straight at Judge Meredith. "The lawyer was Randy Chapman, who is currently the chairman of the ABA's section on aviation law, which is about the highest credential an aviation lawyer can have."

"Randy Chapman is also the lawyer for Brandon Air Lines, the original target of the grand jury's investigation. He was hardly a disinterested party."

"Disinterested or not, his position had merit."

"I didn't know airlines were exempt from the laws that apply to everyone else," Diana remarks in a mocking tone.

Isabel turns her attention back to Meredith. "If revenge was truly our motive, we would've gone after the defendant without delay. In any event, we couldn't let this case disappear. Not only because of all these tragic deaths. Because making public the truth might prevent future tragedies."

"Very noble of you," observes Meredith, "but can't all that be accomplished in the civil litigation?"

"That case might settle, as most of them do. This one won't." The harshness with which Isabel pronounces the word "won't" lends credence to our position. I notice Meredith's eyebrows rise slightly.

"Did you ever consider toning it down some? Bringing an indictment for involuntary manslaughter, for example?"

"We considered it, Your Honor, but we believed this was reckless homicide pure and simple, and we didn't want to water down the indictment with a bunch of lesser offenses. The defendant knew his brother was a drug user. His brother's wife testified under oath she told him that, and begged him not to seek her husband's reinstatement after he was fired by the airline for drug use. Members of a flight crew who had flown with the defendant's brother told the defendant of the dangerous effects of his brother's drug use. Nonetheless, our Mr. Ashmore set about the task of having his brother reinstated as a pilot. He had him tested for drugs, and when his brother failed the test, Mr. Ashmore concealed the results from the airline, his own client. Instead he gave the airline the results of a second test, taken a full day after the first one, presumably to allow his brother to get the drugs out of his system. That the pilot flew this plane and crashed it while under the influence of drugs can hardly be disputed. The autopsy shows massive drugs. The pilot's conversations as recorded on the black box reveal a disoriented and remote man, the common, predictable effect of the barbiturates he swallowed. And perhaps the best proof of all was his inability to pilot the plane properly after encountering routine turbulence, the kind a pilot sees every week, the kind that several other pilots flew right through without any trouble."

I struggle to remain still. Isabel is powerfully educating Meredith as to her twisted version of the facts. Might this later affect Meredith's judgment when he has to make close calls on all sorts of evidentiary issues? I pass Diana a note—"Stop her!"—but Diana remains still.

"The big point to make here, Your Honor, is these are not novel charges. The prosecution didn't manufacture some wild theory of law," Isabel declares.

"Have you ever sought a murder conviction for reckless homicide before?" Meredith inquires in the deep, throaty voice of one awakened moments ago.

"Not personally, no."

"I take it, Madam Prosecutor, you're familiar with the holding of the United States Supreme Court, often repeated, that no man shall be held criminally responsible for conduct which he could not reasonably have understood to be proscribed. Which ruling, I might add, has led courts to strike down a whole lot of statutes and throw out I don't know how many indictments as too vague to give adequate warning of what conduct is forbidden. Are you with me?"

"Yes, Your Honor, I am."

"Do you not see a due process problem here? The defense hasn't specifically raised it—they've touched upon it, I suppose—but I'm raising it right now."

Lifting a thick document from her notebook, Isabel approaches the lectern as Diana steps back to counsel's table. "I have in my hand a rather weighty brief written by none other than Michael Ashmore himself discussing reckless homicide in a case where he obtained a favorable jury verdict on this very same legal theory about seven months ago, so I don't think he's forgotten all about it. Mr. Ashmore has cited in here several cases in support of this theory—none of which, I might add, appear in the defense's moving papers—but all seem appropriate and all were in fact relied upon by the prosecution in our response to this motion to dismiss, which we filed this morning. Most interesting is this paragraph from our Mr. Ashmore which reads as follows." Isabel pauses a moment, then in a slow, emphatic way reads each damning word: "The concept of reckless homicide is so basic to our system of justice that it has widespread support not only in the civil law but in the criminal law as well. Case after recent case in the District has equated a reckless indifference to life resulting in a death with a homicide intentionally caused." Isabel gazes upward at Meredith and continues: "So, Your Honor, to answer your question directly, of course the defendant had notice. He knew about reckless homicide before we did. He told us about it."

Having gone out on a limb to assist the defense, Meredith is not pleased to find the limb cut. "Is all this correct, Ms. Wells?" he interrogates with controlled anger.

Diana cannot yield or apologize—either would be crippling. She charges forward, her tone scissor-sharp, her words shooting forth like arrows. Nothing about her demeanor suggests the slightest touch of remorse. "Let's not lose sight of the ball here," she demands. "This matter is altogether different than the circumstances in the perfume case. There the defendant knowingly and deliberately put a product on the market it knew would do harm to certain purchasers. Here, there was no wickedness of purpose, no attempt to profit, no abandoned and malignant heart. In short, no malice, and malice must be proved beyond a reasonable doubt to convict for murder. The U.S. Attorney knows better than to equate the two cases. One has nothing to do with the other."

Meredith listens impassively. At the conclusion of Diana's remarks, he does not ask Isabel to reply. I know we've lost. Diana looks pale. The media will have a field day discussing Diana's humorous incompetence.

"I deny the motion," is all Meredith says. No cases cited, no explanation, no rationale. Apparently Meredith thinks so little of our motion, he has left us with nothing but four words. I'm livid with Diana for having given Isabel the extraordinary opportunity to depict me as a shrewd and manipulative liar—persuading one court the law was well established when it suited my interest, then challenging that very same law when it applied to me. Sure, the situations are distinguishable, but go tell that to the people who will sit on my jury.

I head for the courtroom door. I'm pushed and pulled by the crowd. I brush lightly against an aging, red-haired woman, who takes out her handkerchief and wipes off her coat where my clothes touch hers. Her look of unmitigated scorn burns through my flesh.

A moment after we arrive home, I lose my anger. I lose it the moment I see Diana weep, lose it forever. She weeps not only from the unbearable humiliation and self-doubt, but from the gripping fear that comes with watching a loved one's life threatened by some irresistible force—a stray bullet flying in his direction, a truck bearing down on an intersection, a jury delivering a verdict of guilty. She weeps with body-shaking sobs and a ferocious gasping for air. She's where I once was: on my bedroom floor. I lie on top of her in a full-body embrace that lasts past dinner and into the evening. We are in our most conservative gray suits, our shoes hugging our sweating feet.

K STREET IS burning—not all of it, but that one long downtown block on which the airline's central headquarters occupy the six top floors of a sprawling concrete and black-glass building. Flames shoot one hundred feet high amidst a dense rising black smoke. Black teenagers smash car windows, tromp on hoods and roofs, pull drivers from their seats. Thank God, no one's killed, but there are raised fists promising more of the same. Violence, as deplorable as it is, does seize one's attention. By morning's first light, the fire is still raging.

My living room is overrun with dusty boxes. Patti removes the documents from the airline's boxes and stacks them in the northern half of the room; the southern half is quickly filled by Jarrad's papers. I estimate we have a million pages of logbooks, correspondence, design drawings, specifications, photos, and contracts involving the J99 and a handful of records about Charlie.

I'm not surprised by the avalanche of documents. Parties required to produce documents they don't want you to see either refuse to produce them (risking a court order overruling the usual objections of relevance or privilege) or, if they know you're understaffed, produce all of them plus tens or hundreds of thousands of other papers that you don't need to see (hoping you'll miss the few pages of importance they've stuck out of order in the oddest places, or you'll not look at all, having neither the time nor resources). Jarrad and Brandon Air Lines have undoubtedly taken to heart the latter approach. What are the statistical odds we'll find, in the little time we have left, the precious few pages buried in these heaps of paper, if buried there at all?

The logbooks aren't easy to find. They are scattered throughout the boxes and arranged without regard to time or place. Nonetheless, we eventually recover them all and organize them ourselves. My worst fear is confirmed: The logbooks have been altered. We find not a single reference to sticking elevators.

Diana and I are forced to spend nearly a week looking through endless pages of useless materials. Rather than preparing for trial, we are drones engaged in document review, ordinarily the work of second-year associates. Patti types countless indexes of documents; even she looks anxious.

Diana has persuaded Judge Meredith to give us a speedy trial date, figuring the prosecution, which has the burden of proof beyond a reasonable doubt, needs more time than we do. This seems at the moment to have been a gross miscalculation. Twelve days until trial and so many things remain undone. We haven't drafted Diana's opening statement, our jury charges, or many of our cross-examination questions. We haven't finalized our voir dire strategy or our list of exhibits. We haven't fully rehearsed our experts nor spoken with several witnesses we expect to call concerning Charlie's piloting skills. Worry is slowly turning to terror.

A lawyer-client relationship should be tailor-made for lovers. The client, for his own good, must tell his lawyer every intimate detail of his sad plight while the lawyer must zealously protect the confidentiality of all their communications. They must be a team with a common mission. That, Diana and I have, but I need a lawyer with more: more experience, more savvy, more influence. I need a bigger-name lawyer who's stood up in court with the media's heat glaring off the reflections of the jurors' eyes. I've considered of late hiring a black lawyer who'd pat me on the back in the jury's presence, who'd openly consult with me before selecting jurors, who'd talk to me as he rose to cross-examine a key witness. In short, a black lawyer whom black jurors would find sufficiently trustworthy to conclude I couldn't be as evil as the prosecution claimed if this fine black professional man so liked and respected me.

A trial lawyer wins or loses—no room for bullshit. Make a mistake, and it's in plain view for everyone to examine. That's how a trial lawyer is ultimately measured, isn't it? Wins or loses, all else just chitchat. How many folks will ever know what it's like to have their work judged with such decisive finality in the public eye? Athletes know. Actors know. Now Diana knows.

I've allowed Diana into waters too deep. Why can't I refuse people I love? Why can't I save them from themselves? The media continues to slaughter Diana for either deliberately failing to disclose my brief from the perfume case (in which case she's acted unethically) or for inadvertently failing to review it (she's blundered badly). Worse yet, the media has gotten wind that Diana and I are lovers. They're treading carefully with snippets like "companions," "former co-workers," "often seen together." They don't want to be accused of spreading vicious gossip or creating a circus atmosphere. They don't want lawsuits. "Anyway," goes one letter to the *Post,* "what relevance would it have even if they admitted to being lovers?"

It is relevant. A lawyer needs to be seen by the jury as an objective truth-giver. He believes in his client with all his heart and mind, but he does so because the evidence compels that belief. He's not biased by any circumstance other than the naked facts of the case. Naked bodies do tend to motivate us to reach conclusions unsupported by the evidence. Jurors, if they believe Diana's my lover, might toss away her arguments as desperate pleas for mercy.

As I'm about to tell Diana we must, by tomorrow, hire a lawyer with a big name and big-time experience (whatever the cost) who will assist her in the beginning and, as he gradually gets up to speed, become lead or colead counsel, I hear her yell out as if she knows what's coming. I look at the red numbers on my alarm clock. Three A.M. I run down the center stairs. "Are you okay?" I breathe upon entering the living room.

"I found something," she says excitedly. "It's a memo from Jarrad."

To be precise, it's Jarrad's Service Bulletin 97-815 released by Jarrad a month ago. She lays out the five printed pages like rare diamonds to be admired.

According to the Safety Board's report, Charlie flew the J99 at a steady altitude and climbed at a constant speed by moving an electric switch up and down with his left thumb, a procedure called "trimming the plane." The J99 Charlie flew could be trimmed electrically from 2.5 degrees to 4.4 degrees (the full nose-down position) in 3.6 seconds. Most pilots rely upon the electric switch to trim the plane, though the J99 can be trimmed manually by fully rotating a wheel in the cockpit nine times for each degree, an agonizingly slow exercise. Without electrically trimming the J99, the pilot must constantly be pulling or pushing the control yoke to keep the nose in proper position.

Jarrad's bulletin informs the airline that it has "for safety reasons" made it "more difficult for the pilot to place the aircraft in a nose-down position." The trim limit has been changed. No longer can a pilot electrically move the J99 to 4.4 degrees. The new limit is 3.5 degrees. In bold capital letters the bulletin further advises: **NEVER MOVE THE STABILIZERS IN TURBU- LENT WEATHER. RELY SOLELY ON THE ELEVATORS FOR ATTITUDE CONTROL.** Hadn't the airline contacted Jarrad about the J99's unsafe performance in turbulence, only to be told that no problem with the plane existed? Do we have a winning theory now—a latent defect compounded by a sudden emergency? I am bursting apart, coming undone. I sing loudly in the shower, making up words as I go.

No one in the airline will talk to us voluntarily—except Jim McKinney, who bravely risks incurring Philip's certain wrath by coming to my home. He carries with him a J99 Operations Manual. Lifting the heavy book with both hands, he thrusts it forward as if it were conclusive evidence of a crime. "Not one word in here telling the pilot to leave the stabilizers alone in turbulence. And not one word about the danger of having a trim capable of movement, electrically, all the way to nose-down. None of Jarrad's test pilots said a word about these things either. Nothing." He puts the manual on his lap. "This was a brand-new plane. Jarrad had a responsibility to train our pilots right. We had no experience with it."

I'm delighted and angry in the same moment. "Jim, there's something I must know. Once the plane went into its dive, could it have been recovered?"

"No way. The whole dive took about seven seconds. That's all. Seven seconds. And given the plane's speed, altitude, and attitude, and the aerodynamic loads at work, no pilot on this earth could have turned that plane around."

Two hours after McKinney leaves, Diana lets out another yell. "When you're hot, you're hot." She beams. This is hot. This is the stuff jurors will remember and maybe hang their verdict on. A few scribblings on the back of a notepad near the bottom of one of Jarrad's larger boxes. The scribblings are of a conversation between Roy Brooks and Jarrad's Vice President for Operations, David Evans, about "freezing elevators." The notes indicate that Brooks wants Jarrad to "fix the problem."

Diana has found what I didn't think we'd have time to locate. I squeeze Diana, I kiss her cheeks. All is forgiven.

I TRY TO contact David Evans. He's no longer at Jarrad, I learn. The company claims to have no forwarding address. Jarrad's in Los Angeles, so we start there. We get phone books for L.A. and the surrounding suburbs. There are three David Evanses listed; none of them, however, has ever worked for Jarrad.

I need Patti, who seems always to know how to accomplish the little things that stump us lawyers. Unfortunately, it's two o'clock, the precise time Patti Banks, day in day out, meticulously prepares her tea and drinks it slowly, savoring it as a prisoner savors his mail. It is her sacred moment of contemplation. Small, sagging breasts and a well-defined, circular mass of wrinkled skin below her eyes make her, by her own admission, "old before her time" in appearance and spirit. By her fiftieth birthday, she figures to look and feel seventy. "Nobody's interested in a woman with morals," she routinely replies even to the most casual questions about her personal life. She will continue, with dispirited resignation, to follow the rules of anyone who pays her until old age overcomes her.

Her divorce after a twelve-year marriage has broken her. (Her husband left to take up with their accountant, whose bills were excessive, but Patti paid them all, thinking at the time they couldn't afford to lose her.) Patti no longer plays tennis or cooks dinner; she cares only about survival in the rawest sense. From a distance Patti is an attractive woman, but the closer one comes, the coarser she looks. Dry, wispy, raven-black hair falls past her shoulders, smelling like rusty copper. She wears loosely flowing dresses reminiscent of those she wore twelve years ago when she had a melliflous voice and a well-shaped body she enjoyed displaying to all interested observers. In those days Patti would find the feeblest excuses to bend or turn, affording pleasurable views of her breasts or buttocks. I don't recall how or when it happened, but over the years she lost her beauty; men's eyes no longer follow her. Had I not known Patti was once married, I would have guessed she was still a virgin by the way she, when seated, regularly clamps her hands over her knees, as if in fear that someone is preparing to pounce on and expose her pale, dry, haggard body to the light.

I decide to wait until Patti's done with her tea, which I know from experience will be not a minute more or less than a quarter past two, at which time I explain to her my predicament. Patti calls the L.A. operator, claiming to be Evans's physician. She's prescribed the wrong heart medicine for Evans; time is critical. The operator puts the call through to Evans's unlisted number.

I explain my predicament to David Evans, who is no friend of Jarrad. Jarrad, he says, fired him after he insisted on changing the trim limit to 3.5 degrees. After Charlie's crash, Jarrad acknowledged the wisdom of the lower limit, but wouldn't let Evans come back.

He's lost everything in the last six months: His stately brick house was taken by the bank, his marriage was eaten alive by the pressures of unexpected poverty, and his daughter, desperate to escape their seedy apartment in a seedy part of East L.A., left with her nineteen-year-old boyfriend. I listen patiently to Evans's horror stories before I ask: "Will you come to Washington to testify if we pay all your expenses?"

"Don't you think I got enough troubles already? I need to find a job. I need to get out of this neighborhood. They do drug deals a block from where I live. They don't even try to hide it."

"It's your chance to even the score with Jarrad."

"I could never even the score. They've put me through hell. They've blacklisted me, I'll bet. That's why I can't find a job."

"Think about it, David. I'll call you in a week or so. I need your help. As bad as things are for you, they're worse for me."

We say good-bye. I thank Patti for her creativity and tell Diana what Evans said. "I don't know if he'll come or not," I admit. "We might have to depose him in L.A., and read his testimony to the jury."

"I want him live," she says. "Anyway, when will we have time to go to L.A.?"

We hear on the evening news that the civil case has been stayed. Randy has for once done me a favor. He's persuaded the court that all deponents will resort to their Fifth Amendment rights now that the criminal trial is about to begin. No more free evidence for Isabel.

At midnight the phone rings. Evans says he'll come. "I'll be damned if I let Jarrad walk away from this. A man's got nothing if he don't have pride."

I'm grateful, I tell him. I'm glad he won't abandon his pride; pride assures dignity.

As I lie in bed, I think what pride can do for a man. Pride, whatever its virtues, doesn't stay with you hour after hour. Pain does.

PREPARE A CASE for trial and you'll understand the moment-to-moment life of a cocaine addict. You'll float skyward when a winning idea enters your brain; you'll drop from a tall building when you find a case that excludes a critical piece of your evidence. The closer comes the day of trial, the harder you work. You become a madman who needs two hours sleep a day. You eat in spurts, sometimes forgetting to seek out food before evening. Every witness looms large: You consider his every habit, his every motivation. What will he say if I ask him the question this way rather than that way? Is he smart, is he honest, is he aiming to shoot me in the groin? For every printed word on every key document, you analyze the writer's intent and speculate on all possible interpretations of ambiguous words, then you decide how to get the writer to tell the jury the interpretation most favorable to your case.

We're rolling here. Those Jarrad documents lifted our spirits. Our jury charges, exhibit list, opening statement, voir dire inquiries: All are drafted. As high as we are, an unexpected visitor gets us still higher. He grabs our behinds and throws us into orbit.

It's one of those remarkable confessions that comes along in a trial lawyer's life once, twice, maybe never. Eddie Perez—now "Eddie, baby," to me—comes to my home uninvited, stands amidst the wreckage that once was my glorious living room, and says in a voice that shakes with authentic truth: "I never deiced Flight five five five."

He wants to say more, so I let him talk. I ask nothing. I sit quietly and wait. Twice in the last week I've interrogated Eddie by phone. Twice I got nothing from him, or so I thought. Somewhere, somehow, I must've moved that brave part of him that puts truth above self.

"There was a lot of planes to deice with not a lot of time. We was going as fast as we could. Flight five five five—the one your brother was on . . ." He halts a moment: a giant step for Eddie to connect the flight to Charlie, to connect numbers to people. He's lost some breath. Calling it Flight five five five is easier on his nerves, but he's not here to make things easy on himself.

"I was about ready to start spraying your brother's plane when I got a call saying not to. So I—"

"From who?" I interrupt. "Who called you?"

He hesitates, shakes his head. He doesn't want to tell me.

I don't want to scare him away. He's probably wondering why he's putting himself in jeopardy for me. He probably figures I don't give a damn what happens to him. It's degrading to confess your sins to people who barely know you. Yet I must ask: "Who, Eddie? You came here to do the right thing. I know you want to tell me."

"Philip Brandon," he says in a low, unsteady voice.

Philip? I've spoken to Philip a dozen times about this crash. Not once has he mentioned he was at La Guardia that night. Then aloud: "Philip Brandon?"

Eddie nods. "I asked him why, and he said we're running behind schedule, and he got reports the plane looked okay as is, so don't spray it. I didn't see no ice on the wings right then, so I figured I'd do what I'm told. I know headquarters is under a lot of pressure to keep planes in the air. Everybody keeps track of on-time arrivals now, and we got all that debt from the takeovers, don't we? Then with the price wars going on, the frequent-flyer programs, salaries, taxes, health plans, it makes them want to cut corners. But whenever I'd find a problem, I'd tell my foreman, 'Hey, I know it's costing money to ground this one, but I ain't an economist. I'm a mechanic.' "

He wants to show me he's honorable. I nod as if to assure him he's not the villain here. He's up against a giant corporation that makes money or dies. Keep talking, Eddie, baby. I understand.

"The pressure's gotten worse. We got more planes this year but less mechanics. Not only more planes, but they're flying shorter routes and on tighter schedules. If we delay one plane, it screws up the whole schedule. If we ground a big jet, a major overhaul can take fifteen thousand worker hours. Half of Brandon's planes are over twenty years old, and older planes, they're going to need more maintenance, that's just how it is. You can't let them fly with leaking fuel tanks and broken gauges, can you? Well, we let them fly, and I'm ashamed of it."

"You will testify to all this, won't you?" Diana asks.

Eddie's eyes bulge slightly. Identifying Philip might have spooked him. "Can they fire me for testifying?" he asks in a whisper. "It took me eleven years to get up to lead mechanic. I got five kids to feed, ma'am."

"They can't fire you," Diana assures him. "We've got whistle-blower laws that protect people like you. People courageous enough to tell the truth."

"You mean stupid enough." He forces a smile.

"You need to tell the jury you didn't deice that plane on orders from higher-ups," Diana commands.

Eddie looks downward. He nods. "I was there when that US Air flight fell into Flushing Bay. I had nothing to do with that one," he adds quickly. "But I saw the bodies."

"You're doing the right thing, Eddie," I say. "I'm grateful beyond words, and I'm very proud of you."

"You'll do well as a witness," Diana chimes in. "The jury loves to hear from an honest man."

"There's one thing they might get you on," Eddie says, either to warn us or dissuade us from calling him as a witness. "Your brother, he had to know his plane wasn't deiced. The pilot's supposed to make the final decision about whether it's okay to take off."

We all understand. Charlie, the prosecution will argue, was too drugged out to make proper decisions. Charlie was the principal player to be held accountable.

"But, Eddie," I remind him, "if you wrote in the logbook the plane was deiced, why would Charlie think it wasn't done?"

Eddie blushes a deep crimson. He had momentarily forgotten his own responsibility for the crash. Confession cannot eradicate all shame, merely soften it. "Mr. Brandon told me to write it," he says bitterly, but the meekness in his voice acknowledges a bitterness turned inward.

Something's happening here I can't quite get my hands around. Logbooks stolen, logbooks altered, one plane among dozens not sprayed. Why would Philip, of all people, have ordered the J99, of all planes, not to be deiced? I plainly told Philip the J99 had icing problems. I pointed the specific evidence out to him.

I know now my first impulse—blame Ruth—was way off the mark. It's one thing to steal papers, yet another to have particular passages erased. Was it merely coincidence the one plane not deiced fell from the sky? Nothing makes sense. Nothing Philip did, and nothing Charlie did. Would Charlie, after two months of total abstinence, have caved in to barbiturates just as he was about to step into the cockpit, then abandon Seconal for a drug he'd never before touched? How did the phenobarbital come to him?

We add Eddie Perez and Philip Brandon to our witness list. Eddie will be a giant roadblock in the prosecution's path. I go to bed early this night, and sleep all the way till morning. I awake with the wild strength a madman feels when he's about to come face-to-face with the object of his madness. Trial starts tomorrow.

PROSPECTIVE JURORS ARE USH-
ered into the dungeonlike courtroom in three waves of forty. I match their
faces to the names and addresses in front of me; I hear them tell Meredith
about their families and jobs. I know who's rich, who's black, who works
for an airline, who's Jewish.

I study their body movements and speech patterns. Most are anxious;
this, they must realize, is a high-profile case. Reporters and camera crews,
initially stationed on the brick pavements leading to the building, are now
infiltrating the second-floor halls outside the courtroom. Soon they will be
inside. The lawyers will be forced to put on their little shows; Meredith,
too, will be under pressure to perform to the media's expectations. I, the
star attraction, can only watch and be watched. I sit with my back straight
(I'm neither lazy nor tired) but not too straight (I'm not uptight or puri-
tanical). I lean slightly forward when Diana wishes to speak to me, and I
sip water gently when my throat is dry. I am a gentleman. I respect the
process and all who participate in it. I don't laugh, don't roll my eyes, don't
shake my head. I am like a dancer who has a highly complex routine to
follow.

I have the uneasy sense no one cares how well I do my dance. These
people here to judge my guilt or innocence don't like me. Why should
they? From comments made by Isabel, and from all they've read and heard,
they know I'm rich, cunning, and without the good manners to believe in
the Lord Jesus Christ, Who will undoubtedly return the favor someday by
letting me burn in hell. I wonder if they despise me all the more for my
weakness and stupidity. Hasn't the good in me made my evil more insidious,
more despicable?

Their stares annoy me. I'm a caged animal to be viewed at their pleasure.

Every whisper is about me, every look is to dissect me. These spectators are here, in the main, to observe and brush against me: The more familiar I am to them, the more lurid will be my punishment.

At times I fear retaliation from some unknown source—a victim's father or brother, an angel sent by God to right the wrong—and I grow hyper-vigilant, examining all those within striking distance. Sensing movement to my right, I turn my head. Isabel is rising from her chair. It's show time.

Isabel approaches the first forty prospective jurors with the poise of one accustomed to public speaking. She begins by invoking the name of Judge Meredith on behalf of her cause: "Judge Meredith will charge you at the end of this case that murder can be committed without the use of a deadly weapon. The question I must ask each of you is this: Can you convict a man for the murders of one hundred twenty people if he had no gun or knife or any weapon in the usual and ordinary sense?" Isabel allows each prospective juror to respond one at a time; only two say no. Both are excused for cause. Isabel continues: "Can you convict a man for murder if he did not intend, in the usual and ordinary sense, to commit murder? This is not an easy thing to do, and if you can't do that, please tell me that. I'll be grateful for your honesty." Again Isabel polls the prospective jurors one by one. Nine admit they could not convict under such circumstances. They, too, are excused for cause. Isabel is skillfully disposing of all those seemingly softhearted jurors without using any of her peremptory strikes. When she asks the panel if any of them would "hold it against her" if, to protect the people's rights, she objected to certain evidence sought to be introduced by the defense, not one hand is raised. Before Isabel returns to her chair, Diana is already on her feet.

"Michael Ashmore has denied all the charges against him by pleading not guilty," Diana reminds the panel. "He has done all the law requires him to do. He does not have to testify and has no burden or duty whatsoever to present any evidence at all, though a great deal of evidence on his behalf will be presented. Will any of you, deep in your heart of hearts, believe that Michael Ashmore is guilty, or has not adequately defended himself, if he does not testify in this case?" Three prospective jurors who waver in their response are excused for cause; all those remaining commit to Diana they will not be influenced by my failure to testify.

"The autopsy of Captain Charles Ashmore showed barbiturates in his body. Do you understand that barbiturates, whatever the amount, will not necessarily affect one's ability to fly a plane?"

"Arguing evidence, Your Honor," shouts Isabel.

The judge nods. "Please move on, Ms. Wells. You know what you're doing isn't right," Meredith reprimands sourly. I wince. The prospective jurors stare at Meredith, then at Diana, searching for clues.

"The air traffic controller told Captain Ashmore to land his plane rather than—"

Isabel objects on the same ground. Meredith sustains the objection. Not to be deterred, Diana launches her most adventurous assault. "Do you believe it is wrong for a United States Attorney to use the power of her office to achieve a purely personal goal?"

Isabel leaps to her feet, demanding she be permitted to approach the bench. Meredith nods. I cannot hear the lawyers' furious whispers, but I suspect Isabel is asking Meredith to instruct the jurors that no evidence exists of any wrongdoing by the U.S. Attorney's office. Hasn't Meredith already heard argument on this issue and squarely rejected the defense's contentions? After motioning the lawyers back to their chairs like a lion tamer with a whip, Meredith sharply sustains the objection but says nothing more, merely ordering Diana to proceed. The jurors now know Isabel's motives are in question.

Diana shifts her attention to those more intimate questions each prospective juror must answer by examining his or her own life. Have you ever had a loved one die? How did you cope with it? How important to you is your family? More important than your civic duty? Than your job? Have you ever taken prescription drugs? When and why and for how long? Have you stopped? Did the drugs help or hurt you? Ever have trouble sleeping? Ever been treated for depression? Ever sued anyone, or been sued? How did you feel about having to testify? Do you believe government employees are as talented as those who work in the private sector? Paid too much, too little? Are air traffic controllers overworked? Under too much pressure? Have you ever traveled in bad weather on any mode of transportation? Did you know the weather would be bad before you began your trip? Do you rely on weathermen? Ever flown on a commercial jet? Was there any turbulence? How severe? Were you frightened? Do you have faith in pilots? Have any friends or relatives who are pilots? What sort of people become pilots? Ever been involved in a car accident? Was it avoidable? Has your car ever gone dead? How often do you have it serviced? Does it upset you when your car malfunctions? Whom do you blame?

After six days, the voir dire is done. Diana and I huddle to decide upon our ten peremptory strikes. We have no trial consultants to help us with jury selection. The better ones cost six hundred per hour, and know less than I do about people in the District.

We don't want people who've been victimized by lawyers, druggies, or large businesses; and we surely don't want African-Americans, though our desires in this regard must be carefully disguised. The United States Supreme Court has held that no lawyer may peremptorily strike jurors based on race, but there's a loophole: If the jury's final makeup matches the percentage of African-Americans in the jury pool, there can be no violation. The danger is, those African-Americans who remain become alerted to our intentions.

We don't talk about our striking one African-American after another; we simply cross through names on sheets of paper. Our liberal souls are violated, our stomachs churn, but we have a job to do. I understand their grievances, the statistics that give them credence, the vulnerability and ambiguity of their daily lives; yet I won't let this knowledge seep into my blood and bones, not now, not here. I'll keep it at some distant border, flashing lights to be avoided. We focus on strategy, not values. I wonder if they know we're excluding them, if they know we're unhappy with ourselves for having to do it.

With our eighth strike, we hit our limit; no more African-Americans, I whisper to Diana. We'll exceed the percentage. She nods. We have two strikes left, four candidates. Diana wants to strike a young woman loaded down with jewelry. "Likely to latch on to some unusual theory of law," she explains. Her next choice is a former drug user. "The reformed ones are always the hardest on the unreformed. A way of redeeming themselves."

I shake my head. "Strike the pilot and the lawyer," I tell her.

"They're your best bets," she answers. "They'll understand."

"Strike them both," I overrule her. "The other jurors will follow them. We don't want any leaders on the jury. We need only one vote," I remind her.

"I want an acquittal," she grumbles, wounded by my jab. "Not a hung jury. Anyway, I got along well with both of them."

"You did," I concede. She's angry. She's lead counsel, and expects the latitude that role brings.

"Yes, I did."

Latitude isn't enough. She wants respect. She wants my respect. "We can disagree, can't we?"

I'm sure she's still burning from the last time we were here; I warned her not to argue that motion to dismiss, didn't I? Of course, she needs reassurance now. She needs to know I still trust her judgment. But I'm not in the reassurance business in court, especially not this court. I'm fighting for my life here. I need her to follow me without debate. The truth is, I trust my instincts more than hers.

"Who makes the final call?"

"I do," I say.

She scratches through the names of the pilot and lawyer, then keeps scratching until the paper wears thin. "The drug user's had his troubles with lawyers. Rent evictions, garnishments, repossessions. He won't like you."

"Let it go, Diana."

The final jury of twelve is a mixed bag. We have two gray-haired engineers who, as lifelong members of this highly technical profession, will likely examine the evidence in a cold, conservative manner and strictly hold the prosecution to its burden of proof; four jurors over sixty years old who, I believe, will be more respectful of my achievements and more sympathetic to blood loyalty; and a retired cop who seems unable to identify with a crime having no intent or contact or taking, calling it at one point "murder in the abstract." Isabel, though, has managed to keep six African-Americans, three of whom are active church members; a shipping clerk who's voted the prosecution's way all four times he's previously served; and a stockbroker who "wouldn't ever bet the farm" on his brother's promises. In the main, I'm uneasy with this jury. There's a hardness in their faces.

Meredith immediately instructs the newly constituted jury to refrain from discussing this case with anyone, including spouses. They're not to read, watch, or listen to any news accounts of this case. "Any juror violating these instructions will be dismissed, and the other jurors sequestered for the remainder of the trial." Even the most trivial pronouncements by Meredith seem invested with the official authority of the state. Without his black robes, Meredith would look ordinary, but as I watch him lean forward and rap his gavel, I cannot imagine him without them.

EDDIE PEREZ IS dead. A single-car crash. No witnesses. Dead at the scene, his 1984 Chevy in a ditch off the side of a narrow, unlit road a mile from his apartment. Police find whiskey on his lips, then more whiskey dripping from an open, slightly cracked bottle on the car's front seat.

I telephone Rosita Perez to offer my condolences. "Eddie never drink whiskey," she swears before launching into a forty-minute description of life's misery. As we're about to say good-bye, she asks: "Who you say you are?"

I have this vision Eddie was murdered, then run off the road, the whiskey poured later. People don't generally lose control of their cars a mile from home where the roads are familiar to them. People don't drink whiskey for the first time while driving alone at night. People will kill, though, when they stand to lose their family fortune.

Visions aren't evidence. Visions prove nothing. I crawl into bed next to Diana, who is already asleep. No need for her to engage in all this worthless speculation. No need for me either, but my mind wanders back to Eddie. Why didn't Isabel ever list Eddie as a prosecution witness if he was the one who supposedly deiced the plane? I hear Diana breathing softly. I rest my head against the back of her shoulder. I need a human touch.

Diana turns gently. She knows, even in sleep, where I am. We're face-to-face. I put my cheek gently against hers, and close my eyes. For the moment I'm at ease. I forget Grace has no one. I forget I've let her part-time baby-sitter go, and hired a conscientious older woman who's available seven days a week; who cooks, cleans, and drives Grace to and from her soccer games and piano lessons; and who, while kindly enough, doesn't connect with Grace, and never will. On weekends Grace watches TV alone and does her homework alone. The weekends were once for Grace and me.

I remember now. I have abandoned Grace only to be with her again. Whenever I assure Grace things will change, she answers with slow, uncertain nods. She's going through her own upheaval. Her father, whom she rarely sees, is on trial for murder. What shocks of terror must she be having to endure alone, hour after hour?

Inch by inch I slide away from Diana, careful not to wake her. I lie flat on my back, and force myself to envision a time when I'm free from pretending I'm not in pain. Only then can I fall asleep.

"LADIES AND GENTLEMEN, I will prove to you during the course of this trial that the pilot who crashed this plane took a lethal dose of barbiturates moments before takeoff, and that such barbiturates caused this pilot to lose all control of his plane upon encountering a mild turbulence that affected none of the many other pilots in the same general air space at the same time. I will further prove to you through the pilot's personal physician and through his former wife that pilot Charles Ashmore had a history of drug use and depression, and that such was well known to his brother, the defendant Michael Ashmore."

With the profoundly solemn demeanor of one who believes history is recording her every word, Isabel recounts her demeaning version of Charlie's life. Charles Ashmore, she declares, was "a man haunted by his father's suicide and his daughter's death." She lays out all the gruesome details: Daddy "hanging by a thick rope" from the living room chandelier, buried later in a Jewish ceremony but not in a Jewish cemetery; Carolyn on fire, her shrieking dance followed six months later by Charlie's testimony against the perfume company. Carolyn's death "pushed Charlie to heavy barbiturates," which in turn pushed him "to the edge." Evidence of his drug use "was plain to all those who would look." When Charlie nearly "crashed his jet on a flight to Minneapolis," declares Isabel, her voice rising to a dramatic pitch, "the copilot and a flight attendant reported him for having been under the influence of drugs. The airline rightfully fired him. His wife left him. He moved in with the defendant. He kept taking drugs. He slept all the time. He looked like hell. He was in no condition to fly a plane, much less a big commercial jet.

"Was all of this known to Michael Ashmore? Of course it was. The man who hung himself was his father too. The girl who was burned up was his own niece. Michael Ashmore was in fact the lawyer who argued the reckless homicide case against the perfume company and won. Did he know about the Seconal? Of course he knew. Better than anyone. He was living in the same house with his brother while all this was going on. If that wasn't enough, he was directly told of his brother's drug use by the Minneapolis flight's copilot and flight attendant, both of whom he himself interviewed. He spoke further and at great length with the airline's CEO about his brother's drug problem. More than that, his brother's wife told him. She told him—no, she begged him—not to have Charlie rehired. And the drug test this defendant had Charlie take, and Charlie failed, resoundingly told him."

The prosecution invariably has the subtle advantage of sitting closer to the jury, sometimes allowing for an intimate feeling between the prosecution and the jurors, which, I fear, is building here. Isabel is effectively making Charlie out to be some drugged-out, suicidal zombie. While despising Isabel for her cruelty, I recognize her act. We lawyers habitually dismember those we haven't met (or met for a few hours with a court reporter between us transcribing every word) based upon the recollections of so-called friends (who seek only to protect themselves) or enemies (who wish only to destroy) along with a few scraps of paper from which we isolate certain words and weave them into our web of half-truths and near-truths. Isabel, having concentrated on one small part of Charlie at one brief moment in time, has distorted the whole of him. Seething with anger, I can only sip my water and sit silently. At this moment I join the great many who hold lawyers in utter contempt.

"This defendant would have you believe he's a kind, loyal family man who did what any decent man would do: come to the aid of a brother in trouble. But once you examine all the evidence, you will see conduct marked not by kindness and loyalty, but by an extraordinarily ruthless arrogance that led inevitably to the horrible murders of one hundred twenty perfectly innocent people—the unknowing, random subjects of the defendant's terrifying experiment with a drug-addicted pilot. What we have here, ladies and gentlemen, and what the evidence will unmistakably show, is a man who took it upon himself to initiate an investigation on behalf of Brandon Air Lines into his own brother's fitness to pilot a plane; who concealed from the airline crucial evidence uncovered in that investigation; and, finally, who had the incredible audacity to make recommendations contrary to the evidence he so improperly concealed. The defendant's recommendations to his unsuspecting client were ultimately followed, as he knew they would be, and were of the same effect as putting a bomb on a civilian aircraft, this bomb having the brain of a disoriented drug user floating in a human body."

Isabel shows the jurors an enlarged photo of the test I withheld from the airline. They stare at it, then at me. Isabel explains the significance of each marking on the exhibit. "Positive for drugs," she pronounces as if delivering the verdict itself. The jurors are eerily still, like insects about to be splattered.

I counsel my clients to take none of opposing counsel's statements personally—"Keep a clear head. It's all an intellectual game," I tell them. As a lawyer, I must freeze out my client's emotions; my job isn't to feel or judge but to win. Now I'm unable to take my own advice. I can't escape the burning fear, the moments of raw humiliation; and I can't stop worrying the jurors, believing a U.S. Attorney seeks nothing but justice, will give greater weight to Isabel's words than is objectively warranted.

Jurors usually lean the prosecution's way. Prosecutors are the ones who, for relatively little pay, protect us from those intent on harming us. Defense counsel get paid to keep out evidence, cast doubt on the truth.

Diana's hand touches mine, her warmth sprinkling over me. We are, thank God, connected by some powerful cord that can't be broken by a stranger's accusations, no matter how odious or true.

"Arrogance, ladies and gentlemen," I hear Isabel repeat with authority, "not kindness but arrogance, triggered the defendant's deliberate acts of deception. Given the defendant's superior intelligence, he was, of course, well aware of all he did and all he risked. It boils down simply to this: At some point this defendant decided he was above the rules, above the law, when as a lawyer and an officer of the court, surely he knew better. Arrogance is blinding, I suppose. Arrogance kept this defendant from seeing the true spirit of the law and from developing a proper perspective.

"Arrogance, surely not kindness, allowed the defendant to knowingly and deliberately put dozens of innocent lives at risk, and arrogance, not kindness, led, ironically enough, to the death of his own brother along with the others he so easily sacrificed. "He"—Isabel points squarely at me—"wrote the script of this disaster, and played the lead role in the immoral drama he created. In short, the defendant made a conscious decision to play God. To be a man, one must refuse to be a god."

Isabel's message is clear: I'm a murderer of the most heinous sort, having deliberately manipulated the very law I'm supposed to guard. Blessed with all of life's advantages, I put at risk the lives of less fortunate others. The local TV stations are likewise incensed. They talk about my "intellect" and my "dominating personality." They show footage of roving black teenagers carrying signs of "Flying High" and "Jew Murderer." Black churches and black colleges, they say, have scheduled debates about the trial, about the airline's discrimination against African-Americans, about the influence of Jews on inner-city life.

All else I've done in my life has been erased. One core piece of evidence stands above all others: I'm a smart Jew who got carried away with his power to manipulate.

A LOW BUZZ of excitement fills the courtroom as Diana rises to make her opening statement. Diana's face is pale, her eyes dull and narrow, as if a thick haze hinders her view. Her legs tremble slightly as she labors unsteadily toward the jurors. I lock my sweating hands and drop them to my knees. Maybe I'm too close to the action.

Diana's gazing in the jury's direction, but saying not a word. What is her first line? We'd rehearsed it fifteen times, what is it? Diana must remember. She looks downward. Is the floor blackening, the lights growing hotter? Will she pass out? Please, God, help her, I cry to myself. I want to plead with Meredith for a recess, but how strange that would seem. Diana raises her eyes. The friendly policeman has a slight smile on his lips, a sweet look of compassion. He wants her to do well. His expression seems to relax her. She begins to speak in a low voice. The jurors strain to hear her, and the more they strain, the more encouraged she seems to become. They want to hear every word.

Her energy increases with each sentence she speaks. The jurors' eyes are riveted on her. "What Ms. Castino has told you is not evidence," she asserts, the color returning to her face. "Evidence will come solely from the testimony of the witnesses under oath. Ms. Castino's comments were nothing more than what she hopes to prove. As this trial progresses, you will learn that Ms. Castino can prove very little of what she has said to you, which in the main amounts to nothing more than speculation, psychological gibberish, and malicious gossip.

"Let's get right down to it. In order to prevail, the prosecution must prove beyond a reasonable doubt the proximate cause of this crash was pilot error; that the pilot error was proximately caused by the influence of drugs; and that Michael Ashmore acted in reckless disregard of human life merely by requesting that Charlie Ashmore be rehired by the airline. The prosecution must prove each and every one of these three propositions beyond a reasonable doubt to obtain a conviction. Not one, not two, but all three. We will show in the course of this trial the prosecution cannot prove any of these propositions—beyond a reasonable doubt or otherwise—for the simple reason that none are true. We will bring witness after witness into this courtroom to show you—though the burden of proof rests with the prosecution—that pilot error had nothing to do with this crash.

"Keep this clearly in mind: Charles Ashmore flew this plane perfectly and in accord with all of the airline's most exacting requirements until his plane encountered heavy turbulence. And we'll prove to you through highly qualified weather experts that this turbulence was indeed heavy, and not merely mild, as Ms. Castino needs you to believe. We'll prove to you the winds were high, fast, and tricky, and that Charles Ashmore likely encountered a deadly wind shear as well. So why didn't Charlie fly around, above or below the turbulence? Because he was directed by supposedly qualified air traffic controllers to fly east. He flew east, and that's where he hit the wind shear, or the wind shear hit him. Does that sound like the reaction of a drug-crazed pilot to you?

"It wasn't only the wind shear that gave Charles Ashmore problems. The plane did too. Ms. Castino didn't bother to tell you the plane's own manufacturer recognized, after this crash, that it needed to alter the design of the Jarrad Ninety-nine, the very plane Charlie flew. Indeed, the plane's design has been altered. The electric trim limit is now far less severe and, in Jarrad's words, 'more safe.' Why more safe? Jarrad now admits the old trim limit too easily allowed the plane to head straight downward. That's not all. Jarrad further admits, in writing, that the stabilizers should never be used in turbulence. That's something they never told Charlie. If anything, Jarrad's precrash manuals would lead a reasonable pilot to believe the stabilizers should be used in turbulence.

"The stabilizers affect the plane's position—nose up, level or, down—as do the more powerful elevators. There's a connection here. The pilot uses the stabilizers to steady the plane, but uses the elevators if bigger adjustments need to be made. What would happen if the elevators didn't work in turbulence? What would happen if they stuck because they'd frozen? The pilot would then have no choice but to use the stabilizers, but we know now from Jarrad's own writings not to use the J Ninety-nine's stabilizers in turbulence. This, I will prove to you, is precisely what happened. The elevators froze, and the stabilizers malfunctioned in the turbulence, causing the plane to go nose-down. Yes, Charlie did have way too much barbiturate in him, but people have different tolerances to drugs, and I'll prove to you that Charlie's tolerance was unusually high. The point is, the weather and the controllers and most of all the plane's defective equipment made this plane go down, not Charlie Ashmore.

"Ms. Castino wants you to believe Charles Ashmore was not only a crazy, drugged-out pilot, but this defendant was just about as crazy to ask that his brother be reinstated as a pilot." Diana shakes her head slowly to convey her disgust. "Put yourself for a moment in Michael Ashmore's shoes. His brother, Charlie, was fired despite having one of the finest flight ratings of any pilot on any airline, and he was fired based upon the suspicions—and I mean suspicions—of two crew members who had no hard evidence, no admissions from Charlie, no visual proof of Charlie taking any drugs. Yes, Michael knew his brother was taking a low dosage of medically prescribed Seconal for insomnia, but he had good reason to believe his brother when

Charlie swore to him the plane's elevators had caused the Minneapolis flight to dive and, if he were rehired, he would completely quit Seconal. These were brothers who were straight with each other, who'd been through a lot together. The evidence will show, ladies and gentlemen, from the time Charlie was rehired to the day of the crash, Charlie not once asked for or purchased medically prescribed Seconal."

Diana continues to sprinkle such phrases as "I will prove" and "the evidence will show" to prevent objections she's treating her opening statement as closing argument; but she is, and Isabel, probably concerned any objections at this stage would appear inappropriate to the jurors, stays silent. Isabel's failure to acknowledge possible alternative explanations to pilot error is allowing many of Diana's declarations to stand unrebutted. I happily sense the prosecution's credibility oozing away like blood from a wound. I glance often at Isabel. She's listening and watching with rapt attention, but like any good lawyer, remains expressionless.

Armed with an array of exhibits already ruled admissible, Diana explains each exhibit at the appropriate moment and in sufficient detail before connecting its significance to her overall case. The graphs and charts we've had professionally done are large, colorful, and a variety of shapes with depth, patterns, and sharp images. Not only do they supply data about the stabilizers, about the weather, and about Charlie's flying record, they concisely interpret the data and reach apparently well-supported conclusions. These exhibits are designed to do the thinking for those jurors who have neither the time nor inclination to analyze any particular exhibit at length; the exhibits come and go in minutes, sometimes seconds, while the trial inexorably moves forward. Diana intends to create an atmosphere so darkened with complexity and doubt that even if the jury as a whole is unpersuaded by our defense, no juror will be comfortably certain who or what caused the crash.

I hear Diana's voice rising. "Michael Ashmore didn't fly or design or build or test or guide this plane in any way. He doesn't own or run the airline. He didn't make and couldn't make the final decision to rehire Charlie Ashmore. This prosecution is nonsense! It's an affront to all law-abiding citizens!"

Diana steps back to counsel's table and flicks a switch. Our computer-animated movie is on. For nearly three hundred thousand dollars, a computer-production company has converted thousands of disparate facts into a coherent, sophisticated 3-D movie of the plane's descent in the storm's midst. The movie, which plays on a high-resolution color television screen for fifty-two seconds, re-creates the flight's path, the growth of storm cells, and the sudden dive. All events are synchronized with the black box and the FDR, their actual times displayed on the screen's upper right corner. Diana stops the movie at various stages to point out the size and location of various "killer weather cells." With the use of different camera angles, fade-outs, and close-ups, Diana creates instantly a series of astonishing exhibits. The various animations create an eerie, ghoulish atmosphere. The jurors can see and hear what Charlie and his copilot experienced in their last moments of life. Death and show business—an unbeatable combination.

Diana says nothing more. She thanks the jurors for their attention, and sinks slowly into her seat. The courtroom is silent. I nod approvingly at Diana, who sits with her back arched, the softness in her face revealing contentment and relief.

WE OFFER TO stipulate that the crash occurred and one hundred twenty died. The prosecution, which usually leaps at any offer to stipulate (since the putting on of proof, no matter how straightforward, always runs the risk of unanticipated responses or sustained objections), does not here. Isabel won't take the safe road, apparently believing it necessary to re-create the naked horror of the crash: the noise, smoke, and blood.

Isabel calls witness after witness to the crash, from those sitting at the gate awaiting the plane's arrival to those living near the crash site. All recount in somber voices the plane's horrifying, uncontrollable descent. These eyewitnesses generally seem reliable. Having little ammunition for cross-examination, Diana wisely keeps her questioning brief and to the point. She gently notes the few inconsistencies in their testimony and has several of them describe the turbulent winds at ground level.

Next come the family members who identify the victims. They are the human faces of lives damaged, left behind. I feel their stares bounce off me like shower water. Over Diana's strenuous objections, the jurors are allowed to see photos of the victims in happier times. This ordeal—proof of the crash and the resulting deaths—takes nearly three days, ending with the hysterical sobbing of a twenty-year-old widow who calls Diana "an agent of Satan." When Diana expresses sorrow for the girl's loss, the girl, her face screwed into an ugly scowl, cries out: "Don't you know how much you and him"—she points directly at me—"are hated? You're lucky nobody's killed you both for what you've done!"

Swarms of reporters daily surround us as we leave the courtroom. Diana won't comment on the case, referring to Meredith's order and the bar's ethical rules, but she tries to look lawyerlike as lights flash. She descends the stairs mindful of keeping her more photogenic side toward the cameras. Curious spectators draw closer. Reporters continue to hound her as she emerges into the heavy night air. I listen to radio accounts of the day's testimony in my car and watch cable news when I arrive home, much of which is incorrect or overblown, adjectives and adverbs flying like missiles headed out to space.

I read the morning and evening newspapers religiously. "At the root of all deception is a lack of courage," says one black reporter who thinks he's doing well by me. Better it be failure of nerve than evil heart and scheming mind. I expect the anger of the black community to diminish with time, but it continues rolling upward as if to defy gravity. My shock diminishes slowly, uneasily, until I believe they're not misguided or ungrateful. They're right; I deserve to die.

I will die. This is what I think upon hearing the coroner's testimony that Charlie took enough phenobarbital to make "most anyone totally disoriented" and "a weaker man pass out altogether or just flat-out die." The coroner "can't imagine a sane man taking so much phenobarbital at any time," much less before stepping into the cockpit of a commercial jet.

Having performed more than ten thousand autopsies and testified before nearly sixty juries, the coroner knows how to maintain a proper posture, project his voice, and look directly at the jurors when reaching the vital parts of his testimony. His sharp chin, hawk nose, and large patches of red, scaly skin above and below his protruding eyes make for an easily remembered face.

"Sir," asks Diana with the admonishing tone of a betrayed friend, "is there some reason you didn't earlier mention the pilot had consumed a fair amount of coffee before boarding the flight?"

"I wasn't asked about it, that's all."

"The prosecutor didn't want to ask you about it, did she?"

"Guess not."

"Coffee is a stimulant, isn't it?"

"Yes, ma'am."

"It would, at least to some extent, counteract the effect of the phenobarbital?"

"To some extent, but it was an awful lot of—"

"Yes or no, sir?"

"Yes. I suppose, yes."

"The flight from La Guardia to National is only an hour, isn't it?"

"I believe that's right."

I watch, analyze, and judge the developing evidence for and against me as if I were trial counsel. In some respects a trial is comparable to therapy: Events are examined, strategies considered, rules analyzed. I've come to know the exhaustion and isolation that follow from having your every misstep scrutinized by those seeking to ruin you. Not yet ready to die, I am more prepared for death than I've ever wanted to be.

I regularly identify with men accused of wrongdoing, men fighting for their survival, men on trial—my ways of keeping sane. In the early mornings when the moonlight is growing dim, I often sink to my knees in awkward silence, needing to believe in something that transcends me, even if it's false. Perhaps the only defense to self-hatred is the belief in one's innocence.

TOM ZACHARY'S HESITANT speech and anxious demeanor convincingly establish his unparalleled desire to escape further association with this unseemly trial. Yet Zachary, Charlie's regular physician, does manage to convey his awareness of FAA rules forbidding drug use within eight hours of a scheduled flight and his unqualified belief that Charlie, by following his prescriptions as to times and quantities, could pilot commercial flights in an unimpaired condition and within the law's limits. "Mr. Ashmore gave me his flight schedule every month and we worked out a conservative prescription," Zachary relates.

"Did Mr. Ashmore keep you advised of all flight changes?"

"I assume he did."

Isabel steps closer to Zachary, then leans forward like a Doberman ready to pounce. "Do you have actual knowledge that he kept you advised?"

"No," Zachary yields, but only for an instant. Her challenge seems to invigorate him. "I do know that Mr. Ashmore was very concerned he took precisely the right amounts of Seconal. I also know if he'd taken more than what I'd prescribed, he would've needed more. He never once needed more."

Isabel nods, looks down at her notes. She's momentarily at a loss. Zachary waits. Meredith waits. The jurors wait. The spectators and reporters wait. All eyes are on Isabel. With each passing second Zachary's remarks take on increasing significance. The jurors have time to think, the reporters to analyze. Meredith jots down some notes.

"Can you tell this court exactly what Seconal is?" Isabel has moved to safer ground.

"It's a barbiturate compound."

"It's a white powder known on the street as red devils or pink ladies, isn't it?" She's trying to make this drug sound sinister.

"That's only because it's packaged in red or pink capsules," Zachary explains. He seems to be gaining confidence. He's thrown Isabel once; maybe he can do it again.

"Did you ever come to know that Charles Ashmore was taking pheno-barbital as well as Seconal?"

Diana jumps to her feet. "Your Honor, that's like asking the witness if he's stopped beating his wife," she complains. "There's no evidence what-soever that Charles Ashmore was ever taking phenobarbital on any regular basis, as the question suggests. Nor is there any evidence that this witness ever prescribed phenobarbital to Charles Ashmore."

Meredith barely looks up when he says: "Sustained. Next question, Madam Prosecutor."

"Let's solve defense counsel's problem, okay? I ask you directly: Did you ever prescribe phenobarbital for Charles Ashmore?"

"No, I did not. Nor did he ever ask me to," Zachary adds.

"I move to strike the witness's unresponsive remarks," Isabel declares sharply.

"So stricken," rules Meredith, who turns slowly to Zachary and warns: "Behave yourself, Doctor. Just answer what you're asked."

Isabel glares at Zachary. "Sir," she says in a hard voice, "would you have prescribed Seconal for Charles Ashmore had you known he was taking phenobarbital as well?"

"Same objection as before, Your Honor." Diana is on her feet, her voice having the calm of certain victory. "It's the same old wife-beating question, only this time we already know from the witness's prior testimony that he did not prescribe phenobarbital for Charlie Ashmore, and this time we have a second flaw inherent in the question, namely, it asks the witness to indulge in rank speculation, and does so about facts which not only aren't proved but have been shown not to exist."

"Objection sustained," says Meredith curtly.

Isabel turns to the jurors, and with a shrug, comments: "If I'm not allowed to get the truth from this witness, I'll stop wasting everybody's time. No more questions for this witness."

Diana is about to object, but it's not necessary. Meredith has that demonic glimmer in his eyes. "That little speech you just heard from Madam Prosecutor, I want you to disregard all of it. Put it totally out of your minds because it reeked with impropriety. Ms. Castino was asking questions she knew were objectionable, and so I wouldn't allow them. We've got rules here. She was violating them, and when she got caught, she pouted about it to you." Meredith turns his attention to Isabel. "Try to make a fool out of this court again, and you'll find your pocketbook a bit lighter. Do it a third time, and you'll spend the night behind bars. You got me?"

Isabel refuses to pull into herself like a frightened turtle. She's still on her feet, her back still straight. "I meant no disrespect, Your Honor. I represent the people—"

"We know who you represent. Now, sit down," Meredith snaps.

Zachary wants to help us, I write. *He feels the heat.* Diana reads my note and nods. Zachary, having prescribed the Seconal for Charlie, must defend that prescription.

"Was it your belief that the level of Seconal you prescribed for Charlie Ashmore was such that Charlie could safely fly a commercial jet?" Diana asks.

"Yes, absolutely. Unless he wasn't taking the Seconal as I prescribed. But I had no reason to believe he wasn't."

"Before coming here today, did you review all of your medical records concerning Captain Charles Ashmore?"

"I reviewed them last week, and again this morning."

"Could you determine from your records the last time you prescribed barbiturates of any kind for Captain Ashmore?"

"Approximately two months before his plane crashed."

"Did he tell you to discontinue the prescription, or did you do that on your own?"

"He told me he was quitting Seconal. He'd been rehired by the airline that very day, as I remember. Said he didn't need it anymore."

"Did you ever prescribe any barbiturate for Captain Ashmore other than Seconal?"

Zachary shakes his head. "Like most of us, he had his habits. Anyway, the Seconal seemed to work for him."

"Please take a good look at Michael Ashmore," she directs him. A moment later she inquires: "Did you ever tell Michael Ashmore you were prescribing Seconal for his brother?"

"I've never spoken with Michael Ashmore, period."

Diana is about to thank Zachary for his time when I slip her another note. *Ask how phenol is different.* She's reluctant, but I nod at her with a tightened jaw and narrowed eyes. Zachary's a friend, I think. He won't hurt us.

Diana sucks up some air and asks: "What are the differences between Seconal and phenobarbital, if any?"

"They have similar properties, similar effects. Why take one rather than the other? Like I said, Seconal comes in capsules. Phenobarbital can be liquid."

"But not Seconal?"

"Not Seconal."

I scribble madly. Diana comes back to counsel's table, glances at my note, and asks: "Could phenobarbital be mixed with a drink, like orange juice or coffee?"

"Yes, it could."

Could the drinker tell? I write. I lay the note in front of Diana. "If the phenobarbital were mixed in with, let's say coffee, would the drinker likely notice the phenobarbital was in there?"

"Talk about speculation, Your Honor," huffs Isabel. "That's the grand-daddy of all speculative questions. I mean, who's the drinker? What's his tolerance? How sensitive is he to changes in taste? How much coffee versus how much phenobarbital? I could go on and on."

"I'm sure you could," agrees Meredith. "And I'm sure I don't want you to. I'll sustain your objection."

Diana has to find a way to ask the question without catching another objection. Meredith will turn on her if he thinks she's making an end run around his ruling. "Dr. Zachary, in your professional opinion, is pheno-barbital odorless?"

"It is."

"If mixed with juice or coffee, can it be smelled?"

"No."

"Is it tasteless?"

"It's tasteless, it's odorless, it's invisible when mixed with another liquid. But an autopsy will easily find it."

Isabel begins slowly with Charlie's ex-wife. No hard questions about drugs, suicide, divorce. She asks Ruth about her work as an English professor at Georgetown, and lets her tell a few amusing stories about her students. She wants Ruth and these jurors to become accustomed to each other; and she wants Ruth comfortable and relaxed when the more sensitive questions are posed.

Ruth enjoys discussing her professional achievements—one year she was voted "Best-Liked Professor," an honor she mentions twice and jokingly compares to winning a Most Valuable Player award in the NBA "but without the Nike endorsements." Her mood grows somber, her demeanor stiff, when asked about Charlie, whom she dutifully describes as a "basically good man, but like all of us, he had his flaws." Their marriage was "good for a very long time," but tragic circumstances—"no one who's not lost a child could possibly know what it's like"—threw their world "out of control." I'm afraid the jurors like her. She's funny and sad, talented and tragic. She's the typical soap opera victim we all love: a sweet person living a wholesome life until cruel fate intervenes.

The jurors learn that cruel fate strikes poor Ruth again, this time in the form of Seconal, a powerful drug her husband "got hooked on." Seconal made Charlie "weak and very sleepy," and he "rarely had the urge even to talk."

Isabel is ready to bring me into this made-for-jurors prime-time show. She asks with authoritative flair: "Did you ever tell this defendant that your husband at the time, Charles Ashmore, was addicted to a barbiturate known as Seconal?"

"Yes, I did."

"And was that before or after Charles Ashmore was rehired by Brandon Air Lines?"

"Before."

"At that same time, did you tell this defendant"—Isabel turns and points to me on cue—"that he should not try to get your then-husband rehired by the airline because of this Seconal addiction?"

"Yes," she says quietly with a downward tilt of her head.

"Did you plead with him?"

"Objection!" Diana hollers out. She needs to disrupt the flow of this examination. "Calls for an opinion, not facts, Your Honor."

Meredith raises his eyebrows. "Overruled," he pronounces with a cutting disdain, his way of discouraging marginal objections. "Witness may answer." Meredith seems absorbed by Ruth's account, as do the jurors, who lean forward or sit straight up, none of them lying back in their chairs.

Ruth conspicuously sucks up air before explaining: "I did plead with Michael. I told him he'd be corrupting his soul if he didn't give the airline the test."

Test? Isabel hasn't asked about any test. This is an ominous sign. Ruth won't need to be prompted. She's moving faster even than Isabel, who must now catch her. "What test?" inquires Isabel, who surely knows the answer.

"Michael took Charlie to get tested for drugs as part of this whole thing to get Charlie rehired. Charlie failed the test. I told Michael to give the test to the airline. That's when I said it'd corrupt his soul if he didn't. Whether he ever gave it to the airline or not, I don't know."

"What exactly did you tell the defendant when you informed him of Charles Ashmore's Seconal addiction?"

"I told him everything I knew. Why Charlie took Seconal, why he couldn't stop, how many milligrams he took and how often. Michael already knew all this, though. Charlie by this time was living in Michael's house."

"Around the time this defendant was making efforts to get Charles Ashmore rehired, would you say your then-husband was visibly unstable?"

"She's not a trained psychologist," Diana protests. "The question calls for expert testimony."

"Overruled," proclaims Meredith without the courtesy of looking at us.

Ruth glances at Meredith, who nods to her, and she's off and running. "Charlie couldn't sleep, hardly ate, woke up screaming half the time. He blamed Carolyn's death on himself. He was supposed to watch her that day, but left her alone with some boy we hardly knew. After Charlie moved in with Michael, we'd still talk by phone once or twice a week. He never sounded good."

"At some point in time, you obtained a divorce from Charles Ashmore, didn't you?"

Ruth's jaw tightens. Her face loses a bit of color. Having given Isabel all she's wanted, I'm sure Ruth's not pleased to be rewarded with an inquiry that points blame, however minor in the overall scheme, straight at her. "I did, yes," answers Ruth, as if stating the words themselves pain her.

"On what day would that have been?" There's a small yet noticeable glee in Isabel's voice that undoubtedly will anger Ruth. Experience tells me that's precisely what Isabel intends. No longer needing Ruth, Isabel will deliberately abandon her now; this is sound strategy. She'll let Ruth raise her voice, grind her teeth. If Ruth is hostile to the prosecution, doesn't that make her earlier testimony against me all the more credible?

"The day his flight crashed," Ruth responds grimly.

"Interesting," comments Isabel. "And, I take it, Charles Ashmore knew—"

"Yes, he knew the divorce was granted," Ruth snaps. "His lawyer told him. Charlie called me, and we talked about it."

"And his reaction?"

"He was sad; so was I. Such is life."

"Did he talk to you about suicide?"

"Ever? Or on that last phone call?" Ruth clarifies, but not wisely. Recognizing her error, she hastily adds: "You mean on that phone call, don't you?"

It's too late. "Let's do it both ways," Isabel says. "First, on the phone call."

"No."

"At any time?"

I watch Ruth closely for hints of Wild Turkey. She tugs hard at the sleeves of her blouse, eyes me, then glares at Isabel. The question, originally meant to be confined to that last phone call, could have been swiftly answered, the inquiry ended. I once told Ruth: Ask an interrogator a question, and he'll ask you two questions about your question. "Charlie did talk about suicide, but not that night. What made him feel that way was Carolyn, not me. He loved his daughter more than life itself."

She's managed to deflect blame from herself. Nothing she did triggered suicidal impulses in Charlie. Carolyn, Carolyn, Carolyn, the very girl whose estate I represented in the reckless homicide case. I'm waiting for Isabel to bat that subject around the park when Ruth adds: "I talked to Michael about that too. Rather, he talked to me. He said Charlie spoke often of suicide, and I said, all the more reason not to get him rehired."

Her voice, remarkably calm, triggers in me a shudder. I'm appalled by her eagerness to do me such grievous harm. Doesn't one ounce of compassion run through her veins? If not for me, then for Grace? Doesn't she care one whit about Grace? Maybe this is her deranged way of coming to grips with me. To be done with me.

Isabel turns to me and in a loud voice demands: "Do you want this defendant to be found guilty?"

I can't win. If Ruth says yes, the jurors will think she has good reason to loathe me, and maybe they should too. If she plays the saint, it will reinforce the power of all her testimony against me.

"Michael was my brother-in-law for many years. I still think of him as family," she says weakly. "So no, I don't. I've had enough tragedy for one lifetime." Quietly she begins to weep.

Does anyone believe those tears are real? Maybe she's overplayed her answer, I think. Maybe she's unwittingly found the only way to help me: proof of her insincerity.

"Would you consider yourself loyal to the defendant?"

"Yes, of course. I've only said these things because I have to. I've sworn on a Bible."

Isabel's done. Meredith calls for a recess. The jurors are excused for their afternoon break. Diana and I huddle.

Ruth has slashed me close to the neck. How to stop the bleeding? "We have to show Ruth is out to get you," Diana decides. "We have to expose her for the bitch she is."

"She abused Charlie," I say bitterly. "The divorce was all her doing."

Diana rolls her eyes. "Come on, Michael, that won't help. It'll only reinforce the idea that Charlie was near the edge."

"By her, not me," I insist. "It shows she was reckless, not me."

"She didn't get Charlie rehired. You did." Diana shakes her head at me, then waits until she has my full attention. "You're not thinking straight. We have to show bias against *you*, not Charlie. We have to attack her credibility, and there's only one effective way to do that." She peers directly into my eyes. "And you know what that is."

"Scorned lover?"

Diana nods. "She wanted you, not Charlie, and you turned her down. That'll make her the slutty bitch, and you the good guy. She's here to get back at you. That's what the jurors must be made to believe."

"Now you're the one not thinking straight," I say flatly. "When she denies everything, what do you have to impeach her with? Not one document, not one witness. She might even say I came on to her."

"Even that will show bias."

"Great. She's biased, and I'm evil. How far will that get us?" I frown. "Let her walk away. Cut our losses."

"It's Charlie, isn't it? Even in death you're looking after him more than yourself."

"Let's not tell the whole country that Charlie's wife was more turned on by his brother," I say with undisguised irritation. "It'll make us both look bad."

"Everybody knows she divorced Charlie. Divorced women usually want other men, don't they? His memory won't be—"

"No," I insist without further explanation. Dignity and loyalty must have their place even when one's life is threatened.

Court resumes. The jurors are back. Ruth returns to the witness chair. Diana stands at the lectern and asks: "Michael Ashmore never encouraged you to divorce Charles Ashmore, did he?"

"No."

"He had nothing to do with your telephone call with Charles Ashmore the day of the crash, did he?"

"No."

"He always spoke well of his brother to you, didn't he?"

"I'd say so, yes."

"He was always loyal to his brother, wasn't he?"

"If anything, he was too loyal," she answers with a small though wicked smile.

Diana looks back at me, a gleam in her eyes. She's going to disregard my instructions. That's what that gleam says to me. She has Ruth in a box, and I doubt Ruth knows it.

"The truth is, ma'am, you weren't always loyal to Charlie Ashmore, were you?"

"It depends on what you mean by loyal," Ruth stammers a bit.

"You don't know what the word 'loyal' means? A moment ago I asked you if Michael Ashmore was loyal to his brother, and you said, 'If anything, he was too loyal.' So you know—"

"I know what the word means," Ruth barks out. "Just not how you're using it."

"All right, let's be specific. You divorced Charles Ashmore despite his pleas you not do so?"

Ruth shrugs. "True, but that doesn't make me disloyal. Divorce was the best thing for both of us."

Diana raises her voice almost to a shout. "Isn't it true that while still married to Charles Ashmore, you tried to seduce Michael Ashmore, and he outright refused you?"

Ruth shoots a look at me, then turns back to Diana. "No, that's not correct," she answers coldly, her sharp tone likely meant to convey a bitter contempt she hopes will deter Diana from pursuing this line of interrogation.

Diana moves toward Ruth, and doesn't stop until inches from her prey. She's ready to lock the door to the box, but she must do it quickly. Diana's losing points with the jurors every moment she continues forward without a big score. She appears to be unduly harassing the witness. "Do you deny, under penalty of perjury, that Michael Ashmore refused your efforts to seduce him?"

She's not closing the box on Ruth. Maybe she doesn't know how to do it, maybe she never saw the same box I did. She's in perilous territory, I think, when Isabel calls out: "Objection. Asked and answered."

"I'll let her answer," Meredith says. He, too, is staring at Ruth.

"I've already denied it once, but since you insist on making a point of it, I'll go you one better. It was Michael who tried to seduce me, and I refused him. About two months or so before Charlie died, if you care to know."

I hear a low gasp behind me. I turn sideways. Reporters write madly; strangers glower in my direction; the jury's eyes are riveted on Ruth. My head is pounding, my throat is dry. I swing back, grab for water. Goddammit, I told Diana! The glass is shaking in my hand. I put it back down before anyone notices.

Diana keeps going. "You would at least admit, wouldn't you, that while you were in college and before you were married, you had a torrid affair with Michael Ashmore?"

Ruth hesitates. She knows many of our Harvard friends could be rounded up and made to testify. All would remember we were together constantly for a year before I left her, and all would remember she swore to even the score someday. Shortly thereafter she married Charlie, which we all took at the time to be her sick way of getting even.

"Yes, I would admit that," Ruth finally answers.

"And you would also admit that Michael Ashmore ended that affair?"

"Yes." No hesitation this time. I figure she's already decided she must tell the truth about those long-ago days.

"And then you married his brother?"

"Yes."

Diana's making headway now. If nothing else, the jurors must be starting to suspect the possibility of bias. "You married Michael's brother to get back at Michael, didn't you?"

"There was an element of that, sure. But I loved Charlie, and always have." Thank God she told everyone (but Charlie) about her desire for revenge. Otherwise, I'm sure she'd deny everything, and imply along the way that Diana belongs in hell.

"An element of that?" Diana repeats. "So part of the reason you married Charles Ashmore was to get back at his brother, Michael?"

"Part of the reason." Ruth shrugs. "But I was young then. I know better now."

"So let me get this straight. You were so mad at Michael Ashmore back then, you were willing to marry his brother simply to get back at him?"

"Part of the reason," Ruth answers sullenly. "How many times do I have to say it?"

"Yet you have testified here today that while married to Charles Ashmore, Michael Ashmore tried to seduce you, and not the other way around?"

"Yes, for the third time," Ruth snaps.

"You would, I take it, consider Michael Ashmore's efforts to seduce you while you were still married to his brother to be a monstrous act of disloyalty?"

"I'm not sure I'd use the word 'monstrous,' but sure it was disloyal."

"What word would you use?"

"I guess 'monstrous' is okay," Ruth says, forcing a wounded smile.

Diana steps away from Ruth and stands by the jury rail, forcing Ruth to look at the jurors. "Are you the same woman I was talking to fifteen minutes ago?"

Ruth frowns. Her eyes narrow. "I don't know what you mean."

"You now accuse Michael Ashmore of monstrous disloyalty to his brother, Charlie, correct?"

"Yes."

"But at the very beginning of this cross-examination, I asked you if Michael Ashmore was *always* loyal to his brother, and you said, 'If anything, he was too loyal.' Do you recall that testimony of yours?"

Diana has found the box, or maybe she's always had it in view. The door is closing. Ruth is still, silent.

"I can have that testimony read back, if you like."

Ruth's eyes widen and her head jerks back as if she's been awakened in darkness by a stranger. She knows those convicted of perjury go to prison. "No, that's not necessary. That's what I said."

"Then I submit to you, ma'am, that if Michael Ashmore had *always* been *too loyal* to his brother, he could not have at the same time committed an act of monstrous disloyalty by seeking to seduce his wife."

"I forgot about his trying to seduce me," she says weakly.

Diana's getting stronger, her voice rising, her hands gesturing. "You forgot that your own brother-in-law recently tried to seduce you while you were still married?" Diana asks incredulously.

"I forgot," is all Ruth can think to say. Maybe she's avoided prison, but she hasn't avoided the jury's ire. Their hard stares, usually reserved for me, have shifted to her.

"Nothing further for this witness," Diana calls out with unmistakable contempt, then bounces back toward me with a surge of energy. She disregarded my instructions, and proved me wrong. That's my girl.

I STEP INTO the grimy, clustered, dark hallways with the uneasy familiarity of one daily compelled to visit a city's seamy side. Lawyers and witnesses shout at each other as packs of distraught, frightened people mill back and forth. Muscular bail bondsmen roam the tile hallways with arrogant smiles and darting looks. Prosecutors plea-bargain, and policemen, eyeing the clamor with disdain, wait hours to testify. Clerks and secretaries are of little help, always ragged and tense, the inevitable consequence of too much work and too little pay. Defendants who fail to appear for scheduled hearings are rarely sanctioned, while witnesses, losing time from work, are compelled to attend the next hearing, often with the same result. Waiting is the hallmark of these proceedings. Judges, lawyers, and witnesses scan the sports pages, work on crossword puzzles, plan lunch, exchange stories.

In sharp contrast, Isabel's examination of Dan Palmer is swift and deadly. In a low, mumbling monotone Palmer answers obediently while leaning forward, his elbows six inches in front of his chest, his neck stretched out as if he's ready to be guillotined in that very chair.

Palmer is made to discuss precisely how his office tested Charlie for drugs—"we followed all the usual procedures, took blood and urine, then sent it all to the lab we've used for years"—and to identify the written test results themselves. Charlie, he admits, tested "positive for Seconal."

"Did you give Michael Ashmore a copy of the results?"

"No, I did not."

Isabel cocks her head to one side. She's confused. Palmer, I know, is telling the truth. The lab sent me my copy directly.

"You at no time gave a copy of these test results to Michael Ashmore?"

"At no time."

Isabel steps back. She's apparently lost at sea. "Did you tell him the results?" she stammers.

Palmer glances at me. He wants to lie, I know he does, but I cannot encourage him. I can only watch and listen. "Yes," he says reluctantly.

Isabel nods, her face reflecting a glow I take to be the relief one feels after narrowly escaping defeat in a decisive battle. Ready to move on, she asks Palmer about his divorce trial.

"Michael Ashmore was your lawyer, wasn't he?"

"Yes."

"And you figured you owed him a favor, didn't you?"

"He won my case for me, if that's what you mean."

"Let me be specific, sir. Did you charge Michael Ashmore or Charles Ashmore one penny for this test?"

"It wasn't very much anyway."

"So there was no charge?"

"No charge."

"Then no invoice?"

"No invoice."

"Who paid the lab?"

"I did."

"If there was no invoice or check or credit card charge, no one looking at the defendant's personal records would know that the test was ever done, isn't that right?"

"I wouldn't know about that," Palmer mutters faintly. "I'm a doctor, not an accountant."

"It wouldn't take an accountant to figure out something smells here, now would it?" Isabel hollers out, her words bouncing off the nearby walls. Before Diana can object, Isabel withdraws her question, her point made. "That's all I have, Your Honor," she says politely, and sits down.

Diana advances to the lectern, and looks kindly at Palmer. "A person can test positive for drugs at all different levels, correct?"

"Yes."

"High, low, medium?"

"Yes."

"When Charles Ashmore's test came back positive for Seconal, was that at a high or low level?"

"Low, very low. Given his body weight, he had to have about five and three-quarters liters of blood, which means he had fifty milligrams or less of Seconal when tested. That's a normal, safe therapeutic dose for a night's sleep. I'd say the Seconal found in his body was negligible."

Satisfied with Palmer's answers, Diana has the necessary discipline to stop her interrogation, thank Palmer, and sit down. While Palmer's a friendly witness, he could inadvertently hurt us.

Meredith adjourns for the day. As the crowd begins to disperse, Palmer strides toward me. "Did I do okay, Michael?" he asks, his breath short from anxiety. "I had to come. They subpoenaed me."

His eyes are fully open, his lips apart. He wants my approval.

"You did great," I say.

He throws himself forward and hugs me. It feels strange, but I don't break away. It's comforting to know some people still like me.

I'M HOLLOW INSIDE, numb outside. I grope not for words but for the proper emotions. Randy, my closest friend for the last decade, is testifying for the prosecution.

No matter how many times Randy has betrayed me these last few months, I cannot fully absorb the shock of it. Each new betrayal stuns me as if it were the first. I hear Isabel, I hear Randy, but must strain to make sense of it all. "Did any of Michael Ashmore's partners consent to his investigation into his own brother's fitness to fly for an airline your firm had represented for many years?"

"None of us knew about it until Michael's investigation was over."

"And none of you were happy about it, correct?"

"None of us."

"Why was that?" asks Isabel. The question is unusually open-ended, not phrased to lead the witness in any specific direction. Isabel wouldn't be so casual, so loose, unless she was absolutely certain of Randy's response.

"A lawyer can serve only one master," is how Randy puts it. "He can't represent a loved one in a dispute with a client who's paying him. His judgment has to be compromised."

"It's a violation of a lawyer's ethical responsibilities, isn't it?"

"Clearly," replies Randy. "But in all fairness to Michael, this was way out of the ordinary for him."

Fairness? Randy's not being fair, I brood. He only wants it to appear that way. The fairer he seems, the deeper he buries me. "Did Michael Ashmore tell you after the fact about his investigation?"

"Yes, he did."

Randy's being coy. He's not answering in a rush, making Isabel ask another question. Another effort by Randy to project an image of fairness.

"What exactly did he tell you?" asks Isabel with mild exasperation. Maybe she's part of the game to make Randy look fair.

"He told me generally what he did and didn't do. He was worried about one thing in particular, and I think that's why he was talking to me at all."

"That one thing was?"

"His brother, Charlie, failed a drug test the airline required him to take. Only Michael knew the test results. He told me he didn't give the airline that test, but later had Charlie take another test, which he passed. Only that later test was given to the airline." Randy pauses a moment, glances at me. "He knew he'd made a huge mistake. He needed to confess to somebody, I guess."

"Was it the considered view of your partners that Michael Ashmore had acted improperly by withholding that first test?"

"Yes," Randy says quietly.

"What did the partners do when they learned of it?"

"Some wanted Michael to take a long leave of absence, and some wanted him out of the firm. Michael got mad and quit."

"Michael Ashmore doesn't like being challenged, does he?"

"Any good trial lawyer has an unconscionably large ego." Randy smiles. "Me included."

Isabel returns the smile, and sits down. It's our turn.

Most trial lawyers agree: Wound a hostile witness in the first minutes, and the jurors will be drowned in his blood the rest of the way. Most alert at the beginning of a cross-examination, the jurors will most vividly remember the witness's performance in the early mind-to-mind combat and will likely form their most lasting impressions of the witness's competency and character based on those first few rugged exchanges. How to wound Randy? The Hudson Escrow Fund, Diana insists. I swore to Randy I'd never tell a soul about the Hudson Fund. My word does mean something, I tell Diana, no matter how desperate my circumstances.

"That man is willing to take you away from Grace, take you away from everything you have," she says in a furious whisper. "I can't believe I even have to convince you."

Do I need to sink to Randy's level? Must I let his behavior determine mine? Wasn't his testimony, while vicious, completely accurate? Then to Diana: "If we nail Randy for stealing monies, how does that change what he said about me? Everything he said was true."

"I'll show you," Diana says, and she's gone, notes in hand, a radiant glow on her face. She would've interrogated Randy about the Hudson Fund whatever my objections. This is her case now. She's in charge. When she says "I'll show you," she means the jury doesn't know that Randy's telling the truth. She means that's her job: to convince the jurors an honest witness isn't honest.

"Mr. Chapman," begins Diana, "are you familiar with an escrow account called the Hudson Escrow Fund?"

A deadly pallor creeps across Randy's face. He's been given a blanket of immunity for his testimony, but it covers only conduct in connection with the plane crash. Randy stares at me with a blur of astonishment. I suppose he never expected me to betray him no matter how deeply he cut me. I take strange comfort in Randy's astonishment. Despite all else I've done, he must still hold me in the very highest regard.

Randy turns in panic to Meredith. "This isn't relevant to the issues of this case."

Diana has her opening. "It goes to impeachment, Your Honor. We'll show this witness was holding monies in trust for a client, and in violation of state law and the bar's ethical rules, he illegally took money from that account for his own personal use. If this witness has committed a criminal act, this jury is entitled to know that in determining Mr. Chapman's veracity as a witness."

"I put the money back," Randy contends in a low scream. "Every cent of it."

Meredith waves his finger at Randy. "What she says is true, then? You took money from an escrow account you were holding in trust for somebody else?"

"For two months or so, Your Honor. I put every penny back with interest."

"You put it all back after Michael Ashmore was told by the client that monies were missing and after Michael insisted you put it all back, isn't that right?" Diana interrogates.

"What does this got to do with—"

"Answer the question," orders Meredith harshly.

Randy frowns as would a child ordered by a parent to eat every last green bean. "That's true but a little misleading. I had every intention of putting it all back before Michael talked to me."

Meredith stops Diana as she's about to ask her next question. In a stern voice he conducts his own interrogation. He elicits every detail of Randy's crime—when, why, and how the money was deposited into the escrow account; when, why, and how it was withdrawn. Randy admits withdrawing ninety thousand dollars to buy in to a growing car dealership. Meredith is appalled. "I'm going to refer this matter to you, Madam Prosecutor, since you are charged with prosecuting all crimes in this District."

Isabel stands. "I didn't know a thing about this, Your Honor."

"Let's proceed," Meredith commands.

Diana wisely waits a moment. She wants the full force of Meredith's contempt for Randy to be felt by the jurors. The jurors, I'm sure, will have no sympathy for Randy. As rich as he is, he should have been able to manage his money. He's a client-rich firm's senior partner earning more money than Zoë Baird, whom the public slaughtered not because she broke the law—because she was rich and broke the law. And she didn't steal anything, not the way Randy did.

Randy had to confess. Any lies could have easily been disproved by bank records showing times and amounts of deposits and withdrawals. I'm glad Randy's sitting. I don't believe he could stand at this moment. He's confessed to a crime under oath in the presence of the national media. The

District bar will be forced to investigate. His license to practice law will be revoked or, if he's fortunate, suspended for a year or two. He'll be remembered not for all the good he's done but for this one transgression. There's no joy in my heart; revenge isn't sweet. All I see is Randy's weeping wife.

"The prosecution made a deal with you, didn't they? You testify for them, and they protect you and the airline, correct?" asks Diana after an appropriate pause.

"They said they wouldn't prosecute me or the airline. That was the deal." Randy's voice is still shaky, his cheeks still pale.

"To be specific, you weren't given the usual transactional immunity but were given complete immunity for any testimony involving this tragic plane crash, which means you can even lie under oath and not be prosecuted for perjury, isn't that right?"

"I could lie—"

Before Randy can finish—I'm sure he's about to add he won't lie though he can—Diana interrupts in her sweetest voice: "You don't have to convince me of that."

Quiet laughter breaks out in the back rows. Rather than pound his gavel, Meredith waits patiently for the laughter to subside, then turns to Randy: "Sir, it's one thing to lie, and still another to boast about having the opportunity to do it, particularly in a murder trial."

"I didn't mean I would lie, just that I could."

"I'll bet you could," retorts Meredith with raised eyebrows, generating another round of laughter. Randy's stiff frown reflects his deepening indignation.

"How did you come to get this privilege to lie?" Diana probes.

"I'd rather call it immunity, if you don't mind," Randy snaps, though his voice is uncharacteristically meek.

"I'd rather call it a cheap way to buy off an indictment, but I'll stick to a 'privilege to lie,' " Diana replies in a hard voice. "Now, please answer my question."

"I'd rather call it a public service," Randy fights back. "Way too many people died. Their families were entitled to know all the facts. I'm not happy about what I did, but I'm not ashamed of it either. For better or worse, I came upon vital information, and was forced to do something with it."

"Spare us all the self-serving 'woe is me' soliloquies and let's get down to the basic facts, shall we? Let's start with this one: Philip Brandon, the

CEO of Brandon Air Lines, fired your law firm a short time after his airline was sued in a federal court for hundreds of millions of dollars, correct?"

"Correct."

"To get immunity, you had to agree to testify against Michael Ashmore, correct?"

"Yes."

"Up until that time, the airline was the prosecution's primary target?"

"Yes, probably."

"On the very day you were given immunity to testify against Michael Ashmore, the airline rehired your firm as their attorneys, also correct?"

"The timing's correct, but the way you put it together gives a misleading picture of what happened. I didn't go to Ms. Castino to get Michael. Or to get the airline back as a client. But yes, the airline was grateful I told them what Michael had done."

"So grateful they were willing to rehire your firm at a cost of about four million dollars a year?"

"They don't just give us four million. We work for it."

"But the fact is, that's what it meant to you and your partners. Four million dollars this year, and four million dollars every year into the future for who knows how long. That's precisely what the bottom line was when you so skillfully talked the prosecution out of indicting Brandon Air Lines and indicting your best friend instead."

"You're twisting it—"

"Then untwist it, sir. Tell us in your own words exactly how it came to be that the target shifted from one huge airline to one single lawyer. You don't need to tell us about the money. We already know that four million a year is a whole lot more than thirty pieces of silver."

"Objection! This is going way over the top, Your Honor."

Meredith shakes his head at Diana. "Calm down, Counsel. Keep it factual."

Randy glares at Diana for a moment, then casts his eyes downward. He's not in control here, can't intimidate anyone. He must rely solely on his wit if he's to escape without further harm. "I went to see Ms. Castino. To tell her she was off base seeking an indictment against the airline. As a matter of law, any such indictment had to fail on constitutional grounds. She said she didn't agree. We argued about it for an hour or so. That's when I told her."

"Told her what?"

"That it wasn't the airline's fault. That Michael hadn't given the airline the results of the test Charlie failed. Had Michael done that, the airline wouldn't have rehired Charlie, and there would've been no crash. The airline was a victim of sorts itself. We wouldn't have said anything against Michael if she'd dropped the case against the airline in the first place. Believe me, we tried."

"Who is the 'we' you refer to?"

"Myself and Philip Brandon."

"Has the prosecution also given complete immunity to Philip Brandon?"

"I believe so."

"Did you two ask for immunity, or did the prosecution offer it to you?"

"It was sort of mutual. Ms. Castino wanted us to testify against Michael, and I said that was a problem. Michael was arguably acting within the scope of his authority as a partner of the firm while doing this investigation for the airline. All of the partners, including myself, could conceivably be charged with criminal conduct, not to mention being named as defendants in any civil suits. She said she could solve that problem by granting immunity to me and my partners. I said it would make sense to give Philip immunity, too, since she wanted him to testify that he never got the failed test from Michael."

"As I understand your testimony, then, you didn't want or plan to tell Ms. Castino about anything Michael did?"

"No, of course not. Like you said, Michael was my best friend. In my heart he still is."

"How touching, sir. But let's get back to the realities of life, okay? Answer this for me: If you had no desire or intention of discussing Michael with Ms. Castino, then how does that square with your earlier sworn testimony that you went to the prosecutor as a 'public service,' that the victims' families were 'entitled to know all the facts'?"

Randy blinks. He's caught in the sticky web he himself has weaved. His breathing grows short, uneven. "It wasn't only Michael's life at stake here," Randy says in nearly a whisper. "If the airline's convicted of a crime, that can be used by the civil plaintiffs in their case. Virtually guarantees them victory, and maybe gets them punitives too. Then you've got the public to consider. Who wants to fly on a criminal airline?" Randy's voice is growing louder, his words now streaming forth. The court reporter is straining to keep pace. "And it just didn't seem right that Philip might lose his entire family fortune because of one accident he had nothing to do with."

Diana's aglow. Her cheeks have the healthy light pink hue of one after a mild workout. Her breathing, her posture, her voice, all reflect inner joy. How many of us get to pay back our old boss in front of a national audience? "Sir," Diana presses forward, "my question to you had nothing to do with Philip Brandon. It had everything to do with your earlier sworn testimony that you went to Ms. Castino because the victims' families were entitled to know the so-called truth. Now you say you didn't want to tell Ms. Castino what Michael had done but were forced to do so when she refused to drop the airline as the principal target. So again I ask you: Which is the truth, which is the lie?"

Randy shifts in his seat, stares blankly at me when he says: "I didn't want to tell on Michael."

"When you complimented yourself on doing a so-called public service, you—"

"I was exaggerating the truth. I apologize."

"You mean you were lying, don't you?"

"I'll leave the word games to you," Randy says nastily.

"But you're so good at them," Diana replies. "And so good at negotiating too. Isn't complete immunity a wonderful thing for someone like you?"

"Objection, Your Honor. When is this going to stop?"

"Enough, Ms. Wells. You've had your fun. Move on," says Meredith gently.

"I don't know if I've made this clear enough," volunteers Randy, "but Michael Ashmore, no matter how busy he's been, has always found time for the sick, the poor, the homeless, the abused. Many of those," he adds emphatically, "were people from the roughest parts of the District." Everyone understands Randy's point: I've repeatedly helped inner-city African-Americans; the cause of racial justice won't be served by convicting one of its most powerful advocates.

Randy seems ready to make amends—after all, how many real friends, if any, does he have besides me?—and Diana seems ready to grant his wish. For nearly an hour Randy puts into evidence my finest moments as a pro bono lawyer. I show no emotion, but find it oddly thrilling to be glorified in public.

Having placed my character into question, Isabel cannot properly object to this rendition of my saintly acts. Randy tells story after story with the alacrity of a coffee-driven talk-show host. I suspect he wants no less from me than absolution, which I (as both victim and newly acclaimed holy man) alone have the power to grant him.

Diana stops when Randy runs out of stories. I grow tense. Isabel, I fear, will focus on that escrow fund. Didn't I have a legal obligation to report Randy's wrongdoing to the state bar? There's a pattern here for the jury to consider. I concealed evidence from the bar with the same "arrogance" I concealed evidence from the airline.

My tension evaporates with Isabel's first words to Meredith. Isabel wants no part of Randy; she dismisses him without a single question on redirect. Isabel must be worried about Randy too. He might retreat from his earlier testimony; or he might impeach himself again. Apparently Isabel has a cautious side to her. Randy would make anyone nervous.

Randy looks directly at me as he walks down the center aisle. I turn away, not as a deliberate gesture of contempt but as a natural, unthinking reaction to his unthinkable betrayal. I'm not distraught; rather, I'm strangely euphoric as if liberated from the shadow of my former self.

THE NEXT THREE witnesses are called for a single purpose: to bolster the prosecution's contention that the airline had good grounds to fire Charlie. Based on these witnesses' collective testimony, the jury might draw the inference that I was reckless to interfere with that well-reasoned decision.

First comes Ted Nash, who has brought the cane he rarely uses. He's looking for sympathy, I figure. He moves toward the witness chair with the enthusiasm of one being led to a hangman's rope.

Nash sets forth in orderly fashion the evidence upon which he based his decision to "terminate" Charlie. He "couldn't ignore" the eyewitness reports of two experienced crew members when coupled with the plane's "sudden dive."

Nancy Dilman, in her middle thirties, has been with the airline for twelve years. Her brown hair is short and neatly combed, her nails manicured, her navy-blue suit well tailored: She has the appearance of a solid, responsible citizen. Sitting upright in her chair, she claims Charlie seemed "too relaxed, as if he were drunk" when she entered the cockpit to serve dinner on that Minneapolis flight. "His face was a little flushed." After thanking her for the meal, Charlie mentioned he was glad to have her in the crew. "The first minute or so he seemed somewhat charming," then his speech became "slurred," and he "tripped over a few words." Under cross-examination,

Dilman admits she has no other evidence suggesting Charlie was under the influence of drugs or alcohol.

Peter Sexton, the copilot on that same flight, is more combative. He, too, maintains that Charlie appeared drunk and slurred his speech; having had more time to observe Charlie than did Dilman, his statements are more damaging. "Slow reflexes," "drowsy," "kind of tuned out," are among his other observations. Unlike Dilman, neither Sexton's appearance nor background inspires confidence. Before being hired by the airline, Sexton was a part-time minister who sold real estate and life insurance to congregation members; for a small extra charge, he drafted wills, using a form he'd copied from a booklet prepared by a local bank. Sexton's neck is filled with tiny shaving cuts, his nasal hair visible in small clumps, his tie too narrow.

Sexton concedes on cross-examination that Charlie's recovery of the plane showed "extraordinary skill." Otherwise, the day is bleak. I grimace at each mention of Charlie's conduct consistent with the classic symptoms of Seconal use certain to be described by the prosecution's expert witness, who waits quietly in the hall.

I arrive home to the usual supply of hate letters. They come from all parts of the country with all sorts of accusations and gruesome predictions. One catches my eye today. I read it again:

They call you cunning, but you're more cunning than they suspect. You fed those drugs to your own brother. That's how bad you wanted my brothers and sisters dead.

If you're going to kill off the African-American community, start with the most spiritual among us. Start with our church leaders. Kill our souls first, and the rest will follow. That's what I mean by cunning.

Burn everlastingly in hell, cunning killer of God. Burn till your skin is all gone, burn just like your victims. May Jesus never forgive you. Just burn, baby, just burn.

I tear the letter into small pieces, then disconnect my phone. I head for the bathroom. Demerol tonight.

THE FAMILIAR SIGNS OF EXHAUS-
tion—skin turned a washed-out yellowy-white while patches below the eyes
darken and elongate, creating the appearance of a partially made-up
clown—have conspired to rob Philip Brandon of that look of invincibility
all of us crave.

Seeming to sense Philip's fatigue, Isabel takes him step by step through
each facet of his "immunity," allowing Philip to explain in his own way at
his own uninterrupted pace what his immunity means to him before Diana
makes her run at him. Isabel doesn't want Philip to endure the humiliation
Randy suffered. Not only is it easier for Philip to tell his story under
friendly questioning, it gives him the appearance of a more candid, straightforward witness. Philip quietly but firmly declares he has "no desire or
intention to tell anything but the truth," which he has "sworn on the Bible
to do."

Isabel will likely keep Philip on a narrow track. She mostly needs him
to say he never received from me results of any test Charlie failed, which
Philip confirms emphatically. "He never told me, or showed me, or even
hinted at it. If anything, I was led in every way to believe only one test was
taken."

"Did you resist rehiring the defendant's brother?"

"I did, yes. But Michael was so hell-bent on it, and he'd done so much
good for us in the past. He said he wouldn't be our lawyer or Charlie's
lawyer, but would act as a board member when doing his investigation. I
was foolish enough to believe him."

"What exactly did he tell you after his investigation was concluded?"

Diana objects, claiming that all such communications are inadmissible.
Treating every serious question raised for his consideration with utmost

care, Meredith has the jurors escorted from the courtroom. He'll hear full argument on this issue, knowing a higher court will be scrutinizing all rulings if the jury finds for the prosecution.

Citing case after case, Diana vehemently defends the widely recognized sanctity of the attorney-client privilege while Isabel, conceding its sanctity, claims the privilege doesn't apply here. Meredith takes little time to decide. "The evidence does not suggest that Mr. Brandon was seeking legal advice. It sounds more like he had it thrust upon him without his consent. In any event, the advice, if that is how it is to be characterized, was more factual than legal. Then there's the uncertain state of the evidence. Was the defendant acting as the airline's lawyer, a neutral arbiter, or as a member of its board? If as an arbiter or a board member, no privilege can be properly asserted, and Mr. Brandon has testified the defendant claimed to be acting as a board member. Finally, the privilege was created for the benefit of the client, not the attorney, and as such can be waived by the client. For that reason and all others, I overrule the objection."

The jurors dutifully file back into the courtroom. Philip resumes his testimony, casting himself as an unsuspecting victim. "Michael lied, it's that simple. I raised questions. I argued. But Michael had the affidavits. He had the blood test. And he knew the law, which he swore was all in his brother's favor."

"Did Michael Ashmore ever tell you his brother was regularly taking Seconal under a doctor's care?"

"No, he never did. Had he done so—and I'm sure he knew this—I'd never have agreed to rehire Charlie. Whether Charlie was getting the drugs legally or not wouldn't have mattered to me. All I know is, it's plain stupid and damn risky for any pilot to be taking any barbiturate regularly. If there was a one-in-a-thousand chance that stuff would've affected Charlie even in the slightest, I'd have said it was way too much. We've got lots of people who can do this job, people who don't fool around with anything."

I FEEL THE weight of the packed courtroom shift as the short silence comes to an end. Spectators, having relaxed for a moment, now lean forward as Diana plants herself directly in front of Philip Brandon.

"Michael Ashmore is not and has never been an officer of the company, has he?"

"No."

"At no time did he ever have the authority to rehire Captain Charles Ashmore, did he?"

"No, he didn't."

"You alone made the decision to reinstate Charlie Ashmore, isn't that correct?"

"Yes. On Michael's legal advice."

Diana pauses, looks at the jurors. "His legal advice? It's odd you would say that. You swore under oath a moment ago that Michael Ashmore was not acting as your lawyer, didn't you?"

"I didn't mean legal advice, just advice," Philip stammers.

"Boy, all this immunity is sure coming in handy in this trial, isn't it?" Diana exclaims mightily, bringing smiles to the jurors' lips. They seem to like her. They rarely smile with Isabel.

"That's enough, Ms. Wells," says Meredith as Isabel climbs to her feet. He motions Isabel to sit.

Diana peers directly into Philip's face. Not long ago she was nothing to him but one of a dozen or so lowly associates assigned to labor on one of many matters on which the airline required advice. "Sir, immediately after the crash of Flight five five five, federal investigators talked with you about Charlie Ashmore, is that correct?"

"Yes."

"Did you tell any of them that you suspected pilot error caused by drugs?"

"No."

"Did you tell any of them that the airline had previously terminated Charlie Ashmore for alleged use of drugs?"

"No one asked."

"So you said nothing?"

"That's right. I answer only what I'm asked."

"They asked you about Charlie Ashmore's record, didn't they?"

"They did. But at that time I was convinced Charlie didn't have a drug problem."

Diana's eyes brighten. "And yet you testified previously, did you not, that you resisted Michael Ashmore's recommendation that Charlie Ashmore be reinstated?"

Philip looks at Isabel for help, but none is forthcoming. "I did resist," he mumbles finally. "I thought it looked bad, that's all. Him being Michael's brother and all."

"And that was the basis of your resistance?" Diana presses him.

"More or less." Philip shrugs, undoing much of his earlier testimony. He's compromised Ted Nash as well.

Isabel's state of tranquillity has vanished. She's writing furiously. This is the nature of most trials: exhilarating moments wrapped in a warm blanket of victory followed closely by a stabbing revelation promising a blood-soaked defeat.

"It is correct, is it not, that the airline is being sued for many hundreds of millions of dollars by the crash victims?"

"Yes."

"And Michael Ashmore has not been sued, has he?"

"No, but he couldn't possibly pay any substantial judgment, so why sue him?"

"But the airline can pay a judgment in the many hundreds of millions?"

This isn't information Philip wants to make available to the national media, whose reporting of it might reach the eyes and ears of the jurors selected for the civil case. "No, it'd probably ruin the airline."

"So the airline is fighting for its financial life?"

"You could say that."

Diana nods with restrained joy. This tells the jurors we have a desperate witness with reason to lie or cheat.

"And you are too?"

Philip stares blankly. What pleasures, I wonder, has all his inherited millions brought him? A loveless marriage with a once-ravishing woman, hordes of groveling politicians without the courage to look into his face, countless friends with favors to ask? Money keeps Philip's arms closed, his body rigid. Isn't every man of great wealth forever dominated by that certain tension that comes with having to keep something hidden, out of reach? Isn't each imprisoned by the nagging fear he'll be nothing if stripped of his wealth? Too much money can be a curse, and Philip is a cursed man, I think. No one but Philip, his wife, and his two children will mourn if their mansion, their yacht, and their Rolls are seized by the banks holding secured loans. "I am fighting too," Philip reluctantly admits, still staring with vacant eyes.

"Is it not correct, sir, that the J Ninety-nine has had twelve or more incidents where the elevators froze and stuck, causing the pilot to lose control of the plane's attitude?" Diana has deliberately shifted course abruptly, hoping Philip won't lock in to his rehearsed testimony with the same ease.

"Not that I'm aware of, Ms. Wells. But you must understand the airline has twenty thousand employees, many of them engineers or mechanics. If there's a sticking problem with an elevator, they attend to it, not me. That's what they get paid to do. Excuse me for being so blunt, but no CEO or board Chairman of a major airline deals with such things, and I'm both. Mechanical problems simply aren't brought to my attention. I invite you to bring any airline CEO to this courtroom and ask him that same question. You'll see what I mean."

Philip has adapted smoothly. Diana raises her voice, hoping to knock him off balance. "Is it your sworn testimony that Michael Ashmore never told you about those twelve sticking incidents?"

"Michael never did, no," answers Philip as if surprised by the question. He's a talented liar.

I lean back in my chair, wondering if we're on the right course. What makes Philip lie so well, I suspect, is confidence. At the meeting where I discussed the rash of sticking elevators, neither he nor Brooks took notes that could now be used to impeach him; and Brooks, as all who know him knows, won't deliberately hurt Philip or the airline. Roy Brooks is ever the Marine infantryman who obeys all orders from his commander without hesitation.

"Of those twenty thousand employees, the one who reports directly to you, and takes instructions directly from you, is Roy Brooks?"

"Yes."

"If he became aware of any significant problems in the company or with its planes, he'd instantly report all that to you, wouldn't he?"

"He's supposed to, Ms. Wells. That's his job, but people don't always do their job."

"But Roy Brooks always does his job, doesn't he?"

"To my knowledge, yes."

"And your principal supplier of airplanes, Jarrad Manufacturing, always does their job too?"

"To my knowledge, Jarrad does. They ought to. They supply about sixty percent of our planes."

"A conversation between Roy Brooks and Jarrad's Vice President of Operations would be something Roy Brooks would tell you about, wouldn't he?"

"Depends on what the nature of the conversation was. Not every conversation."

"Let's suppose the conversation involved a serious design defect in a model supplied to you by Jarrad. Not in one plane, mind you, but in a whole line of planes. That would come to your attention, wouldn't it?"

"It should."

Diana reaches across counsel's table and grabs a memo which she has marked as an exhibit. "I hand you defense exhibit eighty-six," she declares. "It is a phone memo of a conversation between Roy Brooks and David Evans, Jarrad's VP of Operations."

Philip reviews the memo's scribblings for a long while before raising his eyes.

"This memo indicates that Roy Brooks spoke to Jarrad's VP about freezing elevators on the J Ninety-nine, does it not?"

"It does, but I don't know if it's accurate or not. I didn't write it, you know. I've never even seen it before."

"I'm sure you've never seen it before, sir, or else I wouldn't have it here today, would I?"

"Objection!" screams Isabel. "This is the most—"

"Sustained!" Meredith drowns Isabel out, then glares at Diana. "No more of that, you hear?"

Diana nods at Meredith, then quickly returns her attention to Philip. "Does exhibit eighty-six refresh your recollection that there was an issue about freezing elevators?"

"It's possible Roy said something to me about it. Maybe it was the elevators, I don't exactly recall. But if it was, it was something Jarrad ultimately decided was no problem. Remember, Ms. Wells, I'm not an engineer by training. I'm at the airline to increase profits, not fix elevators. If Jarrad says there's no problem, I'm satisfied. Jarrad has the experts."

"It would be fair to say, wouldn't it, that Roy Brooks would not have called Jarrad's VP of Operations about the J Ninety-nine's elevators if they were working fine?"

"I'm sure that's true."

"Is it also true that he would not have ordered Jarrad to fix the problem, as exhibit eight-six indicates, without having first checked with you?"

"Roy probably did check with me, but I don't think I told him to tell Jarrad to fix the problem, but to look into it, and if there was in fact a problem, then to fix it."

"What made you tell Roy Brooks to have Jarrad look into freezing elevators in the first place?"

"I don't remember," Philip says anxiously.

"Come on, sir, the truth now."

Philip winces at the words "the truth now." He falls back in his chair, the dingy walls behind him reminiscent of those listless offices rented in hard times by sole practitioners on the edge of bankruptcy. Philip, I think for the first time, is out of his element. "That is the truth," he asserts with a hoarse growl.

"Turn the page over, sir. Do you see the initials 'PB' followed by the words 'Minn flight'?"

Philip's body tightens. Diana hadn't told him to look at the back side of the page. "PB" undoubtedly stands for Philip Brandon. "Did you tell Roy Brooks to discuss with Jarrad a Brandon Air Lines flight to Minneapolis?"

"I might have," is all Philip will commit.

Diana's fixed stare is reminiscent of a hunter's controlled gaze after having cornered his prey. "You were given a report, were you not, by Michael Ashmore with attached affidavits discussing a flight to Minneapolis by Charlie Ashmore in which his performance as a pilot was questioned?"

"Yes."

"And so you instructed Roy Brooks to tell Jarrad to fix the problem of freezing elevators, and you specifically wanted Roy Brooks to refer Jarrad to that Minneapolis flight as an example of an elevator failure, isn't all that true?"

"I didn't tell Roy to say the Minneapolis flight's problems were caused by freezing elevators," Philip rushes to protest. "Only that it was something to ask Jarrad about because Michael had argued it was."

"Really? I thought Michael hadn't spoken to you about freezing elevators."

Philip shakes his head. "You asked if he'd told me about twelve incidents, and I said no. I still say no. I only remember him mentioning this particular one."

"You didn't just take Michael's word before going to Jarrad, did you?" Diana continues to press. "At the very least, you must have had someone review the logbook of that flight?"

"I'm sure Roy did."

"And if he told Jarrad to fix the problem, he must've seen something in the logbook that supported the possibility of elevator failure, and he must've conveyed that to you before you let him complain to your biggest supplier?"

"I don't know if—"

"I can show you copies of all the logbooks Michael made before first coming to see you about the elevator problem," Diana exclaims gleefully, "if that will help you recall."

Philip's eyes widen. *Diana is implying I have copies of the original logbooks or, at least, copies of those logbooks that evidence the twelve sticking incidents. Surely I could have made several extra copies upon first receiving the logbooks—as lawyers often do—and kept one copy somewhere in the firm the thief or thieves neglected to look; or I could have kept an extra set in my house for safekeeping. Philip doesn't know what cards we're holding. If he gambles I'm without a copy of the unaltered logbooks, he risks being exposed as a liar, a thief, and an unfit CEO.*

Philip takes the safe road. "No, I'm sure something was noted about the elevators on that Minneapolis flight." *Philip doesn't want copies of the unaltered logbooks seen by the jury. He has to give Diana something to avoid that.* "I'm sure Roy looked at the logbook, saw the complaint, told me, then notified Jarrad. Jarrad said the elevators were okay, and that was the end of it for us."

"Did Jarrad do any tests to confirm that?"

"Dozens of tests, if I recall correctly. That's why we did nothing further. Jarrad was very thorough."

"Did you notify the FAA?"

"No," he says cautiously. "I told you, Jarrad did dozens of sophisticated tests. The elevators were okay."

"You didn't ask Jarrad to run dozens of sophisticated tests because of one elevator sticking, did you? I take it you told Jarrad of other sticking incidents too?"

Diana picks up a stack of logbooks—twelve of them, to be exact—and hastily reviews them as she waits for Philip's answer. Philip seems to have lost his confidence.

"There were other reported incidents of sticking as well, but like I said, Jarrad assured us there wasn't a problem."

All my copies of the original logbooks were stolen. Diana's bluffing. Philip's sweating. Diana puts away the twelve useless logbooks, and one by one carries fourteen boxes of paper to the bench, which she has collectively marked as Exhibit 87. "These are all the logbooks, Your Honor, of the J Ninety-nines as of the time Jarrad was running its tests on the elevators. We challenge this witness to find even one report of an elevator freezing or sticking."

Meredith appears confused. Doesn't the defense *want to show* reports of elevators freezing or sticking? He looks curiously at Diana.

"There will be no such reports, Your Honor, because the logbooks have been altered!" Diana asserts in an excited shout. "This was the first step in the cover-up."

"Cover-up?" exclaims Meredith. "You said nothing about a cover-up in your opening."

"We're saying it now, Your Honor. The proof, ironically, is in the lack of proof."

I glance at Philip. He looks faint.

"It'll take him hours to go through all that," Meredith ponders aloud. "I'll excuse the jury for the day, and we can all sit here until he's done."

The next morning the jury returns. Diana rises to her feet. In her most powerful voice she asks: "Have you found even one single reference in all those logbooks to a freezing or sticking elevator?"

Philip, slumped forward, must be at this moment exceedingly grateful he has complete immunity, though the media will not, unlike the prosecution, have any restraints. "I didn't find any," he is forced to admit.

"And yet, hasn't a congressional Subcommittee decided to look into complaints the J Ninety-nines' elevators tend to freeze and stick?"

"As far as I know, those hearings have been postponed indefinitely."

"Who did you talk to, sir, to get that done?"

"Nobody," snaps Philip.

She'll ask nothing more about the hearings, having accomplished her small mission; the jurors have been alerted to the congressional investigation, thus adding credence to our allegations the J99 is defective. Any further interrogation might give Philip an opening to speculate the hearings were postponed because the Subcommittee no longer believed in the validity of the complaints.

Diana edges closer to Philip, her voice rising slowly. She's ready for a full frontal assault. "Were you at La Guardia around the time Flight five five five departed for the last time?" We want Philip to say he wasn't there. Airline computer records pinpoint his arrival into La Guardia five hours before Flight 555's departure and his return at ten o'clock the next morning to D.C. National. Hotel records show he stayed at the La Guardia Marriott that night. Room service brought him a bottle of red wine at three in the morning while he watched a gangster movie that cost nine dollars with tax. We want him to lie.

No such luck. Philip admits to "being at La Guardia late that night" for a meeting with "a food supplier." He's got proof: a letter to the supplier sent the afternoon following the crash confirming the details and date of their discussion. It turns out Philip arranged the meeting twelve hours before it took place.

"You saw Charles Ashmore at La Guardia before his flight took off, didn't you?"

"No, I did not."

"But you had a drink at a bar or a restaurant, didn't you?"

"I did," Philip answers warily. "One of those snack places." He steals a glance at his wife, Emma Larson, a deceptively amiable woman with the delicate, airy features of a gentle, hopping rabbit. She wears a white cotton dress that drops nearly to her white Reeboks. Her short, brushed-back hair, this month a cardinal-red, clashes with eyebrows a coal-black, underscoring the sallow hue of her cheeks.

"And Charles Ashmore was with you then, wasn't he?"

"No, he wasn't," replies Philip after a slight hesitation.

Philip seems to know exactly where the gaps are in our proof. We have no one who saw him at the airport, much less with Charlie. Diana guessed right about the drink, but where does she go from here?

Isabel has probably spent ten to fifteen hours with Philip, explaining precisely what we must prove, how we've questioned the others, what they've said, and how we've tried to catch them in lies. I have no doubt she's helped Philip formulate and memorize answers the prosecution desires. Philip will admit to spending only "two hours" with Isabel, but I know what it takes to get a witness in this sort of shape.

"You paid at the snack place with a credit card, didn't you?" Diana's still guessing, still hoping.

"With cash, I think. It was just some coffee."

We're out of ways to undercut him. No credit card transaction to tell us if Philip was alone, no cashiers who recognize his picture. How much further should we go with this line of inquiry? The more we snipe at Philip, the nastier we seem. We're hurting ourselves. We're making a martyr out of Philip Brandon. All we've got are innuendos, rumors, possibilities. Listening to Philip brings me back to reality. I've gone after elusive shadows that vanish in the light.

Yet Diana, while having gotten nothing solid, seems to have Philip on the run. "You ordered Eddie Perez, the lead mechanic, not to deice this plane, didn't you?" she barks at him.

Philip folds his arms. "That's ridiculous," he chuckles without smiling. "If you look at the records, this flight left the gate on time. There was no reason to rush it. I'd never give that kind of order anyway," Philip backtracks, "not in a million years, but surely not if we're okay on time. What other possible reason is there to do it?" Philip takes a deep, long breath, then slams his open hand on the chair's arm. "What kind of monster do you take me for!"

"Was the plane in fact deiced?" Diana swiftly asks in a tone loaded with suspicion.

Philip takes hold of himself. His voice softens. "I'm sure it was. It's common practice to deice in that kind of weather."

"Did you see it deiced?" she demands.

"No, of course not. I told you, Ms. Wells, I'm not a mechanic."

We have nowhere else to go. It's time to stop. "That's all for you, sir." Diana dismisses Philip with the same acid tone she greeted him. She despises this man, and wants the jurors to know it.

Isabel rises like a queen ready to be crowned: full of confidence and a sense of glory.

"Did you know anyone on Flight five five five other than the pilot?" Isabel asks politely. Philip, after all, deserves respect.

"No one," Philip asserts.

"Sir"—Isabel gestures with a sweep of her arms—"it seems as if the defense is, in its own vague and awkward way, accusing you of sabotaging this flight. What's your response to that?"

Philip's eyes take on a dark glow. "It's garbage, utter garbage!" he thunders. His arms are flailing, his neck reddening, his eyes bulging; he looks as if he's about to burst. "Why in the world would I ever do that? I've worked my heart out for this airline for twenty years! It's at the center of everything I own, everything my family owns!"

Isabel waits for Philip to gather himself before asking: "Sir, you said to Ms. Wells there was more than one reported sticking incident. But where I'm unclear is whether you said they were reported in the logbooks or somewhere else."

"I never did say. That's because I don't know where they were reported," Philip recovers with a small sigh. "They probably came to my attention through Roy Brooks. I never actually read the logbooks until yesterday."

"Is it part of your job as Chairman and CEO to review logbooks?"

"Of course not."

"Is it possible the incidents you learned about were never reported in the logbooks but were the subject of gossip and rumor, and brought to your attention by Roy Brooks when he decided he should follow up these rumors by calling Jarrad?"

"Very possible."

Isabel nods. "I just wanted the record set straight," she says kindly. "It got a little twisted there." Isabel strolls back to counsel's table. She hasn't completely dodged our bullet, but her vital organs haven't been hit. Some bleeding, certainly, but the bandages are in place.

WE BEGIN THIS day with the haunting voices of the dead. Isabel plays the tape from the black box at nine o'clock sharp, taking advantage of the jurors' early morning alertness. Actually, I'd rather them hear the tape now than at day's end, the words not as likely to echo in their brains deep into the night.

With morbid curiosity the jurors lean forward as every word uttered in Flight 555's cockpit is broadcast, many of the more important phrases re-played again and again. I drink water, but my mouth stays gritty. The words "The up and down is stewed" receive special attention, played six times for the jurors. I fear those words, pounded into the jury's collective conscious-ness, will persuade each and all that Charlie was disoriented by the phen-obarbital. Wasn't Charlie, by those words, uttering a cry for help? Would anyone not under the spell of drugs or alcohol say such words, and say them twice?

When Isabel can squeeze not another ounce of horror from this tape, she calls as her next witness Harold Klemmer, an addictionologist from the Mayo Clinic who specializes in treating drug-related illnesses. For an hour Isabel has Klemmer tell the jury of his Yale and Stanford degrees, his thirty years of medical practice, and his best-selling book on the effects of drug use.

While having impeccable credentials, Klemmer doesn't impress me as a likable witness. He's stiff in posture and voice, and speaks as if lecturing at a medical convention, straining to find complex, seldom-used words when simple ones will do, and do better. His white hair, sea-green eyes, and nearly colorless lips accentuate his pallid, horse-shaped face. His white-as-a-bone look reminds me of those self-righteous, bleached-white missionaries who—believed by their African subjects to have acquired their color by eating the bones of other white folks—were naturally seen as the very symbols of death.

"Seconal and phenobarbital have nearly identical consequences. Both depress the central nervous system," answers Klemmer in response to Isabel's first meaningful inquiry. "They both cause drowsiness, slowed reflexes, slurred speech. They impair coordination, and for some they produce a state of intoxication remarkably similar to that of alcohol. Physicians use them not only to treat insomnia but certain mental disorders as well."

"Are these drugs addictive?"

Klemmer nods emphatically. "Once a user is hooked, he's hooked. Barbiturates are the only addicting drugs that can actually kill you if you try to withdraw. It's a horrifying sight. The user's body temperature rises and rises until he becomes delirious. Invariably he is gripped by violent epilepticlike seizures that are sometimes fatal. And all the while he's having these frightening paranoid delusions."

"Do you have an opinion as to whether a man under the influence of phenobarbital or Seconal will be adversely affected in his driving of a car?"

"Of course he will be affected."

"Is the same true of a pilot of an airplane?"

"Yes, only more so. Operating a plane requires more mental agility than driving a car. A Seconal or phenobarbital user is so easily confused he often can't recall how many pills he's taken. That's not surprising because these drugs, designed to make one sleep, disorient an ordinary user at a level sometimes as low as ten to twenty milligrams."

"Can the level of phenobarbital in one's body be measured accurately by a blood test?"

"Certainly."

"Are you familiar with the phenobarbital level in Charles Ashmore's blood as of the time Flight five five five crashed?"

"Given his phenobarbital-to-blood level, he would have had to have taken approximately six hundred milligrams of phenobarbital an hour or so before the flight, which, I must say, is enough to kill a man."

"Is it your opinion, Doctor, that this level of phenobarbital in a man's blood would affect his ability to pilot a jet plane?"

"Affect his ability?" Klemmer snorts. "That's putting it very mildly. I'm amazed he could fly the plane at all."

• • •

DIANA LEANS BACK against the jury rail. "Sir, you've testified in a courtroom before, haven't you?"

"Forty or fifty times," says Klemmer with a glimmer of pride.

"That's a lot of testifying."

"Yes, it is."

"On every one of those occasions you testified for the prosecution, didn't you?"

"Yes, I did."

"And on every one of those occasions you were paid by the prosecution?"

"Yes, I was."

"And you are being paid by the prosecution once again for your testimony here today?"

"The prosecution is paying for my time, not my testimony."

Diana nods with a smile, signaling the jurors of her amusement with Klemmer's fine but meaningless distinction. "I take it, then, that prior to your being asked to testify in this case for the prosecution, you were well acquainted with the U.S. Attorney's office?"

"Yes, I was."

"Did Isabel Castino describe this case to you?"

"Yes."

"Did she tell you about any of the problems that occurred with the plane's stabilizers?"

"No."

"With the plane's elevators?"

"No."

"In forming any of your opinions, then, you didn't take into account any problems that might have been caused by either of these control components, did you?"

Klemmer's lips draw tightly together. "No, I did not," he admits grudgingly.

Diana continues down this path. She asks if he's familiar with the controllers' instructions, the storm's intensity, Charlie's professional accomplishments, Charlie's handling of the plane prior to the onset of turbulence. In those few instances when Klemmer has some information, Diana pins down the nature and extent of his limited knowledge. One fact stands taller than do all others: Klemmer knows only what Isabel has chosen to tell him. After having irrefutably established the source and parameters of Klemmer's information, Diana shoots at him one hypothetical question after another.

Might you have changed your opinion if . . . Would this data have made a difference to you . . . Had you known . . . Each fact helpful to the defense is wrapped in a hypothetical that requires Klemmer to analyze instantly if that fact, standing alone, or that fact, in combination with several other facts rattled off by Diana, might have or would have altered his opinion regarding Charlie's ability to pilot the plane or the ultimate cause of the crash.

Klemmer frequently hesitates, then gives long, winding answers. Rigidly sticking to his initial opinions in the face of evidence he must assume for purposes of the question to be true would make him appear inflexible, or better for us, a whore who will say anything for those paying him. The hypotheticals keep flowing in his direction. If you assume the controller ordered Captain Ashmore to land his plane . . . At what speed and angle would the winds have had to have shifted . . . If you assume Captain Ashmore was flying on course all the way . . . Diana doesn't yield to Klemmer's protestations that such analyses are impossible without further study. She wants him to whine. She wants him to look uneasy, inept, disoriented.

"Sir, do you have a pilot's license?"

"No."

"Ever operated an airplane?"

"I've driven a car. The principles are the same."

"Have you ever consumed any kind of barbiturates?"

"No."

"Then you've never actually experienced what it feels like, have you?"

"No. But I've seen many patients who have."

"Have you ever treated a pilot who was taking barbiturates?"

"A pilot, no."

"Have you ever treated a pilot for any reason?"

"No."

"Sir, in the forty or fifty times you have testified for the prosecution, have you ever testified in a case involving barbiturates?"

"Most involved cocaine or heroin."

"My question, sir, is whether any of these cases involved barbiturates. Yes or no?"

"No."

"Let's see where we are, Dr. Klemmer. You've never operated a plane, never treated a pilot, never taken a barbiturate, and never testified in a case involving barbiturate use, is that all correct?"

"I've already told you all that."

"What you have done is drive a car. Correct?"

"I don't like your attitude."

"Well, my attitude is my attitude. At least it's not for sale."

"Keep to the point, Ms. Wells," admonishes Meredith. "No badgering."

Diana forces Klemmer to admit that factors other than one's blood-barbiturate level are important in determining if one is impaired. "What he's eaten that day, how much he slept the night before, how long he's been using the drug, and, of course, the individual himself. All these are factors," concedes Klemmer uneasily.

"You've never examined, diagnosed, or treated Charles Ashmore, have you?"

"No."

"It is also correct, is it not, that you know absolutely nothing about Charles Ashmore other than what was told to you by Isabel Castino?"

"I reviewed the autopsy report and his two earlier blood tests."

"And that is all, correct?"

"That is all I needed."

"Really now? You don't know Charles Ashmore's tolerance for phenobarbital, his history of use, his willpower, his eating or sleeping habits, do you?"

"No."

"As you've just testified, all these are factors to consider in determining one's ability to resist the effects of phenobarbital, aren't they?"

"They are, but six hundred milligrams is off the charts."

The next outpouring of hypotheticals begins: If Charlie could function normally at two or three hundred milligrams . . . if he slept ten hours the night before . . . if he drank the coffee after he took the phenobarbital . . . if he was highly motivated to get home to the District . . . if he had built up a tolerance . . . Klemmer wavers, fudges. He is breaking down, his confidence eroding.

"Sir, have you ever reached the wrong conclusion in your treatment or diagnosis of a patient?"

"I am not infallible," admits Klemmer, who has by now become accustomed and conditioned to making admissions on virtually every issue he and Diana discuss. He's ready to admit to anything, I think. The sun rises at night. The Pope isn't Catholic. He isn't Klemmer.

"And you could be wrong again here, could you not?"

"I could be. Yes."

"In fact, you reached your opinion based largely on what Ms. Castino decided to tell you, correct?"

"Yes."

"If Ms. Castino supplied you with incorrect or incomplete information, your opinion would be of no value here, also correct?"

"Yes, of course."

"And then there's the copilot, isn't there?"

Klemmer's eyes narrow. "What do you mean?"

Diana's been saving this question for the right time, and the time's right now. Klemmer, the prosecution's designated expert, is tired, suggestible, and unprepared for this line of inquiry. "You know there was a copilot, don't you?"

"Sure."

"You've seen his autopsy, haven't you?"

"He wasn't on any drugs, if that's what you're getting at."

"Exactly. But the plane still went down, didn't it?"

"It went down, yes."

"Doesn't that tell you it went down because of the elevators, and not the pilot? The copilot couldn't save the plane because—"

"Objection! The witness isn't here to speculate about the mechanical defects, if any, of this airplane. He's here to give testimony about the effects of barbiturates. Nothing else!"

"I'll let him answer," Meredith rules. "He seemed happy a while ago to give opinions about the cause of the crash. Let's not stop him now."

Klemmer shrugs. "I don't know anything about planes," he sighs, taking his cue from Isabel's objection.

"That's becoming clearer and clearer," Diana observes curtly.

I turn and look for Randy, who might appreciate Klemmer's predicament. I don't see him anywhere. The District bar has announced it will investigate Randy's admitted embezzlement, and swiftly determine an appropriate punishment. The *Post* recommends disbarment as the "only sensible means of restoring public confidence in our system of justice."

The media spares no one. An hour after Klemmer limps from the witness chair, the local stations condemn his "history of blind allegiance to federal and state prosecutors" and his "unthinking reliance on Isabel Castino's naturally biased view of this case," likely accounting for "his embarrassing failure to anticipate defense counsel's questions." Klemmer, they conclude, was "whiny, evasive, and overmatched." Diana, lauded for her thorough and effective cross-examination, has become the media's darling. How quickly the world turns.

FIVE BLACK TEENAGERS break into a synagogue. They find a middle-aged clerical worker, tie him to a post, and cut him with a butcher's knife. Each boy passes the knife to the boy on his right until the man's naked back is soaked with blood. Arrested hours later, the boys show no remorse. They say they didn't intend to harm the man, only scare him, but his fear provoked them. With each cut of the knife, they found themselves pulled deeper into their own, self-created mystique. The TV reporters like to point out that the beaten man was not Jewish.

What inherent evil do these boys think we Jews possess? Do they believe the myths of perverted courage and dangerous brilliance that allowed us to face God, outwit Him, kill Him, then refuse to repent? Do they resent us for performing the very act that made Christianity possible, thereby leading to that high wall of Christian morality that made rebellion difficult and necessary? If they can't rebel against the very authority to whom they have surrendered their freedom, are we the stranger they must find? All zealots, I think, link truth with innocent suffering.

"Will our jurors feel the same way as those boys?"

Diana knows I mean, specifically, the six black jurors, but after so many years of condemning others for doing what I must now do—consider the character of blacks as a group—I cannot bring myself to say the words. "Those boys were a lot younger," she offers.

I nod. "Maybe it had nothing to do with Jews. Maybe just a random act of violence," I comfort myself until I remember they raided a synagogue. Daddy once said we were the easiest of targets because we Jews had the smell and feel of death about us. I ask Diana: "Should I testify?"

"No," she says gently but with a firmness that has no yield to it. "You'll be forced to confirm everything they've been saying. That you knew Charlie was taking Seconal, you knew he couldn't sleep, you knew he was about to be divorced, and yet you argued with the airline to have him rehired without telling them about any of that. And you hid the failed test. And you knew the airline wouldn't have hired Charlie if—"

"Okay, okay." I wave my arms. "But there's still the question if what I did was truly reckless, given all the many circumstances. I had good reason to believe in Charlie. Any fair-minded jury will see that. I can make Charlie come alive for them."

"Isabel might ask you very specific questions about how much weight Charlie lost, how much sleep he'd get, why Ruth left him," warns Diana. "And there's Carolyn's death and your father's suicide and how all that stuff affected Charlie. And you, too. Maybe she'll try to show you're unstable too. Your father hung himself right after a sit-down dinner for twelve, and your German mother who bravely married a Jew converted right back to a Lutheran. There's more than a few people out there who say she worked for the Nazis before and after she converted back and forth. Not a model of stability for young Michael."

Can I bear nationally televised assaults against those who bore me? My dream last night: I'm wearing a conical hat and a long black woolen coat with a bright yellow star sewed onto its back. Surrounding tenements bar the sun. Stones are thrown at me. I run. A Communion wafer is pushed into my pocket. Iron gates are locked. I'm charged with stealing the wafer and cutting it to make it bleed. The more I protest my innocence, the more crimes I'm accused of committing. Daddy is shot.

It is the same dream Mother had after Daddy's suicide. *It's a dream about God*, I'd told Mother.

About God? No, Michael, it's about me pretending to be a Jew when I wasn't one. When I was a little girl, my daddy used to tell me the Jews were a godless, scheming people who'd gotten rich and influential by attaching themselves to the most powerful Christians. So I thought to myself, what a great sacrifice it would be to become a Jew, how it would show your father how deeply I loved him. It was important to your father that I become a Jew, though he'd never gone to the Jewish schools. And I'd think, the church came from the synagogue, the light before the high altar came from the synagogue's perpetual lamp, the wine and bread of Communion from the Kiddush and matzo of Passover, so the Jews couldn't be as bad as my daddy said, and even if they were, it only made my sacrifice that much nobler.

But you went back.

I would've lost my doctor's license if I hadn't. Maybe my life too. The Nazis didn't want me touching the blood of Jews. After I went back, my former Jewish patients came to despise me. I had a Jewish name, a Jewish husband, and was a Jew so far as they knew.

After Daddy's suicide, Mother told all who would listen that Daddy had "eaten everything on his dinner plate" hours before "it happened," even a slightly stale slice of chocolate cake for dessert. Was that the behavior of a man who had been contemplating suicide, or rather of a man who had acted on a mad impulse? As the weeks passed, she endlessly bemoaned the cake's dryness, disconsolate that Daddy's last sensual pleasure before death was the intake of food that "didn't measure up" to her "usual standards." She should have "kept the cake in the freezer" or given him "the strawberries, they were fresh." A family acquaintance forced to endure one of Mother's rambling discourses despite all polite efforts to extricate herself cruelly remarked in a last-ditch effort to silence Mother (and escape from the funeral home, whose heavy doors must have seemed to have locked her inside) that "maybe the cake had something to do with it," provoking from Mother an hour-long torrent of newly conceived misgivings and rationalizations. Mother blamed her cooking, her moods and her choice of television shows, not once mentioning the possibility that Daddy's death was caused by that which was far more basic and painful.

I ponder how the media's spin on my testimony will affect Grace; every newsworthy word from my mouth will likely be replayed on the local stations. In recent days Grace has been taunted at her ritzy private school by former friends who believe (or have been told to believe) that her father undoubtedly knew that sooner or later a plane piloted by her uncle Charlie would crash and burn.

"Is Grace doing okay?" I ask Diana, who's been talking to Grace more of late than I have. Grace, I think, is afraid to confide in me now.

"Okay," says Diana with a turn and shake of her hand signaling the contrary. "She says she's been talking to God."

"You mean praying?"

"I mean talking. A two-way conversation. She's convinced God will save you. Either He'll come Himself or do it through someone here on earth."

I clench my fists not in anger but with a sharp, helpless anxiety. "This doesn't sound good."

"She's had her mother, her only cousin, and her only uncle all die, and now her father's on trial for murder. What kid wouldn't be a little off the wall? She's afraid of weakness, Michael. She sees people aren't strong enough to fight off death. The weaker we seem to get, the more God visits her."

"Should we take her to a shrink?"

"They'll give her drugs first, talk later."

"No drugs," I spit out. "Not now, not ever!"

"Agreed." Diana nods. "Anyway, it's possible, isn't it, she knows something we don't? Not everything has to be rational. Things happen you can't explain or never expect."

Maybe Grace has talked to God, I think. Maybe God will save me. At least she's not bitter. She hasn't turned on God for allowing tragedy to strike her inner circle with such fatal force.

I go to Grace's room. She's asleep. Looking at her resting tranquilly, her little lungs breathing in and out in harmony with some universal rhythm, drives the pain from my body as if I've been cleansed and warmed by surging water from a hot spring.

Grace must somehow feel my presence. Her eyes lazily open, her brow furls. "What's wrong, Daddy?"

"Nothing's wrong. Just wanted to see you."

"Did Diana tell you?"

"About what?"

"About God coming here."

Just like her father, I think: interrogating even in her sleep. "Yes, she did," I properly admit.

"Do you think I'm lying too? I know she does."

"Diana doesn't think you're lying. She's not sure if—"

"God does come here," she insists.

"How often does He come?" I ask gently. I can interrogate too.

"Whenever I ask Him to." She sits up and says in a saviorlike way: "God was ready to take Uncle Charlie. It wasn't your fault. The plane didn't work."

"What was wrong with it?"

She throws up her thin arms in mild exasperation: "I don't know. It just didn't work, that's all."

"It's okay," I say calmly, but I'm not calm.

"You know something weird? Right at the time Uncle Charlie died, I got this big pain right here." She points to a rib, then grimaces as if reliving the event. "It really hurt, Dad, so bad I almost screamed. I was pressing my hand there as hard as I could. And I looked at the clock, Dad, and saw how late it was. And when I heard the TV, that's what time they said the plane fell."

"Do you think you had a connection with Uncle Charlie that transcended space?"

She frowns. "What does trans . . . ?"

"That went beyond, that overcame space."

She nods. "Because of God, you know. He can do anything. He will save you, Daddy. I promise."

"Okay," I say faintly.

"It's true, Daddy. Somehow He will save you."

I kiss Grace on the cheek. "I know He will, honey."

She pulls me closer to her, and hugs me tightly. "You'll see, Daddy. God will save you."

In the moments each night before I fall asleep, I fantasize meeting my detractors after my acquittal, their ashen faces downward, their voices submissive, their shoulders slumped in the manner of those about to be beheaded. Tonight I drop backward on my pillow as if struck by a heavy object. The room seems to expand. Rainbows of colors rapidly whiten to a sterile, lifeless hue, then vanish behind a black curtain. Hours later I open my eyes with a shudder, finding myself half-naked on the bedroom floor. No matter how this trial ends, I cannot ever be made whole again. I have been damaged in ways beyond repair.

PILOTS LANDING AT D.C. National moments before Flight 555's crash confirm the turbulence, while heavy, was navigable.

"You made it, didn't you?" Isabel asks one pilot who, after acknowledging the obvious, generously adds: "I don't know how useful it is to discuss the weather conditions I encountered. Winds come and go in seconds. If—and I say if—the Brandon pilot encountered the exact same turbulence I did, then I'd say he should have made it through. But I don't know what the turbulence was like in the one spot he was at the moment he was there. Should he have ventured into the area if he knew there was turbulence? I did. Others did. Sure there were cumulus clouds. Sure that gave me concern. But by and large, I rely on my dispatcher and the tower to tell me how bad the storm is going to be ten miles away. Every pilot does."

Charlie's final contact with air traffic control came ten miles from the airport. John Frontera, the local controller who last spoke to Charlie from atop the control tower, was tracking incoming planes by studying "blips" on large radar screens. "Each blip has a data block next to it which prints out the plane's flight number, speed, and altitude," Frontera expounds. "It was too dark to see anything with the naked eye."

"How many planes have you guided to landings in turbulence?" Isabel inquires.

"Many thousands."

"Until Flight five five five, had a single one crashed?"

"No," says Frontera quietly. He looks as if he is about to weep when he says: "The pilot has the ultimate responsibility for making the decision whether or not to land."

I know by the phrases "ultimate responsibility" and "making the decision" he is parroting words fed to him by Isabel, words he'll remember the rest of his life and spit out at anyone questioning his competence or conduct. I write the words *he's scared* and pass the note to Diana, who nods with pinched lips. She's tense and tired. We worked until three this morning preparing for Frontera. He's a key witness. If the jury believes he was negligent in directing Charlie into turbulence, I won't be convicted.

I watch Diana rise. She asks Frontera to listen carefully, then stares straight at him as she plays the tape from the black box:

"We're being bumped awfully hard. Should I try to circle?"

"The storm's spreading. You might hit it worse if you circle. Delta three zero three just landed okay."

"We're starting to get rocked now. Right now. The wind's getting worse."

"I see you on the screen. I can steer you around the worst of it."

"I should try to land?"

"If you think you can, I can steer you around it. I see the storm. Move thirty degrees east and straighten out."

"All right. Thirty degrees east."

"Come back on at five miles."

Moments later the copilot shouts, *"She's diving! She's diving!"* and Charlie mutters over and over, *"Stabilize, come on, stabilize, stabilize . . ."* An instant before the crash I hear rushing air and a scream from the cockpit.

Diana slowly shuts off the tape, all the while eyeing Frontera, whose arms are locked by his heart, which, I'm sure, is beating madly. "That was you talking on the tape with the pilot of Flight five five five, wasn't it?"

"Yes, ma'am, it was."

"The pilot advised you, did he not, that he was encountering severe weather conditions?"

"Yes, ma'am."

"In fact, he specifically told you the plane was getting rocked, didn't he?"

"Yes," Frontera says feebly.

"And you told him you could see where he was and could steer him around it, correct?"

"Yes. Could see him on the screen."

"You told him not to circle, didn't you?"

"In effect, yes," he admits after a long pause.

"And you told him not to circle after he specifically asked you if he should circle?"

Frontera's forehead wrinkles. "Yes, ma'am, but it's up to the pilot to decide for himself whether to land, circle, or execute a missed approach."

"But, sir, you specifically told him, down to the exact degree, where to direct his plane, didn't you?"

"I told him to move thirty degrees east."

"And he followed your instructions, didn't he?"

"As best I can tell, he did. But I would call it more of a suggestion than an instruction."

Diana rolls her eyes in full view of the jurors. In a voice reflecting her utter disdain for Frontera's evasive wordplay, she charges: "You fully expected the pilot of Flight five five five to follow your instruction—or as you euphemistically call it, your suggestion—to move east, did you not?"

"I expected he would."

"Of course you did. Pilots always follow your instructions, don't they?"

"They usually do," he says softly. "Most always."

"You continued to follow Flight five five five on the radar screen after giving the pilot the instruction to move east, didn't you?"

"He started moving east, I know that."

"And it wasn't until after he began moving east that he encountered the turbulence that eventually caused his plane to crash, correct?"

Isabel objects. Frontera mutters, "I don't exactly know what caused the crash, but yes, he hit the worst turbulence after he started going east."

"Did it ever occur to you to place Flight five five five in a holding pattern a safe distance from the storm?"

"The pilot is responsible for finding out the weather conditions and making judgments accordingly," answers Frontera, but those words, too, are Isabel's.

"My question, sir, is whether it ever occurred to you—"

"It always occurs to me to put a pilot in a holding pattern. That's my job. To say go or stay."

"And you said go," Diana declares.

"I should've got Corsett involved," Frontera mumbles.

"Who is Corsett?" Diana asks innocently. Corsett is Frontera's supervisor.

"My boss. He was on a break. I . . ."

"Should have interrupted him," Diana fills in.

"Yeah, I should've," Frontera mumbles again, but I sense he wants all of us clearly to hear those words; he needs all of us to know he feels the proper remorse.

"Did Captain Ashmore respond to your communications appropriately?"

"Yes, ma'am."

"Did he seem mentally alert?"

"He did to me."

"Did he seem in any way to be under the influence of alcohol or drugs?"

"No, ma'am. I'd gotten help if I'd thought that."

Isabel stands. Frontera has been more helpful to us than I'm sure she can bear. "Your Honor, I must object to this whole line of cross-examination. The basic function of a traffic controller is to prevent collisions by providing separation between aircraft. There's no allegation here that this witness, or any other traffic controller for that matter, failed in this respect."

Isabel is ready. She describes thoroughly all federal regulations requiring a pilot to apprise himself of prevailing and expected weather conditions, then sharply distinguishes our circumstances from all those wherein the government was found negligent. "This pilot was fully aware of the very turbulence the defense now contends contributed to the crash. The government has historically been held liable only where it's failed to warn of a hazard known to the controller but unknown to and unknowable by the pilot."

Diana shakes her head as one does when faced with an ironic inconsistency. "If this case is distinguishable from those where the government failed to warn," Diana argues, "it's distinguishable in favor of the defense. Here, the government not only failed to warn, it affirmatively directed the pilot into the storm's most vicious cells."

Meredith spreads his arms and leans back. "I must agree with the prosecution on this one," he rules. "I heard the tape. This witness's instructions did not amount to a clearance to land. Even if they had, issuing a clearance is nothing but a grant of permission to use the runway. It doesn't require the pilot to land on that runway. The witness has it right. The pilot ulti-mately must decide whether to land or circle." Meredith points his finger at Isabel as if she needs reminding: "That doesn't mean the pilot was at fault here. I'm not addressing that issue. I'm only saying that unless more is shown, I can't allow the jury to consider the issue of negligence on the part of the government."

Unless more is shown? We have a controller who not only fails to warn Charlie of the storm but sends him straight into it. We have a controller who tells Charlie not to circle but to land. Unless more is shown? We're beaten on this issue. Diana spends the next hour with Frontera discussing procedures, workloads, stress, and breakdowns; but none of it matters.

Isabel wisely elects to forgo any further examination of Frontera; rather, she announces in her most dramatic voice: "The prosecution rests its case, Your Honor."

Diana springs to her feet. "The defense moves for a directed verdict. The prosecution has failed to put forward sufficient evidence for a reason-able jury to convict," Diana roars. "There's as much evidence of mechanical and weather problems as there is of pilot error!"

The courtroom falls into a hushed silence. I'm stuck to my chair, my muscles stiff. No air leaves my lungs.

"Denied," rules Meredith with disturbing speed. It's now our turn to call witnesses.

THE AIR SEEMS TO STIR AND whir ominously, but actually it's thick and stale, without movement. Danger has its own smell, its own distinctive set of signals. I am shadowed by a profound, merciless, gut-shaking fear—fueled by the dim lights, the low buzz, the highly official surroundings—which tramps beside me like an uninvited, hungry dog. Fear—the one permanent, indestructible part of our being—is immune to all education and reason.

It is my time to stand, take center stage, and tell the whole truth. My legs and arms are moving as they always do when I walk, but the sensation of movement isn't connecting with the appropriate neurons in my brain. I know I'm walking because the chair keeps coming closer, though it remains small and narrow.

I glance at Isabel, who's writing furiously. Questions for me, I'm sure. She couldn't know for certain if I'd testify, and probably figured—if I had the guts to speak for myself—I'd be the defense's last witness. That's why I'm turning common practice on its head and testifying as our first witness—to catch Isabel unprepared, which seems to have been accomplished.

It's not easy to talk. I breathe the way I do after running an hour on the basketball court. I have to calm down. Words are catching in my throat. My head is pounding, my vision's blurred. I sip water. I focus on Diana. I concentrate on what I did, why I did it. Gradually the sweat falling down my chest begins to dry. The words flow forth. At least for the moment, I'm okay. I'm glad I insisted on testifying. I'm glad Diana graciously yielded.

As close as brothers usually are, Charlie and I "were closer," I tell the jurors. We had an "unbreakable bond," we "never lied to each other," we "fought anyone who did harm" to the other. Charlie "swore on our daddy's grave" he'd "dump all his Seconal in the trash" and drop his prescription "forever." And, "true to his word," he did "exactly that." During the two months between his reinstatement and his crash, Charlie flew "all kinds of planes to all kinds of places at all times of day and night, through wind and rain, without one reported problem. Not one." For those two months, Charlie had been a model pilot. "No difficult landings, no dives, no crew members uttering a bad word."

I'm warming up. In a rush of controlled chaos, I chatter on about Charlie's "powerful attraction" to flying: "heroic missions" in Nam, "lives saved," a "religious-type experience." Isabel, surprisingly, doesn't object to my glorification of deeds done in years long past.

Diana slows me down. Deliberately, I'm sure. She asks me short, sharp questions that allow me to point out in exhausting detail the airline's flimsy evidence of Charlie's suspected drug use. Here's my chance to discuss the twelve sticking incidents with the J99's elevators. Here's where I again burst alive: "All of the airline's evidence against Charlie hinged on that one flight to Minneapolis. So, of course, I examined the logbook of that flight. Charlie himself had written in there that the elevators had stuck, and the mechanics on the ground confirmed it. I showed this very logbook to Philip and Roy Brooks. That's what convinced them to take another look at Charlie's termination. Not what I said, but the written records themselves!" I'm in high gear now. I extend the palms of my hands outward, nod my head, thrust out my shoulders. "Was it reckless for me under these circumstances to ask that Charlie's termination be further examined? To ask that those crew members who hadn't been interviewed be now given the chance to speak, and that the sticking problems with the elevators be studied, and that Jarrad be consulted? I didn't think so then, and I don't now."

Diana has me explain my investigation: my sources, my factual findings, my legal conclusions. I admit, without prompting, I hid the failed drug test. I was wrong, I say, but not reckless. Wrong from a purely abstract, ethical perspective, but not reckless to trust a brother I knew wouldn't lie to me. Not reckless to trust the airline's most outstanding pilot. "You must understand," I say somberly. "It had never been reckless to believe in Charlie before, and it wasn't then. I wasn't gambling on a stranger to do the right thing. I wasn't gambling at all. Charlie said he'd quit Seconal, and he did. Charlie had always been a man of his word, and then some. Anyone who'd spent a lifetime with Charlie would trust him with his life and not lose a minute's sleep over it."

Diana nods with a gentle smile, a signal to me, and the jurors, that she finds my last remark well put. She's apparently satisfied I've done all I can. She announces in a triumphant tone that she has "no further questions," then turns confidently to Isabel, declaring "your witness" as if it's purely to our advantage that Isabel cross-examine me.

Isabel won't play the role we have in mind for her—that of a defeated conqueror, who graciously comes to terms with a massive error in judgment. "Your brother lived in your house from right after the airline fired him until the day he died, didn't he?"

"Yes, he did."

"So you were right there with him, an eyewitness to his drug addiction?"

"He wasn't addicted," I correct her. "Like I said, he dropped his Seconal prescription."

"He dropped Seconal, and picked up phenobarbital instead, didn't he?" she comments with intended sarcasm, but in the form of a question to avoid it from being stricken as a gratuitous remark.

Diana, as expected, objects. "The witness cannot answer as to events that took place outside his presence and knowledge," she asserts.

Meredith is about to rule—probably to sustain the objection—when I declare: "I'll answer that question, Your Honor."

Meredith shoots a look at Diana, who, with a shrug of her shoulders, withdraws the objection. I'm on my own.

"I don't believe he took any phenobarbital knowingly," I say.

Isabel's eyebrows shoot up. "Do you actually think he was drugged?" she asks in a rising lilting, mocking voice meant to convey her stunned disbelief. I'm a fool, she's telling everyone with that voice. A desperate, paranoid, self-betraying fool.

"I do," I answer firmly. "Charlie, for one thing, was a creature of habit. He wasn't addicted to Seconal, but he'd gotten used to it. He wouldn't have switched to another drug just like that, and he wouldn't have dared take six hundred milligrams right before takeoff. Like I said, Charlie treasured flying, and he treasured people. He knew enough about barbiturates to know six hundred milligrams might kill him, and kill all his passengers. So it comes down to this: Either he was drugged or he was suicidal, and I know Charlie well enough to know he wouldn't ever kill himself on purpose. Especially not then. His spirits had been on the rise."

"Do you have any *actual proof* your brother was drugged?" she demands harshly.

"I just gave you actual proof. Charlie's character is all the proof—"

"No, I mean *real proof.* Like a witness who saw him being drugged, or an admission by the person who did it or arranged it. Anything like that?"

I lean forward. I raise my voice. "Do you remember what Charlie's doctor said? Phenobarbital can be put into a drink, and Seconal can't. That's why there was a switch in drugs."

"What *proof* do you have that phenobarbital was put into your brother's drink?"

"Philip Brandon was at the airport that night. That's something he's never himself told me even though he and I have discussed this crash a dozen times."

"Is it his duty to tell you—"

"Not his duty, no, but why would he hide that from me? And why would he specifically order that Charlie's plane not be deiced when all other planes were being deiced? Why—"

"Motion to strike!" yells Isabel. "Your Honor, stop this testimony!"

"I'll hear argument on this one," says Meredith. The jury is hurried out of their seats and led out the side door.

Isabel's cheeks are burning. "I'm absolutely appalled, Your Honor. This witness has deliberately told the jury things he knows aren't admissible! He knows it! He just snuck it in, that's the only way I can describe it. What nonsense, Your Honor! He's testifying to some bizarre, made-up fantasy when he claims Philip Brandon ordered that Charlie Ashmore's plane not be deiced. There's not one shred of evidence of that," Isabel storms. "It's objectionable as rank speculation, and if Mr. Ashmore claims he heard it somewhere, then it's hearsay."

Diana stands and with a sweep of her arms declares: "This witness and I were told by Eddie Perez, the lead mechanic at La Guardia for Brandon Air Lines, that Philip Brandon ordered him not to deice Charlie's plane." I hear a loud grunt behind me, see a frown crossing Meredith's face. "Not only is this evidence highly relevant, these statements by Eddie Perez were admissions against interest, thereby making them exceptions to the hearsay rule."

"Your Honor," pleads Isabel, "the prosecution has no way to determine the truth of all this because Eddie Perez is dead. If he were alive, I might agree that such statements fall within one of the hearsay rule's exceptions, but here the confusion is compounded by Eddie Perez's drinking-related car crash, which, unfortunately, killed him. We've got highly unreliable and highly prejudicial hearsay evidence from a now dead witness who can't be cross-examined. The prosecution can't find out from Eddie Perez himself *if* he ever made these sensational allegations, if he was drinking at the time he supposedly made them, if he had a grudge against Philip Brandon of some kind, why he spoke to defense counsel, and so on."

Meredith nods. "I can't allow it in unless you have some corroborating evidence, Ms. Wells. It's too inflammatory and too shaky." Meredith turns to the bailiff. "Bring the jury back in."

The jurors take their seats and await instructions. All their eyes are on the man in black robes. "You are instructed to disregard all testimony from this witness about any orders to deice or not deice the plane of Captain Ashmore." The black-robed figure turns to Isabel and motions her to proceed.

"It is your understanding, isn't it, that Seconal is a highly addictive drug?"

"Objection! Calls for expert testimony," Diana yells out.

"I'm asking for his understanding, Your Honor. Not for an expert opinion."

"Overruled. Witness may answer."

"I'm not a doctor," I say, following Diana's lead. "I don't know if it's addictive for some and not others, or if it's addictive at certain levels and not others. I do know, though, that Charlie stopped taking it."

"If you didn't know if Seconal was addictive or not, how could you have recommended Charlie be rehired?"

I stop. I think. She's cleverly using my words against me. I've followed Diana's lead into quicksand. "I knew he'd quit," I answer.

"How could you know he'd quit if you didn't know whether the drug was addictive?"

"Like I said, I knew Charlie. That was enough."

"You mean the Charlie who failed the drug test and the Charlie who was found dead with a massive amount of barbiturates in his body? That's the Charlie you mean?" she shouts at me.

"Objection! She's badgering the witness!"

"That wasn't meant to be a question, was it, Ms. Castino? Objection sustained."

Isabel keeps her eyes on me. "Sir, did you consult any medical specialists, or do any research on your own to determine if your brother could achieve what he'd promised?"

"I didn't need to," I reply. Maybe I didn't want to consult anyone. Maybe

I wanted so much to believe in Charlie, to end his suffering without further delay, that I refused on a conscious level to consider the possibility that Charlie couldn't be trusted.

"Did you or didn't you?" she barks.

"No, I didn't," I say as calmly as I can. I breathe deeply, and remind myself I'm being watched. A witness who loses his temper doesn't help himself.

"When you conducted your investigation into Charlie's fitness to fly, were you acting as the airline's lawyer?"

I must be careful here. Diana has already argued I was acting as counsel to the airline; I can't contradict her without one of us losing credibility with the jury. Anyway, I'm no longer sure what I told Philip would be my role. I said I'd be impartial, protect the overall interests of the airline; beyond that, everything's fuzzy. I look up at Isabel. "To be perfectly candid, I was acting as counsel for both parties. The Disciplinary Rules permit a lawyer to represent adverse parties when those parties are not in litigation, and they give their full and informed consent to such representation. I had such consent from both parties. Moreover, at the time I was looking into Charlie's termination, the parties were not in a dispute in the classic sense, but were parties with a mutual interest, each seeking to find the truth, and once found, to make a decision based upon that truth."

"Truth?" she roars with deliberate amusement. "So that's why you hid the failed drug test?"

"At the time, I was certain Charlie was okay. I still believe he was okay," I assert with conviction.

"I'm sure none of the dead would agree with you if they could speak."

"Charlie was doing fine until the controller directed him into the worst of the storm," I contend fiercely.

"Move to strike, Your—"

"He was doing fine until the plane iced up and—"

"Move to strike! Move to strike!" shrieks Isabel.

"Sustained!" Meredith shouts over the din. "This witness isn't qualified to speculate on the cause of the crash. Disregard everything he said about the controller, about the ice, about all of it!" Meredith turns and scowls at me. "You're a trial lawyer," he admonishes me. "You know better."

"For once, I sympathize with Mr. Ashmore," says Isabel loudly. "He doesn't know better. That's why he's here now. He's too arrogant to know better."

"That's enough from you, Ms. Castino!" Meredith's anger has shifted from witness to prosecutor. "In another minute I'm going to hold the whole lot of you in contempt, so help me God!"

A moment of silence, followed by a chorus of apologies. None of us wants to go to jail. Meredith nods with disgust. He knows we wouldn't give him the time of day if he didn't have those robes.

Isabel is ready to resume. "You said earlier your brother had a powerful attraction to flying ever since Vietnam, so powerful it was like a religious experience, is that right?"

"Yes," I say cautiously. I think I know where she's going. Charlie, she'll try to imply, was loony about flying, so loony that maybe he'd want to die while in his plane.

"Are you familiar with the term 'fatal attraction'?"

"I am."

"Are you also familiar with what's known as traumatic stress syndrome, an affliction that's caused much mental suffering and instability among men who saw combat in Vietnam?"

Diana warned me not to speak about Nam for this very reason. Yet I couldn't resist praising Charlie in the midst of this storm of condemnation. "Yes, I know what it is, but Charlie didn't have it, if that's what you're getting at. He had no so-called fatal attractions either. I guarantee you have not one iota of proof to the contrary."

"Motion to strike again, Your Honor. This witness is deliberately and improperly answering more than I'm asking."

I listen grimly as Meredith wearily tells the jurors to disregard my last remarks about the prosecution having no "proof." I can't risk any more sustained motions to strike.

"Your brother did find flying to be a *religious-type* experience, didn't he? And didn't he have a powerful attraction to—"

"He wasn't crazy!" I shout. "He loved being a pilot, that's all I meant. For God's sake, does loving your work mean you're crazy?"

"Loving a daughter that's dead, loving a wife who's just divorced you, loving a drug that makes you a zombie, that could make you crazy, couldn't it?"

I shake my head, fold my arms. She's gone too far. "All you've got is speculation piled upon innuendo," I rant. "This is a sad day for justice, isn't it? Using a man's misfortune to condemn him for a crime he didn't commit!"

Meredith glares at me, but I'm glad I said it.

"We're not condemning him for any crime, sir. In case you haven't noticed, you're the one on trial, not him. You're the one who committed a crime."

"WE'VE GOT TO put up or shut up now, don't we?" groans Diana with a shudder. "If we can't link Brandon in any way to this crash, Isabel will tear us apart in her closing."

Anger, worry, grief: They all have their hold on Diana as she paces with a rigid persistence up and down the living room floor. I ache from watching her torture herself. "I should have stuck to my guns," she claims, as if she could have stopped me from testifying if only she had been more firm. She stops, then points an ex-prosecutor's finger at me: "It's one thing to tell me Charlie was drugged, but something else to swear to it in front of God and country when we've got no proof. None, Michael," she cries. "Why on earth would Brandon drug one of his own pilots?"

Diana still has friends at the U.S. Attorney's office in New York who work with FBI agents who in turn know ex-agents we can hire. It's a roundabout route that takes us past Friday midnight. We don't go to sleep until we've hired a team of three ex-agents who promise to begin work at first light.

We wait for their call, which comes forty-six hours later.

"We've pulled all the strings we can," Tommy, the lead ex-agent, reports by phone in his thick Brooklyn accent. "We've checked every prescription for phenobarbital sold in the New York and D.C. areas for the two weeks before the crash, and the name Philip Brandon doesn't pop up on any screens."

Nothing in Brandon's background rings bells, explains Tommy. Brandon has led the usual life of an ambitious businessman. "I guess what we're saying is, Brandon's got no motive to down this plane. None. In fact, just the opposite. The only people we figure got a motive here is some crazy white guy who hates black people or some anti-American nut."

Maybe, I think, there was nothing sinister about Philip's presence at La Guardia that night. Maybe, as he said, he's not in the habit of volunteering information, or maybe he was uneasy about having been at the "crime scene," observing Charlie and spotting nothing.

"Nobody saw Brandon with Charlie at the airport," Tommy sums up.

"All we could come up with was a fight of some kind a few gates from where Charlie's flight took off. But Charlie wasn't involved."

It's midnight, but I call Jim McKinney anyway, something I wouldn't do in more civilized times. Everyone else has ruled out the possibility of a bomb, but no one knows planes like McKinney does. No one's as honest either.

McKinney is surprisingly affable for one so rudely awakened, but his voice reflects his fatigue. "I know you don't trust Brandon anymore," McKinney says dully, "and frankly, I don't either, but what you said in court seems kind of way out. Brandon drugging one of his pilots? C'mon, Michael. He's a bastard, yes, but he's not nuts. And why would he put a bomb on the plane if he was already drugging the pilot?"

"Forget Brandon. Could *anyone* have put a bomb—"

"If it was a bomb, the pilot would've had no time to talk to the tower. When TWA exploded off of Long Island, the pilot said not a word about trouble. There was no time. The bomb hits, it's over. You hear a loud noise, then no more tape. Same with Pan Am Flight one zero three. Both had their tapes go off within one second of the blast. Here we've got the pilot talking about a storm, we've got a plane in heavy winds, then it goes down. That sound like a bomb to you?"

"This plane dropped mighty fast, Jim. Seven seconds. You said so yourself. The TWA flight lasted twenty-four seconds after the explosion."

"With TWA you had eyewitnesses saying they saw the plane bursting apart from a fireball. You had ground radar tracking one plane, then tracking dozens of pieces of wreckage. Nothing like that here. And with TWA, the debris in the ocean showed an explosion occurred in the forward cargo, blowing the suitcases out even before the nose separated from the fuselage. The TWA's front landing gear had damage that could've come only from a huge blast inside the plane."

"But the corpses, they were so mutilated. I saw them."

"I read the reports. Their flesh wasn't shredded the way it would've been had a bomb exploded. No chemical burns on their skin either. And don't forget, TWA went down in clear weather."

"Their flesh looked shredded to me."

"What you saw was impact damage." McKinney pauses. "I'm sorry, Michael, but it wasn't a bomb, and nobody drugged the pilot. What you've got is turbulence and maybe a bad plane. Why did you go off on this thing about Brandon drugging the pilot?"

I say nothing, but don't hang up. I sense he has more to say. I sense it from the frustration in his voice.

"I thought you knew, Michael. That Castino woman had dozens of FBI and CIA people out at the site. People in forensics, explosives, counterterrorism. The State Department went through all their databases of known and suspected terrorists and got nowhere. All the baggage matched up with passenger IDs. Castino had all the experts working on it, and they came up empty. I thought you knew."

I did know. Isabel had told me, though not in this detail. I suppose I can't believe nothing extraordinary happened to cause Charlie's plane to crash. "Plastic explosives," I say. "D.C. National can't detect synthetic bombs." Even as I seek to exonerate Charlie, I'm seized by this horrifying image of Charlie refusing to pull the yoke, his left thumb pushing down the electric switch in a suicidal plunge to the earth. But would Charlie—whose pride wouldn't allow him to accept being fired—have deliberately crashed his plane, the ultimate badge of dishonor for a pilot?

"Good night, Michael." I hear the phone click. Even loyal friends like Jim McKinney are coming to sense a craziness in me they wish to escape.

What's happening to me? I shiver as I lay down the phone. Am I losing all sense of reality? What happened to Charlie up there? What happened to Daddy?

AN INCH ABOVE six feet, thin-boned with short, grayish hair and dark-rimmed glasses, David Evans could easily be mistaken for a university professor or high school librarian if not for his silk Armani suit, his Gucci tie, and the maroon handkerchief tucked neatly into his jacket pocket. His slightly crooked teeth are stained a pale yellow from the coffee and tobacco Diana politely warns him to avoid. "When you've got nobody, and got nothing, the hell with denying yourself the few shitty little pleasures you do have," Evans barks at her, yet he covers his mouth filled with crowns and bridges whenever his lips part into a faint smile, as if unabashed displays of joy are inappropriate for one in his pitiful condition. Diana, though, quickly yields. She wants Evans in good spirits. She wants Evans to like her.

Evans takes his place in the witness chair. Three security officers place on the floor beside him a painstakingly accurate twelve-foot-by-five-foot reproduction of the J99. As rehearsed, Evans explains the functions of the plane's various parts. This is slow going but necessary if the jurors are to comprehend the significance of the elevators and stabilizers. Next into the courtroom comes a replica of the manually operated stabilizer wheel. The wheel must be turned nine times, says Evans, to move the stabilizers one degree.

Diana, ready to get to the core issues, steps closer to Evans and inquires: "Did you speak to Roy Brooks about the J Ninety-nine's elevators?"

"Brooks called me about it. He'd been through the logbooks and found twelve incidents of sticking. He talked about one flight that almost crashed because of it." Evans apparently knows what to say, and seems to enjoy saying it. I'm breathing well. My heart's beating normally.

"Was that a flight to Minneapolis?"

"I believe it was, yes." He has the right amount of hesitation in his voice, as if he'd not been rehearsed.

"What makes you recall he spoke of twelve incidents of sticking? Not eleven, not thirteen, but twelve?" Diana wants to pound home that number twelve. It shows Philip to be a liar, and proves I had a reasonable basis to believe Charlie wasn't at fault for the Minneapolis flight's dive.

"A few times Brooks used the word 'dozen' instead of twelve. I joked once and called it the 'dirty dozen' after the movie because I was saying how this was a dirty business. That's how I remember."

"Why did you say this was a dirty business?"

"Don't get me started," Evans laughs lightly.

"I want to hear all the dirty details," Diana says playfully. The jurors smile. Diana, I think, has them in her grip.

"Okay," Evans says as if readying to aim a lethal weapon. "It's a dirty business because profit's king and safety's not even second. Because when I met with our engineers after getting Brooks's call, they told me they didn't like the trim limit at four point four, and never did. They wanted three point five. The salespeople thought they could sell it easier with a higher trim limit, but the engineers never liked it. A lot of them were also worried about using the stabilizers in turbulence. So I told our CEO about it. I told him we needed to make changes."

"Why did your engineers want to lower the trim limit?"

Evans gathers himself the way one does before uttering the first words of a long speech. "With one press of the button, and in a matter of seconds, a pilot could at four point four drastically change the plane's attitude. The margin for error is unacceptably high. Obviously Jarrad came to agree with me at some point," he says, referring to Bulletin 97–815. "By that time, though, I was dead and gone."

"Dead and gone?"

"Fired," he clarifies. "Sometimes I wish I was really dead and gone."

"Why were you fired?"

"For insisting on the very changes they later made in the Bulletin."

Diana nods. "Tell us why the engineers didn't want the stabilizers used at all in turbulence," she urges gently.

"Extreme gusts and drafts cause rapid changes in airspeed and attitude," explains Evans. "Any updraft or downdraft that tempts the pilot to change trim might reverse itself in seconds. If trim has been applied to the first draft, then the second draft, which will likely be in the opposite direction, will exaggerate the out-of-trim condition."

"So the elevators should always be used in turbulence?"

"Always."

"Did Jarrad conduct any test flights to determine the effect of moving the stabilizers electrically in turbulence or, to take it another step, to determine the effect of moving them all the way to four point four degrees in turbulence?"

"Not when I was there. But I'm sure they did after the crash. It was too late by then for some people," he says caustically, but seemingly with a perverse satisfaction.

"At the time you made your recommendations to Jarrad, what would it have cost Jarrad to put in a safety stop at three point five degrees?"

"About a thousand dollars per plane. Not much when you consider that Jarrad makes billions of dollars a year."

Diana wants to finish strong. She wants the jurors to remember Jarrad could have made the J99 safer for corporate pocket change. "Nothing further, Your Honor," she booms out.

"That'll do it for today," pronounces a weary Meredith six minutes after three o'clock, nearly two full hours before the usual adjournment time. I suppress the urge to slam my fist against the table. Why has Meredith picked this day to stop early? Isabel will now have an entire evening to prepare her cross-examination; and she'll have help. Nine representatives from Jarrad—officers, engineers, lawyers—are in the courtroom, all of whom will certainly provide questions to Isabel.

I wait until we are safely in my car, the doors and windows locked, before

I say: "Something's troubling me. Didn't the FAA review detailed drawings and specifications, then run their own standard tests before approving the J Ninety-nine's design? Why didn't anyone at the FAA say anything? I asked Evans about that, and he told me the FAA guy responsible for giving the J Ninety-nine final approval now works for Jarrad."

"Leave it alone." Diana waves her hand at me. "If we attack the FAA's certification, the jury will learn the FAA reviewed the design and put its stamp on it. On balance, that will do us more harm than good. My guess is the jurors now have some real suspicions about the plane's condition, but if they learn a government agency made up of aviation experts approved the design after running all the necessary tests, they'd be damn reluctant to overrule those experts." Diana's speech is picking up fury. "So what if somebody in the FAA joined Jarrad later on? That's not so unusual, is it? They're in the same industry. And don't even think about calling the FAA guy as a witness. He'll be in the chair for two days with charts up to his eyeballs explaining why the plane was okay, is okay, and always will be okay."

"Consider it dropped," I sigh, disappointed she won't explore the possibility of a wider, more sinister conspiracy. But haven't I already led us down too many dark, twisting paths that promised light but ended with sneak attacks that bloodied our cause?

EVANS IS SHAKEN from the start. Isabel produces two years of poor evaluations signed off by Jarrad's CEO and Evans himself. Apparently Evans was spending more time with his family than the company found acceptable, a deficiency Evans seemed unwilling to correct. "Nobody ever said I'd be fired," Evans advances lamely, the damning evaluations in his sweating hands. His prior testimony that his complaints about the J99 caused his demise at Jarrad has been put into question.

"Weren't there engineers at Jarrad who believed the four point four limit was okay?"

"Yes," admits Evans reluctantly.

"In fact, weren't Jarrad's engineers split pretty evenly about whether to lower the four point four limit?"

"I think more wanted the lower limit," he says hesitantly, "but I didn't exactly take a head count."

Isabel asks if he understood the rationale for the 4.4-degree limit, and Evans, wishing to appear knowledgeable, nicely argues the case for the higher limit. "If a plane was at a high altitude, and an emergency arose requiring the pilot to get the plane down as fast as possible, he could trim it to four point four electrically without having to turn the wheel nine times."

Isabel nods approvingly. Then, in an accusatory tone, inquires: "You flew here all the way from California, didn't you?"

"Yes."

"The defense paid for your flight here, didn't they?"

"Yes."

"And your hotel?"

"Yes."

"You were aware, weren't you, that the plane you flew here was a Jarrad Ninety-nine?"

"Yes." Evans nods. "But it was the only flight I could get on."

"But you did get on it, didn't you?"

"I held my breath, though," Evans adds, but no one smiles. The jurors' faces are cool.

"Held your breath, sir? Isn't it true that other than Flight five five five, no J Ninety-nine has ever crashed?"

"Not to my knowledge, no."

Isabel is on her game today. "Sir, if it would have been so inexpensive for Jarrad to put in the safety stops at three point five degrees, wouldn't you then agree that Jarrad had no economic motive for not doing so, and therefore decided not to do it for reasons other than cost?"

"I don't know." Evans shrugs. "You might be right."

"Let's talk for a moment about that one crash, okay? You're aware, aren't you, the stabilizers found in the wreckage were at their full nose-down position of four point four degrees?"

"Yes, I am."

"Impact damage could not have caused that circumstance, correct?"

Evans nods. "The pilot had to have moved the stabilizers to the four point four position himself."

"You are a licensed pilot yourself, aren't you?"

"Yes, I am."

"As a licensed pilot and as an aviation engineer, you would agree, would you not, that the primary control of an airplane's attitude—that is, the plane's positioning, up, level, or down—is not the stabilizers but the elevators?"

"That's correct."

"A pilot who encounters turbulence should first use his elevators to control the plane's attitude?"

"Yes."

"Always?"

"Always."

"Is this a pretty basic thing that all pilots know?"

"It's pretty basic."

"Isn't this why Jarrad didn't believe a warning about using the stabilizers in turbulence was necessary?"

"You'll have to speak to people at Jarrad about that. What I can tell you is, there's no harm in a warning. Some pilots use only their elevators to control attitude, some use elevators and stabilizers. I wanted to alert the pilots of the J Ninety-nine to use only the elevators in turbulence, no matter what."

"But in controlling attitude, especially in turbulence, no rational pilot would use only the stabilizers and not touch the elevators, correct?"

"I would hope not."

"On the J Ninety-nine, the pilot must manually push back and forth on the yoke to get the elevators to move, correct?"

"Yes."

Isabel hands Evans a chart prepared by Jarrad employees having several colored lines, dozens of numbers, and a second-by-second analysis of the elevators' and stabilizers' movement during Flight 555's final ninety seconds. "By looking at this chart, can you determine whether the pilot moved the elevators during the final ninety seconds of flight?"

Diana objects. The chart hasn't been identified, authenticated, or shown to be an accurate reflection of the events it purports to depict. Isabel contends she's not seeking to admit the chart into evidence but merely to ask questions based upon its information. Meredith allows her to continue.

"If the chart is correct—and I don't know if it is, but if it is," cautions Evans, "then the pilot did not move the elevators during the last ninety seconds of flight, and moved the stabilizers to their full nose-down position. Following the chart, I see the plane nosedived and crashed."

"If the chart is correct, do you have an opinion as to the pilot's actions?"

"He had to be drunk or something," opines Evans with a nonchalance that belies the devastating impact of his words. "He had the attitude indicator right in front of him. That would have told him he was going into a dive. You would think, at that point, he would have used the elevators to counteract the situation. On the J Ninety-nine, like most planes, it takes only one quarter of the elevator power to counteract even this extreme out-of-trim condition."

"In other words, if the pilot had used the elevators, he wouldn't have gotten into this trouble?"

"Assuming the chart is accurate, I would tend to agree. But I don't know exactly how bad the storm was, so I can't say if using the elevators would have definitely averted the crash, but I can say it was suicidal not to use them at all."

Isabel shows Evans a readout of the flight data recorder, which Evans examines and compares to Jarrad's chart. "Does the chart accurately reflect the data from the flight recorder?"

"It does."

"Have you now any reason to believe Jarrad's chart is not accurate?"

"No."

"Do you now firmly believe the pilot erred by not using the elevators under the circumstances reflected by the flight recorder?"

"Yes, I do." With the word "suicidal" still echoing around the courtroom, Isabel returns to her chair. By all accounts, our star witness has been an utter debacle.

WE MAKE THE headlines again. DEFENSE WITNESS CALLS PILOT SUICIDAL, proclaims the *Post*. Evans's crucial testimony about the dangers of the 4.4 trim limit is hardly mentioned. One editorial links Klemmer's comparison of phenobarbital to alcohol with Evans's "he had to be drunk" testimony.

I'm livid with Evans, who apparently felt a need, however unconscious, to reconcile with his old employer. I want to nail Jarrad. "How many sticking incidents have there been since Charlie's crash? When? Where? What kind of weather? What does Jarrad think is causing it? Has Jarrad reported these problems to the FAA? We need to know," I rant.

Diana won't yield this time. "No witnesses from Jarrad. They'll say the design and construction were flawless and exceeded the highest industry standards. They'll tell us how good their engineers were and are, how many awards they've won, how many tests they ran, and on and on. They'll be waving Jarrad's flag in the jury's face hour after hour, and we won't have time to absorb the new mountains of documents they'll give us. We'll be gasping for air."

It seems we've hit rock bottom until I read on page six the airline has moved in the civil case to dissolve the stay it earlier requested. Randy is quoted: "We intend to file our motion for summary judgment as soon as the stay is lifted. A hundred years of well-settled law says no company can be held liable for the criminal acts of its employees. All the credible evidence points to suicide, and suicide is a criminal act. Here, especially. Suicide, under these circumstances, meant murder too."

Lockwood hasn't yet brought me into the civil case. I figure he wants the jurors to be forced to choose between the victims and the airline. Throw me into the mix and the jurors have a way out; they can let the airline off the hook without feeling they've screwed the victims. The airline's cavernously deep pocket is all that stands between me and a multi hundred-million-dollar lawsuit.

Having few stopping points, a trial affords little time for whining or fretting about past mistakes. New witnesses must be prepared, documents reviewed again, strategy constantly redefined. I drop the newspaper in the trash. We must take some risks. Things are getting desperate.

Directing his ruthless, game-day stare straight at Diana, Roy Brooks seems possessed by the commonly felt outrage of the falsely accused; but I suspect his tightened fists and reddening face are all part of an elaborate pretense. Witnesses seized by genuine bursts of emotion are rarely so cagey. Roy is dropping enough seeds of truth to protect against a hurricane assault from his blind side while adroitly denying all wrongdoing. Yes, he spoke to his boss about the J99's elevators, but "only because Michael raised it" as a problem. "Michael was our lawyer," Roy explains. "We weren't going to simply ignore his concerns."

Yes, he talked to Jarrad about the elevators, but "only out of an abundance of caution," never himself believing a problem existed. Sure he mentioned the Minneapolis flight to Evans, but "only to be absolutely thorough" and "investigate every detail to the max." Jarrad, he adds, "followed up" with "a ton of tests" and found "everything to be okay."

Roy admits learning of the "twelve sticking incidents" from me, but can't recall if the logbooks contained notes corroborating my allegations. "I can't imagine anyone in our organization altering any documents, especially ones relating to safety issues," Roy piously observes. "That's why I'm pretty certain the logbooks never had anything about elevators. I didn't need to look at logbooks back then. I just took what Michael said and ran with it. I've done that before with Michael. Wasn't anything out of the ordinary."

He's not denying outright the logbooks once had notes of sticking elevators. He's leaving himself some wiggle room in case we have something; we don't.

"Keep in mind it was Michael who had possession of the logbooks up until the day he was arrested. If anybody was in a position to alter anything, it was Michael, not us."

NOBODY'S LISTENING. THE jurors are looking at Rod Hansen with glassy eyes, the reporters aren't writing, and Meredith, his head dropping every few seconds, is struggling to stay alert. Evans's infamous "suicidal" testimony seems to have made all other comments marginal.

Hansen's doing well. Without the slightest hesitation the dispatcher is asserting that Charlie asked cogent questions about weather reports, flight paths, and crew members. "If he had drugs in him, you'd never know it," he concludes with believable candor. On cross-examination, Hansen admits he's not trained to diagnose drug users, but adds: "Having grown up in the South Bronx, I know one when I see one," managing to evoke a few light chuckles from those glassy-eyed jurors.

We need to hit the drug issue hard. Hansen is followed by Cliff Morgan, a nationally renowned psychiatrist whose specialty is treating the richest among us with drug addictions. Morgan projects a convincing sincerity when he says the "Seconal in Captain Ashmore's body as shown by the failed drug test wasn't sufficiently significant to impair most pilots from flying," implying I wasn't as reckless as the prosecution would have the jurors believe. Morgan isn't as confident about Charlie's ability to fly with six hundred milligrams of phenobarbital in him, but he does the best he can. "It's very possible—given his coherent communications, the coffee, his on-the-mark flight path, and the absence of any comment from his copilot about a piloting problem—that the phenobarbital simply hadn't taken yet. Maybe it would have in another five minutes or five hours, but people react differently to different drugs, especially when they're involved in an activity that keeps their adrenaline flowing."

Isabel gets nowhere with Morgan. After learning Morgan has given testimony "only twice" previously, Isabel inquires why he has testified "so few times," implying that Morgan, if he were truly an expert, would have been called upon to testify with more regularity. With raised eyebrows and perfect timing, Morgan replies: "Because I only testify when I'm doing a public service. I don't need the money." At six hundred an hour, Morgan is worth it.

We go from it wasn't drugs to it was cold, rainy, and turbulent. Donna Hume, who's worked as a meteorologist for the government, an airline, and

CBS news, opines that the turbulence was "intense enough" to cause the crash.

"The surrounding cumulus thunderclouds were unusually dense and well defined and took the shape of rising mounds resembling cauliflowers. That's the most dangerous configuration of all, and the controller should've seen that."

"Was there wind shear at or around the area where Flight five five five began its dive?"

"Based on my analysis, I estimate the wind shear to have been thirty to forty knots and to have changed directions four times in a thirty-second period. It caused Flight five five five to increase in speed, pitch upward, then dive."

"Was this the sort of weather that could cause icing?"

"Perfect weather for icing. On takeoff, it was thirty degrees at La Guardia and sleeting lightly. An hour later at D.C. National, it was down to twenty-eight at ground level. At three thousand feet, it was nineteen degrees."

"And icing could cause the elevators to stick?"

"It could, yes."

I know it won't go so easily for Hume on cross-examination. Like other expert witnesses, she inevitably reaches conclusions favorable to the party paying her considerable fees so she'll be asked to testify at trial, enriching herself further. Hume needs the money. She's a single mother with three kids in private schools. Her ex-husband stopped making court-ordered child payments two months after the divorce was final; he "vanished," Hume tells me, "to somewhere in Arizona" with his new family and got an unlisted number.

"I can't even get laid," Hume confesses the night before she's to battle Isabel. She's happily sipping gin, but her bitterness is steady. "Used to be a girl could get laid if she wanted to. Now with AIDS and herpes and all the other stuff, it's not that easy. They want an AIDS test. They want to know who you're screwing now, and who you've screwed the last ten years. And if they're serious about you, they want to know if your ex is paying child support. It's a bitch. I can't find a decent guy to screw me."

She's always tired, she whines on. She routinely reviews her trio's homework, prepares them for their tests, edits their essays, figures ways to solve their math problems. "They say I yell too much, laugh too little. They would, too, if they had my life. I'm always late, always in a hurry. Wears me out." She admits to blaming every glass of gin, every high-pitched scream, every disintegration into tears, on her low-life bastard of an ex-husband. Friends, she says, have recently come to call her Rain because she's always predicting the worst will happen.

She makes me nervous. She's desperate, strung-out, needy—not the sort of traits that inspire confidence. Of course, she's ours now; there's no time to find someone else. When we interviewed her six weeks ago, she mentioned none of these problems. She was all business, all confidence, all focused.

The morning brings Isabel in cheerful possession of the sharp, cynical tone she regularly uses to undermine a witness's confidence. "You're not an aviation engineer, are you?" Isabel inquires of Hume, her slightly raised upper lip reflecting an undisguised contempt.

"No."

"You're in no way qualified to give opinions about airplanes, to speak on what makes them go or not go, correct?"

"I'm an expert on weather, that's all."

"Expert on weather or not, you don't know of your own personal knowledge that Flight five five five had icing problems immediately before or during its last flight, do you?"

"No."

"You don't know if the elevators stuck or froze, do you?"

"No, I don't."

"In fact, even had there been ice on the elevators, that doesn't necessarily mean they froze up, does it?"

"Not necessarily."

"And even had they frozen up, it doesn't necessarily mean that caused this flight to crash, does it?"

"I really don't know," Hume confesses.

"Then, for all your testimony about clouds and rain and wind shear, you don't know for certain what caused this crash, do you?"

Hume gathers herself. "The weather conditions were such that it's reasonable to believe they caused or contributed to the crash," she answers mechanically.

"But you have no personal knowledge that these weather conditions in fact caused the crash, do you?"

"No."

"All the planes coming into D.C. National at the same time as Flight five five five had the same weather to contend with, didn't they?"

"In general, yes. But I believe Flight five five five went through the worst of the turbulence given where it was when it was."

"Are you aware, Ms. Hume, that the pilot of Flight five five five took a lethal or nearly lethal dose of phenobarbital immediately prior to the flight?"

"Yes," she says quietly.

"And that during the turbulence he put the stabilizers into the full nose-down position?"

"I've been told that."

"You wouldn't rule out pilot error as a cause of this crash, would you?"

"I wouldn't rule anything out or in. I just know the winds were very fierce. Whether that caused the crash or something else did, only God knows."

"THEY'RE GOING TO fire me," McKinney confides. "Brandon said if I testify . . ."

"About the elevators?" I fill in.

"About anything that might hurt the airline in the civil case," he says, the words coming slow and tight. "Or about Sexton."

"Sexton?"

McKinney nods solemnly. "Sexton told me the elevators on the Minneapolis flight probably did stick. Everything happened so fast, I think he kind of froze up—"

"Like the elevators." I can't resist a straight line.

McKinney smiles. "Yeah, like the elevators. He's not going back on what he said about Charlie being drowsy and all, but he thinks Charlie's adrenaline kicked in when the plane got in trouble." He stops, peers at me. "This all helps you, doesn't it?"

Sure it helps. It shows the J99s do have a tendency to ice up and their elevators to freeze; it shows Charlie could do heroic things even if, as Sexton alleges, he was on drugs; it offers further proof that the logbooks were altered; and it supports our contention that Charlie didn't cause that Minneapolis flight to dive, and I wasn't reckless to have him reinstated.

"Will Sexton talk to me?" I ask in a tone that implies he must.

"He won't help you if he can't get immunity. He's worried he might get prosecuted for perjury since he sort of implied the dive was Charlie's fault. He's also worried he broke some laws by not reporting the elevator malfunction to the FAA."

We sit in the massive living room built as a monument to my immortality but which now resembles a graveyard where yellowing papers are stored in rows like corpses in a field. Diana's on the phone with pilots she's lining up as witnesses. McKinney and I are alone in every sense of the word—physically, spiritually, emotionally. It's hard for me to ask him to surrender everything for a man he knows only as the company's ex-lawyer; and it's hard for him to walk away from a dying man crying out for help. We're at each other's mercy.

"I can't give him immunity," I say with a soft groan.

"He knows that. Diana will have to get it from Castino."

"If she can't?"

"He'll deny he ever spoke to me."

"Bastard," I mutter.

"He feels real bad about this," McKinney defends him. "He says he didn't mean to get Charlie fired, but he had to report what he saw. By the time you met with Sexton, Brandon had already laid down the law: Say nothing about the elevators."

I'm sorry I called him a bastard. Sexton will likely lose his job if he testifies, and it sounds like he'll make that sacrifice if he's guaranteed he'll avoid prison.

"Sexton hasn't slept well since the crash. Charlie complained about the elevators the moment the J Ninety-nine went out of control, but Sexton wasn't sure at the time if Charlie was just using that as an excuse. He's heard enough now to know Charlie meant it. Funny, what convinced Sexton at the time that Charlie had to be drugged was the way Charlie recovered the plane. Charlie never broke a sweat. Sexton figured no human could be that cool under fire without being under sedation of some sort. Sexton said his heart was about to break through his skin, and there was Charlie with no emotion on his face at all."

ISABEL WON'T GRANT immunity to Sexton. "Immunity's not candy," she tells Diana, "not something you give out because somebody nice wants it."

I'm steaming. If Sexton were ready to say that Charlie was popping pills every five minutes, he'd get his immunity along with a few pats on the back. Victory apparently means more to Isabel than truth. Victory tells her she has nothing to gain and much to lose by shielding Sexton. Victory can be cruel.

McKinney, though, is still game. He sits with the bearing of a general about to address his troops. His shoulders are straight, his head erect, his jaw jutted slightly forward. He tells the jurors his "explanation" of what happened: "With all the cold and sleet, the plane iced up either at La Guardia or in the air, but somewhere before it hit that storm." So far, so good, I think. McKinney's laying the right foundation. "Why did it ice up? Maybe it wasn't properly deiced at La Guardia, or maybe it was but still iced up in flight. The J Ninety-nine's elevators have a history of icing up."

"What is the significance of the elevators icing up?" Diana asks.

"If they freeze, they stick. They don't work." McKinney turns to me with a somber yet fond look that signals the jurors he wholeheartedly endorses our theory of the crash. He's risking a glorious career for me. Honor means something to this man. "So the plane hit turbulence, and pitched upward. Being the top-notch pilot Charles Ashmore was, he applied the elevators, but they were stuck, so he pushed the stabilizers all the way down. Then they stuck too. The position of the forty-inch jackscrew shows the stabilizers were moved to their full nose-down position by the pilot and not reversed prior to impact."

Beautifully put, I think. In the tradition of our finest trial lawyers, McKinney has taken our adversary's strongest evidence and used it against them. The stabilizers were nose-down because the elevators didn't work. They stayed nose-down because they, too, came to stick. A beautiful summation, a beautiful end to a twenty-six-year career.

Isabel must know the importance of destroying McKinney piece by piece. The jurors seem to have returned to life. McKinney's explanation gives them a plausible basis on which to find in my favor.

Isabel steps toward McKinney. Her eyes are predictably narrow and cold. "Do you, sir, know what speculation means?"

"It means to predict, to guess."

"Exactly. To guess. And guessing isn't the same as knowing, is it?"

"Of course not."

"When you said the plane 'iced up,' you were speculating, weren't you?"

"It was a reasonable guess."

"But you didn't see it ice up?"

"No."

"No one told you it iced up?"

"No."

"No hard data of any kind recorded that it iced up?"

"No."

"That's what I mean by speculation," Isabel booms out. "You also said the pilot tried to use the elevators, but they were stuck, and then he pushed down the stabilizers, and they stuck. All that is speculation, too, isn't it?"

"Any other explanation assumes this pilot forgot everything he'd ever learned, then did everything he wasn't supposed to do."

"Maybe he did, sir, maybe six hundred milligrams of a mind-deadening drug did that to him."

"Have you ever flown a plane, Ms. Castino?"

"No. But that—"

"You have no idea, do you, what it's like to be flying through a storm in a plane that's not functioning properly?"

"Sir, I will ask the questions here, not you."

"What if the elevators weren't working?" McKinney persists. "Do you still think it was pilot error? In that storm? With what the controllers said?"

"Move to strike, Your Honor!"

"Granted." Meredith turns toward McKinney. "Sir, you must confine your remarks to the questions you're asked."

"What about the ones she's afraid to ask?" argues McKinney with a cold rage.

"That's enough now," warns Meredith. "The next time you'll hear the words 'in contempt.' Understood?"

McKinney nods.

Isabel gives McKinney a scornful look of her own. "You don't know of your own personal knowledge that the pilot tried to use the elevators, do you?"

"No."

"Or the stabilizers?"

"I don't know it as a hard fact, but I know it."

"Well, it must be wonderful to know things you don't know. It's quite a trick."

"You seem to have mastered it yourself, Ms. Castino."

Isabel sucks in the stale air. Her cheeks are a bit red. "Do you know of any hard data that shows the J Ninety-nine has been improperly designed?"

"Just the sticking incidents recorded in the logbooks. Nothing else."

"Were there any sticking incidents recorded as to this particular J

Ninety-nine?" Isabel raises her voice. "Any history of icing, any history of sticking elevators?"

I want McKinney to say he couldn't know because the logbooks have been altered, but he's not willing to take that step. Rather, he says quietly: "None that I know of."

"You've heard the pilot's last conversations on the black box, haven't you?"

"Yes."

"Did the pilot ever mention a problem with the elevators?"

"No," McKinney answers after an awkward silence.

"Did he mention a problem with the stabilizers?"

"No."

"And yet it's common practice, isn't it, for a pilot in trouble to report the source of his trouble?"

"Yes, it is. If he knows it."

"If he knows it," Isabel repeats. "Well, sir, if the elevators had stuck, he surely would've known it, right?"

"That's right," McKinney has to admit.

"Because, under your speculative theory, that's why he went to the stabilizers, right?"

"Yes."

"So, for your theory to work, the pilot had to know the elevators stuck, and he had to defy all common practice and all common sense by not reporting the problem, correct?"

McKinney's face contorts as if he'd been hit with a rock. He casts his eyes downward. He looks beaten. "That's a problem with my theory, yes. I don't know why he didn't report it. Pilots are trained to report problems immediately." McKinney looks up. "Unless there was no time. The dive took only seven seconds."

"He had time to tell his copilot 'the up and down is stewed,' didn't he? He had time for that?"

"Yes, but that's about all the time he had," McKinney tries bravely, but it's not enough. All he's done is allow Isabel to pound once again those crazy words into the jury's consciousness. The crazy words of a man flying at high speed to a certain death.

DIANA PARADES TO the witness chair sixteen uniformed pilots, all of whom flew with Charlie during his last two months. Their collective testimony consumes three days, and sorely tests Meredith's patience, who asks more than once if such "repetitive testimony is necessary." Diana merely nods, continuing to elicit from each pilot the same series of answers:

"Charlie was an outstanding pilot."

"Charlie had an Air Transport Rating, the highest rating a pilot can get."

"Charlie had as much experience with the J Ninety-nine as anybody."

"Never once saw Charlie under the influence of drugs or alcohol."

"Every pilot relies heavily on instructions from the air traffic controllers."

"Other planes were landing, so it made sense for Charlie to take that into account."

"Jarrad never told us to leave the stabilizers alone in turbulence, and never told us about any concerns it had regarding the electric trim limit."

"If I'd gotten those instructions from the tower, I would have tried to land too."

In her cross-examinations, Isabel interrogates each witness about the operation and functions of the elevators, seeking to bring back the jurors' attention to what she now believes is the trial's central issue. Nonetheless, Diana is slowly making headway. The jurors are coming to identify with and respect Charlie. A hopeful sign: In yesterday's *New York Times*, it was reported that passengers are beginning to avoid flying on J99s.

Next come my character witnesses, who march to the witness chair, one every thirty minutes. They are an impressive group: federal and state judges, prominent lawyers, civic leaders, business executives, and friends from Harvard, all of whom extol my personal and professional integrity. Isabel asks few questions of these witnesses; by her derisive tone she tells the jurors their testimony is of no value. Yet the jurors are alert, their eyes clear and focused. I sense we're making a comeback of sorts.

"I THOUGHT YOU needed to hear some good news for a change." My hand shakes as I press the receiver to my ear. It's Randy. I'm not sure we still agree on what's good news. I'm about to tell Randy his voice is no longer welcome in my world when he nearly shouts: "We settled the civil case. Lockwood caved! He took forty million, exactly what you offered him in the first place!"

My head's light. I sit on a kitchen chair, my heart filled with a delirious yet unsatisfying joy. I won't be sued for hundreds of millions after all. I won't be filing for bankruptcy. I won't be taking Grace out of her private school.

"Are you there?"

"Yeah, I'm here," I answer, my ear still pressed against the receiver. I want to hear every word.

"Lockwood was afraid he'd lose on summary judgment," says Randy excitedly. "If the judge found it was suicide, the plaintiffs would've been shut out. The big zero."

We're talking lawyer to lawyer here. He speaks the word "suicide" as if I'm a stranger to the pilot. What has all our education done to us? "But you'd never have gotten summary judgment. There were so many facts in dispute," I point out in like kind.

"He's a wimp, Michael. He was afraid he'd lose, period. If not now, then at trial."

I was right about Lockwood: no stomach for combat. Lockwood had to know the jurors, even if they were sold on suicide, could still have nailed the airline for missing Charlie's drugged-out condition. The crash victims, screwed even in death, will shortly be screwed again. Lockwood will soon petition the court for a huge fee, all of which will be subtracted from the relatively meager settlement monies.

"We had some good stuff on damages too," Randy gloats. "We got all the passengers' medical and employment records, and what do you know? Some had serious illnesses, some had been fired from their jobs, some were chronically unemployed. We had felons, we had wife-beaters, we had guys with potency problems. A lot of their relatives didn't want to be in court having to talk about the fuck-ups of their dead loved ones."

At one time I would've complimented Randy on his thoroughness, and meant it. Now I find it offensive. "Who paid?" I ask out of curiosity.

"The airline and the insurance company split it down the middle. Not bad, don't you think? We were arguing suicide, and the policy doesn't even cover that."

"You know it wasn't suicide, Randy. I know you had to argue it . . ." Randy's about to be disbarred or otherwise disgraced, but his opinion of Charlie and me still matters.

"I don't know what I know," Randy admits with a forced laugh. "I'd like to think it wasn't suicide, but you know what? None of the class members have opted out yet. They're all willing to take the deal."

"Not me. I'm opting out on Charlie's behalf."

Randy's voice rises at once in pitch and volume. I'm a loose end he can't clean up. "Don't be stupid, Michael. The only real remedy Charlie's got is a workers' compensation claim restricted to a seventy-thousand lifetime limit, doled out weekly for some thirty years. Don't you see I looked out for Charlie? His estate is sharing pro rata with the rest of the class."

"If there's been willful misconduct by the airline, the workers' compensation laws go out the window. We're not restricted at all."

"You're as crazy as your brother," Randy grumbles.

I can be nasty too. "How's the bar investigation going?" I ask.

"I haven't heard yet," he says curtly. "I'll let you know."

I'm ready to hang up. I say good-bye.

"Good luck, pal," I hear Randy say softly. "I pray for you every night. I really do."

I know Randy well enough to know he's being straight with me. Incredible, isn't it? The man who royally screwed me is now on his knees every night asking for divine intervention on my behalf. "Who is it you're seeking to protect," I ask, disregarding all good manners, "you or me?"

"Both of us," he says with the hearty, engaging laugh that's as familiar to me as the rhythm of my own breath. Randy's contagious way of expressing unbridled joy, one of the many wonderful glues long connecting us, seems hollow now, an echo in a dark tunnel. Joy, like time, is fleeting and irreversible; once lost, it's forever gone.

EARLY IN HIS career, Roy Brooks disliked his superiors; too often they forced work upon him he regarded as menial. Now Roy dislikes his subordinates who aren't sufficiently grateful for his tutelage and complain their work too often is menial.

That Roy is easily embittered and quick to find fault with others has long convinced me that he, despite all his outward manifestations of feudal loyalty, must naturally harbor a secret resentment toward Philip, who, unlike Roy, stands on the mountain's top peak without having ever to scale the rocks. Philip was born on that peak while Roy has had to use all the tools at his disposal to keep from falling to his professional death, knowing always the top peak was not his to claim.

My suspicions are happily confirmed this evening. Roy calls to say I should contact Airport Security at La Guardia and ask for Tony Giordano. "Tell Giordano you know he talked to Philip Brandon the night of the crash. Make him tell you what Philip asked him to do."

Is Roy trying to help me or hurt Philip? I won't ask. I won't deter him from his mission, whatever its ultimate goal is. For the moment I will listen and follow instructions.

"Just so we're clear on all this," he adds, as if my silence has tipped him off to my cynicism, "I'm committed to the airline, not one man. My loyalty is to the stockholders, as it's supposed to be. As much as I like Philip, I'll put him at risk if I must. I'll make that sacrifice."

"Why didn't this sense of loyalty inspire you earlier?" I can't stop myself from asking.

"I wanted the civil case to settle first," he says with a candor untainted by a recognition of wrongdoing. "That was also in the stockholders' best interest."

"I understand," I say empathetically, wanting him to tell me more.

"Loyalty to one man has its limits, don't it? You should know that. That kind of loyalty is what got you indicted."

Roy apparently fancies himself a martyr of sorts: compelled by conscience to inflict suffering on those who have compromised the institution's well-being. Roy himself must know his act of betrayal isn't a "sacrifice" motivated by a generous spirit. He wishes to kill the new king not to serve the king's constituents (who are loyal only to themselves) but to serve himself. But if Roy's selling his soul, without charge, I'm buying.

"Roy, let's not play games, okay? Just tell me what this Giordano guy knows."

"He knows Philip didn't tell the truth under oath."

"Give me specifics."

"This is as far as I'm going," says Roy. "You get your girl lawyer to do the rest. I've satisfied my conscience."

TONY GIORDANO, ENDOWED by nature with a short, wide frame, has apparently developed over the years a backward tilt—like a tree on a cliff's edge that grows backward to preserve itself—affording him the appearance of good posture and breeding. He sits in the witness chair with a straight back and folded hands.

Giordano, not here voluntarily, had to be subpoenaed at his Queens apartment last night at eleven o'clock. Two sheriffs banged on his door until his wife reluctantly opened it.

With La Guardia Security for nine years, Giordano has no blemishes on his personnel record, no complaints from passengers. He says he received a call months ago from someone "high up" at Brandon Air Lines to "stop a pilot from getting on a plane." The "Brandon guy" ordered him to Gate 26.

"Did this Brandon official tell you why he wanted you to stop the pilot from boarding the airplane?" Diana interrogates.

"He just said to do it. Go to Gate twenty-six. Then have him tested."

"Tested for what?"

"Drugs."

He tugs at his shirtsleeve, then at his coarse plaid tie. I'm sure he's suffocating in that chair. Giordano, of course, has reason to be nervous. He never reported this conversation to anyone—not his superiors, not the FAA, not the prosecution. He's virtually certain to be fired before week's end. "I was the only one there at the time," he explains. "That's how I got the call. It wasn't like he was calling me personally."

"Did he tell you the name of the pilot?"

"Charlie Ashmore," the guard says in a hoarse whisper.

"Did he tell you the flight number?"

"Five five five."

"But you decided not to stop Captain Ashmore?"

"It wasn't that. I just didn't get there on time." Giordano takes in a breath. The courtroom is deathly silent. "I was really hoofing it, you know, and I was only a couple of gates away when all hell broke loose."

"And that stopped you?"

"Yeah, it did," Giordano admits. "I had to stop. This pretty big guy, probably in his early forties, was actually assaulting one of the gate attendants. A young woman, no less, and petite, I'd say, about a hundred five pounds dripping wet." Giordano shakes his head with apparent disdain (likely for the jury's benefit) and continues: "Actually punching her. In the damn face, too. I saw blood. The woman was cut near her eye and by her lip. It was horrible."

"So you stopped—"

"Yeah, I had to, didn't I? I pulled the guy off her, and it wasn't easy, I tell you that. He was like a bull with a red towel being flapped in front of him."

"What made him so angry?"

"Well, I later found out the guy was waiting on standby, and was a nervous wreck. It seems his wife had been in a real bad car accident down in Sarasota, and was barely hanging on. He'd told the attendant he absolutely had to get on that plane. She had three seats left, and five standbys. She followed the airline's policy of giving the seats to Platinum and Gold-level passengers first, so he didn't get on. People still at the gate said he was screaming at her, but she wouldn't budge. And the three standbys apparently just scampered on, not wanting to give up their seats. When the gate door closed, he just lost it."

"Did you call for backup?"

"I didn't have time. As soon as I saw the fight, I rushed over to break it up. After I finally got the guy settled down, the woman started bawling. She was going to sue, she said. She was going to get her husband to beat him up. A lot of nonsense. I walked him away from the gate, and called for backup. Then I went running to Gate twenty-six."

"Did you see Charlie Ashmore?"

"He'd already boarded the plane, and kicked off from the gate. So I called back the Brandon guy to tell him what had happened. He got all worked up, and hung up on me. That's the last I talked to him."

"You don't recall his name?"

"He never said it, or if he did, I didn't pick up on it. He just said he was with Brandon Air Lines, and needed that pilot tested for drugs. He gave me his cellular number."

"Did he say why he believed the pilot needed to be tested?"

"No. Just said, do it. Said it like he had the authority to order it. Like he was in charge."

Diana nods at him. "That's all, Mr. Giordano."

"Can I say something more?"

"About what?" Diana asks warily.

"About why it wasn't my fault I didn't get there on time. It wasn't just the fight. The Brandon guy screwed me up too. He said the pilot wasn't at the gate yet, but was on his way. Usually the pilots board thirty to forty-five minutes before the flight, so I figured I had time. Even if the pilot beat me to the gate, I could've gone onto the plane, and escorted him off. But he got there only a couple of minutes before takeoff. The gate attendants said he was the last guy on. He walks on, and immediately kicks the plane back. He's gone like a puff of smoke."

GIORDANO'S TESTIMONY HAS cast a peculiar multicolored light on these proceedings, some rays so dark as to blind, others illuminating paths newly paved with concrete evidence. The most dazzling of these rays has exposed

Philip, and left him floundering half-naked before a titillated jury. I'd bet my last dollar Philip was the mysterious caller and, so, must have seen Charlie that night. Who from Brandon Air Lines, other than Philip, was at La Guardia that night? Who, other than Philip, knew Charlie and was familiar with his so-called drug problem?

That Philip lied will naturally elevate in importance the issue of reasonable doubt and likely give a modicum of credence to my sabotage theory, which, while still lacking hard proof, has gained the allure of a cover-up. While these developments are encouraging, all else is bleak. We now have a witness who claims Charlie was believed to be sufficiently unstable as to warrant his being taken, forcibly if necessary, from his assigned flight, such claim reinforced by an actual instruction to Airport Security to accomplish this very feat. It is, as we lawyers say, "a belief that was acted upon," which lends credibility to the proposition that the belief was actually held.

Giordano's late arrival, coupled with a Brandon employee's late instruction, might have once worked to the benefit of the civil plaintiffs, but does little to help me avoid my share of responsibility—unless the jurors, believing the airline or Airport Security had the last clear chance to prevent the tragedy and thus had a greater hand in the crash than did I, find my recklessness, however egregious, not to be the proximate cause of the crash. Hope isn't gone from my soul, but its breathing is growing faint.

Hope doesn't seem to be rising in Philip either, who had to know, after Giordano's incriminating story, he'd be recalled as a witness; yet he radiates a sense of detachment, as if he's playing himself in the movie version of the trial. I'm reminded of those concentration camp prisoners who refused to see corpses they stepped over; others wouldn't believe the smoke from the crematoriums came from burning corpses.

"Mr. Brandon," Diana begins, "you were the one who called Airport Security and spoke to Tony Giordano the night of the crash, weren't you?"

"Yes," says Philip mechanically, having already admitted to being at La Guardia that night.

"And you instructed Mr. Giordano to stop Charlie Ashmore at the gate and test him for drugs?"

"Yes, I did."

"And so you lied under sworn oath to me, to this jury, and to this court when you said you didn't see Charlie that night, didn't you?"

Philip could say he'd seen Charlie acting "unstable" shortly before that night, but didn't decide until that night to have Charlie tested; but he seems a bit too rigid in body and spirit to be flexible in his response. To lie convincingly takes not only great concentration in the first instance, it requires admirable mental agility to sustain the lie as the interrogation wears on, and questions designed to expose the same lie are posed from different angles, with different phrases, in different contexts.

"I did see Charlie that night," Philip says, and leaves it at that. He doesn't explain, justify, or elaborate. He says what he says as if he is a remarkable man for having had the courage to confess his lie and is fully deserving of generous praise for his heroic deed.

Diana proceeds, without a hint of surprise, as if she's always known Philip to be the consummate liar, precisely the kind of bastard who cannot be trusted. Her voice is laced not with the rage betrayal evokes but with a thoughtful cynicism. "You said earlier you had coffee that night, and according to the autopsy, Charlie did too. I take it you two had coffee together?"

"We did."

"Did you arrange in advance this meeting?"

Philip shakes his head with much effort. "It was by chance. We saw each other and decided to get some coffee. After a while I began to notice he wasn't completely right. He had a dazed look over his eyes. He was slurring some of his words. I asked him when he was flying. That's when he looked at his watch and got right up. Said he was late. Had to go. I said maybe he should sit this one out, fly back tomorrow. He looked at me with this irate expression and said, no, he was going out tonight. He'd never missed a flight, and wasn't about to miss one now."

"So you let him leave?"

"I wasn't about to wrestle him to the ground, Miss Wells. Anyway, I couldn't have if I tried. Charlie Ashmore was a very powerful man."

"You mean he wasn't at all in a weakened state?" asks Diana innocently, but I detect a note of excitement.

"I didn't say that," Philip admonishes her, the first sign of life in him, though his voice has a hollow echo to it.

"Was he, in your opinion, weakened at all?"

"I assume he had to be, but I wasn't going to find out. I thought the wise thing was to call security, which I did the moment Charlie walked away."

"On your cellular phone?"

"Yes."

"And when the security guard called to tell you he'd missed Charlie, what did you do?"

"The plane was gone, Ms. Wells."

"Did you try to reach Charlie while the plane was on the runway?"

"No," Philip answers softly, but his face, a shade whiter, and his breathing, a bit quicker, betray a rising panic; yet, for purposes of this trial, he is on safe ground. His voice, which I would have surely recognized, is nowhere recorded on the black box. Philip folds his arms, looks away.

Diana leans toward Philip as if ready to spring upon him. "You drugged Captain Ashmore, didn't you?"

"I am insulted that—"

"Yes or no, sir?"

"No. A thousand times no."

"You told Eddie Perez not to deice—"

"That's a hideous lie," Philip interrupts with a cold fury.

Diana steps back. "I'm sorry you're so offended, sir, but if I recall, it was just a few minutes ago you confessed to all of us here that you, a key witness in a murder trial, did in fact tell a hideous lie."

"It wasn't hideous, just stupid. An error in judgment. I tried to help Michael, but now I look bad."

"You tried to help Michael?" Diana, turning to the jurors, rolls her eyes and chuckles. "At such risk to yourself? How kind of you, Mr. Brandon. If I'd known that, I wouldn't have bothered you with all these foolish questions. Silly me, I thought maybe you lied to protect yourself."

"I knew it would help the prosecution's case if they had an eyewitness to Charlie being disoriented that night," declares Philip correctly.

"Lying would also help you, sir, since you failed to stop Charlie from getting on the plane. And it certainly helped your airline in that big damage suit, didn't it?"

"Yes, all that too," he concedes with a nod.

"Maybe I'm missing something here, but weren't you the one who actively sought immunity from the prosecution in return for testimony against Michael, and then in fact went after Michael when you were called as a prosecution witness?"

"I didn't go after Michael full force, as you now know. I've been working with him a long time. That means something to me."

"Aren't you, sir, just full of contradictions?" Diana remarks disdainfully. "Or should I be more blunt and use the word 'lies'?"

"Use any words you like. I know I'm telling the complete truth," he asserts. "Charlie was under the influence, and I tried to stop him from flying. The Airport Security screwed up, not me. I tried not to let the whole weight of this come down on Michael's head, but you, in all your wisdom, have now accomplished just that."

I sit perfectly still, but my blood is racing. We've thrown Philip into a corner, and he's bit us in the neck. The jury now has an eyewitness—albeit a confessed liar—who claims Charlie was disoriented moments before boarding the flight. While all other witnesses against me could only measure and speculate, Philip saw. That's the kind of testimony that gets a jury's engine running.

Fatigue rules Rosita Perez: dulls her voice, slumps her small shoulders, slows her speech. Her pitted face, while gaunt, sags by her chin as she labors to and from the kitchen with all the energy of a bored and aching eighty-year-old woman.

Her apartment is distinctive for its crucifixes, which line the otherwise bare walls and adorn the glass coffee table. The crucifixes come in all sizes and colors with intricate interior designs. All else in these cramped quarters is cheap: plastic kitchen chairs, beaten-up refrigerator, twelve-inch black-and-white TV, moth-eaten carpet.

I don't want food or drink, I tell Rosita. We're here to talk. We're out of witnesses. To underscore the urgency of our visit, Diana and I stand. We stand, and we pace.

"Your husband told us he was ordered not to deice the plane. We think he must've told you that too," I say.

"Your husband was willing to testify to that. He wanted to do the right thing," Diana chimes in.

"And now he's dead," Rosita Perez bluntly points out. She puts down the Cokes and cookies she's brought us despite our protests. "You understand what that means to his children?"

"We need your testimony, and we need it tomorrow. You must say what Eddie was going to say," Diana pleads.

"They will kill me too." Rosita shudders.

"Nobody killed your husband," Diana says with a note of bewilderment. "It was a car accident."

"Eddie never have whiskey," Rosita answers firmly. "I tell everybody that, but nobody do anything."

"You're our last chance," I advise her. "Everybody on Eddie's crew says

Eddie was going to spray my brother's plane himself. None of them can say if he did or didn't. They were all busy with other planes."

"If I say anything, will they take the money back?"

"What money?" Diana jumps in.

Rosita points to the Cokes. "Drink something, okay? Sit down." Rosita Perez sits on the sofa, and touches each of the crucifixes on the coffee table. We sit too. We want her to relax now. We want her to talk. "After Eddie die, they pay me twelve hundred dollars from Eddie's insurance. But Mr. Brandon, he call me and say they give me another ten thousand dollars because twelve hundred, it wasn't enough and Eddie do such good work for them. He send the money right into my checking account. Like magic, you know?"

"We can't give you money," Diana rushes to say. "It's not permitted. It's buying testimony. We'd all get in trouble."

"I live here with the mice and the roaches," Rosita explains. "The real ones and the human ones too. I been robbed twice in the last year." She looks up at us, one of the crucifixes in her hand. "I'd like to live somewheres else, but with Eddie gone, it's hard just to pay rent and doctor's bills. Being afraid all the time, it makes you tired, don't it?"

I nod. Fear and fatigue, I understand.

"I'd ask Mr. Brandon for more, but maybe he get mad. They owe me that money, I know that, but still he get mad, don't he?"

"Why not use the money he's already given you to move?" Diana asks.

"No, no," Rosita says quickly. "I save that money for when we have nothing. No food, no good clothes, nothing. I know that day's coming."

"I wish you were more like Eddie," I comment out of frustration. "He was willing to testify." It's a low blow, but fear has a way of cooling the heart.

"I don't want them blaming Eddie for this," she holds on.

"We'll make it clear Eddie had to follow orders, then bravely told the truth," Diana assures her.

"How brave is it to tell your wife?" She looks squarely at Diana.

"Eddie was a man of honor. He was ready to testify." Diana squirms away.

"Can you . . . make me testify?" Rosita stammers.

"We can make you come to the courthouse, but we can't make you repeat anything your husband said to you," I reply with a candor that hurts.

She nods gratefully. She respects me for telling the truth, I think. "Mr. Brandon," she mumbles, "he should give me more."

She wants to tell us. She needs a push. "Why, Rosita? Why does Brandon owe you?" I interrogate as if the jury were listening.

She puts down one crucifix, picks up another. "He tell Eddie not to spray the plane that go down. Eddie was very sad about it all the time. Scared too. He know about something they don't like anybody to know."

"I know you'll help us," whispers Diana, eyeing the crucifix. "I believe it's God's will."

Rosita looks down, bows her head. I think she's praying.

"YOUR HONOR, THE defense said in their papers, and again last night, that they had no further witnesses. Now, without any notice to the prosecution, they spring this last-second surprise on us, and expect us to roll over and let them have their way. Well, we're not prepared to cross-examine Rosita Perez, and shouldn't be forced to do so today or any other day," argues Isabel with an exasperated contempt. "The defense knew long ago who Rosita Perez was, and where she could be found. Why they waited so long to give notice of her appearance as a witness is beyond me, but I submit the defense long ago waived their right to call her. The prosecution, for its part, stands ready, as scheduled, to begin closing argument first thing this morning."

Judge Meredith turns to Diana. "Why did you wait?" he asks in a low growl. I'm glad the jury is spared the sight of his displeasure with us.

"We apologize to this court and to the prosecution, Your Honor, but the truth is, we didn't know what Rosita Perez could or would say until last night. Undoubtedly, in an ideal world, we would've known sooner, but our resources are limited and the demands of this trial leave us little time for investigative work."

"They had months before this trial began to interview this witness," Isabel points out.

Diana is arguing the wrong point. We're calling Rosita Perez to rebut Philip's testimony. I knock on the table. Diana glances back at me. I mouth the word *rebuttal*. She turns to Meredith. "The prosecution is missing the point here," she transitions smoothly. "Rosita Perez is being introduced as a rebuttal witness. To prove Philip Brandon lied. We couldn't have known Mr. Brandon would lie until he did."

"Exactly what is this witness being brought here to rebut? The prosecution is entitled to know."

"She will testify that Philip Brandon did order Flight five five five not to be deiced, and that such orders were given directly to her husband, Eddie Perez."

"And who told her that?" Isabel rants. "Who told her?"

"Her husband."

"Her husband?" repeats Isabel. "Not Philip Brandon, but her husband?"

"Her husband told her, and he had no reason to lie."

Isabel turns to Meredith. "That's not admissible testimony, Your Honor. Two hundred years of law say it's not."

"Two hundred years of justice say it's a prosecutor's job to find the truth, not block it," declares Diana.

Isabel keeps her eyes focused on Meredith. "Your Honor, this isn't even a close question. The proposed testimony is classic hearsay. All this witness can and will say is she was told this or told that. She has no firsthand facts to report. Worse yet, she's reporting what was allegedly said to her by her husband, who's now deceased. Oral communications by a deceased person are barred as well, so we've got a double whammy here: hearsay from a deceased." Isabel shakes her head with the annoyance of one forced to engage in unnecessary debate. "As this court well knows, statements from a deceased are allowed only if made as dying declarations. But Eddie Perez died in a car accident, and was found dead at the scene. These statements, whatever their value, weren't made as Eddie Perez lay dying."

Diana's voice is laced more with rage than irritation. "Ms. Castino is deliberately omitting a key exception to the rule. Eddie Perez was admitting to a wrongful act. Admissions against interest are admissible, hearsay or not."

"He had no liability for it," Isabel counters. "It's an admission against the airline, not himself."

"That's not right, Your Honor," Diana thunders. "In fact, nothing's right about all this! Shouldn't the jury be allowed to hear that Philip Brandon did exactly what he said he didn't do? Shouldn't they be allowed to hear that this plane wasn't deiced and so the elevators were naturally more susceptible to freezing and sticking? Shouldn't they know there's further support for the testimony of Michael Ashmore himself, who laid out his view that deliberate acts led to the downing of this plane? And don't the

FAA and all the citizens of this nation who travel by air need to hear all this?

"I recognize there are certain highly technical rules about what evidence comes in and what doesn't," Diana continues, "but if there were ever a time to bend the rules a bit, this is that time. I beg you, Your Honor, let the truth be heard! Cast away all those little lawyer rules and little ways of thinking, and do what makes sense!"

"That was a very moving speech, Ms. Wells," observes Meredith in a mean-spirited voice that portends doom. "But those little lawyer rules you refer to, they're what I've got to go by. I'm a judge, not a vigilante. I'm bound by rules for reasons that do make sense. If you want the rules changed to suit your purposes, go lobby the legislature or your bar association. Don't lobby me."

"I'm not lobbying," Diana claims. "I'm merely pointing out the—"

"Do you seriously contend, Ms. Wells, that the hearsay rule and the dead man's statute aren't applicable here?"

"Getting at the truth is more important than either or both of those rules. After all, what is a trial other than a search for the truth?"

"If you don't know, Ms. Wells, I'll tell you. A trial is a search for the truth within a certain framework of rules that assures the court the evidence being heard is reliable and relevant. The rules say that evidence given about what another person said, especially one who's deceased, isn't reliable enough. So I've got no choice but to grant the prosecution's motion and exclude this witness. If I don't follow the rules, who will?"

THE LAWYERS CONFERENCE with Judge Meredith in chambers to debate the precise words the court will use to instruct the jury on the applicable law. I wait with all the reporters, gawkers, gossipers. The lawyers emerge with poker faces, but I sense Diana's unhappy. She nods somberly when I ask if "things went okay" with Meredith.

Maybe Diana's nervous. It's time for closing argument. Who wouldn't be a little nervous? Isabel herself looks a bit pale as she rises. Isabel is in her dark blue skirt and jacket, her hair freshly washed and brushed. In contrast to her inviting appearance, her voice is harsh as if to emphasize the harsh verdict these jurors must rightfully deliver.

"I believe you will do the right and honorable thing here," she preaches to them. "I believe you won't be led astray by desperate smoke screens designed to separate you from your common sense. I believe you understand the defendant made all this happen, that he single-handedly persuaded the airline to rehire his drug-addicted brother by deliberately and maliciously concealing the very evidence that confirmed the extreme danger of allowing Charles Ashmore to pilot any sort of plane, much less a sophisticated, high-tech, newly operational jet aircraft. The defendant accomplished this feat because he was the airline's chief counsel. The airline's key executives put their complete trust in him, as he knew they would, and he recklessly abused it. I ask you: Does a man who recklessly gambles on the lives of innocents deserve your sympathy? Those innocents and their loved ones paid the ultimate price for the loss of his gamble. Now it's his turn to pay—not with his life, as these innocents did, but with prison time. All things considered, no matter what you decide, he'll get off far easier than those he condemned to fiery, terrifying deaths. For thousands of years philosophers have debated the mark of true evil, and if there's a common thread running through their thinking, it's this: True evil takes hold and flourishes in one's indifference to the lives of strangers."

Isabel steps to the rail separating her from the jurors and pauses. She wants to have a silent moment with them, I think. She wants them to contemplate what's been said. She raises her arms, rocks slightly back as she begins again: "I'm sure I need not remind you of the pervasive havoc drugs have inflicted so mercilessly upon our communities. But I do wish to remind you how you can stop it. Ladies and gentlemen, you are in a unique position to send a loud and powerful message. Not only to this defendant—who God knows needs one—but to every drug user and every drug dealer across this country. Make it clear to every one of them that we cannot and will not tolerate drug use, especially when it finds its way into the heads and hearts of those most responsible for guarding the public safety. For God's sake, do not let this man walk away because he's rich and prominent. Because he's not personally stained himself with the filth of drugs. In his own special way, this defendant is as ruthless and cunning as any murderer I have ever had to prosecute!"

Isabel walks along the rail in each direction, inches from the jurors in the first row. I know she wants to connect with them in every way she can, to have them see her as a kind, down-to-earth person forced to defend humanity from the likes of me.

"To find this defendant acted with reckless disregard, all you need do is consider the testimony of the defendant himself," she contends with a kinder yet relentlessly adamant tone. "Consider that even now he seeks to persuade us he isn't reckless by advancing theories themselves so reckless and devoid of factual support they persuade us of the very thing he argues against. Here's a trained lawyer—a man taught to think analytically and to rely on hard evidence—who tells us his brother was drugged by someone who supposedly put a deadly quantity of barbiturates in his drink. Proof for this? None. Proof that this theory is preposterous? Plenty. It's not disputed his brother, as this defendant always knew, was a big-time user of barbiturates, and as two credible airline employees have testified, was on a barbiturate or some similar drug on a prior flight which dived and nearly crashed. We're not talking about Snow White here. We're talking about a lying drug abuser and a lying lawyer who teamed up to deliver the big lie. Now the defendant's at it again. Now he's on to a whole new set of lies.

"Theories of unknown conspirators doing unspeakable things for unknown reasons are about as desperate as it gets for a defendant in a murder trial. This, I submit," declares Isabel, pointing at me, "is one desperate man. He has no real evidence."

Isabel is fixed now at the center of the jury box, her hands clutching the rail separating government from citizen. "They're throwing everything at the wall, hoping something will stick. If the pilot wasn't drugged, then maybe the elevators stuck. But 'maybe' isn't good enough. For all their wailing about the J Ninety-nine's elevators, the defense hasn't put in one iota of evidence that this particular plane's elevators ever froze or stuck on this or any other flight.

"The standard for conviction is proof beyond a reasonable doubt, not any doubt. If the standard was proof beyond any doubt, then every criminal would go free merely by denying his guilt since that would cause some doubt, wouldn't it, no matter the evidence? We wouldn't need prisons anymore. Just swear you're innocent, thereby creating some doubt, however tiny, and go home. No, it's reasonable doubt, and there's nothing reasonable about any of the defendant's arguments in this case.

"They can blame the plane, the weather, the controllers, or anybody and everything, but when all's said and done, common sense tells you a man with six hundred milligrams of a powerful barbiturate in his body cannot have the wherewithal to maneuver a plane in turbulent weather. Common sense tells you a barbiturate abuser who learns hours before his flight that his divorce is final, and then is found with a massive load of barbiturates in his body, wasn't coincidentally drugged somewhere by someone wanting to kill him. In all my years as a prosecutor, I've never heard a more desperate, more reckless argument than that.

"I challenge defense counsel to explain why the pilot didn't speak up if the plane wasn't properly deiced at La Guardia or if the plane froze up in flight. No one disputes it's the pilot's obligation to make sure his plane is in every respect ready for takeoff. We submit there was no ice, at takeoff or in flight, but if there was, this pilot was apparently too drugged out to know it. And we submit further that if this pilot did in fact dive on a prior J Ninety-nine flight due to the elevators icing up, shouldn't he have been extremely sensitive to this whole supposed problem? Wouldn't it have been incredibly reckless for this pilot to get into another J Ninety-nine in cold, rainy weather without checking for ice? The answer's simple: Either there was no ice, in which case the plane itself wasn't at fault, or the pilot was reckless for not checking or reporting the ice. And what made him reckless was the phenobarbital, which had the potential at six hundred milligrams to dull his brain down to the level one reaches immediately before passing out.

"You cannot fully assess this defendant's testimony without taking into account his lifelong habit to lie and conceal. I'm not just talking about his big lie—telling the airline everything was okay with his brother when he surely knew it wasn't—but all those little lies over a lifetime that add up to a habit. You heard his own best friend and former business partner testify that this defendant told not one of his partners that he was seeking to persuade the reluctant CEO of the firm's biggest client to rehire his brother. He told not one of his partners that he was putting at serious risk the firm's vital business relationship with the airline. And, of course, he told no one he'd outright lied to the airline until things had grown dire.

"This defendant didn't begin his lying in this courtroom, or months ago to his partners, but years before that. He grew up in a house where he was taught to lie, where he was taught to help conceal his father's sick pretense. Born and raised as a Jew, his father pretended all his adult years to be a Lutheran, and this defendant helped him do it. I say this not as criticism, but by way of explanation. The facts are, this defendant from an early age developed a habit of concealing and lying as a way of protecting family members from perceived harm."

My face burns whenever I hear Isabel say the word "Jew." How far will we fall merely to claim victory? How many prejudices will we stoke, how many lives will we harm? As nasty as these arguments are, I remain still with folded hands, but imagine—as I've done daily throughout this trial—a time when I can peer into Isabel's face and feel nothing but the ordinary sensation recorded in one's brain upon recognizing an acquaintance whose connection has dissolved into a distant, barely recalled memory.

"To find this defendant guilty of reckless homicide," Isabel wears on, "you need only find his recklessness contributed to the crash. You need not find it was the sole cause, or even the primary cause. Just that it was a contributing cause. This isn't merely my interpretation of the law. This is the law you will be instructed to follow by Judge Meredith."

My chest tightens. My breathing stops. All my self-restraint dissolves. By Judge Meredith? No, that's not possible. That is not the law! Isabel's declaration kicks me in the belly, momentarily knocking the wind from me. Not the sole cause? Not even the primary cause?

Isabel continues to elaborate on the importance of this coming instruction: "Even if you find the airline was partly to blame, and the manufacturer was partly to blame, and the same was true about the weather and the controllers, you must still convict the defendant if you find that the pilot's ability to operate the plane was adversely affected by the phenobarbital in his body, and that this circumstance contributed to the crash." Isabel's strong voice and oratorical flair are blending together. The uneasy, feverish whispering of the crowd, followed by the knocking of Meredith's gavel, spurs her forward. I don't hear the final minutes of Isabel's argument, absorbed as I am by looming shadows of a living death.

HERE'S DIANA'S JOB for the next two hours: Artfully sum up thirty-seven days of testimony by weaving the highlights into a series of coherent, compelling arguments that will persuade these jurors I'm not a murderer, and failing that, persuade them the prosecution hasn't proved beyond a reasonable doubt I'm a murderer.

"You're one of the good guys." Diana winks at me as she rises to speak.

She's remarkably calm as she faces my twelve judges. She's grown in these last thirty-seven days, I think. She can pull me from these rising waters.

"The prosecution has utterly failed to prove guilt by any standard," she announces confidently. "Their so-called proof is based largely on guesswork and sensational allegations, all designed to persuade you to do something no jury has ever before done: convict a man of murder who neither intended nor desired to cause the slightest harm to anyone; who wielded no weapon of any kind and had no physical contact with those harmed; who was several times removed from the event causing harm; and who had nothing to do with the turbulent weather, the plane's faulty design, or the controller's remarkably poor judgment. To convict this man of murder would be a giant step toward creating a society where a man could be imprisoned for virtually any deed that later went wrong. Frightening, isn't it? Big Brother is coming our way. That giant step you ought not take is his giant step.

"If anyone is guilty here, it's the airline for letting the plane fly knowing of the sticking elevators; it's the manufacturer for negligently designing and constructing the plane; it's the controllers for directing the pilot into the storm's path; and it's the U.S. Attorney for bringing a case which dishonors her office and sadly diminishes the credibility of our judicial system."

Diana takes a breath. She slows down. Time to move from broad rhetoric to minute analysis. She begins with computer simulations showing to one hundredth of a second the close timing of the dive with the storm's onset, then launches into an examination of the key testimony supporting our version of the truth.

Meredith lets her go past her four-hour limit. She chats pleasantly about the subtleties of each piece of evidence as if discussing her boyfriend's habits with her closest girlfriends. She's got her rhythm.

At the end it's Diana who points to me. "To call this man a murderer is not only absurd but truly horrifying. It is the nightmare example of pros-ecutorial abuse."

She takes one long last soulful look at her twelve newfound friends, then comes back to me at counsel's table.

The jury leaves the courtroom to begin its deliberations. This grueling exercise is finally done.

GRACE HUMS QUIETLY to herself while Diana stares aimlessly. I slump in my kitchen chair as if tied down by heavy ropes. None of us has the energy to rise, much less clear the dirty dishes covering the table. The jury's been out an unbearable two days.

I push down on the wooden arms and struggle mightily to free myself from the chair. I labor toward the radio, find a station with a fast beat, pump up the volume. Music gives me the energy to deal with tedious tasks.

The Stones come on. I'm singing, actually singing. "I can't get no . . . satisfaction . . ." I wave my arms, tap my feet. Diana lets go a small smile.

The music brings Grace to her feet. "Dance, Daddy!" she yells in delight. She throws her arms around my waist, and we swing to and fro, avoiding the table, the garbage, the dishwasher. Another song, another dance, followed by "an even better song to dance to," Grace swears. Every song, it turns out, is better than the last one.

I'm beat. I head for a chair, any chair. "C'mon, Daddy," she pleads. She holds on to me, unwilling to let me go.

I tickle her, my only way to escape. She giggles and squirms away. I've got her on the run now, and in a playful moment I tackle her lightly to the floor, and with one hand pin back her arms. My free hand tickles her. She flails her limbs furiously to no avail.

"I give!" she yells. "I'm stewed! I give!"

I let her go. My eyes blur in confusion. I'm not certain what I actually heard. Stewed? Is that what she said?

"What did you say?"

"I give." She fights her way to her feet, still giggling.

"No, before that."

"Stewed? Is that—"

"Have you heard the black box?" I ask accusingly. "What Uncle Charlie said?"

"No," she replies innocently.

"Were you making fun?"

"Of Uncle Charlie?"

"Of him or me. Stewed means drunk, doesn't it?"

"You're not drunk," she says, a bit bewildered.

"What does stewed mean?" Diana cuts in.

"Uncle Charlie and I made up the word. We made up a lot of words. We just put 'stuck' and 'glue' together. It means really stuck, as stuck as anything can be."

"How do you spell it?" I ask.

"S-t-u-e-d."

I SWORE TO myself I wouldn't allow Grace to see or hear any part of this trial, and despite Diana's pleas, I would've honored my pledge had Grace's comments not been so dramatically important.

There's no guarantee, of course, that Meredith will allow Grace to testify. The evidence is in, the jury is out; nothing but the most extraordinary circumstance would convince a presiding judge to halt a jury in the midst of deliberations to have them hear additional evidence. Yet Diana offers no apologies. She explains with straightforward candor how Grace's proposed testimony came to our attention.

Meredith turns to Isabel, who from her chair ridicules our "last-ditch effort to create a circus atmosphere."

"On your feet, Madam Prosecutor, if you wish to address this court."

Isabel climbs out of her chair, her face flushed. "It's one last crucial witness after another," she sneers. "We've got ourselves a rightfully scared defendant who's now calling on his own daughter purely to gain the jury's sympathy. It'd be an outrage if it wasn't so pitiful, though I don't doubt he could use the sympathy," Isabel gloats with a malicious chuckle, provoking a smattering of laughter among those loyal to the prosecution.

"Your objection is overruled," Meredith slams her. "Without sympathy," he adds, triggering laughter from those few aligned with the defense.

GRACE SITS WITH her hands dutifully folded, her feet an ample distance from the floor. To many of the spectators' delight, Grace wiggles her dangling feet, momentarily breaking the tension.

As required by the evidentiary rules, Diana establishes Grace's competence to testify by asking preliminary questions about her age, friends, and school. Grace answers each question crisply. She seems to adore the attention, the lights, the cameras. Yes, says Grace, she understands the difference between the truth and a lie; knows she must tell the truth today; and is aware she has taken an oath to do so.

"Grace, did you and your uncle Charlie play any special games about words?"

"Yes," answers Grace sweetly.

"Why?"

"It was fun. And Uncle Charlie said words are important. For learning."

"Did you have a secret word for being stuck?"

Grace nods. "Yes, if something was really stuck bad. So bad it was like glue. Being stuck like with glue."

"What was that word?"

" 'Stued.' Stuck like glue."

"You combined the words 'stuck' and 'glue' to come up with 'stued'?"

"Yes, it was fun."

"Did you have any other secret words?"

"Lots of them."

"Did you have one for escalators?"

"Dancing steps."

"And for elevators?" I hold my breath. *Please, Grace, don't fail me. Not like the others. Please, Grace.*

"We called elevators ups and downs."

"So if your uncle Charlie said, 'The up and down is stued,' what would he mean?"

"The elevator is stuck. Stuck bad."

"The elevator is stuck," repeats Diana. "Could the word 'stued' have meant anything else?" She is gambling now, but she, too, has come to believe in Grace.

"No," Grace answers innocently. "Not if Uncle Charlie said it. It was our secret word. Uncle Charlie wouldn't say 'stued' if he didn't mean stuck. You see, we made it up, so it couldn't mean anything else. Same with the up and down."

"Thank you, Grace. That's all I have. You must wait here until Ms. Castino is finished, okay?"

"Sure. Be happy to tell her the same thing," she replies pleasantly, evoking a slight smile even from Meredith.

Isabel must be careful. She can't be perceived as attacking a child. Remaining a courteous distance from Grace, she asks gently: "Grace, may I ask if you discussed with anyone what you would have to say here today?"

"No one told me I would have to say anything," she corrects Isabel, like a seasoned veteran of litigation wars.

"Excuse me," Isabel retreats. "Maybe I said that badly. What I mean is, did you talk with your dad or Diana Wells about what you would say here today?"

Grace nods. "With both of them."

"What did you tell them?"

"Same as I've said here."

"Did either of them give you any advice? Suggest what you might say?"

"My dad did."

"What advice did he give you?"

"To tell the truth at all times, no matter what."

Isabel remains still. She's being buried, and everyone knows it. "Did your dad tell you what the words 'stued' and 'up and down' mean?"

"Those were my uncle Charlie's words. My dad didn't even know what they meant till I told him last night."

Isabel edges a bit closer to Grace. "Are you angry with the prosecution, Grace? For bringing this criminal action against your dad?"

"Yes, ma'am."

"You would do anything to help your dad not be found guilty of a crime, wouldn't you?"

"Yes."

"You might even lie if you had to, wouldn't you? Nobody would blame you. We'd all understand."

"I would lie for my dad, I would," answers Grace thoughtfully. "But I wasn't lying today, ma'am. Everything I said was true. I swear it."

EXTRAORDINARY CIRCUMSTANCES REQUIRE extraordinary measures. Upon our request, Meredith will allow each side ten minutes to argue the merits of Grace's testimony. Reversing the usual order, Meredith instructs Diana to proceed first.

"The last piece of the puzzle has been put into place," argues Diana with an easy confidence. "Fittingly enough, put there by a child. A witness free of corruption, a truth-teller of the purest sort. It took a child to tell us what the words 'the up and down is stued' meant. It took a child to lead us into the light of understanding.

"Keep in mind that none of this child's testimony has been contradicted, impeached, or in any way disputed. What's the impact of her testimony on this trial? It's huge, absolutely huge. It confirms everything the defense has contended throughout this entire proceeding. It confirms the elevators were badly designed. It confirms Charlie Ashmore's alertness and understanding of the problem. It confirms why he pushed the stabilizers all the way down. Most of all, it confirms that these particular elevators at that particular moment failed to work. Given such evidence, you must acquit Michael Ashmore."

Isabel shakes her head and chuckles. She faces the jurors, then eases toward them. "Did you notice that not once did defense counsel mention that Grace's last name was Ashmore, or that Grace just happened to be the defendant's only child? Do you think it's possible this poor child, who has no family other than this defendant, might be motivated to make up a story that allows her dear dad to go home with her? Don't get me wrong, I blame not the child. She's as innocent as Ms. Wells claims her to be. The young and the innocent, though, are easily led.

"No, I blame not the child but the parent and the lawyer. I blame them for shamelessly exploiting this young girl. I blame them without hesitation because it stretches all good sense to its breaking point and beyond to believe that this defense team of two very brilliant lawyers—who had no explanation whatsoever for what these words meant throughout the entire course of the civil proceedings in federal court, throughout all the grand jury proceedings in this court, throughout all our pretrial discovery, and of course, throughout all the argument and testimony in this very lengthy trial—would have this supposedly perfect explanation literally fall into their laps two days into your deliberations. How utterly fateful and lucky and convenient. Nobody, and I mean nobody, knew what those words meant for all this time until, we're supposed to believe, last night. And who solves the supposed riddle? None other than the defendant's daughter herself!

"Now, that's one for the books, isn't it? Saved in the nick of time by his lovely, young daughter who deciphers the incoherent mumblings of her uncle just before the verdict's delivered. Well, where's Grace Ashmore been all these months? Who in this country hasn't heard those unintelligible words broadcasted time and again on their local stations? Who hasn't read them in their local papers? To believe the defense, you'd have to believe everybody heard and read them except for Grace Ashmore, who I'm sure had no interest in following the reports of her own father's trial," chuckles Isabel with a roll of her eyes. "I don't mean to be cynical, but isn't all this a bit surreal? Where has Grace Ashmore been before today?

"Grace Ashmore's appearance says one thing louder than all else: The defense doesn't believe in their own case. They're so sure they're going to lose, they've desperately dragged before you the defendant's own flesh and blood to do a wild, wretched song and dance. I believe your collective wisdom will allow you to see this charade for what it is. I submit again to you that Michael Ashmore is a convincing liar, and I submit further he'd have no difficulty convincing his own daughter to lie as well. He's incorrigible, he's shameless, and he's a murderer!'"

WE GET THE call at eleven. The jury's reached a verdict. We stumble into my car. Have I shaved this morning, combed my hair? I rub my face, brush back loose strands of hair. I look at myself to be sure I'm wearing a tie.

Standing room only in the courtroom. My legs are heavy as I trudge past rows of solemn faces that seem to merge together into one free-floating ball of flesh. This room, always tiny, is closing in on me. I'm jumpy as I force myself to sit.

None of the jurors is looking at me. They're looking down, or into the crowd, or at Meredith: everywhere but at me. Generally I find this sort of avoidance to be a discouraging sign, but at this instant I believe they're about to set me free and don't want to be accused of doing so merely because they have a personal fondness for me.

In another minute I'll know for certain. Meredith calls on the bailiff to read aloud the verdict. The bailiff, an elderly black man with a songlike voice, dons his glasses and starts with the name of the case. Maybe I'm imagining it, but today his voice is uncharacteristically loud and harsh, echoing as if in a locked tile chamber.

I hear the word "guilty." I hear the phrase "for the reckless homicide of . . ." Names are pronounced, counts enumerated. He's going slow, but so many names. I can't keep track. After a while I realize the bailiff is reading the names of the dead passengers and crew. I'm guilty, he keeps saying. Reckless homicide. On count nineteen, on count twenty. Guilty, guilty. I turn to Diana. Her eyes are wet, her head is down. I won't see her anymore, not in the way I once did. I won't touch her flesh again.

Grace is screaming. I hear her screaming, though I know I'm only imagining it. It will happen, though. Diana will see her tonight. Grace will ask where I am. Diana will tell her. Grace will scream, I know she will. She'll scream until her little voice gives out.

On count ninety-six, guilty. On count ninety-seven . . . Are people applauding? I think I hear flesh slapping together, but I'm too dazed to turn my head and look.

My hands are jerked from my sides, locked together with irons. A uniformed sheriff orders me to be still. Judge Henry Meredith is pointing at me. "Life" is a word I pick up amidst the torrent thrown at me. "A tragedy of herculean proportions," Meredith opines, "that didn't have to happen. Deceit made it happen, drugs made it happen, and a complete and stunning disregard for the lives . . ." Meredith seems to be gathering more force with each phrase. I watch his lips move, his arms swing. I'm growing faint. My legs, no longer heavy, feel like Jell-O falling from a spoon.

"I don't impose this sentence lightly," Meredith explains. "Life without parole is, for some men, a sentence worse than death. But given the evidence here, my conscience requires me to do no less, and the law permits me to do no more."

I'm circled by three sheriffs who push me toward the courtroom's side door. I turn to Diana. "We'll appeal," she cries out softly, her chin jutted forward. I nod at her, and go quietly with the sheriffs. I have no fight left.

Long before fully awake, I'm gripped by a tightness and pounding that carry me from a heavy, sweat-filled sleep to a consciousness wishing to be stripped of memories. I awake slowly, as if traveling trough centuries without a sense of where I've been or where I'm headed. I know only I'm below something of substantial weight, pressing uncomfortably against my chest; but nothing visible is there. I climb to my feet in dozens of tiny movements.

My sense of time has become distorted: An hour seems endless; the days pass quickly. I regard my smallest achievements—sleeping four consecutive hours, eating a full plate of potatoes—as evidence of growing strength, much as a dying man is comforted on the eve of his death by his ability to leave his bed to urinate.

I'm in Lorton's Maximum Security Facility. We all have our own cells, as none of us is deemed sufficiently trustworthy to have neighbors within stabbing or strangling range. Nothing pretty about my cell: a hole in the floor for a toilet, a thin, bumpy mattress, ants and roaches trapped in spiderwebs along rusted iron bars.

Lorton's seven prisons contain eleven thousand inmates. All but six hundred are black, the great majority in their early twenties. Fifty percent are here for murder, rape, or robbery; virtually all have suffered or profited from illegal drugs. The guards are quick to tell me I fit the mold: a murderer involved with drugs.

The guards have developed a common way of speaking: lips that move with an angry tightness and lungs that regularly produce a heavy sneer. They delight in reminding me that I've murdered more innocents than any man or woman in Lorton; I surely deserve whatever comes my way. I despise these men but cling to their sides. I'm eyed, pushed, and poked by inmates whenever I'm led from my cell. I stick out.

Every prisoner knows who I am. I'm that rich, lying white Jew bastard who let all those brothers and sisters go down in flames. I'm that Jew-boy who's still alive, that satanic challenge to every able-bodied homeboy who wants to redeem his life by killing the slaughterer of innocents. I'm that evil, dangerous stranger whose crime was accomplished not in the usual manly fashion with guns or fists but by cowardly deception and intellectual gamesmanship. I thrive by influence and manipulation. Who here is more frightening, or more vulnerable? I'm alone. I'm unarmed. I have no one to help me.

This first week I have laundry detail. Maybe, says a broad-shouldered, small-eyed guard, if I sort the laundry right, they'll let me plant grass next week. He chuckles loudly. Everyone finds my presence here strangely satisfying.

I follow him to the laundry room where huge machines whir on as if in agony. The narrow, twisting halls stink of urine, vomit, and unwashed bodies.

The guard says deals are done in this room. "Tell me if you see drugs or guns," he orders me. "You work with us, you'll do all right."

I nod, but have no intention of reporting anything to anyone. The guards can't protect me every minute of the day; and it takes only seconds to slit a man's throat, cut open his chest, and rip out his still-beating heart.

I keep an examining eye on all who wander in and out of this open area. I let no one approach from my blind side, subtly turning and shifting in slow, unobtrusive movements designed to alert no one to my fear. In time I notice a man glaring straight at me, his prison clothes pulled tightly against his muscular frame and thick arms. I look away, and pull laundry from one machine, shove it into another.

He edges closer to me, his glare hard and constant. I continue with my tedious tasks as if his approaching presence is of no concern to me. I give no hint of surrender.

He's still coming, and picking up speed. I turn in time to see him wickedly thrust his forearm at me. It catches me flush on the left temple, blurring my vision, and I go crashing to the floor.

I refuse to stay down. My head's pounding as I push myself to my knees. I'm about to stand when I let out a low, painful grunt. A vicious kick to my belly has knocked me off balance.

I'm back on my knees. He's hovering over me with that same nasty glare. I fight my way upward until I'm erect. I don't back away. I glare too. I'm seized by a savage energy, inspired by that instinct which draws and binds one to life.

He hands me a thick-handled broom. "Clean up this shit hole, slave boy. I be back for you later. I best see not a speck of dirt." He begins to walk away.

"Don't go," I say.

He stops, turns. "You don't say nothing to me, slave boy, less'n I tell you to talk. You got that?"

I hold the broom upside down, its bottom at my waist. "I just wanted to thank you for the broom," I say respectfully, then swing it as I would a baseball bat. The wood whips through the air with a loud whoosh, and strikes him at high speed across the chin. He folds up and drops to the floor like a punctured balloon.

I don't leave the laundry room. I keep on with my work until my fellow inmate regains consciousness, and slowly drags himself off the floor. He eyes me, eyes the broom in my grasp, and walks away. For the moment I'm proud. For the moment I won't think about tomorrow.

THICK GLASS IS in my way. My hands paw it as if it were Diana's flesh, but it's transparent, supercooled silicon dioxide. Diana's warm body is on the other side. We pick up our telephones.

"What happened?" she asks with a soft nervousness. She points to the reddish-black bruise on the side of my head.

"I wasn't paying attention." I shrug. "Hit my head going into my cell."

She closes her eyes, shakes her head. "Please take care of yourself, okay?"

"I'm worried about you too."

She allows a small, grateful smile before getting to the day's business. "I filed our notice of appeal yesterday. We're going to get a new trial, I just know it. Meredith's instructions were dead wrong."

"And in the meantime, how are you going to live?"

"Like I always have. One breath at a time."

"You've got no income, no savings, no clients. You pay your rent with credit cards. You've missed your last two car payments." I drop to my most somber, fatherly voice. "Now, listen to me. You sell whatever stocks I've got left, you sell all my bonds, and you liquidate my entire pension fund. Then you keep half of everything. I'll pay whatever taxes must be paid."

"You need that money for Grace," she insists. "Anyway, I sold some jewelry and furniture I didn't really need. I'm doing okay. I've gotten a few calls too. Lawyers here in town referring criminal matters to me."

"That's good," I say softly, "but I'll go you one better. Starting today, you pay no more rent. You move to my house. It'll be good for you, and very good for Grace."

Her eyes dim. Her cheeks turn inward. "Strange, isn't it?" she mutters. "You move out, I move in. That's not how it's supposed to work."

"I wasn't counting on a prison sentence." I'm muttering too.

"I wasn't counting on losing your case. I—"

"You have absolutely nothing to apologize for," I say fiercely. "You were great in there."

"If I was so great in there, why are you in here?"

I don't answer her. "I'll pay for utilities, food, everything. You'd be doing me and Grace a huge favor."

"Sure I'll do it," she says graciously. "Thank you."

I nod happily. Grace needs an adult who loves her.

"Oh, yeah, almost forgot," she says with a familiar rush. "It was on the radio. Brandon's wife got picked up for DUI. The local news guys gave him a hard time about it. You know, how after he's said in interviews how terrible drugs were for pilots and then there's his wife driving and drinking."

"Drinking? Or was it drugs? You seem to be saying both."

"I'm not sure. I heard DUI. Then the talk about drugs. Why?"

"I don't know. Something." I close my eyes. Something is circling me, something about Philip, something he said. Something about him knowing firsthand. While he was testifying? Before that? Roy was there, wasn't he? Yes, in the conference room. We were talking about Charlie. Rehiring Charlie. Philip said something about his wife, something about insomnia. Slurs her words . . . Barbiturates, she's on barbiturates. My eyes leap open. She's on barbiturates!

"Check out what she was arrested for," I say breathlessly. "See if it was phenobarbital."

"Phenobarbital?"

"We looked under the wrong name," I nearly shout. "Philip's wife goes by Emma Larson, not Brandon. She was writing short stories when Philip married her, and wanted to keep her name. If she was arrested for phenobarbital, get those ex-agents checking again. Check for phenobarbital pick-ups under the name of Emma Larson."

I SIT WITH difficulty. I'm in handcuffs. A prison guard with dark glasses and a loaded rifle keeps me in his direct view.

It's hard to breathe in here. The windows and doors are tightly shut. The ceiling fan is still. The vents are quiet. Mounds of dust gather in the room's corners, stick to the walls' many swirling cracks, and lay in clumps on the moldy green carpet.

It's a long, narrow room reminiscent of a street alley to be avoided. An assortment of old, mismatched chairs grouped in an uneven semicircle faces a desk distinguished for its array of deep, twisting scratches. Removable plastic tiles in bleak gray cover the low ceiling. Justice isn't only blind, it's out of money too. Yet I'm grateful to be here. As dilapidated as are Meredith's chambers, they undeniably constitute, when compared to my eight-foot-by-eight-foot cell, a magnificent architectural achievement that at once awes the senses and inspires the heart. Beauty and riches, I think, are measured not by their intrinsic nature but by their relative worth.

Judge Meredith has a cynical though curious edge to his voice upon greeting Diana and me. He mentions casually our notice of appeal, and says he believes his jury instructions were proper. Certainly, adds the judge solemnly, he acted always in good faith and always to further the cause of justice.

Meredith isn't often reversed—he's savvy and has friends on the appeals court—but legal commentators have in the main condemned his instructions and predicted a heavily divided appeals court. It's likely Meredith will encourage a resolution if one is in sight. To be found in error in this most high-profile case would surely reduce the odds of his joining his buddies on the appeals court.

"I trust you've come up with something pretty big." Meredith nods at Diana almost playfully, but an ominous undercurrent tugs at his voice. "If you haven't, if you've got us all together here for some hysterical plea based on some marginal new evidence, I'll encourage the prosecution to file a motion for sanctions."

"It's big," Diana promises. "If you don't see it that way, I'm sure the court of appeals will. Not to mention all of our media friends."

Meredith's voice turns cold. "All right, let's hear it."

Diana slides to the edge of her wooden chair and leans forward. "A team of former FBI agents have found that a woman named Emma Larson purchased six hundred milligrams of phenobarbital two days before February the sixth, the day of the crash. Emma Larson is Philip Brandon's wife."

"It shows access to the phenobarbital," Meredith ponders aloud. "But it's still a long way from proving sabotage, isn't it? Interesting, though, but—"

"I've got Emma Larson's doctor in your reception area. I'd like to bring him in here. There's more to the story."

"Bring him in," Meredith concurs.

An elderly gentleman sporting suspenders and bow tie, Richard Hodge is escorted into these chambers by Diana, who guides him to the empty chair beside Meredith. Hodge tells us he's been Emma's personal physician for two decades. For the past eighteen months he's been prescribing phenobarbital for Emma's insomnia. He has Emma's records with him.

"It's correct, isn't it, that you prescribed six hundred milligrams of phenobarbital for Emma Larson two days before Thursday, February the sixth?"

"Yes, on that Tuesday. It was a ten-day supply."

"And between that Tuesday and Thursday, you received a second call from Emma, didn't you?"

He nods. "On that Wednesday, to be exact. She said she needed more phenobarbital. She said she'd misplaced what she had."

"All six hundred milligrams?"

"That's what my notes say."

"Were those six hundred milligrams in liquid form?"

"Yes. She always took it that way."

"So you prescribed another six hundred milligrams on Wednesday, February fifth?"

"Yes, I did. She'd never lost any of it before, and I knew she couldn't have taken all that phenobarbital in so short a time. Otherwise, she wouldn't have been so clear-minded."

Diana turns to Meredith. "We have the pharmacist who actually filled both prescriptions. He's in your reception area as well. He'll say he personally handed both prescriptions to Emma Larson that week. He knows her by name and by face. He's been filling all her phenobarbital prescriptions for the past year."

"How many darn people you got out there?" Meredith asks with raised eyebrows. He looks a bit comical with that gesture, though it's probably more a function of his wardrobe than his demeanor. It's Saturday. He's in plaid shirt and brown trousers, looking mighty ordinary. He turns back to Hodge. "The court thanks you for coming here. I expect there's a chance we'll need you again. Maybe as soon as a week or two."

"I'll be in town," the doctor says while rising from his chair. He leaves the chambers without looking at any of us. A stranger to a strange proceeding, he seems eager to return to familiar territory.

Diana follows him out and returns in minutes, the reception area adjoining these chambers. The pharmacist, a former Marine captain, has the look of a man who could still pummel you to death if the need arose.

"I'm Roger Owens," he explains. "I have records with me that show Emma Larson picked up six hundred milligrams of phenobarbital on Tuesday, February fourth, and another six hundred the next day. When I asked her how come she was back so soon, she said she'd either lost the pheno or somebody stole it. Then she said something like she knew she hadn't lost it because she always put the pheno on her sink counter, and that's exactly what she'd done this time." Owens speaks firmly, looks right into Meredith's eyes. His neatly combed sandy hair, wiry build, and piercing gray eyes suggest a rugged, honest man. Most jurors would find him utterly convincing.

I can see the heat building on Meredith's face. "Bring Mr. Brandon here," he commands.

"We'd like to bring in Randy Chapman first," Diana says. "We want to build so many walls around Philip Brandon, he can't go anywhere but run in circles."

NONE OF US leaves Meredith's chambers. Within the half hour we're told Randy has been interrupted in midconference call by two sheriffs who now have him in their car.

Meredith seems edgy. He squirms back and forth in his seat, folds his arms, kicks against his desk. He's looking at Isabel.

"Madam Prosecutor, we must be very careful here. We must allow nothing to compromise our search for the whole truth."

"Of course not," says Isabel with an indignant lift of her chin.

"It'd be only natural for you to want the facts to come out in support of the verdict you've already got," Meredith chides her.

Isabel is leaning forward, but not in her familiar, ready-to-spring-at-you way. Her body seems bereft of energy, her lean more akin to a slump. Her chin is a bit low, her arms hang lifelessly. Guilt wears you out. Guilt pounds and stabs at you. "I'm disappointed, Your Honor, you have so little faith in me. To the contrary, I'm determined to find out if my trust was betrayed. If so, I want the killers to pay with their lives."

Meredith allows a contrite smile. "We're all on the same page, then. When Mr. Chapman gets here, no holding back."

We wait in awkward silence until there comes a rapid knock followed by a door pulled back. Randy enters with the confused scowl of a man unaccustomed to taking orders. He's in his lawyer clothes, looking as if pursued by ghosts.

"Sir," warns Meredith, "the court has learned of disturbing new evidence that strongly suggests the possibility of sabotage. I'll leave the details to Ms. Castino, who will inform you of your rights."

"My rights?" queries Randy.

"Yes, your rights," Isabel confirms. "You have the right to—"

"I'm under arrest?" Randy interrupts. "For what?" Randy points to himself. "Me?"

"You're under arrest for the first-degree murder of one hundred and twenty persons."

"Oh, that's just preposterous," Randy barks at Isabel. "What kind of scam are you running here?"

Isabel's chin jerks back. "This is no scam, I assure you. We have new evidence from independent sources that confirms the logbooks were indeed altered, the plane was deliberately not deiced, and most astonishing of all, the pilot was drugged."

I listen without expression—a habit I perfected over the course of my trial—but with a tingling amusement. What new evidence do we have about the logbooks and the deicing? I don't mind Isabel stretching the truth as long as her exaggerations don't undermine our ultimate objective.

"If you really think I'm guilty here," Randy answers, "then why is Michael still in prison clothes?"

"She's got something real," I call out to my old friend. "This isn't a game."

Randy fixes his eyes on me. He trusts me, I know. Memories of all those nights we sweated together and shared never-forgotten secrets cannot ever be completely erased.

"Philip Brandon had six hundred milligrams of phenobarbital in his possession two days before the crash," I say. "Not five hundred, not seven hundred, but exactly six hundred. And all of us here know Philip had dropped me to work with you on stopping the takeover."

"You're bluffing. I know you, Michael. This isn't real," Randy erupts. "For Christ sake, Philip wouldn't sabotage his own airline. He'd have no reason to."

"We don't have to prove motive," Isabel responds. "Just intent."

"Why don't you just take the high road?" Randy snaps. "Admit you screwed up by going after Michael, and let that be the end of it."

"Maybe you'd like a status report on the FAA's testing?" Isabel replies sharply. "They're about done, so I'll give you a sneak preview of what they're going to conclude. The design of the J Ninety-nine is faulty. The elevators do in fact tend to ice up, and wind-tunnel tests show ice forms unevenly on the wings, causing one side of the plane to drop precipitously."

"You and Philip let me take the fall, didn't you?" I can't resist asking Randy. "And worse than that, you let die all those trusting souls who believed the airline would take care of them."

"If Philip did something crazy, that's Philip, not me," Randy squawks, but he's answering a different question.

"He was looking to you for advice," I reply. "He was ready to follow anyone who showed him a way to survive."

"Give us Brandon, and we won't go for the death penalty," Isabel offers.

"I couldn't give you Philip even if I wanted to," Randy groans. "I don't know the first thing about that phenobarbital you say he had."

"You don't need to know all the details," Isabel presses him. "Just that you knew Brandon was going to sabotage the plane."

"But I didn't know," Randy swears. "I still don't know."

"Brandon altered the logbooks, ordered the plane not be deiced, and drugged the pilot. This much we're sure of. If you can't corroborate any of these three things, then you're on your own. You can leave right now. We go for the death penalty against both of you."

"That's crazy," Randy whispers. "You've got nothing against me."

"Crazy or not, you've got five minutes to think it over," Isabel adds. "Then we get Brandon in here. We ask him to testify against you. If he talks first, you won't ever get a deal from us."

"You're so vague about everything," Randy complains in uneven gulps. "What are you offering? Complete immunity, a fine, what?"

"It depends on what you say," Isabel replies. "The more credible, the better. The more specific, the better. The more important, the better."

"She's got more against you than you think," I chip in, hoping to move the ball down the field.

"I might know something about the logbooks," Randy stammers after an unbearably long silence. "But I'm not saying anything until I know what I'm getting for it."

"If it's good stuff, and I'm convinced you did nothing to cause that plane to go down, I might let you walk."

Randy nods happily. I sense the price is right. He's buying. "Philip did have those twelve sticking incidents erased. How he did it, who he paid, I don't know. He said he was doing it to save the airline."

"How did Philip get my copy of the logbooks?" I throw at Randy.

"I took them myself one night and gave them to Philip. That's when he told me he was going to have them altered, and of course, later they were."

"And you never reported any of this?" Isabel declares in the form of a question.

"It was done purely to help the airline in the civil case. It never occurred to me it'd become an issue in some criminal prosecution," Randy explains. "Anyway, Philip had every right to take back his own company's documents. That's no crime. Plus, we figured Jarrad had all the experts. If anybody understood the intricacies of the J Ninety-nine's design, it was Jarrad's engineers. They said it was okay. We knew Jarrad had too much to lose if one of their planes went down, so we figured they were being straight with us."

"Philip got too good a price for the J Ninety-nines to give them back, and Jarrad wasn't about to admit to a design defect without a fight," I remind Randy.

Randy doesn't look at me when he says: "After Charlie's plane went down, we panicked. I'm not proud of it, but that's the best way to describe it. It wasn't that we thought the elevators caused the crash, we just didn't want it to look like they did. We wanted to play it safe, that's all."

"Too bad you didn't want to play it safe with the airline's passengers," I admonish him.

"You've broken a lot of laws," Isabel announces with judgelike solemnity.

"All we did was screw around with some logbooks," Randy maintains.

"Is that all?" Isabel answers in her most cutting voice. "Well, let's see now. You've falsified logbooks that were at the center of a murder trial. That's called obstruction of justice. At the same time, you've criminally defrauded the FAA by covering up reports of a defective design. And that's the small stuff. The worst of it is, you knowingly allowed defective aircraft to fly unsuspecting passengers, a felony in itself, and since one of those aircraft crashed as a result of the defect you knowingly concealed, that's felony murder, pure and simple. Under the laws of the District, any person involved in a felony which causes a death, however unintended, is guilty of murder in the first degree. In this case, it's one hundred twenty murders."

"But you said the pilot was drugged," Randy protests. "I did nothing to drug—"

"I could indict you on both grounds," Isabel hammers him. "Felony murder if it was the plane, or plain old murder one if it was the drugs. I'll take a conviction on either theory."

Randy looks numb. He barely moves his lips upon conceding his soul: "I'll say whatever I have to say about Philip. That he altered the logbooks, that he defrauded the FAA, that he knew defective aircraft was in the air."

"That's a start, but it doesn't get you all the way home. First base, maybe. It gets you a deal for reckless homicide, a crime I'm sure you're well familiar with."

"Not good enough." Randy shakes. "I never told Philip to drug anybody, if that's what he did. And I never told him to do anything to that plane."

"Did Philip Brandon have Eddie Perez killed?"

"How would I know?"

"Maybe he'll kill you, too, now that you're talking to the U.S. Attorney."

"I'm not talking to you people," Randy storms. "You're talking to me!"

"Brandon won't know that," Isabel points out. "We might let it be known you're spilling everything."

"This is bullshit!"

"Your best bet is to work with us. Give us something solid against Brandon on murder one, and we'll let you walk."

"I'll approve that," Meredith pronounces.

"There you go," says Isabel. "A risk-free plea bargain. The judge has already approved it."

"If he did have Perez killed," Randy speculates, "then won't he do the same to me?"

"You're the one who got all this started," notes Isabel with a slightly demonic glee. "You're the one who put us on to your friend. Now it's all turned around on you. So nobody's going to shed any tears for you, Mr. Chapman. You've got to tell us about motive," demands Isabel, "if you expect to get anywhere."

"I thought you didn't need motive."

"C'mon, Randy," I urge him. "Philip's not going to protect you if it means prison for him. What did you tell him to do about the Subcommittee, about National? He was looking to you for advice."

"Those conversations are privileged, Michael. You know that."

"Not if a crime was planned," Isabel joins in.

"It wasn't a crime," swears Randy. "It was a plan of action. I didn't specifically advise him to bribe anybody."

"Bribe who?" Meredith asks. The judge is leaning forward, his elbows spread wide, his locked hands resting six inches from his chest. All eyes are riveted on Randy.

"Dan Howley. An aide to the Chairman of the Subcommittee. I had lunch with him. I told him the airline was prepared to cooperate fully with the Subcommittee, but felt it could do so more effectively if it knew what info the Subcommittee had about the elevators. Our people could then determine if that info was accurate or not before the hearings started. This way time could be saved, and the hearings made more meaningful. And maybe, if the airline wasn't cornered and wasn't forced to fight, a resolution could be quietly worked out that would benefit the flying public."

"Did he buy that?" Isabel probed.

"He was uncomfortable with it at first, but said he'd talk to his boss about it. Then I said it would also help if we knew the sources of the info they were getting. He said with a sort of a laugh, 'You mean our Deep Throat?' And so I laughed too, and said, 'Of course, that would help.' Then he turned cross, and said he couldn't ever do that. I said okay, and started talking about other things. I figured I'd better build more of a rapport with him before going back to those deep waters again. So we talked for about an hour, had a few glasses of wine. He told me his son was very sick. The insurance company was giving him a hard time about coverage. He asked me if I could suggest a lawyer to him. I said sure, maybe I'd make a few calls for him myself. Off the books, of course. I knew on his salary he couldn't pay a lawyer much."

"And did you make the calls for him?" Isabel presses.

"I never had to. I told Philip about the conversation, and he said he'd handle it from there. I never heard from Howley again."

"Did Brandon meet with Howley?"

"That's everything I know," Randy insists. "What base am I on?"

"Let's see what happens with Howley first. Meanwhile, I'm having you fitted with a wrist bracelet electronically wired to FBI headquarters. Go home, and stay there. You're under arrest."

DAN HOWLEY'S POLYESTER clothes stick to his body, and his longish, plastered-down hair, which no longer conceals the growing bald spot toward the back of his head, seems to swallow a narrow, gently featured face that grimaces at Isabel's every inquiry. Lean-shouldered yet fleshy around the waist, Howley looks to be in his mid-thirties.

"Mr. Howley, I intend to be completely candid and up-front with you. Randy Chapman has already confessed to arranging a meeting between you and Philip Brandon. We also know, having subpoenaed your bank records, that you deposited a half million dollars the very day Flight five five five crashed.

"We have little doubt, sir, that after the public hears Mr. Chapman's confession, there'll be calls for congressional committees to investigate. Hundreds of witnesses will be subpoenaed. Reporters will be everywhere. Everything you've ever done will be found out and examined. Every tax return, every girlfriend, every expense form," she warns. "But if you weren't the architect of this plane crash, but only a messenger for someone above you in the food chain, then we can bargain. There's no need for you to get crushed."

The interrogation of Dan Howley is painful for all forced to watch. Howley, who strikes me as a decent sort, is so unnerved he cannot speak without saliva accumulating on his dark red gums and parched lips, which he is forced to wipe away with his increasingly soggy handkerchief. With much stammering and noticeable reluctance, he eventually confirms, in whole, Randy's version of their meeting; he next moves on to his breakfast, the following morning, with Philip Brandon, which, it turns out, took place on February the fourth, two days before the crash and the same day Emma's phenobarbital disappeared from her sink counter.

It is here that Howley digresses; to "keep his sanity," he says, he must tell us that at the time of his meeting with Brandon, his seven-year-old son was suffering from acute lymphoblastic leukemia, which, by producing an overload of immature white blood cells, was methodically killing him hour by hour—crowding out his red blood cells, invading his liver, destroying his capacity to fight off infections. The Howleys had tried every treatment they could afford: blood transfusions, chemotherapy, antimetabolites. Nothing had retarded the growth of the white cells. Specialists in New York urgently recommended an immediate transplant of healthy bone marrow.

"The doctors said he'd die in four to six months without the transplant," said Howley, heaving with every word. "But the insurance company said transplants weren't covered and, anyway, the leukemia was a preexisting condition, so we had to pay them back for all the chemo and transfusions. It was a horror."

"Tell me, Dan"—Isabel, who refuses to slow the pace of her questioning, is at least willing to afford Howley the illusion of affection by calling him by his first name and doing so with a convincing show of warmth that might have a touch, however faint, of genuineness—"what did Philip Brandon ask of you on February fourth?"

"He said he knew about my son's illness, and felt very bad about it. He said he'd pay for the transplant and all the past bills if I'd just tell him who Deep Throat was. He assured me no harm would come to this man. And he'd give me a half million in cash, and pay me whatever else I needed once I found a donor. If everything came to less than a half million, I could pocket the difference."

"That's a lot of money."

"It saved my son's life."

"So you told him who Deep Throat was?"

"Yes," Howley admits. "And I told him he'd be appearing before the Subcommittee first thing Friday morning, February seventh."

"And Deep Throat was Charlie Ashmore, wasn't it?"

Howley begins quietly to weep. His face is lined with the sort of wisdom, pain, and dark humor that alert a discerning observer to his suffering, frequent rallies, renewed suffering. "I killed that man, didn't I? I killed over a hundred people." Howley shoots a fearful glance in my direction.

"Tell us how Charlie came to you," I ask after a respectful silence.

"He just popped into our offices one day," Howley explains slowly, wiping the water from his cheeks.

"What did he tell you?" I persist.

Howley straightens himself and gathers his wind. "He said he'd been fired, all because the airline was covering up a design defect in the J Ninety-nine. So when his J Ninety-nine went out of control, the airline blamed him rather than admit the plane's design problem. He gave me logs which showed J Ninety-nines had stuck at least a dozen times. I spoke to my boss, and we both thought there was something there to investigate. But still we were a bit on guard. Maybe this was merely a disgruntled ex-employee with a personal grudge to settle.

"Anyway, I called Charlie to come back, and he spoke to a few of the Subcommittee members in my boss's office. He got them pretty riled up, I'll say that. Once they found out from Charlie's former military commanders that Charlie was a man of honor and sacrifice with extraordinary piloting skills, they couldn't wait to get things going, and make Charlie their first witness."

Charlie, I think, must have somehow gotten these selected logs from my personal files, which he must have copied one night after I'd left the office. I didn't realize until this moment the lengths to which Charlie was willing to go to clear his record. I look back at Howley, whose eyes are fixed on me.

"Charlie made us all promise not to tell anybody he was behind the Subcommittee's call for hearings. Especially you, Mr. Ashmore. He told me you were counsel for the airline, and it would put you in a terrible conflict, which he didn't want to inflict on you.

"Funny enough, right after he convinced the Subcommittee to go forward, he got rehired by the airline. But by then it was too late to call things off. And to Charlie's credit, he didn't want to."

"Charlie," I say for Isabel's benefit, "believed in doing the right thing."

Howley casts his eyes downward as does a religious man in a house of worship. "I'm sorry for what I did. I got your brother killed. I hope you can find it in you to forgive me, but I'd understand if you can't."

I take a breath. "I would've done the same thing if I were you." I watch Dan Howley lift his eyes and nod gratefully. "How is your son doing?" I ask.

"Much better, Mr. Ashmore. He got the transplant."

"Philip Brandon is the one I can't forgive," I say bitterly.

ALL MY SENSES ARE AT THEIR peak. As Philip labors past me, I behold every part of him razor-sharp, as if he were being held fast under a brilliant cold white light. I see the tiny blackish-gray stubble under his nose, the pencil-thin blue veins crisscrossing his eyelids, the sore-red pimple below his right ear. I breathe in his stale cologne, taste the nicotine on his breath, and hear the saliva gurgling in his throat inches above the thunderous pounding of his heart. I am already envisioning Philip in his grave, the dirt being sprinkled on his coffin.

I sit, under guard, as Philip takes his seat across from me. He knows why he's been brought to these chambers, but to reinforce the message, Meredith warns Philip that all he says today will be recorded by—Meredith points to a frail young woman frantically punching keys—an official court reporter. Philip neither nods nor speaks, though his blinking eyes and fingers, tapping in machinelike bursts against his knees, betray a jittery weariness.

Philip points to me, and asks in a voice intended to reveal his displeasure: "What is he doing here?" He underscores the word "he" with the grating tone one uses to describe a foul, irritating habit.

Isabel has invited me here precisely because I make Philip nervous. I know when he's lying, when he's about to break. Philip knows I know. Anyway, I'm entitled to be here; at bottom, it's my innocence we're discussing.

"If I were in your shoes," Isabel notes, "the only thing I'd be worrying about is a murder one conviction. Because it's coming. I'd say in three to four months, you'll have the most hated face in America."

"If you thought I'd done something so wrong, you'd have done something about it a lot sooner."

Isabel looks straight into Philip's face when she says: "We just wanted to give you time to hang yourself." She means not with a rope but with the talk that panic incites.

Philip turns his chin upward, looks away. He isn't yielding. He remembers what I've taught him: Never show weakness to those who are preparing to leap your way.

Isabel's look has turned into a white-hot glare. "We intend to indict you and your wife for the murders of one hundred twenty people," she says acidly.

"Emma?"

"We know from both her doctor and her pharmacist that she was the one who personally ordered and picked up the six hundred milligrams of phenobarbital two days before the crash, gave it to you, then personally ordered and picked up another six hundred milligrams for herself the next day."

Philip comes to a complete halt. He stops tapping his fingers, he stops looking at me, he stops taking normal breaths. I can still sense Howley's presence here, though he departed twenty-six hours ago. "Emma did nothing," Philip maintains.

"We have also subpoenaed the bank records of Dan Howley," Isabel continues. "They show he deposited exactly one half million dollars the morning of the crash. Where, sir, do you suppose Howley got that kind of money? On the day of the crash, no less?"

"It didn't come from me," insists Philip.

"That's a lie," observes Isabel coldly. She rises to her feet and flips a switch. "As the sports guys say, 'Let's go to the videotape.' "

The videotaped confessions of Randy and Dan Howley are played. Having heard these confessions live, I'm more interested in Philip's reactions than in the faces on the small screen. Philip sits stiffly, much of the time shaking his head.

"I did nothing wrong," Philip swears, "no matter what those two say. They're just lying to save themselves."

"And you're the last honest man, right?" Isabel mocks him.

"Those confessions, what do they say? Nothing! Do they say I did something to the pilot? Or something to the plane? No, of course not! You've got no evidence any responsible jury would listen to."

"Do you deny, sir, that you've spoken to Dan Howley?"

"I might have, but if I did, I don't recall it. The name means nothing to me."

Isabel pulls from her briefcase printed phone company records. She points out a connection from Philip's private business line to Howley's home. The call was made one day before the crash.

"Could you have dialed a wrong number, and just happened to get Dan Howley?" inquires Isabel with an amused disdain. "We can find out the odds of that from our statisticians."

Philip smiles faintly, but his chest caves inward as if crushed by a giant iron ball. "I spoke to Howley," Philip concedes in agony. "I didn't want to tell you that because I knew you'd think I did something sinister. Exactly the opposite. Dan Howley wanted something from me, not vice versa, and he's the one who brought up the subject of money. But I refused to pay him. Now he's exacting his revenge."

"You spoke to him about Charlie, too, didn't you?"

"This is all bullshit," Philip mutters. "I want a lawyer."

"You spoke to him last night, didn't you?"

"Didn't you hear me? I want a lawyer."

"You might first want to hear the tape of last night's call. If you still want a lawyer after that, you can call one, and we'll lock you up."

"You mean . . . my phone was tapped?" Philip's chin jerks back slightly. He isn't ready for this bullet.

"Pursuant to a court order, yes."

Philip glances pleadingly at Meredith. "Is this all legal?"

Meredith nods. "I signed the order myself."

Philip takes a breath and slumps backward. His face is knotted in a painful grimace. I know that look.

"But once you get a lawyer," Isabel warns, "you're on your own. We'll make no deals."

"Put on the tape," mumbles Philip.

Isabel nods, then flips a switch:

I can't afford any big legal bills, Mr. Brandon. These people are serious. If I don't tell them about the money, they'll keep after me.

You haven't done anything wrong, Dan. Neither have I. Just stay calm.

Can I tell them about the money?

They'll use it against you if you do. They'll crucify us both.

A half million is a lot to hide.

It's none of their business how you got—

Why did that plane go down? I need to know, Mr. Brandon. I feel like I killed—

The pilot, that's why. I told you he was unstable. I told you that from the start. But he died right after I told you he was Deep Throat.

It was an accident. A terrible accident.

Isabel shuts off the tape and glares at Philip. "On the tape, Dan Howley says he told you, before the crash, that Charlie was Deep Throat, and you don't take exception to that remark. You simply say the crash was an accident."

"I do want a lawyer," Philip whispers. "I do."

"And after the crash, the Subcommittee naturally became convinced that Charlie, while maybe reliable years ago, had become a big-time drug user and was, during the time he spoke to them, completely untrustworthy. They figured the Minneapolis dive was probably his fault after all, just like you were telling Howley. So the Subcommittee dropped their hearings, Brandon's stock price shot up, and National didn't go through with their takeover."

Philip's cheeks are a sickly gray. His lips, while moving, produce no audible sounds.

"Then there's the bribe," Isabel steams along. "You told Howley not to tell anybody about the money, and he said, 'A half million is a lot to hide.' Tell us what money you were both talking about."

Philip seems to have run out of believable lies. He turns away, lowers his eyes. "The great lie of this universe," he mutters, "is that we control our lives. We don't. We put money in a market that zooms up and down for reasons that can't always be logically explained. We go to war because somebody somewhere decides to take land from somebody else. We fly in a plane and it crashes. We're all at the mercy of somebody else," he laments, his words ejecting forth in spurts, as if an aching tightness has gripped his throat.

"Terrible choices are sometimes pushed into your face. That's what happened to me. I didn't ask to be born a Brandon. I didn't ask to be in charge of the family fortune. You might think I was living a dream, but no, you can't imagine the pressure of it. So many times I wished I could just be, even for a day, one of those invisible workers in the plant. Go home when the day's over, no worries about stock prices or bank loans. It makes you crazy after a while." Philip looks around the room. He's searching, I think, for a tender look, a friendly nod. "None of you want to understand," he wails. "You think I'm an animal. I'm not."

I sense a change in Philip. I sense he's no longer denying the deed but merely denying he's any less human for having committed it. I sense it not from his words but from the plaintive cry in his voice.

"Philip," I say, "if you keep silent now, you'll be convicted in full public view and surely go down in American history as the antihero. This is your last chance to do the right thing in the right way."

He wants to confess; he wants us to know he has a spark of humanity about him. If only we can prove to him we not only understand but forgive. No, he's not an animal. Animals kill purely for survival. Men torture and kill to preserve symbols and quell the fear inspired not by their victims but by their own ordinary, decaying selves.

"We understand what it had to be like for you," I say. "Your father's like a god to most people. If you'd let the airline fail, the pain of living would've been unbearable."

Isabel, a quick learner, takes my lead. "We are not condemning you. All of us have our breaking points. But we must know precisely what happened. The public's safety demands it. And while we firmly believe we already know," Isabel adds, "we need you to fill in the details."

Philip smiles wanly. I suspect he's glad, though mildly afraid, we understand and, at some level, forgive. "What about Emma?" he asks. "She had nothing to do with this."

"Give us all the details, and we'll leave Emma alone. You have my word on that."

"I'm not an animal," Philip repeats with a slight tremble. "Most nights I wake up screaming. Dead bodies floating in my head. I know what I've done."

THE TAPE IS running. Philip sits with his fists clenched on his lap. His voice, while soft, can be heard.

"I told Charlie I knew he was Deep Throat, and if he testified about the elevators, I'd lose the airline, and he'd eventually lose his job. National wouldn't want a troublemaker. No airline would. But Charlie, he kept saying no. He would testify, and that was it. The elevators posed a danger to life. He had a duty.

"So I got us two extra-large coffees, then poured in the pheno with the cream and sugar. I didn't want Charlie to get on that plane. Just to go to the gate all drugged up, and get stopped by security. They'd test Charlie, and we'd immediately fire him, then leak the story to the media. It would totally ruin Charlie, and make him useless to the Subcommittee. How could they dare trot Charlie out as their star witness when he'd just been found with a ton of drugs in his body? And worse yet, just as he was about to board a plane? The Subcommittee would have to fold its cards, our stock price would shoot up, and National would be thwarted. It was a good plan. It would benefit thousands and thousands of stockholders—most of them ordinary Joes—at the expense of one man, who I'd intended to give generous benefits to anyway.

"What ruined the plan was that damn security guard not keeping his priorities straight. And Charlie not drinking his coffee until the last moment. I couldn't call security until Charlie had the coffee.

"Crazy thing was, the plane wouldn't have gone down if the elevators were working. Charlie was on track till the storm hit. I guess the pheno didn't hit him as quick as most people, though at the end he was starting to lose it. That weird stuff about the 'up and down is stewed' instead of just saying the elevators were stuck. That's the pheno working."

"It wasn't the drugs," I'm quick to agree. "It had to be the plane, or else the copilot would've saved it."

"It was the coffee, I guess, that kept the pheno from working sooner." Philip looks straight at Isabel. "You see what I mean? If I'd wanted the plane to go down, would I have given Charlie coffee? Would I have called Airport Security?

"Right after I talked with Airport Security, I called the lead mechanic. As an extra precaution. Told him not to deice Charlie's plane. We couldn't spare the time and, anyway, I had reports it looked okay. He was a little edgy about it. He said his crew had been working real hard, deicing all the planes at their gates, and Charlie's plane was next. What was he supposed to do about the logbook? he kept saying. Wouldn't it look funny that all the planes were deiced except this one? He was trying to force my hand, you know. Trying to make me feel I had to deice it. So I did him one better. Write down it was deiced, I told him.

"I figured it was okay because the plane would in fact be deiced once we switched pilots. I'd just tell him later I changed my mind.

"Then I called Charlie on his cellular phone. He was probably within a minute or so of getting to the gate, so I played my last card. I told him his plane hadn't been deiced, and wasn't going to be, so he had no choice but to let someone else fly. That's why I told the mechanic not to deice it. As a way of forcing Charlie not to fly.

"I don't think Charlie believed me. He said I wouldn't do such a thing, and even if I had, it was a short flight and he'd make it anyway. Maybe he was just testing me, or maybe he believed he could do anything any time with any plane no matter the conditions. But here's where things got positively screwed up. The mechanic gave Charlie the logbook that said the plane was deiced. He wasn't supposed to give it to Charlie. He was supposed to wait until the next pilot."

"He didn't know there would be a next pilot," I point out.

"I couldn't tell *him* that, now, could I? The hell of it is, I hadn't even planned to call the mechanic, it was sort of an impulse," he groans. "I guess I got this sinking feeling that Charlie would somehow con the security guard or intimidate him. Charlie was good at both. He conned his own brother, didn't he?"

Philip seems to be happily convincing himself that while foolish and unlucky, he'd done nothing malicious or evil. He, too, had been a victim of forces beyond the control of mere humans, though he, of course, had set those forces in motion.

"The real villain here is Jarrad, not me," Philip concludes. "Jarrad designed those defective elevators, and wouldn't admit to it."

"But you drugged Charlie, then told Perez not to deice the plane," Isabel declares. "Either act makes this reckless homicide."

"It's not murder," Philip objects, "because I tried to stop Charlie from getting on that plane. The security guard—"

"It's reckless homicide even if we take as true everything you've said," Isabel contends. "You recklessly and deliberately created an unacceptable risk to the public safety."

"You people got reckless homicide on the brain," Philip snaps.

Isabel leans in on him. "Did you have Eddie Perez killed?"

"No." There's a point beyond which Philip won't go, no matter his need to confess. He knows we have no proof.

"Then we're done here," Isabel says. "I go for life imprisonment, at a minimum."

"Don't judge me by this one thing I've done," pleads Philip in a bitter, throaty voice. "I've lived a life. I've done many good things. I didn't want those people to die!" Philip reaches out and grabs Isabel's arm. "I hated what I had to do! I've cursed my fate every day and night since that plane went down. Many times I've wished I had died on that plane!"

Judge Meredith rises from his chair and points to my armed guard. "Get those chains off that man!"

The guard looks at me, then at Meredith. He remains still.

"Do it now," commands Meredith.

"Judge, I've got no authority—"

"I am all the authority you need," Meredith booms out. "Unchain that man now, or I'll see to it that you be put in chains yourself."

The guard unlocks my chains. I wiggle my hands and feet. I'm free.

Diana is hugging me. She's sobbing. Her body's heaving. The wonderful feel of her soft, moving flesh warms and inspires me. I'm going home, I think. I'm really going home.

Meredith picks up his telephone. Moments later three sheriffs enter and take Philip Brandon away.

THE MEDIA'S CALLING it Crashgate. Philip's videotaped confession has been blasted onto the airways. Prison authorities, on guard against suicide or murder, keep a close watch on Philip.

The media's praise for me knows no bounds, their form of penance. In a nearly full-page editorial, the *New York Times* applauds the FAA's decision to ground all J99s until design and construction errors are fully corrected, and credits me with "having achieved a higher level of safety for the flying public." In a feature story, the *Post* condemns as "anti-Semitic trash" all prior references to my religion (which at the time it typically quoted at generous length).

I relish the hero worship: the writers who ask about the "seamy side" of the airline industry, the lawyers who wish merely to be seen with me, the women who smile and touch me. After two weeks, I'm still game if they are.

I'm back at my old firm today. It's a marvelous sight. There's a sense of decay here. The airline has again yanked its business from the firm, and everyone's scrambling to find a savior. It won't be Randy. While spared an indictment, Randy was disbarred the day I was released from prison. I pass by his office. It's barren. No furniture, no art, no lamps. It's like a tornado had blown all that was Randy's out of sight.

My partners plead with me to come back, all of them groveling in their own special way. It's great fun watching them humble themselves. Those who most strongly insisted on my leaving are the most outlandish in their praise. I don't tell them immediately of my intention to start my own firm with Diana; I allow them the time to perfect their groveling techniques. They need the practice. They know the words but deliver them without the ring of truth so necessary for a successful groveler.

After a few hours I leave. No matter what they say or how they say it, I'm not buying. I'm merely window-shopping. I'm looking at the dogs in the window.

MEDIOCRITY AND OBSEQUIOUSNESS, mixed together with a splash of treachery and heated on a low, steady flame, have finally produced the hearty ambrosia on which Roy Brooks has longed to feast. After years of obeying and agreeing, Roy Brooks has been anointed by the immortal King William to lead Brandon Air Lines past the thick black clouds (which Roy, in part, saw months ago but stayed the disastrous course) that threaten to blow it not only off course but off the map. Roy, the airline's new CEO, will not defend Philip's actions, which he finds "shocking" and "outrageous," and has come to form an alliance with King William, who, with great sadness, has branded his son "an outlaw." Roy, while promising the FAA "full disclosure" of all the airline's records, has publicly urged Jarrad to "step up to the plate" and "fix these elevators." (He's also called upon Jarrad to "reimburse" the airline for the "financial harm" it will incur during the time of the fix.)

I've come to see Roy—not to request but to demand Charlie's money. I won't let Roy get self-righteous. I won't listen to "I didn't know" or "Philip was possessed." Roy knew the J99s weren't safe. He'd seen the logbooks.

Roy should drop to his knees and thank God the civil case has already been settled. What massive damages would a jury have awarded innocent victims of a terrorist act committed by the airline itself through the scheming of its highest-ranking officer? Surely the airline would've argued it's not liable for an employee's criminal act, but what sane judge would have dismissed such a case and not allowed a jury to hear it?

I tell Roy I want ten million dollars by tomorrow. He knows Charlie's estate (and Charlie's alone) never settled with the airline.

"Ten million?" gasps Roy.

"If it makes you feel better, I'm not keeping any of it. I'm setting up a foundation for families of crash victims."

"It's way out of line," he sulks.

"Okay, twelve million."

"What—"

"The longer I wait, the higher goes my number."

"I know your little tricks, Michael. Don't screw around with me."

"Fourteen million, and that's a bargain. If it goes to a jury, I'll ask for sixty million in punitives, and get it."

"You think you're so smart, don't you? Hell, if your brother's wife had gotten her divorce papers one day later, she would've gotten all the money."

"I guess there is a God out there somewhere."

"Ten million's too high," he says adamantly.

"Now it's fifteen, and in five minutes I walk out of here. That's when I don't settle at any price."

"Maybe there's another way to resolve this," he offers. "Maybe your new firm can do some of our work. Maybe all of it. You'll be a fifty-lawyer firm in six months."

"I don't want your business. It costs too much."

"Don't be so sure of yourself, Michael."

"I'll be delighted to fight this one out with you, Roy. You won't find twelve jurors anywhere in this country who'll like you or Philip. In fact, you're my first two witnesses. You guys will bring down the airline's stock price by thirty percent."

I hand Roy a settlement agreement, and write in "fifteen million dollars" after the words "in the amount of." Roy signs it. We don't shake hands, we say no good-byes.

It's brilliantly light as I begin my journey home. Grace and Diana are waiting. We have theater tickets. We're going to watch people pretend. I'm told this is what families do when they lead normal lives. It's called a night out.